Allegra angled a glance at him, a slight smile on her lips.

"I know you tease and beguile and play the part of being enthralled by me. But those are just the tools of a rake's arsenal. I'm not sure I truly believe it."

Afterward Will couldn't recall just what pushed him over the brink. Perhaps it was because she looked so delectable, her soft cheeks ruddy from the cold, her dark eyes sparkling a challenge. Or maybe he only followed the lead of the curving feather of her silly bonnet, which bobbed in the slight breeze to caress the cheek he yearned to touch. Whatever the spark that set him off, he found himself drawing her closer.

"Believe it," he murmured….

JULIA JUSTISS

Rogue's Lady

HQN™

ISBN-13: 978-0-373-77223-0
ISBN-10:   0-373-77223-8

ROGUE'S LADY

Also by Julia Justiss

To my son Matt as he leaves high school for the wider world: Like Allegra, may you hold fast to your dreams, and like Will, may you set forth to make them come true.

Rogue's Lady

CHAPTER ONE

STANDING AT THE LIBRARY window, staring numbly at the bare late-winter garden below, Allegra Antinori scarcely registered the footsteps approaching from behind her.

"So this is where you've been hiding."

Wincing at the breathy, little-girl voice—so at odds with the venomous tone in which the words had been uttered—Allegra reluctantly turned to gaze into the hard blue eyes of Uncle Robert's wife.

Twitching her expensive, jet-trimmed black shawl into place, the young woman continued, "Poor Robert might have been too ill these last few months to prevent your lounging about, but it's more than time you made yourself useful. Cease your sniveling and go help Hobbs bring the trays of meat and cheese up to the dining room. The mourners will be arriving shortly."

After weeks spent at her uncle's bedside as he slowly slipped toward death, Allegra was too drained and forlorn to challenge, as she would have otherwise, the woman's petty tyranny. "Very well, Aunt Sapphira."

Those gentlemen-bewitching blue eyes shot her a

look that would have frozen the Thames. "It's *Lady Lynton* to you now, wench. I may have been forced to humor Robert and take you in after your parents died last fall, but you'll stay on *my* terms now. Regardless of the airs you like to give yourself, you're not really a member of the family and I will not tolerate your pretending otherwise."

Devastated as she was by the loss in quick succession of the three people dearest to her, Allegra could not allow that claim to go uncontested. "Uncle Robert may not have been my uncle, but he was my mother's dearest cousin—no matter how much you'd like to deny it," she said.

"Perhaps by birth, but everyone knows Lady Grace's whole family disowned her when she married your father. An itinerant musician—and a foreigner, no less! I suppose she learned some grasping Italian ways from her husband, for she certainly managed somehow to keep a hold over Robert. Letting her family run tame in his house whenever they came to London! But he can intervene for you no longer. If you wish to keep a roof over your head, you'll abandon those pretensions or I'll send you packing, see if I won't! Now, go about your work."

Smoldering fury momentarily overwhelming her grief, Allegra vowed she would be thrown out on the street tonight before she would curtsey to this female barely older than herself or call her "Lady Lynton."

"I should be happy to help provide for the guests… Aunt Sapphira," she replied, holding her ground and staring directly into the eyes of the woman who had beguiled her uncle into marriage a mere six months after the death of his beloved first wife.

Apparently realizing she could push Allegra only so far—or not wishing to lose a free extra servant when she expected a houseful of guests—Sapphira looked away first.

"Make sure you do whatever else Hobbs needs," she said, turning to inspect herself in the library mirror. "And I'd better not see your dark face in the parlor while the guests are here. Why Robert acknowledged any connection to a chit who looks more like a Gypsy than a proper English girl, I'll never understand."

With that parting shot, Sapphira smoothed her guinea-gold curls off the porcelain perfection of her brow and walked out.

Her meager strength drained by the confrontation, Allegra sank down on the sofa. She'd rest for a few moments and then go help Hobbs.

For the hundredth time she deplored the susceptibility of the male species to rosebud-pink lips, gentian-blue eyes and blond curls above a well-curved figure. She only hoped that in the year her uncle had been married to Sapphira, he'd never learned how selfish and ruthless was the heart under that outwardly perfect form.

Suddenly released by her uncle's death yesterday from the sickroom that had been her focus for weeks, Allegra had been drifting in a fog of lassitude and despair. Better to have something, anything, to fill the empty time now heavy on her hands, since she was still too weary and heartsick to decide what she should do next.

For a moment, the sense of being utterly alone in the world overwhelmed her. How she wished Uncle Robert's son Rob had made it home to see his father one more time before his death! To share with her the agony of his loss, as with elder-brother affection he had befriended her during her childhood visits.

But the cousin Rob she had always—and secretly still—idolized was Captain Robert Lynton now, gone these three years with Wellington's army. Having survived the slaughter of Waterloo, he was presently on staff duty in Paris.

Surely when the news of Uncle Robert's death reached him, Wellington would let him come home, she thought, her spirits brightening.

Not that it would make much difference to her future. Much as she loved her uncle, only the sudden death of her parents at a time when Papa's finances had been in unusually dire straits had forced her to London to beg his assistance. She'd never intended her sojourn at Lynton House to be more than temporary. But Uncle Robert had already been ailing when she arrived, putting plans to move elsewhere on hold while she tended him—his beautiful new wife, she recalled with a curl of her lip, having professed a horror of the sickroom. With a roof over her head—however precariously, given the rancor in Sapphira's eyes—and time to prepare, she would far rather find some other way to support herself than remain here on the new Lord Lynton's charity, and at Sapphira's mercy.

Not when she'd grown up in a family worthy of the name. Staring into the cold hearth, Allegra smiled. There might have been lean times, but so remarkable was her father's musical talent that another patron, or a commission for a new ballet, concerto or sonata, always turned up in time to avert disaster. For the virtuoso and the beautiful wife he called his muse and inspiration, being together was worth every trial. Raised in the circle of their love, Allegra had never given a thought to her status in the wider world.

She would need to give it a great deal of thought now. Sapphira had just made it perfectly clear that, having resented every kind word and every morsel of food her uncle had provided during Allegra's six months at Upper Brook Street, she intended to transform Allegra into an unpaid servant.

But deciding how to avoid that fate would have to wait until later. For now, Allegra thought as she hauled her weary body off the sofa, she would serve her uncle one last time by helping Hobbs and the staff prepare the meal for the mourners who were coming to honor the late Lord Lynton.

HOURS LATER Allegra was carrying a load of empty platters down to the kitchen when Hobbs returned from escorting out the last of the guests.

"I'll take those now, Miss Allegra," the butler said, hastening over to relieve her of her burden. "'Twas good of you to lend us a hand. Me and the staff be right sorry for your loss. Lord Lynton were a fine gentleman."

"He was indeed," Allegra said, touched and grateful for the deference the butler continued to show her, despite the fact that by now the staff must know their mistress was trying to relegate Allegra to a position among them.

"You been at the master's bedside near without pause these last weeks. Why don't you go up and rest?"

Truly, she was so tired she was swaying on her feet. "Thank you, Hobbs. I believe I shall."

As she started toward the main stairs, Mrs. Bessborough, the housekeeper, put a hand on her arm, her face creased in concern. "Excuse me, Miss, but…" She exchanged a distressed look with the butler. "Oh, Miss, I'm powerful sorry, but her ladyship directed me to move your things out of the blue bedchamber."

Allegra stopped and exhaled a sigh. Despite the press of guests today, Sapphira certainly hadn't wasted any time enforcing Allegra's change of status.

"It's all right, Bessie." She patted the arm of the woman, who, like Hobbs, had known her since she'd first toddled into the Lynton kitchen clutching her mama's skirts some twenty years ago. "Would you show me to my…new accommodations?"

"Yes, Miss. Follow me." Shaking her head and clucking her displeasure, the housekeeper preceded Allegra up the service stairs.

As Allegra expected, the housekeeper did not stop until they reached the attic rooms where the female servants slept. "*She* told me to put you in with the maids, but there's this nice storeroom under the eaves that held the late Lady Lynton's trucks. Sam helped me move them so we could get a bed in. I'm afraid 'tis a bit cramped, Miss, but you'll have privacy."

The woman's kindness brought tears to Allegra's eyes. "Are you sure, Bessie? I don't wish to get you into trouble with Aunt Sapphira."

The housekeeper sniffed. "Seeing as that one don't never set her dainty foot to any stairs but the ones to her bedchamber, she'll never know. And to think, the poor master's not yet cold in his grave! I never thought I'd live to see such a thing. What do you mean to do, Miss?"

Allegra walked over and sank gratefully onto the bed. "I'm not sure yet."

"You play the pianoforte and the violin just as beautifully as your pa ever did, God rest his soul. Might you be a musician like him?"

"Were I married to a musician, we might play together, but as a lone woman, I'm afraid 'twould be nearly impossible to establish such a career."

"Might you go on the stage? When you was a girl, you used to chatter on about all the theaters you'd visited."

During her father's occasional stints as a musician in theater orchestras, the family had struck up an acquaintance with a number of actors and theater managers. But

while she could envision becoming a musician with enthusiasm, neither dancing nor acting held any appeal.

"No, I don't think I have the talent to become a Sid-
dons—or," she added, chuckling, "the desire to display
my legs in breeches roles, like Vestris."

"Well, I should hope not!" the housekeeper exclaimed,
looking properly shocked. "The best thing woulda been
to find a fine young gentleman to marry you, which we
all was hoping the master would do. But then he fell
sick…" The housekeeper sighed, her voice trailing off.

Mrs. Bessborough might never have set foot in a
Mayfair ballroom, but she knew very well that with
Allegra's mother discredited by her runaway marriage,
entering the aristocratic world into which her mother
had been born, difficult enough a feat for Allegra with
Lord Lynton's backing, would be impossible now in the
face of Sapphira Lynton's opposition.

"I doubt Uncle Robert would have arranged a
match, even had he lived." Nor, Allegra added silently,
had she any desire to insinuate herself into the closed,
self-important world that had rejected her mother simply for marrying the man she loved.

"I don't suppose you know some nice young gentleman musician?" the housekeeper continued hopefully.

Allegra's thoughts flew back to an incident eight
months ago, just before her parents fell ill. Mama had
called her aside to confide that a handsome young violinist in her father's orchestra had requested permission
to pay his addresses—and been refused.

"You mustn't think Papa is not concerned with your feelings, rejecting Mr. Walker without even consulting you," Lady Grace had assured her. "More than most parents, we believe loving the partner you marry is of absolute importance! Had we any suspicion that your affections were engaged, Papa would have told Mr. Walker to proceed. But since we did not, with Napoleon now banished to St. Helena for good, Papa has other plans for you."

Gratified as she was to learn of the musician's admiration, Allegra quickly confirmed that she was more curious about her future than disappointed that Papa had spurned her suitor. But though she pressed Lady Grace to say more, with a laugh and a kiss, her mama told her Papa would speak to her himself when the time was right.

Allegra smiled sadly. Whatever Papa's plans had been, a virulent fever had carried off both him and her mother before the "right" time arrived. Leaving Allegra unwed, unattached and alone.

"I'm afraid there's no one," Allegra replied, swallowing hard at that forlorn truth.

Where in the world was there a place for Allegra Antinori? she wondered. But fatigue overwhelming that despairing thought, she lifted a hand to smother a yawn.

"Shame on me!" the housekeeper exclaimed. "Here I be rattling on when I expect all you want to do is fall into that bed and sleep for a week. Things will look better tomorrow, I daresay. Now, let me help you out of that gown and let you rest. I'll send Lizzie up in the morning with your chocolate."

"Thank you, Bessie," Allegra said, gratitude again bringing tears to her lashes as she turned to let the woman undo her stays. Once tucked into bed, she pulled the covers over her head and went instantly to sleep.

ALLEGRA AWOKE to pale sunlight making a faint warm square on the quilt covering her. Disoriented, she stared up at the small, high window through which the sunlight was streaming before recalling where she was and why.

The pain of remembering Uncle Robert's death exceeded her sadness in being evicted from the blue and gold brocaded bedchamber that had always been hers and her mother's when they visited here. Shivering in the cold, she got up quickly and dressed in a plain round gown she could manage on her own, then grabbed the lap desk Hobbs had set on Aunt Amelia's trucks and climbed back on her bed, wrapping the quilt around her. Now, before Sapphira woke and sent for her to perform some task, she should ponder what she meant to do.

Though she had as yet only a hazy idea what that might be, she did know that she could not remain at Lynton House. She refused to jump at Sapphira's bidding, nor did she wish to endanger her friends on the staff by making them choose between supporting her and obeying their mistress.

So what did she wish to do?

More than anything she wanted a place to settle in

and call her own…not a dreary succession of rented rooms with their mismatched and tattered furnishings which, using imagination and careful economy, her mama made into a home, only to begin all over again when Papa's work took them to the next town and the next. Her mother might have been born a viscount's daughter, but Lady Grace prided herself on how well she'd learned to deal with the most unprepossessing of accommodations, to direct a handful of servants when times were good, to cook, clean, mend and entertain without assistance when times were lean. Along with music, dancing, literature, needlework and the deportment required of a lady of birth, she'd made sure Allegra acquired those more practical skills, too.

Yes, Allegra thought, she'd love to have a permanent home and a position in which she could exercise her talents, perhaps provide some useful service.

Suddenly she recalled the visit she and her mother had paid years ago to Lady Grace's former governess. After a career serving the children of the viscount's family, that lady had retired to a snug cottage on a small parcel of land surrounded by a large kitchen garden and an orchard.

Ah, that would be security indeed, to possess a sturdy house on land of one's own, something that did not depend upon the whims of society, that no disapproving relation could ever take away!

Perhaps she should seek work as a governess. A governess at a country estate with an extensive library and

fine pianoforte, where she might spend her nights playing or reading after instructing her young charges in
music, dance, literature and geography. Where she might
set the little girls on her lap, as her mother had done
with her, and teach them to embroider and mend, or
help with the babes in the nursery. Since it was nearly
certain, she thought with a deep pang of regret, that she
would never marry and have children of her own.

Of course, a governess could be dismissed just as
quickly as an unwanted relation, nor could one count
on obtaining a pension and a house, even after a lifetime
of service. She'd have to choose her position carefully.

She would begin a list of her qualifications and
start looking for an employment agency immediately,
she decided.

Allegra had just begun her list when, after a knock
at the door, the maid Lizzie burst in.

"Oh, Miss, 'tis so exciting! Hobbs said a letter just
come from France and the young master—that is, the
new Lord Lynton—be on his way home!"

Rob was coming home! A frisson of joy penetrated the
grief lying heavy in her heart. "When?" she demanded.

"Hobbs didn't say, Miss, but the staff thinks 'twill
be soon." Setting down her tray, she added, "Mrs. Bessborough said to tell you to take heart, 'cause things was
gonna be different around here!"

After thanking Lizzie and assuring her she need not
come back to fetch the tray, Allegra gestured the maid out.

Rob would soon be here. Allegra closed her eyes and

savored the thought, as comforting as the scent of the hot chocolate. Warmed by the first good news she'd heard since her parents expired what seemed a lifetime ago, Allegra sipped the frothy beverage, a wistful smile on her lips as she remembered her last visit with Rob Lynton.

Blond, handsome, five years her senior and very much on his dignity as an Oxford man, he'd discouraged her from trailing after him as she had when they were both younger, saying it was past time for her to tidy her hair, modulate her voice and behave like a proper young lady instead of a hot-tempered hoyden who argued with him at every turn. Though he'd refused her pleas for a renewal of the fencing lessons begun on her previous visit, he'd unbent enough to challenge her at chess, trounce her at billiards and allow her to ride with him in the park in the early morning when no one of consequence might observe his ramshackle cousin trotting at his heels.

The ache in her heart sharpened as she recalled that moment in the park when the romantic—and admittedly hoydenish—sixteen-year-old she'd been had suddenly decided her dearest wish was for Rob to realize she *was* a proper young lady, and the only lady he wanted. Casting covert, adoring glances at him as they rode, she'd envisioned him galloping up to her father's lodgings, leaping from the saddle, declaring his undying love, and swearing his life would be meaningless unless she agreed to become his wife.

That had been…six years ago? Though she needed

a gallant knight's rescue now more than ever, she'd long outgrown that adolescent dream. Still, just knowing Rob was coming home sent a bubble of excitement and anticipation rising in her chest.

The young Rob she remembered would be a man now, a seasoned soldier who had survived desperate battles and gone on to keep the peace in a restive Paris. Decisive and commanding, he would be more than capable of prying the reins of his household from the clutches of his stepmother.

Bonaparte had just made his break from Elba, sending Rob racing to Belgium to coordinate the gathering of Wellington's forces, when Sapphira began her assault on his father's sensibilities, so Rob had never met the late Lord Lynton's young bride. What would he make of his new "mama"? Allegra wondered.

Send her to the rightabout immediately, pouty pink lips, gilded hair, jutting bosom and all, Allegra devoutly hoped. But though Rob wasn't elderly or grieving for a beloved wife's touch, he *was* a man. She couldn't be certain he would prove any more immune than Uncle Robert to Sapphira's charms.

She should go forward with her plans to find employment elsewhere, Allegra concluded as she finished her chocolate, firmly banishing the stubborn relics of her old romantic dream. Though she would stay and see Rob established here as Lord Lynton before she embarked on a new life, the nauseating possibility that Sapphira might succeed in cozening Rob as successfully as she had beguiled his father made Allegra determined to have alternative plans for her future in place by the time Rob returned.

With one last sigh over the handsome countenance she so vividly remembered even after all these years, Allegra set aside her cup, took up her pen and went back to her list.

CHAPTER TWO

ON THE OTHER SIDE OF TOWN, a knock at the door of his Chelsea parlor distracted William Tavener from his reading. Glancing up as the door swung open, he discovered his cousin Lucilla, Lady Domcaster, standing on the threshold, hands on hips as she surveyed the small, untidy space. In her elegant ruby pelisse and bonnet, she looked as out of place in his shabby sitting room as her expression of distaste proclaimed her to feel.

Covering his shock—and a surge of gladness—at seeing his favorite childhood cousin after a gap of two years, he rose from his chair and drawled, "Lucilla, my dear, what a surprise! Not a wise move coming here, you know. Leave immediately and I shall swear I never saw you."

With a sniff, Lady Domcaster advanced into the room. "Oh, rubbish, Will. And you may save that forbidding look to intimidate your boxing opponents. You know it won't frighten me. Gracious, what a dingy set of rooms!"

Realizing with perhaps too great a sense of relief that Lucilla wasn't going to allow him to scare her off, he gave an affected sigh and gestured languidly to the sofa. "Come in then, if you must. My apologies that the accommodations aren't up to your standards. Though I'd still advise you to reconsider this call."

"If you'd answered either of my two notes," Lucilla replied as she seated herself, "I wouldn't have to do something as scandalous as visiting my bachelor cousin in his rooms."

Will brought one hand up over his heart. "Dear me! My wicked reputation. Is Domcaster likely to call me out?"

"Oh, I can handle my lord husband," Lucilla assured him, a sparkle in her eye. "Besides, the on-dit says you only seduce married ladies in their own boudoirs or in love nests of their providing. Now, since I've already committed the impropriety of coming here, you might as well offer me refreshment—if there's any to be had?"

"Give me a moment and I'll see if Barrows can scare up some wine." After delivering her a courtly bow, which she waved off with a grin, he entered his chamber to hail his valet, friend and man-of-all-work.

Barrows stepped back so abruptly, Will knew he must have been listening at the door. "Quite an astounding development!" Barrows said in an undertone. "Shall I fetch wine or stay to play chaperone?"

"Wine," Will replied softly. "The better to send her on her way more quickly."

"Excellent point," Barrows replied and headed toward the back exit.

The errand gave Will a moment to trap the joy his cousin's unexpected visit had surprised from him and bottle it back under the urbane, bored demeanor he affected.

"Wine is forthcoming," he announced as he walked back in. "So, to what do I owe the honor of this highly irregular visit?"

"Did you not even read the notes I sent?" Lucilla asked with a touch of exasperation.

As if he would not have immediately devoured the contents of the first correspondence he'd received from any relation in nearly two years. But afraid, if he called upon her as she'd bid, he might not be strong enough to resist the temptation to renew the friendship they'd shared in their youth—a liaison that would now reflect no credit upon an otherwise respectable matron—he'd chosen not to go to North Audley Street.

Warmed as he was by her persistence in seeking him out, it would still be best for her if he rebuffed any attempts to renew that connection. Not correcting her mistaken impression of his indolence, he gave her instead a lazy grin. "Refresh my memory."

"After being buried in the country producing off-spring for years, now that Maria and Sarah are old enough to acquire a bit of town bronze and with Mark reading for Oxford, Domcaster agreed to my having the Season in London he's long promised."

"Your many friends must be ecstatic. Why contact me?"

Lucilla shook her head. "Don't try to cozen me. When I walked in, before you put your mask-face back on, I could tell you were as pleased to see me as I am to see you. I've missed you, Will!"

Before he could divine her intent, she came over and seized him in a hug. Shocked anew, he allowed himself just a moment to fiercely return the pressure of her arms before setting her gently aside. "Lucilla, you unman me."

"Oh, do drop that irritating manner and let us speak frankly. I expect you believe that my being seen with you can do my reputation no good, but what I propose will change all that. Fortunately, there is still time for you to make a recover before you succeed in isolating yourself permanently from good society."

He'd suspected she wanted to quietly resume their friendship, interrupted by both their coming of age and her marriage. Surprised once again, he said, "That sounds foreboding. I tremble to think what you intend."

"I intend to put a period to your career as a some-time gambler and full-time beguiler of ladies no better than they should be! Though I might have been buried in Hertfortshire raising a family, my dear friend Lydia here in London has kept me fully informed. Domcaster said one must expect a young man to sow some wild oats, but really, my dear, you're nearing thirty now. 'Tis past time you settled to something more useful than fleecing lambs at whist and seducing other men's wives."

"They were not all of them wives," he pointed out, amused. "'Twas a fair number of widows sprinkled in."

"A good thing for your health. I understand some

not-so-amenable husbands of several of your paramours almost insisted on grass for breakfast."

"Since I was always able to persuade the injured party to swords rather than pistols, there wasn't much danger. You know how good I am with a blade. Honor upheld, no one hurt."

"Heavens, Will!" Lucilla exclaimed, laughing. "Trust you to leave both the lady *and* her husband satisfied."

Will reached down to pick a speck of lint off the sleeve of his best jacket. "One must have a little excitement in one's life, Lucilla."

"Indeed." Lucilla shook her head. "Although I should think your bouts at Gentleman Jackson's—yes, Lydia has kept us informed about your boxing career!—would satisfy that desire! You've always been such a scrapper. I never understood why Uncle Harold refused to purchase you a commission. You could have been decimating the ranks of French cuirassiers instead of setting your lance at every loose-moraled woman in London."

A vivid memory flashed into mind…his uncle impatiently dismissing Will's plea to buy a set of colors, replying he had no intention of wasting his blunt sending Will where he'd only get his worthless carcass skewered by some Polish lancer. Though Will should have expected that, even with a war on, Uncle Harold would not consider the army in dire enough straits to require the dubious services of his late sister's troublesome orphan.

"Someone must care for the poor unloved ladies," he said after a moment.

Something like pity flickered briefly on Lucilla's face. "You would know about the unloved part! I still think it atrocious the way Aunt Millicent—"

Will put a finger to her lips before she ventured into territory he'd rather not examine. "Enough!" He smiled, letting his affection show through this time. "You were ever my champion, even when we were quite young. Though what you saw in a grubby urchin who was always spoiling for a fight, I do not know."

"Courage. Dignity. A keen sense of fair play," she answered softly. "Or maybe," she added with a grin before he could act on the compulsion to defuse her praise with some witticism, "it was just that, unlike Uncle Harold's obnoxious son, you did not believe yourself above riding and rousting about with a mere girl."

"What a pair we were!" Will chuckled. "You, at least, overcame your wild youth. I do appreciate your loyalty, you know."

A knock indicated the return of Barrows, who entered to serve the wine before quietly bowing himself out again.

"I wasn't able to do anything useful for you when we were children," Lucilla continued after sipping her wine. "But I vowed that someday, if I had the chance, I would. As the wife of an earl—who just happens to be related to two of the Almack patronesses—I have an unassailable position in society, a whole Season in which to wield my power, and I've decided it's time you assumed the place to which you were born."

Will spread his arms wide. "Behold me occupying that position! Baron Penniless of Rack-and-Ruin Manor."

Ignoring the bitterness in his tone, she nodded. "Exactly. You *are* still a baron. Uncle might have shamefully neglected the property put under his guardianship, but Brookwillow still possesses a stout stone manor house situated on a fine piece of land. Both need only an infusion of cash to put them to rights. You merely need to leave off pursuing light-skirted matrons and start looking for a wealthy bride. And I intend to help you find one."

The idea was so preposterous, Will could not help laughing. "My dear, you are a dreamer! I hardly think I would be of interest to any *respectable* woman—unless she's attics-to-let. Even should I manage to charm some tender innocent, no papa worth his salt would countenance my suit."

"Nonsense," Lucilla returned roundly. "You speak as if you were steeped in vice! You've only done what most young men do—game and seduce women all too willing to be seduced—albeit with a bit more flair. Indeed, I suspect Uncle Harold is proud of your reputation, though he'd never admit it. However, as head of the family, he *will* support your efforts to become established in good society."

"He told you that?" Will asked, astounded.

"Why should he not? Since to do so," she added dryly, "costs him neither time nor blunt. With your breeding and family connections, charming an innocent shouldn't prove much of a challenge. You're quite a handsome devil, you know, and what girl can resist the lure of a rake's reputation?"

He stared at her a moment. "Given my 'rake's reputation,' what does your lord husband have to say about your running tame with me?"

"You know Marcus always liked you, even when you were milling down every boy who whispered behind your back at Eton. He agrees that you ought to assume the responsibilities of your rank." Lucilla giggled. "And knowing how he detests London, you may easily understand why he was happy to agree that you stand in for him as my escort to every party, ball and rout I choose to attend."

"He trusts me that much—in spite of my reputation?"

Lucilla's face grew serious. "He knows you would never do me harm—and so do I. Besides, the girls and their governess are with me, so we shall appear quite the family. Now, what we need to find you is a gently bred lass from the lower ranks. Despite Uncle Harold's support, with your…limited means, 'tis best not to aspire to the hand of a duke or earl's daughter. Perhaps a chit whose family wishes her to acquire a title…especially if she had a nabob grandfather to leave her his wealth!"

Holding up his hands, Will shook his head. "Lucilla my dear, I appreciate your kind intentions, but spare me! I've no desire to become a tenant for life."

"What *would* you become, then? 'Tis past time to

cease drifting as you have since leaving Oxford. Would it be so bad to find a kind, sensible girl to care for, who will care about you? One whose dowry will allow you to repair the manor house, refurbish your land and begin living as befits a Lord Tavener of Brookwillow?"

She gestured around the room. "You'll never convince me you'd be sorry to give up *this*. Only think! Instead of a rented room—which hasn't even a pianoforte!—you might recline in your own music room at Brookwillow. Become a patron of the arts, sponsor musicales and theatricals. Write music as you once did. Fill the library with all the rubbishy books you used to bring home from Eton and Oxford." She giggled again. "Much to the horror of Uncle Harold."

Will smiled. "The only thing more awful to our uncle than a nephew who wrote music was the idea of one becoming a scholar. I once choused him out of 200 pounds by threatening to accept a position as a don at Christ Church."

"Did they really offer you a post?" Lucilla asked, diverted. "I think you might have been a good one."

"No, I was wise not to accept it, even if I was angry at the time with Uncle Harold for not buying me that commission." And despairing of what his future could offer, with a crumbling estate, no money and no chance to harness his few talents to earn any. "There wouldn't have been any married ladies of wealth there for me to pursue."

"True. But you're bored with that now."

He raised his eyebrows. "Am I?"

"Yes. Lydia reports you've not been involved in any new scandal for months. I understand you even rebuffed Lady Marlow's quite flagrant lures."

"Please, I beg you will not repeat that. Only consider my reputation!"

"No doubt 'twas your reputation as a lover that led her to pursue you." She gave him a wicked look. "Employ those talents to charm your well-dowered maiden and you will both be happy! Marriage can be much more than a dreary arrangement based on wealth and position, as I can attest with *great* satisfaction."

Hoping to throw her off, he gave her a lascivious look. "You certainly have the offspring to prove it."

"'Tis another benefit of wedlock," she replied, not at all embarrassed. "You might have a son."

Will shuddered. "I can't imagine anyone more ill-suited for the role of father. With my parents dead since I was a lad, what do I know about it?"

"You certainly know what *not* to do. Now, once the Season begins, I'm hosting a dinner for Lydia's niece Cecelia, after which we will proceed to Lady Ormsby's rout. You can make your first appearance then." She cast a discerning eye over his attire and frowned. "It will give you enough time to get to the tailor and have some new garments made."

"I am attending this rout, am I?"

Her face softened and she reached over to take his hand. "Dear Will, forgive me! I know I am terribly managing—which, I suppose, is what comes of running a household that includes a score of servants and three active children! I just want you to be happy, living in a place and a style worthy of you. I want you to have a chance to find the family you were robbed of as a child. I can't make up for the lack of the commission or change the standards that forbid a gentleman from pursuing a career as a musician or scholar, but I can do this. Won't you at least *try* to become respectable? If we don't find an heiress to your liking, you can always go back to living the way you are now. What can you lose?"

"Several months of pursuing willing widows?" he suggested. But Lucilla was right. He *was* bored with the emptiness of his life, dissatisfied, restless, yearning for some indefinable something more.

He was by no means sure that acquiring a wife would satisfy those longings, however. "I doubt I have the temperament for matrimony," he objected. "I've lived on my own so long, I don't know that I could tolerate having a woman about all the time."

"You've always enjoyed my company, haven't you?"

He grinned. "Ah, but I don't live with you day in and day out."

"Well, married couples needn't live in each other's pockets, either. Indeed, much as I adore Domcaster, with his duties on the land and in town and mine with the house and children, we often go for days seeing each other only at dinner…or at night. Among all the young ladies on the Marriage Mart, surely you can find one who would be that congenial."

"Perhaps," Will temporized, not really putting much credit in that happy prediction. Certainly he had no illusions of tumbling into some great love match, as his cousin had. Save for Lucilla, the one relative who had inexplicably taken into her heart the fractious boy everyone else rebuffed, he knew about as much about familial affection as he did about fathering.

Indeed, the people to whom he was closest, he thought with a wry grimace, were neither of his own kin nor class. Barrows, now his valet and companion, a scruffy gutter rat he'd rescued when they were both boys. Maud and Andrew Phillips, the elderly caretakers of what was left of his crumbling estate, who'd shown him all he knew of parental affection. A pang of guilt pierced him that he'd not made the trip to Brookwillow to visit them in months.

Perhaps, if he could tell them he'd acquired the means to restore his ravaged estate and make easy their declining years, he might not be so reluctant to make the trip.

Even as he told himself it was highly improbable that Lucilla's scheme could achieve that result, he heard himself say, "Very well, send me a card. I'll make myself presentable and attend."

"Wonderful!" Lucilla rose and gave him another hug. "Come for dinner next week. Domcaster is looking forward to talking with you." As he walked her to the door she added, "I should have thought the last rich widow you dallied with would have kept a better kitchen. You look half-starved. You don't need any money for the tailor—"

"No," he interrupted, feeling heat flush his cheeks. Since his luck at the tables had been out of late, her comment about his ability to provide himself with food and raiment cut a bit too close for comfort. "My dear, my time with Clorinda was spent dining on delights far more arousing than any chef could devise."

She batted his arm. "If you're trying to put me to the blush, you're all out. Domcaster says I have no sensibility at all. Very good! I'll send you the invitation."

He bowed. "As you command, my lady."

"Stuff!" she said, making a face at him. "No, you needn't see me to my carriage," she added as he opened the door and made to walk her out. "My maid Berthe is waiting." She pointed down the hall to a young woman who stood by the staircase, a liveried footman beside her. "Until next week, then. It is good to see you again, Will," she added softly before she turned to stroll away.

"You, too, Lucilla," he murmured, returning her wave before she disappeared down the stairs.

Slowly Will reentered his room and sat back down in his chair. Lord Tavener of Brookwillow Manor. Could he really become such a man? Restore his house, revive the land, take up his music again, build a true scholar's library? Find someone who wished to share that life?

It seemed too good to be true…but in the last nine years, he'd not found any other way to achieve that dream. He discovered quickly enough after leaving Oxford that gaming, the only source of income open to a gentleman of no resources who wished to remain a gentleman, provided too irregular an income to facilitate the restoration of his birthright, nor after meeting his basic needs was there ever enough left to invest in some capital-generating venture. Nothing less than a substantial influx of cash—the sort that could be provided by the richly dowered bride Lucilla proposed to find him—could accomplish the task.

Already in poor condition at the time of his father's death, Brookwillow had been too modest a property and too needful of time and serious investment to set it to rights to induce his uncle and guardian, the Earl of Pennhurst, possessed as he was of so many grander and more extensive lands, to bother with it. The last time Will had visited his estate, rain was dripping through the dining-room roof and birds nested in the upper guest chambers. The Phillipses managed to keep the servant's quarters and kitchen habitable, but could do little with the rest.

As for the land, a few tenants still worked small plots around their cottages, but there weren't nearly enough acres under cultivation to produce a saleable crop. Not that, after spending his youth at boarding schools, he had any idea how to go about transforming the estate into a productive agricultural property.

In short, his indifferent uncle's provision of the bare modicum of a gentleman's upbringing had left Will with few resources and no useable skills. His only innate talent, beyond music, scholarship and a way with cards and horses, seemed to be the ability to beguile bored women into his bed. Though at first that unexpected aptitude had amused him and kept loneliness at bay, of late, even this facility had lost its charm. And no matter how many sessions he battled every contender who dared challenge him at Gentleman Jackson's, he could no longer box away the sense of emptiness inside.

While he was pondering the possibilities, Barrows walked back in. "So to what did we owe the honor of Lady Domcaster's most improper visit?"

Will smiled. "It seems I am to become a respectable member of the gentry, Barrows. Leave off gambling, shun immoral women, and find a tender bud of an heiress who will embrace me willingly, love me madly and hand over her fortune so I can restore Brookwillow."

Picking up the glass Lucilla had left, Barrows drained the last of the wine. "Do you know anything about charming a respectable maid?"

"About as much as I do about farming. But Lucilla insists I have naught to lose by attempting it. Perhaps 'twill be entertaining to attend some ton parties."

"You've always derived enjoyment from your cousin's company," Barrows pointed out. "And I have perceived of late that you seemed disinclined to accept some of the lures cast at you. Why, Lady Marlow practically—"

"Not you, too," Will groaned.

"If pursuing the improper sort of female has left you dissatisfied, attempting to entice the other sort might at least add a spice of variety to your life."

"I expect we shall see. Count how many coins we've

set aside, won't you? It seems I must visit the tailor. I'm to make my grand entrance soon at Lady Ormsby's rout."

"At once, m'lord." Raising the glass to him, Barrows walked out.

Add a spice of variety to his existence. Yes, entering the ton should do that. After a lifetime of being an outsider, the child not wanted, the student left behind at school during term breaks, he had no expectation that Lucilla's experiment would do anything more.

CHAPTER THREE

Two weeks later, as she helped Mrs. Bessborough stack freshly laundered sheets in the linen press, Allegra reflected wryly that the changes the housekeeper had predicted had begun sooner than—and not at all in the manner—that good woman had predicted.

Captain Lord Lynton had still not arrived, although the household continued to expect him at any moment. Apparently unconcerned with how Lynton House's new owner might view her actions, however, the day after her husband's funeral Sapphira summoned a small army of merchants and craftsmen to measure windows, floors, mantels and stairs. She intended, Allegra overheard her telling friends, to refurbish her late spouse's fusty old town house from attic to cellars.

And so she had, banishing the Chippendale mahogany furniture and brocaded hangings and replacing them with draperies in the startlingly bright colors she preferred and furnishings in the new Egyptian style.

When Hobbs, begging her pardon, objected to her wreaking a similar transformation upon the library until the new master determined what he wished to have done with his private domain, she'd sacked him and hired a sharp-faced younger man. She'd gone on to demote Cook to a mere assistant and hire a French chef whose expertise, she informed Mrs. Bessborough, would better please her discriminating guests.

"I visited Mr. Hobbs during my half-day," Mrs. Bessborough said, pulling Allegra out of her contemplation. "So sad it was to see him, stripped of his duties, and he a man still in his prime!" She shook her head. "I expect at any moment *she* will turn me off, as well."

"You needn't fear that," Allegra assured her. "Whatever her failings, Aunt Sapphira is clever enough to understand that with Stirling still finding his way about his butler's duties, the household would come to a complete halt without your steadying hand at the reins."

The housekeeper sniffed. "Indeed, for who would smooth down Cook's hackles or calm the maids after one of Monsieur Leveque's tantrums? *She* oughta be grateful you're here, too, speaking that Frenchie's tongue sweet as a lark and soothing his devil's temper like you do. I declare, even with the both of us, sometimes 'tis a pure miracle she gets her morning chocolate and her fancy dinners on time!"

At a jangling sound, Mrs. Bessborough glanced over at the bell case. "The front parlor—that will be the mistress. Now, where is Lizzie?"

"I'll go." With a half-smile, Allegra added, "Aunt Sapphira is probably looking for me anyway."

Wondering what chore her aunt would try to foist on her now, Allegra gave the last sheet to the housekeeper and took the stairs to the parlor.

Allegra suspected Lady Lynton's speedy sacking of Hobbs and demotion of Cook was intended both to begin restaffing the household with key employees loyal only to her and to deprive Allegra of anyone in authority who remembered her as a valued family member instead of a poor relation kept to do Sapphira's bidding. Welcoming the struggle as a distraction from her grief, since the new butler's arrival Allegra had been fighting a small rearguard action to stymie Sapphira's attempts to relegate her to servant status.

The day of his arrival, most certainly upon Sapphira's order, Stirling had stopped her in the hall and commanded her to clean the fireplaces in the guest bedrooms. With a hauteur that would have done Lady Grace proud, Allegra raked the man with a frosty glance and informed him that as Lord Lynton's cousin, she would determine for herself which tasks, fit for a gentlewoman, she wished to perform. Shrewd enough to realize the imprudence of challenging Allegra—at least not until the new master returned and made her position clear—he'd since ignored her.

Allegra also refused to Sapphira's face any chore the widow tried to assign her that did not fall, by Allegra's definition, within the scope of a lady's duties. Though her aunt had several times vowed she'd have "that ungrateful foreign brat" thrown into the street, nothing so dire had come to pass. Allegra concluded that Sapphira either did not trust her new butler to lay hands on a self-proclaimed lady—or realized she could not count on any of the footmen to assist Stirling in carrying out an order to eject her husband's unwanted relation.

Balked at forcing Allegra into menial duties, Sapphira countered by devising a never-ending succession of the most tedious but genteel chores she could imagine. Wondering whether she would be taxed to answer letters, sort the tangle of embroidery threads in Sapphira's sewing basket, pour tea or fetch the shawl, fan, sewing scissors or other item Sapphira inexplicably could not locate, particularly when there was an audience to watch Allegra do her bidding, Allegra knocked on the parlor door.

She entered to find Sapphira entertaining Lady Ingram and Mrs. Barton-Smythe, the two among her friends Allegra most disliked. At least, she thought with relief, it wasn't any of Sapphira's sycophant admirers, who, emboldened by her husband's death, paid her calls nearly every day.

After glancing at her when she walked in, Sapphira looked away, pointedly ignoring Allegra as she returned her attention to her friends. Allegra set her teeth and waited.

"You hadn't heard?" Lady Ingram was saying. "The divine Lord Tavener gave up Clorinda a month ago. Felicia Marlow's been trying to fix his interest—to no avail. Now, *there's* a man who could distract one from one's grief!"

"Such presence," Mrs. Barton-Smythe sighed. "Such eyes! Such physique!"

"Such *technique,*" Lady Ingram riposted, setting the women giggling.

Such a conversation to be having with a new widow, Allegra thought, her small store of patience exhausted. Compared to Rob, she doubted she'd find this Lord Tavener so "divine."

Pasting a smile on her face, she dipped a graceful curtsey. "Aunt Sapphira, how might I assist you?"

Her expression disapproving, Mrs. Barton-Smythe said, "Anyway, I understand Tavener's finally looking to marry. That should set off some fluttering in the dovecotes of London!"

"Indeed!" Sapphira replied. Finally deigning to ac-knowledge Allegra, she turned and waved an imperi-ous hand at her, like a sovereign giving permission for an underling to approach. "I find the parlor chilly, Allegra. Fetch my shawl. And do put an apron over that gown while you help Stirling polish the silver, for if you spoil the dress, I shan't buy you another!" Turning to her friends, she said with a shake of her head, "So thoughtless—but what can one expect of a chit of her background?"

Curling her nails into her palms to stifle the first response that sprang to her lips, Allegra laughed lightly. "Poor Aunt Sapphira, grief is making you forgetful! Polishing silver is a footman's task, as you know quite well. Although," she added in a thoughtful tone, "forgetfulness *is* said to be a sign of an aging mind. By the way, dear aunt, should you not take a seat out of the sunlight? 'Tis so injurious to the mature complexion."

Sapphira had opened her lips, probably to give Allegra a set-down, but at that last remark, alarm flared in her eyes. Clamping her mouth shut, she jumped up from the sofa and hurried over to the mirror.

Just then the front door knocker sounded. "Answer that before you get my shawl," Sapphira ordered as she peered into the glass, searching her reflection.

Suppressing a chuckle, Allegra exited the room and walked down to the entry hall. Bypassing with a rueful shrug the footman who stood ready to perform that task, she threw open the door.

Allegra's breath caught and her hand clutched the doorknob as her gaze locked on the tall officer in scarlet regimentals. "Rob!" she gasped.

A thin scar made a white arch over the left eyebrow of a face bronzed by a life in the saddle. Standing on the threshold was not the lighthearted Oxford student she remembered, but someone older, rather stern-looking, every inch the seasoned commander who had led men in battle.

Still, with his hair the color of ripe wheat and his deep blue eyes set off by the brilliant red of his uniform, Rob Lynton was even handsomer than the university student of six years ago. She exhaled in a rush as something fluttered in her chest.

He was staring at her, as well. "Is that—Allegra?

Heavens, how grown up you look! But what are you doing answering the door?"

"Oh, R-Rob!" she stuttered, his dear face suddenly reminding her so vividly of his father's that grief razored through her, bringing tears to her eyes.

Seeing them, his expression softened. Stepping past her to close the door, he murmured, "Ah, Allegra, 'tis a heartache indeed," and drew her into his arms.

Savoring the feeling of his closeness, she clung to him, fighting the urge to weep. A sharp "harrumph" made her straighten. She turned to see Stirling watching them, disapproval on his face.

Eying her askance, he inclined his head to Rob and said icily, "How may I help you, soldier?"

With one hand resting on her shoulder, Rob looked him up and down. "It's 'captain' to you, sirrah. And who are you? Where is Hobbs?"

"Rob, this is Stirling, your, ah, new butler," Allegra interposed.

Stirling's face registered shock, followed by an almost comical dismay. "Lord Lynton, f-forgive me!" he stammered, bowing low. "Please allow me to express my own and the staff's great pleasure at your safe return!"

Frowning, Rob glanced around the entry at the crocodile-legged table and brightly striped hangings. "Is this home?"

"Perhaps I should take you in to meet Sapphira," Allegra suggested.

Rob grimaced. "Ah, yes, my lovely new mama. No

point postponing that pleasure, I suppose. My batman will be arriving shortly," he said to Stirling. "Assist him in stowing my kit." Turning his back on the butler, he grasped Allegra's arm. "Shall we go?"

Stirling bowed deeply as they passed. "At once, my lord, Miss Allegra!"

"You've become quite a beauty, little cousin," Rob said as he walked her up to the parlor. "But what were you doing in the hallway, answering the door in that old gown? Why aren't you wearing proper mourning?"

Flushing with pleasure at his first remark, Allegra hesitated before responding to the second. As satisfying as it might be to pour into his ears all her anger and resentment toward Sapphira—and as promising as Rob's initial comment about his stepmother had been— bitter experience had taught her caution.

It would be wiser to keep her own counsel until Rob observed for himself the changes that had been wrought in his absence. If he were no longer the fair-minded individual she'd known…if Sapphira managed to win him over in spite of the alterations she'd made, he would neither take kindly nor give much credence to any negative opinions Allegra voiced now about his stepmother.

And if Sapphira did win him over, Allegra would offer Rob the report about his father's last days that she'd promised herself to deliver and leave Lynton House as soon as she could arrange it.

Leave Lynton House and Rob…her childhood hero

and the one remaining link to her idyllic past. The thought cut too deeply, so she thrust it away and focused on the query to which she could safely reply. "I was not…very well circumstanced when I arrived," she said, shame scouring her at his disapproval, "and haven't yet the funds to purchase mourning gowns."

"Then my father's wife should have ordered some for you," Rob said flatly.

"We'll talk more about it later," Allegra replied as they arrived at the parlor. Knocking once, she pushed the door open and escorted him in.

"Aunt Sapphira, ladies," she said as he bowed. "May I present Captain Lord Lynton."

The babble of conversation faded into shocked silence. Lady Ingram and Mrs. Barton-Smythe hurriedly stood and dropped curtseys, while Sapphira froze, staring at Rob's unsmiling face. Then she rose as well, one hand at her throat—and fainted.

As an opening tactic, Allegra thought as she watched Rob rush to catch his stepmother before she crumpled to the floor, Sapphira's swoon was masterful. In one action, she both emphasized her role as his father's fragile, grief-ravaged widow and bought herself time to assess her stepson's reaction.

Her sardonic amusement deepening, Allegra observed how, while fluttering and moaning as he lifted her onto the couch, Sapphira managed to rub her impressive bosom against Rob's coat, insuring he could not fail to notice her feminine charms, either.

Though Rob caught Sapphira and set her gently back onto the couch, his expression remained guarded—as if he mistrusted her performance as much as Allegra did. Nor did he display any of the panic or agitation with which men often reacted to feminine tears and trauma. Some of the tension in Allegra's gut eased.

Coolly Rob turned to Sapphira's callers. "Begging your pardon, ladies, I must ask you to excuse us. I'm sure my stepmother will send you a note when she is feeling more the thing." He swept them a bow, leaving them with no choice but to murmur expressions of solicitude and take their leave.

After directing the footman who showed them out to summon Lady Lynton's maid, he went to the sideboard and poured a glass of wine. When Sapphira opened her eyes and gazed dazedly around her, he presented it.

"Please sip this, ma'am, while we wait for your maid to assist you. I regret the distress my sudden entrance evidently caused and beg leave to wait upon you later when you've recovered."

Taking the glass from Rob—and making sure her fingers brushed his, Allegra noted—Sapphira took a tiny sip and gazed up at him. "Lord Lynton—our own dear Rob! Pray excuse my weakness, but when I saw you standing there, looking so much like my poor Robert, I was…quite overcome."

Rob removed his fingers. "Indeed. I expect you will grow accustomed to the likeness, since I intend to sell out and remain in England."

"Oh, Rob, that's great news!" Allegra said, speaking for the first time since the little drama unfolded.

Ignoring her, Sapphira gave him a weak smile. "Then I will have you to advise me? What a relief! Managing a household is such a burden for a woman alone, especially as I am still so much cast down…" She allowed one crystalline tear to bead on her long lashes.

At that moment, Hill, Sapphira's dresser, appeared along with Lizzie. Allegra noted that after Hill assured Rob she and Lizzie could manage taking her ladyship up to her chamber, he made no further attempt to assist her. He simply watched as the women supported Sapphira out of the room, a thoughtful expression on his face.

When the trio had gone, he turned back to Allegra. "I notice you didn't offer your help."

"I expect Aunt Sapphira would sooner accept the hand of an urchin off the street than take mine," she replied.

"You don't get on?"

After briefly considering a more detailed response, Allegra said only "No."

Rob studied her, his gaze progressing from her simply arranged hair to her gloveless hands to her worn gown. His eyes returning to her face, he said, "I have an appointment with the solicitors soon, but when I return, I should like to talk further."

"I'd like that, too. You…" She paused, her eyes filling with tears. "You must wish to know about Uncle

Robert's last days. He often spoke of you, and I promised to convey his blessings."

"I didn't know how ill he was until…" His own eyes sheening with moisture, Rob broke off and swallowed hard. "In his last letter, he said only that he'd been ailing with some trifling thing that would soon pass. When I heard nothing further, I should have realized that something was amiss—but there was always one more duty to perform, and the weeks slipped by."

Shocked, Allegra looked up at him. "You didn't know how desperately ill he was?"

"If I had, I would have come home at once! But after that one letter, Papa didn't write again. And his fine new wife sent me…nothing. I didn't even know you were here. I'm glad he had some family with him at…at the end."

"Oh, Rob," she whispered, tears starting again as his face contorted. While he looked away, fighting for control, she took his hand. He gripped hers hard for a moment before turning back to her.

"Thank you for being here, Allegra. I want to know everything, but later, when I have more time. Now I must go up and change for the appointment. Walk up with me, won't you?"

Letting go of her hand, he motioned her to precede him. In silence they entered the hall and walked up the stairs. Distracted by a renewal of her grief, it wasn't until Rob stopped at the door to the blue bedchamber that she remembered.

Flushing, she motioned toward his room farther down the hall. "I'll leave you to finish your preparations. Please do send for me when you get back, and good luck at the solicitors." After squeezing his hand, she made to walk past him back toward the service stairs.

He caught her shoulder. "Come now, Bessie can manage without you for a few hours. Why don't you rest while I'm gone?" With a smile, he opened the door to the blue bedchamber and gave her a teasing push.

Caught off-guard by that action, she stumbled. By the time she'd righted herself, her flush deepening as she tried to think of something to say, his sharp gaze had scanned the obviously unoccupied chamber.

"You're not staying here?"

She summoned a smile. "I have…other accommodations now."

His lips tightened into a thin line. "I see. Yes, we shall certainly talk later."

"Of course. I hope your meeting goes well." Turning again, she walked away, acutely aware that instead of continuing on to his room, he remained in the hallway. She felt the force of his gaze upon her until she disappeared behind the door to the service stairs.

THE IMPERATIVE of revisiting for Rob the last few weeks of his father's life brought Allegra's muted grief back to sharp, aching focus. Not feeling up to a battle of wills with Sapphira, she climbed the stairs and slipped inside her little attic room.

A few hours later, after reviewing her time with her late uncle and choosing the details she would recount to Rob, she reread the note she'd just received from Mr. Waters at the employment agency, summarizing their interview earlier in the week.

Her qualifications looked excellent, he wrote, and given the gentility of her carriage, voice and demeanor, he felt certain he would have no trouble obtaining a post for her as soon as he received her letters of reference.

Sighing, Allegra cudgeled her brain trying to determine whom she might approach to obtain such letters. Giving up the effort for the moment, as she had often these last few months when she struggled with some problem, from her reticule she drew out her most prized possession—her father's last letter, written when he knew he was dying.

The vellum was smooth and worn from use. Just holding it gave her comfort, nor had she any need to unfold it to recall the words written within.

"My precious daughter," Papa had begun in a struggling hand, "I now accept that this feeble frame has refused my will's demand to recover. But before I go, I must tell you that while music was my life, you and your mother have been my heart, my soul, my spirit and my joy. Though I rejoice that soon, she and I will be together for all eternity, my heart breaks at leaving you alone. You must not be afraid, *carita.* Always remember you possess your mother's grace and the Antinori fierceness."

The writing growing steadily more illegible, he concluded, "With your courage, intelligence and spirit, all will be well in the end. Adios! Your adoring Papa."

At this moment as never before, Allegra felt truly alone in the world. A rush of panic and despair escaped her attempt to supress it. Would everything ever be well again?

A knock sounded at the door, interrupting her thoughts, and Lizzie popped in. "The Captain be wanting to see you in the library." Belatedly adding a curtsey, Lizzie continued, "At your convenience, he said." She sighed. "Oh, Miss Allegra, ain't he just the handsomest man you ever saw? And as gentlemanly as handsome!"

Calling Rob's face to mind steadied Allegra. With her old friend returned, she wasn't completely alone. "Handsome and gentlemanly indeed," she agreed. Resolute and gallant as a knight of yore, she added to herself, picturing him again in his regimentals. If only her childhood hero might ride to her rescue.

A sudden flare of hope made her straighten. Even as a boy, Rob had followed his father's lead in supporting her and her family. He'd chastised his friends when they teased her and once knocked down another boy who called her a "dark-faced foreigner." Might he offer some more attractive alternatives for her future?

She mustn't depend on anyone but herself now, she reminded. But though she told herself she should count only on delivering Uncle Robert's messages to Rob before going her own way, Allegra could not forestall a swell of excitement.

Not sure whether he would include Sapphira in their

discussion, Allegra was relieved when she entered the library to find only Rob within. But seeing him seated behind the desk where she had so often found Uncle Robert, she had to take a deep breath.

"Allegra, come in!" he called. "Some wine?"

After pouring them each a glass, Rob ushered her to the sofa and took a seat beside her. "First, accept both my condolences and my apologies. You must have thought me an unfeeling beast! I didn't learn until I talked with Bessie this afternoon that you lost your parents last fall. Please believe that I would have written at once, had I known. I can only be glad that after that awful event, you had the good sense to come here to Papa."

Determined to banish the threatening tears, she took a sip of her wine and composed herself. "It was…a dreadful time. I think we helped each other, Uncle Robert and I."

"You certainly helped him! Bessie told me he was already ill when you arrived. That you put aside your own grief and devoted all your time to entertaining and tending him…and at the last, to keeping vigil. Chores his new wife did not feel up to performing, I understand."

Allegra shrugged. "He was almost as much a father to me as my own. It was a pleasure to spend time with him." Amazing herself, she felt compelled to add, "Sapphira is rather young, and has neither the sensibility nor the skill to be of much assistance in a sickroom. I believe she has been all her life much cosseted and indulged."

Rob grimaced. "So I gathered upon entering my

front hallway. I thought at first I'd stumbled into the wrong house! I stopped to see Hobbs this afternoon and learned I have him to thank for sparing this room from invasion by crocodiles and lacquered paint. I've reinstated him, by the way."

"I'm so glad! But—what about Stirling?"

"Sapphira can provide him with references—assuming she is up to that task. You are also young, but you seem to have managed the duties of the sickroom quite well."

She smiled. "Oh, but consider my unconventional upbringing! From plucking chickens to make a healing broth to brewing tisanes to soothe the throat of an ailing soprano, there are few nursing chores I've not done. But enough of me. Let me tell you about Uncle Robert."

For the next half hour, Allegra sketched for Rob all the events of the last few months of his father's life, touching on his humor, his faith, his courage and the great love he bore his son. "Toward the last, he dictated several letters for you. As he requested, I left them there, in the desk drawer."

Rob nodded. "I found them after returning from the solicitor's office. But what of you, Allegra? What do you intend to do now?"

She faced him squarely. "You needn't worry that I mean to be a charge upon you. I've inquired about a post as a governess."

"My fiery little cousin a governess?" He grinned and shook his head. "The girl who dressed down a duke in the park for having the temerity to ride by too closely to her mount? Who would have come to blows with that numbclutch Eton mate of mine for calling her a silly, lisping foreigner, had I not intervened? Heaven help the unlucky family that hired you!"

Allegra felt her face heat. "I admit, I was a trifle… boisterous as a child. But I've long since mastered my temper."

"Have you?" he drawled, his amused tone suggesting he didn't believe it for an instant. "I hope you're not set on the notion of becoming a governess, for after consulting Papa's solicitors, I have other plans."

Did he mean to assist her after all? Trying to restrain her soaring hopes, she replied, "Other plans?"

"Though you may not know it, for Papa lived simply and such worldly considerations were obviously never of any importance to your parents, the Lyntons are quite wealthy. Which doubtless explains my father's appeal to a chit of Sapphira's age," he added acidly. "Despite bestowing a sumptuous jointure upon his widow, Papa left a sizeable estate. It was his wish that you have the means to reclaim the place in society that should have been yours as Lady Grace's daughter."

For a moment Allegra stared at Rob, uncomprehending. "You mean…he left me a bequest?" she said at last.

"A bequest? Ah, well, yes, I suppose you could call it that. You shall have a handsome sum to serve as your dowry, along with the funds to purchase gowns and all the other necessary fripperies so that you may attend the afternoon calls, rout parties, balls and such that will lead to becoming betrothed to a worthy young man who will cherish and protect you for the rest of your life."

"And then I live happily ever after?" Allegra gave a bitter laugh. "The idea of entering that world is just as much a fairy tale. Even girls Mama came out with, ones she considered good friends, gave her the cut direct after she married Papa. Aside from Uncle Robert, not even her own family recognized her. What makes you think they would accept her daughter?" *What makes you think I want them to?* she added silently.

"Ah, but you are wrong. Lady Grace's papa would have welcomed her home at any time, but she refused to take up her 'proper' position among her own class if it meant being separated from your father. True, the highest sticklers may not receive you and Almacks might be beyond your touch, but a sizeable part of the polite world will be quite willing to accept the ward of Lord Lynton and granddaughter of Viscount Conwyn."

She held her hands out at her sides. "Accept this 'dark-skinned foreigner'?" she asked skeptically, Sapphira's oft-repeated disparagement of her ebony hair and olive skin echoing in her head.

Smiling slightly, Rob studied her, the intensity of his gaze sending a little shock through her. "Not all men like a blond-and-pink princess," he said softly after a moment. "Some prefer a more…earthy, exotic lady."

The appreciation in his eyes deepened to something hotter. Allegra felt her cheeks flush, her mind suddenly buffeted by so many contradictory ideas and emotions she could not frame a reply.

One practical observation in that flurry of thoughts steadied her. "But what of a sponsor? You must know Sapphira would never…" Her voice trailed off and she grimaced as she imagined the probable response, were Rob to have the temerity to ask his stepmother to introduce her.

"Oh no, Sapphira isn't…temperamentally suited for the role. Besides, she must be in deep mourning for at least six more months, while by the time the Season begins, you need only don black gloves. I shall invite Cousin Letitia Randall to stay with us. She knew your mother well. That is, if you will agree to a presentation?"

Her immediate response was to decline, but she bit it back. Rob was being kind and extremely generous. Though she had decidedly mixed feelings about entering society, with the arrogance of one born to that privileged world, he would never understand why she would not leap for joy at this chance to claim a place within it. And despite his assurances, he must know that he would need both determination and perseverance to overcome what she suspected would be a rocky reception by the ton if she accepted his offer.

Unless…

She recalled the look of heated appreciation in Rob's eyes. Suddenly her mind was overwhelmed by a resurgence of the wild hope she'd never quite managed to extinguish. Only one thing would make Rob's generous offer truly a dream come true.

Dressed in lovely clothes, hair upswept and her mother's pearls about her neck, might she capture the heart of this "parfait, gentil" knight for her own?

If she could, if she could bring Rob to realize that the wild girl of whom he'd always been fond was now an accomplished, desirable woman, one with whom he wanted to share his life, it would be a more marvelous resolution to her dilemma than she dared believe possible.

Instead of going alone into the world, she'd be able to remain here with Rob, Bessie and Hobbs, the only people still on earth who knew and appreciated her— and not as a servant, but as a daughter of the house. Marrying some ton gentleman so as to reclaim her mother's place in society held little appeal, but if that ton gentleman were Rob, she would gain not just social acceptance and a secure future, she would have won her secret heart's desire and a love to last a lifetime.

A love like her parents'.

Despite the difficulties her mother had experienced because of marrying her father, Lady Grace and her husband had been happy. Having grown up in the charmed circle of their devotion, Allegra couldn't envision marrying someone, as Sapphira obviously had, only to secure wealth and a comfortable position in society. Nor did she think she could tolerate marrying a man who deigned to give her his name and heirs but not his loyalty or affection.

If she married, it must be to a man she desired, respected and loved without reserve. A man who pledged his love and fidelity in return. Someone trustworthy, steadfast and honorable—like Rob.

Could she win his heart?

"Well?" Rob interrupted her racing thoughts.

"I…I'm not sure," she said, her mind still entrapped in glorious speculation.

He grinned. "Then say 'yes.' I'll write Cousin Letitia tonight. You'll doubtless want her assistance in purchasing that wardrobe of gowns and such. With the Season soon to start, you need to begin on that at once. Lady Ormsby's rout is barely a month away."

He rose to his feet. "If you'll excuse me, I must go wait upon Sapphira and inform her of our plans."

Allegra shook her head, sure of only one thing about Rob's audacious scheme. "Sapphira is not going to like this."

Rob laughed out loud. "No, I expect not," he said as he advanced to the door. "I knew the Lord would send some ray of sunshine to brighten the bleakness of father's passing." Pausing on the threshold, he looked back to add, "By the way, I told Bessie to move your things back into the blue bedchamber." He snapped her a salute. "Welcome back to the family, Allegra."

For long moments after Rob walked out, Allegra sat motionless, hardly able to believe her entire circumstances had changed so dramatically in the space of a single day.

There was no reason not to accept this offer. If her fondest desires about Rob were not realized, if she found society not to her liking or the ton rebuffed her, she could always use Uncle Robert's legacy to purchase the property for which she'd been pining and carve out a life for herself there.

Either way, she would have a permanent home of her own that no one could ever take from her.

No more creeping down service stairs, suspended between two worlds. Uncle Robert had loved her as she loved him. He'd appreciated and valued her enough to leave her an inheritance, thought her deserving of a place in her mother's society. Perhaps deserving of his son's love?

A deep gratitude sharpened the pangs of loss. How she missed that gentle, quiet, loving man! Knuckling the tears from her eyes, she vowed she would justify the confidence he'd placed in her, make Rob proud he'd welcomed her back into the family.

And just maybe, she concluded with a tremor of exhilaration and longing, she would gain Rob's love and a secure place to belong.

CHAPTER FOUR

THREE WEEKS LATER, Will sat at Lady Domcaster's dinner table, a smile stamped on his lips as he cut his gaze to the head of the table, trying to catch his cousin Lucilla's eye while giving nominal attention to the young lady seated beside him.

"I declare, Lord Tavener," Miss Benton-Wythe exclaimed in her flat, nasal voice, "when the governess opened her door and the chicken Harry had hidden flew out, flapping and squawking, she shrieked so loud we were like to die laughing!" Apparently envisioning that occasion, she went off into a fit of giggles.

Wincing, Will turned to his other side to address the honoree of the evening, Miss Cecelia Rysdale, daughter of Lucilla's friend Lydia. "Miss Rysdale, do you recall any similar amusing events from childhood?"

Color came and went in the young lady's cheeks as she hastily dropped her eyes to her plate, muttering an unintelligible syllable Will took to be "no." 'Twas about the extent of the response he'd been able to eke from her during the course of this interminable dinner.

Having no idea what one talked about with young

ladies, he'd first mentioned the progress of the peace accords in Vienna, then asked about the current offerings of the Philharmonic Society, then attempted to elicit opinions on the performance of *Hamlet* now at Covent Garden. After these conversational overtures evoked puzzled silence, a rather desperate compliment about the young ladies' bonnets finally drew a response from Miss Benton-Wythe.

Though not even the mention of fashion managed to entice Miss Rysdale into speech, her companion more than made up for her silence. Miss Benton-Wythe launched into a detailed description of the design and construction of her headgear, and having begun, needed no encouragement whatsoever to keep on chattering.

Will calculated that over the course of this dinner, Miss Benton-Wythe had produced enough words to fill three conversations, all delivered in a penetrating voice and punctuated by high-pitched giggles that were giving him the headache. He wished he'd stuck to a monologue about diplomacy.

Finally catching Lucilla's attention, he cast her a beseeching look. Though she returned him a stern glance, the corner of her mouth twitched as she rose, signaling it was time for the ladies to leave the table.

Will leapt to his feet. "Ladies, my pleasure," he told the two girls as he bowed.

"La, my lord, 'twas my pleasure, too," Miss Benton-Wythe said, giving him a frankly assessing look.

Hard-pressed to suppress his relief, Will watched

Lucilla lead the women from the room. Thank heavens all the attendees at this dinner were proceeding to other engagements, sparing him the necessity of sharing brandy and cigars with the male guests, mostly fathers of Miss Rysdale and her friends and mostly unknown to him. He understood now why Domcaster, despite his obvious affection for his wife, had chosen to return to the country.

Even as Will nodded and smiled, the gentlemen started to follow the ladies out. When the last one exited, Will sat back down and took a long, fortifying pull on his wineglass. It appeared this business of finding a rich wife would be even more distasteful than he'd envisioned.

He had just finished the wine when Lucilla returned. "Bless you, cousin," he said. "Two more minutes and I would have cast myself facedown into the syllabub."

Though Lucilla clucked in disapproval, her eyes danced. "I'll allow that Miss Benton-Wythe's voice is a trifle…grating."

"I should have enjoyed hearing more of Miss Rysdale's. But after I delivered a very mild tribute to her appearance, she looked as if she thought I meant to ravish her upon the spot and spent the rest of the meal communing with the china."

Lucilla sighed. "Someone must have carried tales to her about your wicked reputation. She is rather timid."

"Perhaps I should have reassured her that I do not seduce children," Will returned. "I must warn you, grateful as I am for your support, if this is a sample of what

I can expect in the Marriage Mart, I'd rather resign myself to my rooms in Chelsea."

Lucilla shook her head. "Not all the eligible young ladies are being fired straight from the schoolroom, as Cecelia and Miss Benton-Wythe are. You shall encounter a much larger variety shortly at Lady Ormsby's rout. Besides, you promised to be my escort for the Season and I'm not about to let you wiggle out of that! Let me collect my cloak and we can be off."

"Will there be a card room? Winning a few hands of pique would help restore my good humor."

"Yes, there should be some play. And I don't mean to be unreasonable. Once I've introduced you around— and you have stood up with me twice, for I must dance!—if you meet no lady who engages your interest, I will cede you to the card room."

"In that case, I am yours to command," Will said.

An hour later, wearing the most beautiful gown she'd ever owned and knowing she looked her best, Allegra stood in the shadows of Lady Ormsby's entryway. A Lynton footman had caught up with them just as they arrived with a note for Rob from his estate manager that, Rob said, apologizing to them for the delay, required an immediate response. Retreating out of the press of arriving guests, she waited with Mrs. Randall for Rob to complete his business so they might go up.

She should be giddy with anticipation at attending her very first ton party. Instead, she was tense and wary despite the promise of having Rob beside her all evening, looking, she thought, a pleasant flutter in her chest as she gazed over to him, handsomer than a prince in his elegant evening attire.

Unfortunately, in the three weeks since Rob had dramatically altered her life, it had quickly become evident that Mrs. Letitia Randall, the cousin he had invited to London to fill the roll of chaperone, was no match for the cunning—and malice—of Sapphira Lynton.

Beginning soon after the slamming of the door and the wail of weeping that had followed Rob's proclamation of Allegra's change of status, Lady Lynton had done all within her power to circumvent and frustrate Rob's intention to raise Allegra to a place within the ton. With a feminine guile that was impossible for Allegra to prove and would be difficult for Rob's masculine mind to comprehend, her intervention had been by indirection or subterfuge.

"La, I'm much too cast down to traipse all over town spending Lynton's blunt," Sapphira had proclaimed when the meek Mrs. Randall asked her to advise them on the acquiring of Allegra's wardrobe. "I suppose I could pen a note to the modistes I favor, recommending styles, colors and fabrics for Allegra's gowns. Fitting her out fashionably is going to be difficult, though, Tall Meg that she is."

And write she had, Allegra thought, clamping her lips together as she wondered just what exactly Sapphira had penned. For had Allegra not insisted upon following her own judgment, honed by years of observing costumes in opera and the theater, the modistes would have persuaded Mrs. Randall into purchasing Allegra a wardrobe of pink and white frocks profusely trimmed in lace and ribbon that would not have become her in the least.

While Lady Lynton also proclaimed herself too ill to accompany them paying social calls, she expressed an avid interest in discovering from Mrs. Randall each morning where they planned to visit. On numerous occasions, as they alighted from a hackney at the house of one or another of the ton's hostesses, Allegra spied Lady Lynton's carriage just leaving.

When they entered the drawing room thereafter, Allegra was met with stilted politeness, speculative looks—or outright silence, as conversation ceased while the ladies already present turned to stare at her.

Sapphira's heavy floral perfume hanging in the air like the scent of smoke after a candle is snuffed, it was obvious from the careful omission of any inquiry about Allegra's parents that someone had just re-illumined all the details of Lady Grace's scandal. At times, annoyed and frustrated by the hypocrisy, only Allegra's desire not to embarrass poor Mrs. Randall prevented her from boldly asking if her hostess had met Lady Grace after her marriage…and had that lady ever had the privilege of hearing her father play?

Even more dispiriting, since returning her to the family, Rob had left her entirely in Mrs. Randall's care. She'd seen him but seldom and until tonight, had had no champion to stand beside her in the glare of society's faintly hostile scrutiny.

She wouldn't have minded the female disdain had she felt she was making some progress in luring Rob to act upon his observation that his little cousin had become a desirable woman. Though on the few occasions they'd met at home, she'd seen the same heated appreciation in his eyes, she could hardly bewitch him if he was so seldom present to be bewitched.

Thanks again to Sapphira, she thought with irritation. Apparently not content with her initial attempt to entice Rob, the first night he'd dined at home with them, Sapphira had been at her most alluring, gazing up at Rob, soliciting his comments and opinions, leaning down to display her bosom while passing him dishes, letting her fingers rest on his during the exchange. Grimacing with a distaste that was thrilling to Allegra, Rob had pointedly pulled his hand free, then quit the dining room as soon as dessert was served. He'd not eaten a meal with them since.

Thank heavens Sapphira had such overweening confidence in her own appeal that, since Rob resisted her, she'd not be able to conceive of him admiring any other woman. For if she ever discovered Allegra's secret hope, she'd make life even more miserable for her.

But possessing the Antinori fierceness, Allegra wasn't about to give up yet. Somehow she would find more opportunities to be with him—and make the most of the ones she had, like tonight.

Cheered by that resolution, she gave Rob her most glittering smile when at last, his instructions to the footman complete, he returned to offer each of them an arm.

"Are the loveliest ladies at the party ready to greet their hostess?"

"With you beside me, I'm ready for anything," Allegra said, and put her hand firmly on his arm. Together they mounted the stairs to Lady Ormsby's ballroom.

IN THE RECEIVING LINE upstairs, after smiling and bowing through a long round of introductions, Will led Lucilla toward the ballroom, doing his best to look as if he were interested in the proceedings. To his greetings, he'd received mostly blushing monosyllables from the younger maidens, speculative looks under veiled lashes from the older ones—and boldly inviting glances from two well-endowed widows.

"Perhaps my wicked reputation has preceded me," Will told his cousin. "I seem to terrify the infants."

"They will find you charming enough once they converse with you. But upon first meeting, you tend to wear a stern, rather intimidating look. Please remember that the young ladies you are greeting are not rival pugilists you are about to confront in the ring! Smile, speak only of something unexceptional and you will put them at ease."

"I have confined myself to the unexceptional!" Will protested. "'Miss Westerly, what a charming gown. The blue quite lights up your eyes.' I daresay I've never uttered so much treacle in a single evening. Now, several of the matrons seemed much more…rewarding of my efforts." He sighed and looked at Lucilla, a twinkle in his eyes. "Having bowed before innocence all evening, I find myself thirsting for a taste of plain, straightforward sin."

While Lucilla batted him on the arm and called him "incorrigible," Will scanned the room, looking for the two widows who'd given him come-hither glances. Once he'd danced with Lucilla, he might seek out their company. He deserved some amusement after enduring an entire dinner with Miss Benton-Wythe.

As Will paused at the entrance to the ballroom, his gaze drifted to a trio of guests who had just ascended from the entry below. He was about to turn away when the image before his eyes registered in his brain and he froze in midstep.

Outlined against the black-garbed older lady leading the group was a much younger woman in a diaphanous gown of pale gold. The burnished glow of the material set off the faintly olive hue of the skin perceptible above her gloves and the modest décolletage of her dress. Staring now with avid appreciation, Will noted the lovely line of shoulder and neck—and the voluptuous curve of bosom concealed beneath the gown.

Throat drying and fingers curling in his gloves, he spent another instant regretting the neckline hadn't been cut lower, allowing bystanders a better look at that tempting lushness. All his senses humming, he forced his eyes upward.

Her face, with its high cheekbones, narrow nose and wide forehead, was the same exotic tint as her chest and shoulders. If she'd not deigned to try to mask her unfashionable coloring with rice power, very likely she'd employed no artifice to thicken the luxuriant lashes that framed those large dark eyes. Whether or not the ripe apricot hue of her full lips stemmed from nature or artifice did not affect his immediate, powerful desire to kiss them. His body tightened at the thought.

Who was she and what was she doing here? he wondered. Looking like an exotic Eastern princess, she seemed as out of place among this crop of pink-and-white-gowned debutantes as if one of the glasshouse orchids his classics professor used to grow had suddenly sprouted in a field of demure English daisies.

A jerk at his arm pulled him from his rapt contemplation of the newcomer.

"Will, what is wrong?" Lucilla asked.

"That girl in the saffron gown." Will angled his chin toward the doorway. "Who is she?"

His cousin looked in the direction he'd indicated. "The one walking with the woman in widow's black?" When he nodded impatiently, she continued, "Miss Allegra Antinori. Despite the foreign name, she's from the Montesgue family—Viscount Conwyn is her grandfather. She's the ward of a distant connection of her mother, Lord Lynton—" Lucilla indicated the blond gentleman escorting the two ladies "—whose cousin, Mrs. Randall, is her chaperone."

"Allegra," Will repeated, the music of her name lingering on his tongue. "And she's unmarried?" If unwed and possessed of an entrée to this gathering, she must definitely be on the Marriage Mart. Lucilla's idea of beguiling a well-bred maid suddenly seemed much more appealing.

Lucilla glanced at his face, no doubt perceiving the avid interest in his eyes. Thankfully she didn't cast her glance lower, or she might have discerned rather pointed evidence of the strength of that interest.

"Yes, she's unmarried and eligible—I suppose. Though I don't know if the dowry left her by the late Lord Lynton would be adequate to your needs."

Ignoring for the moment the matter of wealth, the hesitation in Lucilla's voice prompted him to ask, "You 'suppose' she is eligible?"

Lucilla sighed. "'Tis a rather old scandal. Her mother, Lady Grace, Viscount Conwyn's youngest daughter, ruined herself by running off with a foreigner. After her parents' deaths, the girl returned to live with the Lyntons, who were the only of her mother's relations who did not shun the connection after her mother's misalliance. But for that one blot upon the family escutcheon, Miss Antinori's breeding is unexceptional—though the highest sticklers would probably not agree. Still, if her fortune is sufficient, she has a chance of making an acceptable match. At least I hope so, not being one for holding the sins of the parent against the child."

"You never did so in the past," Will murmured, feeling another level of connection to the alluring Miss Antinori.

Just then, the girl looked up and caught him staring at her. As her dark eyes locked on his, Will's nerves tingled and a warmth swept through him, as if he'd suddenly stepped from shadow into sunlight.

Despite the information Lucilla had just given him indicating Miss Antinori's reception by society might be uncertain, at discovering herself to be the object of scrutiny, the girl neither blushed nor looked away. For a long moment, she held his gaze coolly. Will felt the charged force of the link between them, like the tension on the lead between a trainer and the green colt he is trying to master.

Then, lifting her chin and squaring her shoulders, she turned her face away, took Lord Lynton's arm and walked with him into the crowd of guests.

Shaken by that wordless encounter, Will turned back to Lucilla. It seemed there was not enough air in the room, for he had to catch his breath before he could speak. "Despite a childhood spent banished from society," he said at last, "the girl seems poised enough. Where did Lady Grace and her daughter end up?"

"Her father was a musician, I'm told, so—"

"Don't tell me she's the daughter of Emilio Antinori!" Will interrupted, the vague flicker of recognition in his brain suddenly flaming into focus.

"Why, yes. You've heard of him? Well, of course you would have," Lucilla concluded, "as interested in music as you've always been. He was good, I take it?"

Will laughed, his gaze following the girl as she made her way through the room on her escort's arm. "'Good' is hardly adequate to describe the work of Emilio Antinori. The man was a genius, not just the most talented violinist since Haydn, but also a composer whose works rival in depth and complexity those of Bach and Beethoven. I once had the privilege of watching him play. Amazing."

Though he'd attended the concert more than ten years ago, Will could still hear the high, pure vibrato notes, see the flying fingers that made the intricate progression of arpeggios seem effortless while the intensity of melody held him mesmerized. If he'd had a fraction of the talent of the great Antinori, he would have turned his back on his heritage and become a professional musician.

With an ache of regret that the world had lost such a talent, Will came back to the present to find Lucilla watching him, a faint smile on her lips. "Do I get my dance now?" she asked. "Or, given that look in your eye, must there be introductions first?"

"You can present me to Miss Antinori?" he asked eagerly.

"I met her while paying afternoon calls. She seems nice enough. Her cousin and sponsor, Robert Lynton, the new Lord Lynton, was a classmate of Domcaster's at Oxford."

"Rob Lynton? Yes, I remember him from school. Present me then, if you please."

Lucilla's smile faded. "There's one other complication you should know about. With Lynton sponsoring Miss Antinori, one would expect Lady Lynton to be her chaperone, but apparently the two do not get on. I don't know Robert's stepmother—she made her bow after Domcaster and I retired to the country. I'm told that after several years as society's reigning Diamond, she married the late Lord Lynton only last year."

Will recalled a well-curved blond beauty with blue eyes and a coquettish manner ill-suited to her status as a new bride. "I believe I have met Lady Lynton."

"As a handsome man with a rakish reputation, I imagine you have," Lucilla retorted with a sniff. "Though she makes quite a display of mourning, I've heard Sapphira Lynton has never gotten over being society's darling, the only child doted on by her papa. The Lyntons are quite wealthy, which I suppose explains why she accepted that offer out of the scores she's reputed to have received. Though I also understand that while her husband lay dying, 'twas Miss Antinori who nursed her relation while Lynton's 'distraught' wife consoled herself with her cicisbos."

Having already formed a dim opinion of a lady who'd been casting out lures to other men when the wedding ring had scarcely settled on her finger, Will could readily believe it. "And the happy family resides all together? Quite an accomplishment."

Lucilla chuckled. "It must be indeed. I'll present you if you insist, though I'd much rather your interest were piqued by a chit of more…conventional upbringing."

"Like Miss Benton-Wythe?" he asked dryly. Before Lucilla could answer, he grinned and added, "Didn't you say you'd not hold her mother's lapses against Miss Antinori?"

"One always hopes the brave soul risking censure by doing the good deed will not be one's friend or relation."

"Given my past, I can hardly hold the prospect of scandal against her," Will pointed out.

"Which is precisely why you need to approach only girls of unquestioned reputation!" Lucilla retorted. "Very well, I'll present you. Although—" she gave him a rueful look "—for the reasons we've just mentioned, Lynton might well prefer that I not present *you* to his ward."

"So the two black sheep do not further sully each other's wool," Will surmised.

"It would be more prudent," Lucilla agreed.

His cousin was right. For a long moment, Will hesitated, torn between Lucilla's sensible advice…and the remembered force of Miss Antinori's gaze.

It was only an introduction, he reasoned. The girl might turn out to be a beautiful widget, as feather-brained as Miss Benton-Wythe or as tongue-tied as poor Miss Rysdale. Though given the cool confidence with which she had held his gaze, he didn't think so.

Enough pondering. He would do it, Will decided. Nodding to Lucilla, he offered his arm. Together they set off toward where Miss Antinori and Lord Lynton had disappeared into the crowd.

"One final matter," Lucilla murmured as they approached. "If after the introductions, Lynton allows you to converse with the lady, I beg you will not distress her by inquiring about her scandalous father—no matter how much you admired him as a musician. I imagine that's one topic she wishes to strictly avoid."

In the next instant, they reached their party and Lucilla called Lynton's name. With his ward on his arm, he turned toward them—and Will sucked in a breath.

Miss Antinori seen close up was even more enchanting than Miss Antinori viewed from a distance. Her glossy dark hair, piled atop her head in an intricate arrangement threaded through with gold ribbon and pearls, just reached his chin. Her perfume, a spicy waft of lavender, enveloped him as she gazed up, those dark, extravagantly lashed eyes wary. His gaze roved across the satin plane of her cheeks down to the lush fullness of her apricot lips.

Sweat broke out on his brow and he had to remind himself to keep breathing. But then he couldn't help himself, he simply had to sneak a quick glance downward, across the elegant curve of neck and shoulder down to that voluptuous, mouth-watering swell of bosom.

Oh, that he might repeat that journey of the eyes with his fingertips, his tongue!

While the rush of sensation in his body threatened to

overwhelm him, Will tried to remind himself that Miss Antinori was a lady—an innocent, virginal maiden. He must not think of her in this way, no matter how much she reminded him of the delightfully passionate and inventive ballerina he'd once had the pleasure of loving, before a peer with a larger purse had stolen her away.

As if in a daze, he heard himself murmur a greeting to Lynton and the chaperone, who responded in turn. Not until Lucilla presented him and he saw Miss Antinori curtsey was he finally able to wrench his mind free of the sensual fantasies. Seizing the hand she offered, he bowed and touched his lips to the air above them, rich with her potent scent.

"Miss Antinori, it is my profound pleasure."

CHAPTER FIVE

A FLURRY OF THOUGHTS whirled through Allegra's mind as the dark-garbed gentleman bowed before her, the clasp of his hand making her fingers tingle beneath her gloves. So this was the "divine" Lord Tavener Sapphira's friends had discussed with such relish. Was he mocking or admiring her?

Though Rob had complimented her appearance tonight, he had not examined her as thoroughly as the bold-eyed man bowing over her hand, who'd tried to stare her out of countenance a few moments ago. Not at all ashamed of her parents or her upbringing, she'd met the man's gaze proudly…and felt a sharp, strong sensation almost like a shock, so unusual and unexpected she'd had great difficulty maintaining her composure.

As with his profession of "profound pleasure" in meeting her just now, she wasn't sure whether he'd intended to admire or disparage. So how to respond?

Excruciating politeness would be best, she decided, trying not to be distracted by her still-tingling fingers. "I am equally pleased to meet you, Lord Tavener," she said coolly, removing her hand from his disturbing grip. If he'd meant to mock, she'd just returned the favor.

He seemed to understand that, for as he straightened, he grinned at her. "A lady as clever as she is lovely. Now that is a double delight," he replied.

As she let herself inspect him, another shock rippled through her. Heavens, he was arresting! Low as her opinion of Sapphira and her friends might be, she had to concede they had not underestimated Lord Tavener's appeal.

Broad of shoulders and whipcord lean, he emanated an aura of strength and confidence that was almost menacing. Dressed all in black save for his cream patterned waistcoat and snowy cravat, he wore the elegant clothes negligently, as if his appearance was not of much importance to him.

When she shifted her eyes farther upward, she felt again that odd, sizzling sensation. Though not precisely handsome, his face with its sharp chin, molded cheekbones and high forehead brushed by a lock of dark hair gave the impression of roughness and power. Suddenly she recalled the Michelangelo sketches Papa had once shown her, studies made by the master before he began his sculpture.

Recalling also the unclothed nature of those studies, her cheeks heated as she finally met his gaze. Eyes of a striking ice blue captured hers. Dazzled, drawn to him, for a moment she had the ridiculous idea that he could see straight into her soul. A smile curved his lips, setting off a fascinating slow scintillation in those blue, blue eyes. Scarcely breathing, Allegra could not look away.

"Like what you see?" he murmured at last.

His entirely inappropriate words broke the spell, made her realize she'd been staring at him just as rudely as he had at her earlier. Though she felt the heat in her cheeks intensify, having avidly observed gallants at the theater as they wooed the actresses, Allegra didn't need the conversation she'd overheard in Sapphira's drawing room to recognize she had just met a rake of the first order.

"Do you like what you see, sir, when you gaze in the mirror?" she flashed back.

His smile widened. "That depends on who I see in the mirror with me. I note that, being still in black gloves, you cannot dance. I am promised to Lady Domcaster for the next set, but afterwards, might I have the honor of strolling with you?"

He was dangerously attractive, with those mesmerizing eyes and that knowing smile. In her circumstances, however, the last person she needed to encourage was an out-and-out rake. Still, he was Lady Domcaster's cousin, and that lady, niece to one earl and wife to another, was impeccably well-connected. It wouldn't do to offend her.

"If you wish, Lord Tavener, I should be happy to stroll with you," she said, disturbed by an unwanted jolt of anticipation at the thought.

"That, among other things, I most devoutly wish," he replied. "Until later, Miss Antinori." With a bow to

Mrs. Randall and Rob, he walked off, Lady Domcaster on his arm.

"Damn and blast!" Rob swore under his breath, confirming Allegra's impression that Lord Tavener was not a gentleman he wanted her to know. "I realize you could do naught but accept, Allegra, but I wish it had been nearly any other man present who paid you his respects."

"Dear me!" Mrs. Randall quavered. "Is Lord Tavener not good ton?"

"Until Lady Domcaster took him up this Season, he wasn't," Rob retorted. "Although that's not entirely correct. There's nothing at fault in his breeding. His father was a baron, albeit an impecunious one, and his mother a Carlisle. Her uncle, the Earl of Pennhurst, was appointed Tavener's guardian after his parents died when he was just a lad—and did a rather poor job of it. Ignored Tavener for the most part and neglected the small estate he inherited, which is now said to be in ruins."

"Poor boy!" Mrs. Randall said.

Rob grinned wryly. "He didn't let himself be ignored at school, I promise you! We were at Eton and Oxford together, though being younger than he and moving with a different set, I didn't know him well. Always spoiling for a fight, ready to take on even lads much bigger and older. Almost always won, by the way. He's now accounted one of the foremost amateur pugilists in England."

"It sounds as if he were angry with the world," Allegra said. As well he might be, she thought with an empathetic pang, after losing his parents and being thrust into an indifferent world.

Rob shrugged. "Perhaps. Anyway, since Oxford he's lived in London, keeping himself afloat with a mix of gaming and…and—" he lowered his voice as color stained his cheeks "—ah, associations with ladies of large fortune."

"Married ladies," Allegra surmised. "In other words, a rake."

While Mrs. Randall gasped, Rob confirmed Allegra's impression with a nod. "A notorious one, who has never before bothered to make an appearance at ton events. He and Lady Domcaster are close friends from youth, so with Domcaster still in the country, I suppose he must be acting as her escort. Though were she my wife, I doubt I'd permit him to do so, never mind that they are cousins."

"Is she in danger from him?" Allegra inquired.

"Probably not," Rob conceded. "Domcaster's no fool. Besides, I seem to recall that he and Tavener were friends at Oxford, perhaps because he was then courting Tavener's cousin, whom he later married. Most likely Tavener's attempting to establish himself—at Lady Domcaster's urging, I would guess."

Like I am, Allegra thought.

"Good breeding or no, you'd do well to be on your guard, Allegra," Rob warned. "If he says or does anything that gives you alarm, leave him at once."

"Thank you, Rob. I will do so," Allegra said.

Not that she'd needed Rob's warning. With his intense eyes and beguiling charm, Tavener put her in mind of a peer who'd pursued a young actress friend the summer Allegra turned fifteen, when her father was playing in a theater orchestra. Knowing her strict papa would not approve her close association with a thespian, she'd had to sneak out to visit Molly, eager to learn what the vivacious, experienced girl could teach her about love and life.

Her lordship's campaign began just after he attended their first performance in the town near his ancestral manor. Through Molly's ploy-by-ploy description and her own observation, Allegra had eagerly followed the progress of his courtship, from the gifts, notes and ardent poetry to Molly's eventual, enthusiastic capitulation. The physical particulars of which a prosaic Molly had explained in frank detail, Allegra recalled. Something hot and giddy churned in her belly at the memory.

Putting a hand on her stomach to quell the sensation, Allegra told herself to beware. Molly had so vividly described the feeling of physical attraction that, though she had never experienced it before, Allegra realized the reaction Lord Tavener evoked in her was desire.

'Twas disconcerting to discover one could feel lust for one man while pining for another, but she supposed she should not be surprised. Molly's rake had demonstrated quite convincingly that true affection and desire could be entirely separate entities.

Charming as Lord Tavener might be, she could not afford to head down the path Molly had strolled so

eagerly. No matter how compelling Tavener's eyes—
or how strong the shock to her fingers when he
touched her hand.

Rob cleared his throat, pulling Allegra from her
thoughts. A military gentleman approached, one of
Rob's friends, and was duly introduced. After conversing for a few moments, he drifted off.

A few matrons, acquaintances of Mrs. Randall,
stopped to chat. Allegra grew painfully aware that for
most of the long interval after Lord Tavener's departure,
though a number of gentlemen passing by gave her
admiring looks, none save a few of Rob's friends approached seeking an introduction. Rob optimistically
predicted that she would find her way in society eventually, but after the last few weeks of calls that had
elicited raised eyebrows and unspoken censure, Allegra
wasn't so sure.

Then, with a relief that was stronger than it should
have been, she looked up to see Lord Tavener approaching. She tried—and failed—to steel herself against the
flutter in her belly when he took her hand.

After bowing to Rob and Mrs. Randall, he announced, "My cousin abandoned me in the ballroom in
favor of tormenting several of her disappointed former
suitors. Miss Antinori, are you ready to stroll?"

"Perfectly ready, sir," she agreed and tucked her
hand on his arm. Acutely aware of a renewed tingling
sensation in her fingertips, of the masculine aura that
seemed to surround him, she let him lead her off.

To her relief, he made no attempt to maneuver her toward the doors opening onto the terrace, guiding her instead out of the press of guests toward the wall, where they might make a circuit of the chamber.

"Do you know you are the most stunning creature here?" he asked. "Going through the moves of the country dance, waiting until I could return for you, seemed an eternity."

Though the trajectory he'd chosen to walk her on might be proper, his conversation certainly wasn't. "I imagine Lady Domcaster would be devastated to hear that," she replied a bit acerbically.

As if startled, he stopped and turned to her, his brilliant blue eyes lighting again as he smiled. "That wit again! Bravo!" Moving closer, he squeezed her hand, his voice taking on a caressing tone. "I knew the instant I saw you tonight that you would delight…all of me."

It was delicious nonsense…but it was also highly improper. Regretfully Allegra halted and removed her hand from his arm. "Lord Tavener, may I remind you that this is not the Cyprian's Ball and I am neither a lightskirt nor a loose-moraled matron whose fancy you can capture. If you would return me to my chaperone, please?"

Having braced herself for irritation or anger, she was totally unprepared for his peal of laughter.

While she looked on, wide-eyed, he controlled his mirth. "Blast, Miss Antinori, but you are quite right. Pray accept my apologies! It's just that, having gone about so little in good society, I have no idea how to talk to a gently bred maiden. My attempts at Lucilla's dinner earlier were abysmal failures. You are so lovely, I was distracted clean out of renewing those efforts."

The appealing look from those penetrating blue eyes proclaimed his absolute honesty. Allegra simply couldn't help it—she was charmed...and curious.

"Excuse me, but I can't believe you could fail to entertain even a young, inexperienced maiden. *Especially* a young and inexperienced one."

"Oh, believe it! Either my appearance, my compliments—or the tales told about me—frightened one young lady into a silence that lasted throughout the meal. My conversational attempts with the other met with total failure until a desperate remark about fashion set her off on a monologue so full of tedious detail, I was ready to stab myself with a dessert fork just to escape the room."

His look of comical dismay set her chuckling. Before she could reprove his exaggeration, he continued, "You laugh, but 'tis no jesting matter! I'm sure in my absence, if you were not already aware of it, Lord Lynton has acquainted you with my scandalous reputation. My cousin Lady Domcaster insists that I try to reestablish myself. However, if I am not able to successfully converse with *proper* ladies, I might as well abandon the attempt at once. Unless..." He drew the word out, gazing down into her eyes.

Intrigued in spite of herself, she echoed, "Unless?"

"Miss Antinori, in addition to being the loveliest girl

in the room—no, forgive me, but you must allow the compliment, for it is simple truth—you have shown yourself both observant and clever. Might I impose upon you…might I beg you to instruct me?"

She stared at him. "Instruct you?"

"On how to make proper conversation that is agreeable to young ladies. I know about as much about respectable females as I do about the mysteries of the Orient. Unless I learn, and learn quickly, I haven't a prayer of being received by the families of eligible young women." He paused, frowning. "May I be shockingly blunt?"

"I prefer plain dealing, sir," she replied, caught up in his tale despite her better judgment.

Once again that smile lit up his eyes. "I thought you might! Lucilla insists I should look for a wife—a rich wife with a fortune that could restore my estate, of whose dilapidated condition I'm sure Lynton already warned you."

He gave her a wry, self-deprecating look. "Frankly, though I'm an amusing enough fellow when I choose to be, I sincerely doubt any respectable lady will want to take on so unlikely a husband. But I've promised Lucilla I'd make an attempt, so here I am, self-accused of being both a fortune hunter and a rake, throwing my poor body into the fray. A rake who earnestly seeks to be reformed. Will you not have pity and rescue me, Miss Antinori?"

Beneath the flippancy of his words she sensed a

social isolation almost like her own. Perhaps because of that, she was tempted to accept his challenge. Except that behind the arresting intensity of his gaze lurked something deep, sensual. That same masculine allure that had led Molly to capitulate all those summers ago and warned Allegra that spending time with Tavener, despite his avowed desire to reform, would be dangerous.

"It would be more proper for Lady Domcaster to instruct you," Allegra replied at last. "Not that I am not fully qualified," she added quickly. "Mama instructed me in all the intricacies of ton behavior, and in matters of propriety, Papa was even stricter."

"I'm sure they were, with so precious a prize to guard. Still, I should very much like to pursue your acquaintance. You would find me a willing pupil."

Much as she tried to tell herself that his outrageous request was just another tool in his rake's arsenal, she couldn't shake a sense that, on some level, he was quite serious. Before an unwanted sympathy for his position— and her strong attraction to him—led her to capitulate, she replied, "Tutoring you would not be…wise."

At her refusal, the hopeful look in his eyes faded. "Then I am doubly sorry. To lose your instruction, and to have begun so badly with you."

Not knowing what to say, she did not reply. Tavener offered his arm, she took it, and in silence they resumed their circuit of the room.

After a few moments, he sighed. "Though I shall

probably have to beg your pardon once again, before I return you to your chaperone, I simply must say this."

As she tried to arm herself against whatever impertinence he meant to utter, he bent that compelling gaze upon her once more and said, "Miss Antinori, I must tell you how much I admired and respected your father. He was a true genius, and the musical world is much the poorer for his premature passing."

For a moment, she thought she must have imagined his comments, so thoroughly had it been drummed into her head that she must on no account mention her parents. "You…knew my father?" she asked at last.

"No, but I did have the honor of hearing him play once, when I was at Oxford. Such passion! Such skill! I'm a bit hand of a violist myself, and have attempted to play some of his compositions, which are as beautiful as they are difficult. You must be so proud of him."

"I am proud of him," she whispered. A combustible swirl of grief, anger at having been forced to deny her parents, delight and gratitude at encountering someone who admired her father choked her into silence.

After three weeks of circumspect behavior, of confining her conversation to inquiries about the health of persons she knew little and cared less about or innocuous remarks about the weather, Tavener's introduction of that taboo topic electrified her. Prudent or not, she decided on the spot to encourage his friendship.

Looking up into the blue eyes that once again seemed to sense the turmoil in her soul, she said,

"Thank you. It is a great joy to speak of him. And Lord Tavener, though I still think Lady Domcaster's qualifications for instructing you far exceed my own, I would be happy to help you practice your conversation."

She was rewarded with a smile of such brilliance, she had no difficulty believing he'd made a long series of conquests. Sternly she reminded herself that, regardless of how great an admirer of her father he might be, she must not join their number.

"Excellent!" he exclaimed. "You shall not regret it, I promise. Would you like a glass of wine before we begin?"

Agreeing that would be very nice, she let him lead her off to the refreshment room.

They were nearing the exit of the ballroom when Allegra heard ahead of them a familiar tinkling laugh. She gritted her teeth as, through the passing guests, she saw Sapphira Lynton poised on the threshold.

CHAPTER SIX

FOR SEVERAL MOMENTS Lady Lynton stood in the doorway acknowledging greetings from acquaintances, framed by the pediment-topped opening like an actress by the proscenium. Though she was properly attired all in black, from the way the silken gown hugged her curves, its bodice cut low over her generous breasts, the dark color emphasizing the porcelain perfection of her skin, she managed to make mourning dress look provocative.

Not that the gown was styled or the bodice cut more seductively than those of other matrons, Allegra had to allow. The impression of allure was more in Sapphira's air and manner—which did not, Allegra thought, setting her lips in a thin line, appear to be that of a widow suffering excesses of grief.

"Quite an entrance, don't you think?" Lord Tavener murmured in her ear. "She should have been on the stage."

Startled almost as much by this cynical assessment as by how closely it mirrored her own opinion, she turned to face him. Though she knew she should refute the statement, she found herself saying, "Indeed."

Before she could think of something more appropri-

ate, Sapphira spied her. Her gay smile fading, Lady
Lynton stared without acknowledging Allegra almost to
the point of insult before at last nodding. Then, taking the
arm of an admirer who had rushed up, without saying a
word to Allegra, she walked past her across the room.

Almost a cut direct, it was a snub such as Sapphira
would probably never have dared administer had Rob
been beside Allegra. A snub that telegraphed to everyone present just how little Lady Lynton thought of her
late husband's distant cousin, though Allegra was a
guest in Lady Lynton's own home.

Allegra felt her stomach churn with embarrassment.
Having just had demonstrated to the world and her
escort how undesirable a person she was to know, she
turned to Lord Tavener, lips trembling with fury. "Perhaps you would prefer to take me back to Lynton now?"

He raised his eyebrows. "Why would I wish to do
that? Because a certain former ton Diamond has exe-
crable manners? Lady Lynton's lack is not *your* fault,
Miss Antinori."

She gave him a searching glance, but could detect
no mockery in him. "You are probably the only one—
or should I say the only *gentleman*—in this room of
that opinion."

"Sadly, society seems to contain fewer and fewer
men of perception."

Unwilling to surrender her fury—not sure she could
bear to endure his pity—she said stiffly, "If reestablish-
ing your reputation is important, you have just seen that

being in my company will not advance your goal. I expect it would be best that you return me to Lynton."

"Oh, no, Miss Antinori!" he said with mock sternness. "You shall not that easily renege on your promise to instruct me. Unless…" His expression sobering in earnest, he continued, "unless you fear being seen with me may discredit *you*. A fear which, regretfully, may have merit."

An almost grim expression flitted across his face before he fixed his eyes on her again, their blue depths no longer ice, but flame. "Loath as I would be to lose your company," he said in a voice as dynamic as his eyes, "I could not allow myself to bring you harm. If you wish, I shall of course return you to your chaperone."

He did not wish to risk discrediting *her*. That avowal flowed over her like a cooling breeze, carrying off her anger, while the sincerity of his concern flooded her aching heart with a healing balm. A strong sense of connectedness once again bound her gaze to his.

They *were* connected, she realized. Both outsiders looking in upon a world that might not deign to accept them. And though prudence whispered that each would fare better fighting separately the battle to gain access to the ton, his kindness in wanting to keep her from harm was the first she'd received from anyone of her class save Rob.

Not only was he kind—and perceptive enough to see beneath Sapphira's blinding veneer of beauty—he had both known and appreciated her father. How could she send him away? Despite the simmer under her skin at his nearness that whispered of the danger he posed.

His gaze was still fixed on her, awaiting her answer as if there were nothing in the world more important to him. "I suppose it would be more prudent for both our purposes that we not associate with each other but…but if you are willing to run the risk, Lord Tavener, so am I."

Once again, the brilliance of his smile caught her off-guard. "Indeed I am, Miss Antinori. Now, some wine?"

Keeping her hand tucked under his own, Tavener walked her to the refreshment room and signaled a waiter to bring them each a glass. As they sipped, he said, "So, Miss Antinori, how should I address an innocent young female?"

"You need to wed an heiress, you said?" When he nodded, she continued, "Whether or not she is handsome, such a girl will probably be surrounded by suitors. Though she may well have heard every extravagant compliment that could be devised to her appearance, you should still be prepared to praise her. But only in general terms," she cautioned. "Celebrate her loveliness, her beauty, her perfection, perhaps even her eyes or her countenance, but nothing else… specific."

"Like her lips—or shoulders—or bosom?" he asked, his eyes slowly inspecting those parts of her as he named them.

A little shiver sped down her backbone and her

breasts seemed to swell and tighten under his lingering gaze. Shaking off the sensation, she pointed an accusing finger. "That is exactly what you must *not* do!"

His eyes, which had gone heavy-lidded, snapped wide as he jerked them back up to her face. "Right! Loveliness, beauty, eyes, countenance. No bosom." He sighed and shook his head. "This is going to be difficult."

A laugh bubbled up her throat, which she choked into a cough before it escaped. Correctly interpreting what she'd uttered, Tavener grinned at her.

She shot him a severe look. "Lord Tavener, are you serious about trying to find a respectable bride?"

His blue eyes turned penitent. "Yes, Miss Antinori."

"Then, I beg you, try to overcome your rogue's responses and pay attention."

He nodded. "I am duly rebuked. What else should I say to the young lady?"

"After a proper compliment, it would be good if you could question her about her interests, if you have knowledge of them. If not, comments about the weather or events taking place in society are always acceptable. And current fashion, of course."

He groaned. "Are we back to remarks about bonnets and the state of the roads? If being 'proper' means I have to confine myself to uttering such swill, perhaps I should give up now and emigrate to the Americas."

Though Allegra couldn't help but sympathize, having just endured three weeks of social calls that focused on those same numbingly innocuous topics, she said, "Pray, do not despair yet! You may speak about the theater, concerts or exhibitions currently taking place. Or if you invite the lady to ride or drive in the park, you may discuss horses and carriages. Literature, if the young lady enjoys it. But generally not politics."

He chuckled. "So I discovered! For all the recognition it sparked in my dinner companions tonight, the Congress of Vienna might have taken place on the far side of the moon."

Allegra shook her head in sympathy. "I'm afraid young ladies are not encouraged to study—much less to venture opinions—on such matters, which some consider beyond their understanding."

"But not beyond yours?" he guessed.

"My upbringing was not precisely…conventional. Such foreigners as we encountered in our travels were often bid to dine, and rather naturally, Papa wished to discuss the turmoil on the continent."

"I should like to hear more about your proper but unconventional upbringing."

The interest he was expressing in who she really was, rather than in the society maiden she had to appear to be, drew her as strongly as his physical appeal. Resisting it, she said, "Perhaps another time. But to continue your lesson, neither should you discuss any purely masculine pursuits, such as cockfighting or boxing."

She remembered then that Tavener was a boxer—a

very accomplished one, if Rob's impressions were correct. Perhaps that was responsible for the slight aura of danger that hung about him as negligently as the black coat stretched over those broad shoulders.

Allegra slid him a glance from under her lashes, trying to imagine that lean, powerful body stripped of jacket, waistcoat and cravat. Balanced on the balls of his feet, shirt open at the neck, sleeves turned back as he circled his opponent, fists up and ready, his fierce blue gaze focused… She shivered as a thrill of attraction and trepidation rippled through her.

She started from her reverie to find his head bent, his face so close she could feel his breath on her cheek. That intense blue gaze focused on her, he said softly, "What else can I touch upon, Miss Antinori?"

Ah yes, *touch*… Her eyes strayed to his mouth, hovering near hers. The top lip was firm, almost stern, but the bottom lip was plump, sensual. Allegra had a sudden memory of Molly and her rake standing in the shadowed wings of the theater, the man slowly pulling Molly's head down as he slanted his mouth over hers. A memory of Molly's sigh…

Tavener looked like a man who knew a great deal about kissing. He looked as if he wanted to kiss *her*.

Her heart commenced pounding and heat suffused her. Beginning to understand the sensual spell Molly's rake had cast over her that long ago summer, alarmed by how much she yearned to lean up and brush Tavener's lips, Allegra jerked away. "You may touch upon many topics, my lord, but you must not look at me—at a young lady—like that."

He smiled, his eyes still heated. "Like…what?"

"Like you were about to kiss her!" Allegra blurted.

"Do you want me to kiss you?" he murmured.

"My lord, you are hopeless!" Allegra declared, once more stifling a laugh. "If you are to make any progress at all, you must cease uttering such provocative comments."

"Is Lord Tavener annoying you?" a stern voice asked.

So absorbed was she in her conversation with Tavener, Allegra had become completely oblivious to their surroundings. She looked up to see Rob gazing at them, arms folded, a disapproving frown on his face.

"Not at all, Rob. He has been quite…entertaining."

The glance Rob gave Tavener was distinctly unfriendly. "You were gone so long, I grew concerned. Mrs. Randall begged me to fetch you. A number of people have stopped by, desiring to make your acquaintance. Let me return you to her now."

Allegra couldn't imagine that she had truly been in such demand, but judging by the almost hostile look on his face, Rob was determined to separate her from Tavener.

Before she could reply, Tavener said, "I've no doubt there are others anxious to meet her. Excuse me, Lynton, for monopolizing so lovely a lady. Miss Antinori, I hope you will permit me to call. As you have just noted, I still have much to learn."

"I should be happy to receive you, Lord Tavener," she replied, curtseying to his bow. Then Rob seized her hand and propelled her toward the exit.

Glancing over her shoulder, Allegra saw Tavener standing motionless, his bright blue gaze following her as Rob walked her away. Something sizzled in the air between them before Rob steered her through the door.

"Unfortunately you cannot cut the connection, Allegra," Rob said as he hurried her into the ballroom where Mrs. Randall waited. "Still, I cannot help but think it highly imprudent for you to spend much time with him. You can hardly hope to encourage more eligible gentlemen to pursue you if you allow that…that man of questionable character to hover around you."

"Perhaps you need to stay near and protect me," Allegra said, half in jest.

To her surprise and delight, Rob tucked her hand more firmly under his arm. "Perhaps I should. In any event, I shall insure that none but eminently respectable gentlemen approach for the rest of tonight!"

From that moment, Rob proceeded to be as good as his word. For the time they remained at the rout, he hardly stirred from her side, escorting her to meet his friends, obtaining her refreshments, and when not conversing with other guests, focusing all his attention on her.

Twice during the succeeding hour she saw Lord Tavener among the guests and wondered if he would approach. Each time, Rob took a protective step closer, as if to warn the man off. Like that valiant knight of old…although in this case, she wasn't sure she really wanted his protection.

Soon after, Mrs. Randall professed herself tired and Rob summoned the carriage to convey them home—to Allegra's gratification, seating himself beside her.

As the carriage bowled along, Mrs. Randall nodded off while Allegra and Rob sat in companionable silence. Content to have Rob at her side, Allegra mused over the events of the evening.

In the past few weeks she'd seen so little of Rob. He seemed to always be away on business or meeting friends at his club. He had not accorded her as much time or attention as he had tonight—after reclaiming her from Lord Tavener—since the two private interviews he'd given her the day of his arrival.

Could he be jealous of Tavener? she wondered with a little thrill. Probably not, she conceded. Still, if having Lord Tavener dance attendance would prompt a protective Rob into spending more time with her, perhaps she should openly encourage that gentleman.

She'd have to use the diversion Tavener created cautiously, though. Attractive the man certainly was— perhaps too attractive. The heated sort of feelings he generated could not be permitted to go beyond titillation, no matter how much they intrigued her, lest she endanger her reputation. Besides, she recalled with a sigh, even for an actress who was free to pursue such attraction, lustful adventures seldom ended well.

Molly's handsome rake had broken off their affair after only a month, leaving her friend brokenhearted.

Nor was there any question of a more serious relationship between them. The likelihood of a man who openly admitted earning his rogue's reputation turning into the sort of faithful, devoted husband she required was slim. She had no desire to spend her life worrying and wondering whether her husband was truly in London on business—or dallying with another of the women he could charm so easily. In any event, her dowry probably wasn't large enough to tempt an offer from a man who needed to refurbish his estate.

Though her parents had loved each other dearly, Allegra was now paying society's price for Lady Grace succumbing to her attraction to the wrong sort of man. The bitter aftermath of her parents' and then Uncle Robert's deaths had burned into Allegra's soul the realization of just how alone and without resources she had been left, caught between two worlds, truly at home in neither.

Uncle Robert's bequest had given her the opportunity to change that. More than anything, she wanted a home and a place of her own. Regardless of Lord Tavener's potent allure, Allegra didn't intend to throw away her one chance at a secure future by becoming beguiled by a rogue.

Still, encouraging Lord Tavener's attentions would set her on a risky path, walking a thin line between friendship and the power of his dangerous charm. But if doing so would jolt the handsome, honorable, peerless man of character she wanted into realizing he wanted her too, surely the risk was justified.

Smiling in the darkness, Allegra edged closer to Rob. She would look forward to Tavener's admittedly amusing company and repay his friendship by helping him reform his behavior so he might woo an heiress to restore his estates. And with Tavener goading Rob into staying near, maybe she'd finally be able to bewitch the man of her dreams.

As long as she stayed sensible, how could she lose?

CHAPTER SEVEN

ALLEGRA HAD an opportunity to put her resolve into practice the very next afternoon. To her delight, one of the gentlemen who called to pay his compliments after meeting her at Lady Ormsby's rout was Lord Tavener.

Unfortunately, Rob was not present to see how Tavener's eyes brightened when, after pausing on the threshold as the butler announced him, he located her on the sofa, flanked by a widowed friend of Mrs. Randall and one of Rob's military mates.

Of course, the smile that sprang to her lips as she saw *him* would also have served to increase Rob's determination to keep watch over them.

But why should she not smile at Tavener? she asked herself. They were to be friends and accomplices of a sort, she assisting him to more successfully beguile heiresses, he helping her to fix Rob's interest. She dismissed a guilty little pang that while his purpose in seeing her had been freely expressed, she had no intention of divulging her private reasons for encouraging his calls.

A little voice warned that she should be careful what she asked for. By his own words last night,

Tavener admitted he'd earned his rake's reputation.
While the danger of his company might keep Lynton
on the alert, she must stay on her guard lest Tavener
use his mesmerizing eyes and tremor-inducing touch
to lure her into a situation that could destroy her plans
for a future with Rob.

Tavener nodded to her before seating himself beside Mrs. Randall. To Allegra's gratification, however,
when the military gentleman stood up to take his
leave, Tavener quickly claimed the place beside her.
Their other caller also rose to depart, leaving Allegra
with Tavener as Mrs. Randall walked her old friend
to the door.

"Let me tell you again how much I enjoyed our conversation last night," Tavener said. His gaze roving over
her, he added, "As lovely as you appeared then, you
delight the eye this afternoon in that sea-green frock,
reminding me of a goddess just arisen from the waves."

Though he brought his eyes back up to her face,
something in his smoldering look and the caressing
note in his voice intensified the warmth within her,
pooled it sweet and thick as honey in her belly. Heat
flushed her face as she recalled that the goddess who'd
emerged from the sea had been clothed only in her
natural beauty. Was that how Tavener envisioned her?

If so, she needed to redirect his thoughts—and her
own. Forcing her eyes away from the power of his gaze,
she said reprovingly, "A rather unacceptable greeting, my
lord. Not only am I dark where she was fair, a compli-

ment that mentions the birth of Aphrodite cannot be considered proper. I'm afraid you still have much to learn."

His brows lifted in surprise for an instant before he laughed. "Touché, Miss Antinori. So you know the story?"

By the dancing light in his eyes, she knew *he* knew she'd caught him trying to sneak an impropriety past her. Disarmed by the swiftness of their wordless communication and happy at knowing she could speak freely about her family with him, she couldn't make herself scold. "Yes," she said instead. "Though music was his passion, my father interested himself in all the classic forms of art and literature. My mother read the fables to me as a child."

"Ah, then I know the perfect excursion to suggest. You did tell me that it was acceptable to discuss topics pertaining to a lady's interests, did you not?"

"I am gratified that you remember something of my instructions," she returned severely, not willing to let him off entirely unscathed.

"Oh, I did listen, most carefully. It's just that impropriety comes so much more naturally to me."

He gave her a half regretful, half roguish smile so utterly charming, for a moment she was lulled into wondering what other improprieties he might be contemplating. Catching herself, she determined to steer the conversation back on track.

"If you wish to accomplish the purpose you described to me last night," she admonished, "you shall have to embrace propriety wholeheartedly."

Chuckling, he slid a quick glance up and down her figure. "I can assure you, I am most anxious to do so."

He might just as well have run his hand along her torso, so keenly did she feel that glance. But before she could protest again, his face sobered and he held his hands palm-out in a gesture of surrender. "Let us cry pax! I shall follow your excellent advice and behave myself now. Did your father ever take you to see the Elgin marbles?"

Relieved—and a tiny bit disappointed—that he'd decided to play the gentleman, Allegra shook her head. "No. They are…carvings, I presume?"

"Remarkable ones, dating from the age of classical Greece. Lord Elgin, when he was ambassador to the Sultan in Constantinople, sent a team of artists and craftsmen to Athens, intending for them to sketch and make plaster molds of the sculptures in the Parthenon, the temple to Athena," Tavener explained. "Upon discovering that the Turkish authorities in control of the city were allowing these treasures to be ground into lime or sold off, he decided instead to buy as many as he could and transport them back to England.

"Greek art represented the highest expression of civilization, Elgin believed. He wanted both to save these irreplaceable objects from destruction and enlighten and inspire his fellow countrymen when they viewed them. So, would you—and Mrs. Randall, of course—like to come and be inspired, Miss Antinori?"

"I would, very much!" Allegra declared. Thrilled at

the prospect of an excursion whose object was of much greater interest to her than the shopping expeditions and stilted, tedious afternoon calls that had occupied her recently, Allegra looked over at her chaperone, now returning to her seat. "Lord Tavener has invited us to view some Greek sculpture. Should you like to go, ma'am?"

"Sculptures?" Mrs. Randall echoed. "At the Royal Academy?"

"Not far from it," Tavener replied. "The collection is housed in a building on the grounds of Burlington House. 'Tis more like a shed, actually, and the space can be rather cold and damp. If you would rather not go, ma'am, I could escort Miss Antinori in my curricle. We could take a turn through Hyde Park on the way back. That would be quite unexceptional, would it not?"

"Of course." Mrs. Randall nodded. "I must confess I am not a great admirer of carvings, particularly if they are housed in some chilly place. But if you wish to, Allegra, and Lord Tavener drives his curricle, you may go."

Allegra glanced over at Tavener, her eyebrows raised. Though he returned her gaze with a look of bland innocence, it did not escape her that he had just cleverly disposed of her chaperone—in an entirely proper way. But the idea of viewing Greek art—and indulging in more of Tavener's deliciously improper conversation—was too appealing for her to cede to the caution that should have made her overrule an excursion without her chaperone.

"Shall I return for you in an hour?" he suggested.

She gave him a stern look meant to inform him she knew exactly what he'd just done. His answering grin once again told her that he realized she'd seen through his ploy.

Suppressing the desire to grin back—like two children sharing a guilty secret—she said, trying to infuse her voice with quelling hauteur, "An hour would be acceptable."

Accordingly, some ninety minutes later, Tavener handed her down at the entrance to Burlington House. "It seems a rather inauspicious place to house ancient treasures," she remarked, gesturing toward the low-roofed building at the side of the grounds to which he was leading her.

"Lord Elgin had hoped to construct a museum to display them," Tavener replied. "But after leaving Constantinople, he was captured and imprisoned for two years in France. When he at last arrived home, he discovered that his wife had…bestowed her affections elsewhere, leading to a divorce trial whose expense and publicity were ruinous. Needing to recoup some of his investment, over the last few years he has attempted to sell the works to the British Museum. One hopes, recognizing their value, that Parliament will approve the purchase and have them installed in a place worthy of their beauty. But now," he said as he held open the door for her, "you will see for yourself."

Allegra was about to speak when her gaze, adjusting to the darker light within the shed, focused upon the first sculpture. Her reply was lost in a gasp of wonder.

Precisely delineated in white marble was the head of a stallion, his mane cropped, his nostrils flared. So perfect in every detail was he, she felt she might rub his neck and feel beneath her fingers the warm, velvet texture of his skin.

Shaking her head in awe, she looked over at Tavener. A brilliant smile lit his face and he gestured her forward. "Go on. There's much more."

She walked ahead to examine bas-relief panels of figures seated on banqueting stools, the folds of their draped clothing looking as if they should ruffle in the breeze. Another displayed a man striding purposefully forward, drapery swirling about his muscular legs. Yet another, a rearing centaur grabbing an attacking male figure by the neck.

So exquisite was the work, she was not even embarrassed at discovering a number of the male figures were completely nude, though that fact did make her grateful Tavener had found a way to prevent Mrs. Randall from accompanying them.

The final work held her once again transfixed. The statue of the young woman was fully formed, the figure standing with arms at her sides and one leg slightly forward, a column capital balanced on her head.

"She is one of six maidens," Tavener said at her shoulder, "who supported the porch of the Erechthion, one of the smaller temples below the Parthenon. Though she seems to be carrying the weight of the world, unlike the other figures, she was lucky enough to keep her head."

"I cannot imagine how one could carve so large and perfectly formed an image," Allegra marveled.

"There were originally some fifty even larger statues in the temple's pediments, most of which were lost in an explosion when the temple, which the Turks were using as a powder magazine, was attacked by the Venetians. The largest statue, a thirty-three-foot-tall image of Athena made of ivory and gold, masterwork of the sculptor Pheidias, stood at the center of the temple."

"Was that also destroyed in the explosion?"

"Perhaps. In any event, no trace of it remains."

Fascinated, for a long time Allegra wandered back and forth examining the variety of figures carved onto the frieze panels, which Tavener explained represented a festival procession to the temple. From the clothing and the objects carried by the figures, Allegra tried to guess their occupations and envision what their lives might have been like.

Certainly musicians were well represented. Would her father's status—and her own—have been higher in this ancient culture?

After studying the panels one last time, she took Tavener's arm and let him lead her out of the shed.

"You enjoyed the carvings?" he asked as they walked back to the curricle.

"They are incredible!" she exclaimed.

His fierce blue gaze, free this time of any teasing sensual overtones, caught and held hers. "I knew you would love them," he said simply.

Allegra could neither explain nor put a name to the emotion that flooded her as their gazes locked. Though all the suggestive remarks he'd already addressed to her argued that by no logical measure could Tavener be considered "safe," still she couldn't shake the strong sense that in his company she was protected, valued…at peace, as she had not been since the loss of her family.

Then his eyes darkened with a heat she did understand, sounding a warning in her brain that allowed her to break free of his spell. Pulling her gaze from his, she murmured, "Thank you for bringing me."

"It was my pleasure." They had reached his curricle, the sense of connection still humming between them. When she relinquished his hand after he'd assisted her into the vehicle, she felt somehow…bereft.

To distract herself from that disturbing reaction, as he set the curricle in motion, she said, "You seem remarkably knowledgeable about the artifacts. How did you learn about them?"

"My classics professor was acquainted with Reverend Hunt, Elgin's chaplain whom he sent to negotiate with the Athenian authorities about the acquisition of the antiquities. Hunt described to him how it came about."

"You are quite the scholar," she said, intrigued to discover a more serious side to this beguiling rogue.

"Shockingly unfashionable, but I once thought there

could be nothing more satisfying than spending a lifetime immersing oneself in the texts of the ancient Greeks and Romans. The plays of Euripides, the tragedies of Homer, the natural science of Aristotle— almost everything worth reading was written by them. However," he continued with a self-deprecating twist of the lip, "my uncle said he'd be damned before he'd allow me to disgrace the Carlisle blood by becoming, as he put it, a common clerk."

Though the words were pronounced casually, Allegra sensed an undercurrent of bitterness and regret. Sympathy filled her, but before she could express it, he continued, "Luckily, I soon discovered the superior delights to be found in…tasting the company of a beautiful woman."

Taking his attention from his horses, for a brief moment he focused that intent gaze on her mouth.

Warmth coiled in her belly again as she forced herself to look away. Reminding herself she must not succumb to the blandishments of a rake, however scholarly he might be, she struggled to refocus the conversation. "Does it seem likely that Parliament will approve purchasing the marbles?" she asked after a moment. "Such beauty begs to be treasured."

"Indeed it does," Tavener replied softly, the heat of his quick glance making her wonder if he meant more than the sculpture. "Some argue that, rather than saving the works, Elgin butchered them by removing them from the site and contend he should not be rewarded for his piracy."

"But if the Turkish authorities were not protecting the works, surely Lord Elgin can be forgiven for transporting them where they might be preserved and appreciated," she said, relaxing a bit now that Tavener had returned to his story, easing the subtle tension sparking between them.

"Elgin certainly believed so," Tavener replied. "Still, the marble frieze on which the figures were carved was part of the temple's structure. Elgin's detractors point out that chiseling out the figures defaced the building and destroyed the setting in which they were meant to be displayed."

"Ah, I see. But would the works have survived, had they been left intact?"

He smiled at her. "That is the real question, is it not? I happen to believe Elgin's action was justified. I suspect, however, if the Greeks ever overthrow their Turkish masters, they may hold a different opinion."

Before she could comment, Tavener laughed. "Lord Elgin isn't the first man connected to the sculptures to fare badly at the hands of public opinion. The great Pheidias himself, creator of the Athena statue and overseer of all the artistic work on the acropolis, was caught up in the political wrangling of his master Pericles, ruler of Athens. Falsely accused of fraud and sacrilege, he was banished from the city."

"How awful!" Allegra exclaimed. "To have created such beauty and then be banned from ever viewing it again."

"He had his justification in the end," Tavener replied. "The Peloponnesians commissioned him to create an even larger statue of Zeus for the temple at Olympia, which later became known as one of the seven wonders of the ancient world. A precedent that should give Elgin hope."

"In what way?" she asked, glancing at him curiously.

The yearning she read in his eyes before he lowered his gaze to the horses sent a little shock through her. "That even those estranged from home and kin might someday find a place to be useful and belong," he said softly.

He seeks the same thing I do, she thought, his words resonating within her. The sense of connection she'd felt earlier surged through her again.

While she curled her fingers in her gloves to resist the urge to place her hand over his, he continued, his voice once again teasingly light, "Let us hope it proves so for poor Lord Elgin. But now that we are entering the park, we must banish such scholarly topics."

Blinking, Allegra realized that they had indeed arrived at Hyde Park without her being at all aware of their transit through the streets, so thoroughly had she been engrossed in Lord Tavener's story. Just as she'd sat enthralled as a child, listening to her mama's tales.

"Hyde Park during the promenade hour is society's stage," Tavener was saying, pulling her back to the present. "And society, my dear Miss Antinori, is all about frivolity. So unless you wish me to be thought a very dull escort indeed, you shall have to put off that serious expression. Or perhaps I should say something to bring a delicious blush back to your cheeks."

"And confirm you are a rogue?" she countered, the mere hint of his saying something worth blushing over sending the heat through her again. "I thought you wished me to help you overcome that reputation."

"You can't expect me to be reformed overnight," he reasoned as he slowed the horses and guided them onto the carriageway. Spared now from having to attend as closely to his cattle, he turned and fixed her with that flirtatious gaze which she was coming to anticipate and to which, alas, she responded all too readily.

"You cannot fault me for wishing to admire the beauties of the present as sincerely as we've just admired those of the past. Have I told you how charming you look? Despite the lack of classical drapery—though I should very much like to see you garbed as a goddess— you are as lovely as any Greek nymph. Lovelier, for you are not cold marble, but warm flesh."

His eyes holding hers, he took her hand and kissed it.

Energy seemed to arc from his gloved fingers into hers. As he straightened, Allegra was suddenly conscious of his sheer masculine power, his broad shoulders blocking the sun, his eyes lazy-lidded over the blue fire of his gaze, the erotic curve of his lips. A shimmer of excitement spiraled in her belly, pooled low at her hips, tingled in her breasts.

He leaned toward her and for an instant, she thought

he meant to kiss her, right here in the park. Panic break-ing his sensual spell, she pulled away.

"M-my lord!" she exclaimed, her breathing shaky. "I thought we had established that a gentleman does not compare a lady to…to a Greek nymph."

Abruptly he straightened, his eyes snapping wide. "Drat!" he exclaimed and uttered a rueful laugh. "You are quite correct, Miss Antinori. But propriety of speech is deuced difficult to maintain, especially when one's companion is so utterly lovely. I don't expect you could help me out by contriving to appear a bit less beautiful?"

He arched an inquiring eyebrow, for all the world as if he'd just uttered a reasonable request. Surprised and diverted, Allegra said, "Would dull homespun suffice? I wore enough of it growing up to prize my new gowns, but I did promise to assist you."

He made a show of studying her, then shook his head. "Grateful as I am at your willingness to eschew your fashionable new frocks, I fear 'tis not the gown that fires the attraction, but the compelling lady wearing it."

Though she could not help but feel a feminine gratifi-cation at his remark—and the frankly admiring look that accompanied it—his words still skirted too close to the edge of what was acceptable. "Flatteringly said, my lord, but you must remember the Marriage Mart is not comprised of worldly-wise widows or experienced matrons. Any reference to the *wearing* of a gown would put a young maiden to the blush. You must try harder—or refrain from compliments altogether, for the present."

"I stand rebuked," he said with a nod. "Though I could scarce be harder," she thought she heard him mutter before her attention was attracted by the approach of two riders, who slowed their horses to keep pace with the curricle. Though Allegra did not recognize them, their elegant attire and languid air proclaimed them to be dandies of the first stare.

"Tavener!" the nearer one called. Riding a black gelding, he was garbed in dark blue, his blond locks falling fashionably over his forehead. "Who is the lovely Venus you are escorting? Pray, introduce us!"

"Indeed, do!" the man's dark-haired companion said, his eyes raking up and down Allegra's figure.

Liking the second man's blatantly assessing glance even less than the slight innuendo of the first one's greeting, Allegra turned away, her cheeks coloring.

Any doubt that she might have misinterpreted the nuance of the two men's behavior disappeared when she felt Tavener stiffen beside her. "If you want introductions, solicit them from the young lady's guardian, Lord Lynton."

"Trying to keep her for yourself, are you? Sly dog!" the second gentleman riposted.

Allegra felt an increase of tension in the tall man beside her even before a look of trepidation replaced the fatuous expression on Dark Hair's face. As she glanced up curiously, a little shock went through her.

In place of the lazy-eyed, teasing acquaintance of a few moments ago sat a stranger who radiated menace, his jaw set and his feral, icy gaze fixed on the second gentleman. Allegra shivered, glad that look was not directed at her.

"I'm sure you'll wish to apologize to the lady before you take your leave, Fitzhugh," Tavener said softly. "Or must I teach you some manners?"

"N-no need to get yourself into a pelter, Tavener," the man stuttered. "Apologies, ma'am," he said, quickly doffing his hat to Allegra. "Meant no offense." Before she could murmur an acknowledgement, the two men wheeled their horses and rode off.

Shaken by the encounter, it was several minutes before Allegra could bring herself to look back up at Tavener. Though his expression was no longer quite so forbidding, he drove in tight-lipped silence, staring straight ahead.

Saddened and a bit angry at having the mood of the afternoon spoiled, at last Allegra ventured, "I take it those two gentlemen were men I should not know?"

Tavener looked back at her and sighed. "I doubt your chaperone would approve an introduction. Fitzhugh and Markham, rakehells and gamblers both, have never to my knowledge sought out the company of innocent maidens."

Comprehending after a moment what he must mean, she said, "So they thought I was your…oh, my!" She put her hands up to mask her flaming cheeks.

Why would they assume that? she wondered, anger, distress and humiliation warring within her. Her carriage dress was a model of high fashion and modesty, and since she'd barely glanced at them, surely nothing in her manner could have prompted such an assumption.

At that moment, Tavener guided the team off the carriage path and pulled up the horses. Turning to face her, regret and a simmering anger in his eyes, he said, "I must apologize. I truly thought it would be safe to drive you in the park in the middle of the afternoon, but it appears I was mistaken. Though I would hardly call those gentlemen 'friends,' we are acquainted. 'Tis my blasted reputation that led them to presume…what they did."

He gave a short, bitter laugh. "I warned you an association with me might endanger your good name. I hardly expected to find that assertion proved so quickly."

This time Allegra did not stop herself from laying her hand atop his. "You cannot be sure your reputation prompted their behavior. It must be well known that you are escorting Lady Domcaster this Season as you look about for a wife. You are not responsible for the vileness of their presumptions…any more than I was responsible for Sapphira's rudeness at Lady Ormsby's rout."

Eyes studying her face, as if seeing her in a different light, he said softly, "Though I still think you are mistaken, 'tis kind of you to try to ease my chagrin."

Allegra laughed shortly. "Thank heavens Sapphira was not present! She would have delighted to see me mistaken for a Cyprian."

Tavener lifted an eyebrow in surprise. "Her dislike of you is that great?"

"I'm afraid so. She believes my breeding and lineage

should bar my even attempting to enter society and is furious that Uncle Robert's bequest has elevated me above what she considers my proper place." Suddenly recalling that she ought not be discussing family matters with one who was almost a stranger, she flushed. "Forgive me for prosing on a matter in which you can have no interest."

"You are mistaken. I'm interested in everything about you. But perhaps I should return you home."

The incident having spoiled her enjoyment of their excursion, Allegra nodded. "I am feeling a bit weary."

"We'll leave at once." After backing the horses and turning the curricle toward the exit, Tavener added, his voice carefully neutral, "I shall endeavor to convey you home without any additional untoward events."

"Truly, you mustn't blame yourself," Allegra repeated, not wanting him to think her desire to return home was prompted by a reluctance to be seen with him. "Even if a previous association with you led those…gentlemen to jump to false conclusions, you quickly made them aware of their mistake. Lord Lynton himself could not have dismissed them more blightingly, as if I were a gently bred maiden whose innocence must be protected."

Tavener glanced over at her, a slight smile on his lips. "You are a gently bred maiden whose innocence should be protected," he pointed out.

Recalling her youth hobnobbing with musicians and theater people, Allegra sighed. "If you knew some of the things I'd done and witnessed growing up, you wouldn't think so. Certainly society would not."

"Society can be a dolt," Tavener said with some vehemence. "But if you are gracious enough to agree to continue our friendship, I shall make sure in future not to endanger you. We shall not stir a foot from your door without your chaperone at our side to maintain propriety."

The strong connection she felt to him and his forceful handling of the unpleasant incident just past led Allegra to reply, "On the contrary, in your company I do not feel endangered—but very safe. And I shall be honored to consider you a friend."

Tavener was far too attractive for her to safely relax her guard around him, but though she'd surprised herself with the forcefulness of that avowal, still she knew what she'd just said was entirely true.

By his expression, she saw she'd surprised her escort as well. "You leave me with nothing to say but 'thank you,' Miss Antinori," he said, his voice low.

Conversation ended as they reached the street, which seemed more than usually crowded and required Tavener to keep his full attention on controlling his horses.

As she had while returning from the musicale the night before, Allegra had time to reflect on her excursion with this dangerous and very appealing gentleman.

She had best not underestimate that appeal, she thought, recalling the remarks that had heated her blood and made it difficult for her to concentrate on

maintaining a proper conversation. And yet paradoxi-
cally, there had been moments when she felt more at
ease with Tavener than she'd been with anyone since
losing her family.

She supposed she ought to be grateful that if she
must cultivate the acquaintance of some other gentleman in order to excite Rob's interest, the man to whom
that task had fallen was turning out to be as complex,
interesting and worthy of friendship as Lord Tavener.

A man who'd also, for a fraught moment, made her
long for his kiss—in a way she had never, a little voice
added, longed for Rob's.

Shocked by the thought, Allegra gave a little gasp.
She looked up quickly, but her escort, occupied by the
traffic on the roadway, did not appear to have noticed.

From whence had that nonsensical notion come? she
wondered. Of course she wanted Rob to kiss her! Hadn't
she dreamed for years of having him carry her off across
his saddle bow? And of course, when he did, she would
experience the same warmth in the belly and tingling in
the breasts she felt when Tavener fixed her with one of
his hot gazes, or murmured his delicious improprieties.

Which was precisely the point, she reassured herself.
Rob had never looked at or spoken to her thus, so how
could she have felt such reactions? Far too proper and
honorable to trifle with the sensibilities of a virtuous
maiden, he'd never allow his desire to be revealed in
warm glances or tempting speeches, most likely not until
after his chosen lady had consented to become his wife.

She knew she hadn't mistaken the gleam of sensual appreciation she'd seen several times in his eyes, when he didn't realize she knew he was looking at her. Maybe she ought to somehow inveigle ways to get him alone and encourage him to act on his attraction. Perhaps if she could entice him to acknowledge his desire, he would recognize it was permissible to see her as more than the kindred spirit of his youth. That it was a natural and honorable progression to allow himself to view her as a woman, a lady for whom he could feel both love and passion.

Encouraged by that conclusion, she was smiling again when Tavener pulled up his horses at the Lynton town house.

CHAPTER EIGHT

AFTER ESCORTING Miss Antinori to her front door, Will set off toward home in thoughtful silence, his mind replaying the incident in the park.

He would indeed like to keep Allegra Antinori for himself, he thought ruefully. But as loath to bring harm to her as he would be to injure Lucilla, he must in future be more careful. No more excursions without her chaperone, alas. And if men like Fitzhugh and Markham were going to come sniffing around—with her allure, how could any man resist?—he would also have to watch his conversation, that he give none of them any cause to treat her with the insulting familiarity Fitzhugh had exhibited in the park.

At least, he'd have to watch what he said when there were others nearby. Recalling some of their warmer exchanges, he had to smile. Clever and worldly enough to have caught some of his sensual references, she was still an innocent—a combination as fascinating as it was unique.

Both his senses and his extensive experience with women promised him that beneath the untouched exterior of that luscious body lay a depth of passion just waiting for the right man to awaken it. Ah, that he might be that man!

Damping down the immediate surge of desire the idea evoked, he sighed. 'Twas a shame she was not the opera dancer or chanteuse her dusky beauty hinted at. Were she a lady of small virtue, he would know just how to proceed, luring her into a delightful game that would lead eventually to its inevitable, satisfying conclusion.

But Miss Antinori was a genteel virgin. The fact that she responded—and knew she responded—to the sensual banter he couldn't seem to refrain from indulging in around her both excited and disturbed him.

Theirs could be no casual, mutually enjoyable tryst. If she followed where desire prompted him to lead her, that road must end in marriage.

Which was exactly what Lucilla was urging. But not with Miss Antinori. His cousin had made it clear last night that though she had nothing against the girl personally, given her dubious upbringing and the tarnish on his own reputation, he ought to bypass her and pursue a lady of unquestioned character.

He had to admit that along with his curiosity to discover if Miss Antinori would be as intriguing in daylight as she'd been in the glow of the candelabra, irritation at Lucilla's sensible advice had prompted him to call on her. As he'd suspected, a further acquaintance with Miss Antinori only confirmed the qualities of wit and intelligence he'd glimpsed the previous night. In addition to the ever-present sensual allure, she was an interesting and delightful companion.

But it was more than that. Some…connection he couldn't put a name to drew him to her, something he'd never felt before. The strength of that pull was both compelling and unsettling.

He enjoyed women, the warmth of their voices, the softness of their bodies, the rush of sexual release they afforded, and several times his chere-amies had gone on to become friends. The feelings Miss Antinori engendered, however, were stronger, sharper…different in a way beyond his previous experience.

Through hard and bitter effort he'd carved himself a small, relatively secure niche in an indifferent world, peopled it with a few friends on whom he could depend. Though by no means sure he was suited for matrimony, he supposed he could enlarge that small store of affection to include fondness for a wife. But some instinctive premonition warned him that Miss Antinori might elicit in him feelings far more intense than mere fondness.

For an instant, a sick feeling resonated in the pit of his stomach, a muted echo of the desperate loneliness and isolation he'd felt as a child. He had no desire to stumble into wanting something—or someone—so keenly that he risked a devastation similar to what he'd felt as a five-year-old when he lost his parents and with them, his whole world. Perhaps it would be prudent to abandon his pursuit of Miss Antinori.

Even as the thought formed, he shook his head and

laughed. 'Twas no reason to turn so melodramatic. Miss Antinori posed no real danger; he was only unsettled because she didn't fit neatly into either of the two categories into which he'd previously divided all women—"virtuous lady" or "knowing wench."

And as little suited for it as he might be, he mustn't dismiss out of hand the idea of matrimony—not while it represented a chance to restore Brookwillow. Since Miss Antinori was the most interesting eligible female he'd met, he might as well charm Lucilla into investigating whether the girl's dowry would be sufficient for that purpose.

There was no assurance he'd be able to win her even if he tried. Lord Lynton had already made it abundantly clear he would not encourage Will's pursuit.

His amusement faded as he recalled the look Miss Antinori's escort had given him when he'd walked into the ballroom and found them together. Under eyes as cold as the English Channel in January, Lynton's lips had settled almost into a sneer, as if Will were polluting the purity of the girl's hand by holding it. A reaction that immediately inspired in Will the desire to pull her closer.

The young Lynton he'd known at school had grown into exactly the sort of gentleman that drove Will to prod and needle until he found some pretext upon which to challenge him to a bout of fisticuffs. A man so supremely confident of his own self-worth, so arrogantly dismissive of those who did not meet his standards. A man who'd possessed from birth all the advantages of breeding, position and wealth.

A wolfish grin stole over Will's face. He would have to pursue Miss Antinori, if only to further disgruntle the Peerless Hero. He simply couldn't walk away from the challenge she presented, just as he'd never turned his back on a fight, even as a scrawny lad set upon by bigger boys.

He thrust out of mind the small voice whispering that losing his heart to the intriguing Miss Antinori might batter him more severely than the worst beating he'd ever suffered as a pugilist.

STILL SMILING, Allegra was climbing the stairs to her bedchamber when Hobbs waved at her from the first-floor landing. "Master Rob be wishful of seeing you in the library at your convenience, Miss Allegra."

Delight and anticipation filled her chest. "Tell him I'll be there shortly." Hurrying to her chamber, Allegra called Lizzie to help her quickly change her gown. What might Rob want to discuss with her?

One window of Rob's library overlooked the back garden, the other, the street, she recalled. Had Rob seen her returning with Tavener? If he was summoning her immediately after viewing them together, might he be jealous—or at least disapproving? If so, perhaps her scheme was working!

As soon as Lizzie had her afternoon gown pinned in place, she hurried down to the library.

She entered to find Rob sitting at his desk, a scowl

on his face. Hoping she knew the reason for it, she said brightly, "Good afternoon, Rob. My, what a frown! Is something wrong?"

As he saw her, his brow cleared and he put on a smile of his own. "Please, sit. No, nothing is amiss—that is, nothing that cannot be corrected."

Allegra took a chair. "How can I help you, then?"

Rob opened his mouth, closed it and sighed. "'Tis a delicate matter," he began again. "One does not wish to offend Lady Domcaster or the Carlisle family, but drat it, you simply mustn't encourage Tavener! I realize there's nothing you can do to forestall a morning call properly paid, but you need not go driving with the fellow!"

Savoring the jealousy she hoped was responsible for some of Rob's vehemence, Allegra replied, "But he drove his curricle, with us in the open for all to see." Wanting to emphasize how carefully she'd observed the proprieties, she added, "We visited the Elgin marbles and the park, which Mrs. Randall said was perfectly unexceptional."

"With any other gentleman it would be unexceptional, but Tavener—! And he took you to view the Elgin marbles? Blast, the ton will think you a bluestocking, which is almost as bad as being a rogue's flirt!"

"How dare you!" Allegra cried, anger evaporating her satisfaction at his concern. Not even from Rob— especially not from Rob—would she allow her character to be maligned. "I am not a 'flirt,' I am a lady!" she said hotly. "You, of all people, should know that."

Rob made a restraining gesture. "Yes, yes I do, so don't unleash your famous temper on me. That's precisely my point. You and I know you're a lady, but society must be persuaded of it. A campaign that cannot go well, my dear, if the world sees you always in Tavener's company."

Though Allegra had to allow the truth of that, as her anger dissipated, disappointment grew. Rob seemed more concerned about preserving appearances than jealous of her spending time with Tavener. "I must remain at home until some gentleman of whom you approve invites me to drive?" she asked.

"Of course not. You may pay calls and shop—"

"I own more gowns now than I could ever wear out and I've already paid calls on every society lady Mrs. Randall recommended," she countered, not at all interested in continuing those tedious activities. "Am I to be restricted to no more lively entertainment than that?"

Suddenly realizing that this might be the perfect opening to advance her desires, she rushed on, "I haven't a horse, so I can't ride with you, but might we continue the fencing lessons you began before you left for the army? I should love to learn more!"

Rob laughed. "Heavens, no! 'Twould not be suitable. Besides, the last thing I want is to equip you with a sword so you might try to skewer me the next time I offend you by chastising your behavior!"

"Chess, then. You used to enjoy our games."

"Playing chess with me would hardly meet the goal of exposing you to the wider world."

A dismaying thought struck, almost too awful to voice. Forcing herself to articulate it, she said softly, "Do…do you not want to spend time with me? If 'tis that, you need only say so and I'll not—"

"No, of course it isn't that," Rob interrupted, looking harried. "It's just—you're not a child anymore, Allegra! Despite our family connection, 'tis not seemly for us to spend time together alone. Besides, how can I make the ton aware of what a jewel has come into their midst if I bury you here at Lynton House?"

As a reaffirmation, it wasn't all she might have wished. Still, he was acknowledging he knew she had grown up…and would not the fact that he considered it improper for them to spend time alone indicate that he did indeed find her an alluring temptation he needed to avoid?

Unlike a certain other gentleman, who seemed to delight in temptation.

Heartened by that conclusion, she replied, "Might you drive me in the park, then? Just once or twice, until other suitable gentlemen ask for that honor." Riding in his curricle wouldn't have quite the intimacy as a game of chess or a fencing match at Lynton House, but it would allow her to converse with him in relative privacy. If they just had enough time together, surely he'd realize how much he prized her company.

Rob frowned thoughtfully. "Yes, I suppose that would be possible. I'm not engaged for tomorrow afternoon, I believe. Should you like to drive in the park then?"

"Above all things!" She gave him a radiant smile.

"Very good. We shall start there. You mustn't lose heart, Allegra. There are many upcoming events at which you will be able to meet eligible gentlemen. A little persistence—and prudence—in discouraging Tavener, and I'm sure you'll find the right gentleman to wed."

Recognizing dismissal when she heard it, Allegra rose. "I'll leave you to your work, then."

Rob sighed. "There's a shortage of millet for the Weiss farm and an outbreak of sore-hoof among the sheep on the Cumbrian estate. And the seed grain to order—but I don't mean to prose on about matters in which a lady could have little interest and even less understanding."

"Ah, but you are wrong!" Allegra protested. "Though we moved about quite often, I've always been interested in farming. I'm sure I would understand, if you explain it."

"But I don't wish to explain!" he retorted impatiently. Sighing again, he patted her hand. "Let us not brangle! I don't mean to chastise, but you shall have to curb that argumentative nature if you want to win a husband. A man doesn't like a woman who tries to intrude in his business—or wishes to dispute with him constantly."

Allegra swallowed her first, biting response. "Yes, Rob," she said after a moment, struggling to quell her irritation. "Shall we see you at dinner tonight?"

"No, I'll be at my club." He grimaced. "Meaning no disparagement of present company, I prefer not to dine with my stepmother. I swear, if she reaches for my hand again, I may forget the duty I owe to my father's widow and pack her off to the family estate in Cumbria."

That's a resolution she could wholeheartedly approve, Allegra thought, wishing she had a club to escape to. "I understand. Until tomorrow afternoon, then?"

He gave her a salute. "Until tomorrow."

Allegra's smile faded as she left the library. She'd been right; Rob truly disliked the notion of her spending time with Tavener. However, trying to master a sense of disappointment, she wished he had a less restricted view of a woman's role—and seemed to view their upcoming outing more as a pleasure and less as a military strategy.

But that was only evidence of his good character, was it not? she reassured herself. Honorable as he was handsome, having recommended she have a Season, Rob would think it unsporting to trade upon their former closeness to forward a match between them before she'd had time to meet other eligible gentlemen. And though he might be a bit…high-handed at times, doubtless due to habits of command ingrained by the army, she still had no doubt which man she'd prefer.

She would have Rob to herself for several hours tomorrow. She'd just have to make the most of it.

GARBED IN THE PALE YELLOW carriage dress she felt showed her at her best, Allegra eagerly accepted the groom's hand up into Rob's curricle. Nervously she adjusted her skirts as he set the horses in motion. With her opportunities to engage his heart and mind so limited, she wished to take full advantage of this rare chance.

"You're looking especially lovely," Rob said, making her glad she'd considered her choice of gown so carefully. "Let's go see how many hearts you can ensnare."

Resisting the strong temptation to confess 'twas only one heart she wanted, she replied, "And you, sir, are just as handsome in that bottle-green jacket as you are in regimentals. Have you sold out, then?"

"Yes, I completed the business yesterday. I shall miss the Regiment…though not the battles. Despite all the talk about courage and valor, war's an ugly business."

"What of the peace, then? With Boney exiled for good, I've heard many English aristocrats are flocking to visit the continent. Is Paris as beautiful as they say?"

Eyes on his horses, Rob shrugged. "Napoleon pulled down parts of the old city to create wide boulevards and erected stolen Egyptian monuments in some squares to celebrate his glory, which makes it overall a vast, drafty place. I much prefer London."

She could hardly fault that response by a good Englishman, Allegra told herself, damping down a niggle of disappointment. Another idea occurred, much more to her purpose. "And the ladies? I've always heard how beautiful and elegant they are."

Rob shook his head. "Beautiful perhaps, but as shockingly frank and forward as their gowns were low-cut. Faithless flirts, the lot of them! Give me a quiet, modest, pretty-behaved English lass any day."

Allegra fell silent, mulling this bit of information. Quiet. Modest. Pretty-behaved. Not argumentative, as he'd thought her yesterday. She truly had learned to curb her temper—usually. But how did she go about proving she possessed the qualities he admired to the man who still saw her as his hot-tempered hoyden of a cousin?

Unfortunately, it appeared she shouldn't try teasing or flirting or trying to play on the sensual attraction he felt for her. Unsure how to proceed, she picked up the conversational thread she'd begun. "How did you find Spain and Portugal, then? I've always envied your chance to travel abroad." How she would love someday to visit her father's Italy…especially with Rob as her companion.

Rob laughed. "Would that our positions had been reversed, not that I would wish the conditions I experienced during my 'travels' on any gently bred female! The sea off the Iberian coast looks beautiful, I'll allow, but the country inland is rocky, dry and mostly barren. How I pined for the green forests of home! Now that duty no longer calls me away, I shall be happy never to leave England again."

"I can see that making long marches in every sort of weather and spending the night who knows where might have given you a distaste for exploring," she allowed.

He laughed again and shook his head. "Some of the billets we found—no, I shall not miss that! But the friendships I forged there are past price. That camaraderie and the knowledge that I served my country in its time of need, I shall always treasure."

"As well you should!" Knowing his preference for home, she found Rob even more noble for having put aside his own desires to endure nameless privations in the fight to defeat Napoleon.

Besides, preferring home and hearth was an admirable trait in a husband. And wasn't settling down in a permanent location what she wanted too?

By now they'd reached Hyde Park. To her surprise, it was much more crowded than when she'd accompanied Tavener here. "What a throng! Is today a preferred visiting day?"

"No, 'tis the usual afternoon hour," Rob replied. "I expect you were here too early the other day—fortunately, for there would have been fewer people of rank to notice you with Tavener. Did you meet anyone, by the way?"

"No one he wished to present," Allegra replied, heat flushing her cheeks as she recalled the rude appraisal she'd received from Tavener's rakish acquaintances. No need to further inflame Rob's dislike of Tavener by revealing that incident, despite being able to describe how quickly her escort had routed the two rogues.

Rob snorted. "That I can believe. We shall go about changing that at once. Ho, Sir Thomas, well-met!"

Rob pulled up the curricle beside a gentleman on a bay hack, whom he introduced as his old Oxford mate, Sir Thomas Reede. Before Sir Thomas could ride off, a landau approached them, bearing another of Rob's friends, Mr. Richard Radsleigh and his mother. After presentations were made all around, calls promised and an invitation to Mrs. Radsleigh's upcoming rout secured, they drove on.

Allegra's hope for more private talk with Rob was frustrated as it seemed around every bend of the carriage trail they met another of Rob's friends, often in a carriage accompanied by female relations. Soon Allegra's head was swimming with names she would never all remember.

Though their arrival put an end to the private chat she'd wished for, still it was a novel experience to be the center of attention. To receive compliments from the gentlemen and invitations to call from their ladies.

And what a large number of friends Rob had! Though 'twas hardly surprising, given his sterling character, that he had earned the affection of so many.

Sitting in the midst of the latest gathering, smiling up at Rob as he joked with Colonel Jessamyn and several former company mates, Allegra reflected that simply gazing at the object of your admiration could be satisfying. Even, she added with a mental sigh, if that person's stated goal was to show you off to other prospective suitors.

As HIS HORSE PICKED its way through the crowd, Will chided himself again for succumbing to the urge that had propelled him to ride at a place and time he normally avoided. Until now, he'd not had enough interest in the parade of society ladies displaying themselves for their prospective beaux—and gentlemen preening before the ladies—to endure the slow pace resulting from this packing of so much humanity on trails he preferred to gallop. There was, however, some amusement to be had in watching the demimondaines flirting with their admirers while well-bred ladies pretended to ignore them—and greeting acquaintances startled to find him here at this hour.

Finally, he spotted the reason behind his compulsion to ride seated in a curricle some thirty yards away and surrounded by mounted guardsmen. He noted Lord Lynton at the vehicle's reins and smiled. Should he join them and turn Lynton's pleasant expression into a frown?

He urged his horse forward until forced to halt by the press of vehicles, still twenty paces from his quarry. Perhaps he'd wait until the guardsmen departed before trying to approach further. Anyway, 'twas a pleasure just looking at her, radiant in a gown and bonnet that borrowed brightness from the sun itself as it cast a golden halo about her olive face and dark eyes. Those apricot lips parted slightly as she smiled up at her escort.

Then his contented smile faded. The gaze she had fixed on Lynton was more than admiring—one might almost call it adoring. Then Lynton said something that made her laugh, blush—and snuggle closer to him.

Suddenly Will felt sick, as if an opponent he deemed

less skilled had unexpectedly landed a punch to his gut. So the wind sat in that quarter, did it?

So shaken was he by the discovery, he was nearly out of the park before he realized he'd turned his horse toward the exit. Pulling up, he tried to regain his composure.

There was no reason to feel this keen, deep-seated sense almost of—outrage at discovering Miss Antinori's favor rested on her cousin. Surely he wasn't coxcomb enough to believe he alone could bring a smile to those mesmerizing lips. After having shared a single stroll through a ballroom and one carriage ride, he could hardly have any claim over her, nor could he accuse her of deliberately throwing out lures to entice him.

Though enticed he certainly was.

Just because she responded to Will—and she did respond to him, of that he was certain—didn't mean she couldn't harbor a tendre for Lynton. The man was a distant relation she'd known and probably admired from childhood. Lynton possessed fortune, breeding and he was a handsome military hero, too—the very stuff of a young girl's dreams.

Had Miss Antinori encouraged him only to pique Lynton? If she had, Will didn't really blame her. Though somehow he couldn't make himself believe that.

Not that it mattered. Conveyed in one look was all the evidence he needed to persuade him to take Lucilla's excellent advice and find another lady to charm.

And yet…something simmered between them when he was near Miss Antinori, something beyond mere attraction—something she felt as strongly as he did. Will would bet the last of his dwindling stack of guineas on it.

So, how to proceed? If he looked at it from a different angle, his discovery of Miss Antinori's inclination for Lynton made it easier for him to continue pursuing her. Not even he was chuckleheaded enough to lose his heart to a girl who was pining for another man. Then too, if Miss Antinori's hopes were fixed on Lynton, Will had no chance of winning her hand and disappointing Lucilla, who wanted a more conventional bride for him.

By maintaining the connection, he could obtain the lessons he needed in the proper deportment around young maidens, amuse himself in Miss Antinori's engaging company—and annoy Lynton. Which, in addition to the innate enjoyment Will would derive from it, might assist the lady by spurring on her disapproving suitor.

His mind made up, Will turned his horse toward home and urged him to a trot. Refusing to admit he had any reasons other than those he'd just detailed for deciding to continue his acquaintance with Miss Antinori, he set his mind to savoring the possibility of seeing her again.

CHAPTER NINE

A WEEK LATER, ALLEGRA SAT in the carriage beside Rob on their way to Lady Harrington's musicale. He had initially been uneasy about allowing her to attend a musical event, concerned that her appearance at such a function might remind the ton of her father's profession. But then Mrs. Randall, who usually meekly agreed with whatever pronouncement Rob made, ventured to disagree.

"I understand—and indeed share—your concern, dear Lynton, but I most particularly desire to attend. So I asked Lady Lynton, whom I'm sure you must agree possesses an impeccable knowledge of the ton, her opinion on the matter. She assured me that at so large a gathering, Allegra will hardly be noticed."

She could well believe Sapphira had said exactly that, Allegra thought acidly. But 'twas another proof of Rob's kindness that he put aside his own misgivings so as not to deny his timid cousin the pleasure of being present at an event she'd expressed a strong desire to attend.

Gazing admiringly up at Rob, so handsome in his elegant evening coat and crisp white cravat, Allegra admitted she was anticipating the evening as well—particularly with Rob at her side.

Since her drive in the park with Rob, she'd attended three small dinner parties and been called upon by several gentlemen, activities only mildly more amusing than shopping or paying morning calls. Growing up surrounded by professional musicians, she'd had the pleasure of listening to practices or performances almost daily. Not until she came to London into the silent isolation of tending her dying uncle did she realize how great a part music played in her life. With the resources of the metropolis now available to her, she hoped tonight's event would be the first of many musical evenings.

Lord Tavener had called as well, though she'd acceded to Rob's wishes and refused his invitation to drive. The rather stilted conversation produced by her other gentlemen visitors made her appreciate all the more his teasing wit—and regret having to turn down his tempting offer.

Perhaps she would see Lord Tavener tonight, she thought and felt an immediate kick in her pulse. Having his clever and amusing commentary on the performers and personages present would add further luster to what promised to be a wonderful evening.

Excitement bubbling up, she turned to Rob. "What musical groups will play tonight? Soloists? Ensembles?"

"I don't know. I expect there will be some of both."

"There might be a chamber orchestra and perhaps some dancing after," Mrs. Randall inserted.

"An orchestra? Oh, that would be a treat!" Allegra felt her already giddy spirits rise further. "I suppose they might begin as wind or string ensembles before combining to perform as an orchestra."

Rob cleared his throat. "Allegra, I'm sure I hardly need remind you that if you happen to be…acquainted with any of the performers, you must not converse with them. A nod of acknowledgement, perhaps, but no more! Indeed, it would be best if you contain your enthusiasm and appear to be only mildly entertained, as any well-bred maiden would."

Allegra's soaring spirits fluttered downward. What if Mark Harden, who had often played first violin when her papa was concertmaster, happened to be one of the musicians? Must she cut this man who had often teased her as a child?

Not that Harden, doubtless knowing the rules of society as well as Rob, would feel slighted if she did not speak to him. She didn't really stand on terms of intimacy with the man; Papa had always kept his family at a distance from the other performers, especially as she grew older. Still, an anger she could scarcely restrain bubbled up at the notion that she must mask her enjoyment, pretend to be just another society maiden who found music "mildly entertaining" and considered conversing with a musician beneath her. She pressed her lips firmly together to keep from returning a sharp comment.

Yet this was the society she was attempting to enter, she reminded herself. Only the stark truth that she would have to embrace his world if she wished to marry Rob kept her from telling him here and now that if she must pretend to be someone she was not—and live that lie forever—it might be better for her to abandon the idea of a presentation.

Had Sapphira anticipated her quandary? Allegra wondered suddenly. Was this why Rob's stepmother, notably uninterested in the enjoyment of anyone save herself, encouraged Mrs. Randall's desire to attend this event? Had that been the real meaning behind the odd comment Sapphira had tossed her as they passed on the stairs tonight, that she trusted Allegra would doubtless find at the musicale a convivial group with whom to converse?

Rob must have taken her lengthy silence for modest, quiet and pretty-behaved agreement, for he leaned over to pat her hand. "Don't worry, Allegra. Letitia and I will insure that only presentable gentlemen are allowed to approach you. As long as you confine your remarks to a general mention of the performances, those gentlemen will pronounce you a well-brought-up lady—and a lovely one."

With a growing sense of incredulity, she realized not only did Rob not recognize the repressed anger beneath her silence, he thought she was worried—and ashamed!—that someone in the ton might remember she was Emilio Antinori's daughter.

It took all the control over her temper developed after a tempestuous youth to avoid snapping that she was proud, not ashamed, of what Papa had been, and that 'twas ludicrous for the members of his precious society to think less of her for being the daughter of a cultured, intelligent man whose genius far outshone them all.

While she ground her teeth to keep from speaking, the carriage swayed to a stop.

"Be a good girl and I guarantee the evening will be a success," Rob advised, giving her nose a tap before he exited the vehicle.

A good girl? she thought angrily as Rob handed them down from the carriage. He'd consider her "good" as long as she appeared demure, agreeable—and did everything she could to conceal whose "girl" she really was. Though Rob's advice was only sensible in view of her circumstances, she could not prevent herself from feeling more irritated with him than she'd been since his return.

He led them toward a columned front door flanked by flambeaux and staffed by half a dozen servants who were assisting the arriving guests. After handing over their cloaks and greeting their hostess, Mrs. Randall preceded them into the ballroom, where chairs had been arranged. While her chaperone claimed places for them beside Lady Maxwell and Mrs. Anderson, two of her widowed friends, Allegra scanned the assembled guests.

If Lord Tavener were here, she could discuss the music with him. Not only had he already broached the forbidden topic of her parentage, he alone among the ton members she'd encountered seemed to think no less of her for being a musician's daughter. Indeed, a musician himself, he'd heard her father play and admired his genius.

Whatever he spoke about, his comments would be intelligent and amusing. Most likely he'd follow up his observations with some outrageous remark designed to make her blush and reprove him. Then, after appearing to listen closely to her reprimand, he'd deliver another teasing comment that would have her blushing—and laughing—again.

She smiled at the memory, realizing how much, in trying to please Rob by avoiding Tavener's company, she'd missed their exchanges. Despite the need to guard herself from his sensual appeal, she had to admit she felt more at ease around him than with anyone else in London.

Certainly more relaxed than she was while trying to impress Rob—who smiled indulgently and tapped her on the nose. Not since her hoydenish youth had she been so tempted to slap him.

But after a thorough inspection of the assembled crowd she had to conclude, with a sting of disappointment sharper than she liked to admit, that Lord Tavener was not among the guests. Shortly after, the music began.

A string quartet—mercifully, its members all unknown to her—performed first, giving a masterful rendition of a Mozart violin concerto. As the graceful chords soared over her, Allegra felt her agitated spirits begin to calm. By the end of the first movement, her irritation had dissolved as she lost herself in the glorious interplay of melodic themes. Loath to hear the last note, she clapped enthusiastically after the quartet finished—until, with a little frown, Rob reached over to stay her hands.

"There will be an intermission before the next group begins," Mrs. Randall said hastily to cover the awkward moment. "This would be a fine time to introduce Allegra to more of society. Lynton, might you fetch us a glass of wine while you discover which suitable gentlemen are present?"

"Excellent suggestion, ma'am. I'll go at once." After bowing, Rob walked off.

Just as well that he left, Allegra thought resentfully, since she was once again feeling out of charity with him. Her interest wandering from the conversation between Mrs. Randall and her two friends, she was gazing across the room at the cornice carving of winged cherubs, defiantly humming the last musical theme, when a familiar voice startled her.

"At last I find you alone," Lord Tavener said, inclining his head toward her chaperone, apparently too engrossed in her conversation to have noticed his approach. "If I may be so bold?" He indicated the chair beside her.

Her spirits leapt in anticipation. "I should be delighted," she said. As he seated himself, the heat and scent of him, shaving soap and warm male, washed over her, quickening her heartbeat and causing her breath to catch.

"You must allow, there has been precious little private chat during my morning calls. How are you to instruct me if we never have a chance to talk?"

Allegra felt her cheeks warm at his reproof. "I am sorry, my lord. I have missed our conversations."

"Not half as much as I! Obviously I have not been amusing enough, since I've been unable to convince you to drive with me again." Leaning closer, he murmured, "It's your fault, you know. 'Tis nearly impossible for a man to think of something clever while his senses are being assaulted by the beauty of the lady beside him."

He fixed on her that intense look that always made it difficult for her to breathe. As if his brilliant blue eyes could truly emit fire, she felt the skin of her cheeks, her lips, her throat heat as his gaze traveled slowly downward.

Never before had she been so conscious of the bareness of her chest and shoulders, the upper curve of her breasts above the décolletage of her gown. When his gaze halted there, she felt the nipples concealed beneath their covering of azure blue silk swell and burn.

"My lord!" she protested. "You are gazing inappropriately. Again."

He jerked his eyes up. "Sorry! But you have no idea what that tiny ribbon of black lace trimming the edges of your sleeves and bodice does to a man."

"For shame, Lord Tavener!" she said severely. "'Tis *mourning* lace."

"My point exactly. I am *trying* to be proper, but you distracted me. Again."

She could not help it; laughter bubbled up, dispelling the sensual tension. "I see it still requires much work to make you a fitting companion for a gently bred lass."

"As I have already admitted. So, you will drive with me again? Or have you irritated Lynton sufficiently that you intend to renege on our agreement?"

Surprise and dismay flooded her as guilt pricked sharply. "Irritated Lynton! Why would you think such a thing?"

He gave her a glimmer of a smile. "I saw you with Lynton in the park. The way you were gazing at him... well, it wasn't a 'cousinly' look."

Allegra felt her face burn. She could deny his assumption—but she couldn't bring herself to sully the relationship they'd built by playing false with him. Taking a deep breath, she said, "I...do care for Lynton. But you mustn't think I encouraged you only to catch his attention! I truly enjoy your company."

His smile widened. "Thanks be to God! I shall not have to search my soul for some shred of honor powerful enough to compel me to stop calling on you. So, is the diversion working?"

Encouraged that he had taken her confession so well, she found herself admitting, "For a while, it seemed to be. But of late, he only seems interested in introducing me to every eligible gentleman of his acquaintance."

"Perhaps you need to rattle him again by spending more time with me. Let me call tomorrow and arrange another outing—with Mrs. Randall accompanying us this time."

Perhaps they could be allies after all, just as she'd hoped. But honest allies now, both of them fully cognizant of the other's goals. "So—you're not angry with me?"

His expression gentled. "I could never be angry with you."

Relief, surprising in its intensity, filled her as she met his gaze. Yes, he was temptation—he could not help but tempt, so powerful was the masculine appeal in every line of that lithe body, those feral eyes, the sensual lips.

But something beyond the physical drew her to him. An intuitive understanding seemed to connect them— an intellectual bond she'd never experienced while conversing with any of the proper gentlemen to whom Rob introduced her. As if she'd known him most of her life, as she had Rob, rather than barely more than a week.

Dare she let herself acknowledge that bond, despite the danger he posed?

Even as she debated the wisdom of such a step, he placed his hand over hers. "Shall we be friends, then?"

Any rational reply she might have made was lost as a tingling sensation, more arousing than brotherly, radiated from the pressure of his gloved fingers all the way to her shoulder. The familiar warning bells clanged in her head.

Despite their clamor, Allegra didn't want to pull her hand free. As if she were iron to his magnet, this simple touching of fingertips infused her with the desire to move closer still.

Helpless to look away, she watched the blue of his eyes deepen as his expression changed to a focused intensity she recognized all too well. Before she could force herself to break the contact between them, Tavener suddenly released her fingers and sat back.

"Help me here," he said, his voice strained. "I'm about to say something else inappropriate."

A guilty thrill of feminine satisfaction rippled through her at this confirmation of how much her nearness affected him—followed, for some unaccountable reason, by a deep tenderness.

"You should say, my lord," she advised, "'I'm delighted that we are in agreement, and I shall look forward to calling on you tomorrow.'"

He nodded, humor replacing the desire in his eyes. "Not precisely what I should *like* to say—but no more on that, so you may be easy. You see, already your instruction is bearing fruit. But I sense gentlemen approaching, doubtless your guardian bearing more worthy candidates to your hand. Shall I leave now, or linger and give him the pleasure of dismissing me?"

She glanced behind them. Two men had indeed nearly reached them, but not escorted by Rob. Before she could ask Tavener to identify them, she sensed him stiffen.

The gentlemen bowed before her chaperone. "Mrs. Randall, will you allow Tavener to introduce us to your lovely ward?" the tall blond man asked.

Interrupted from her conversation, Mrs. Randall looked up with a start. One hand fluttered to her throat as she glanced from the smiling faces of the newcomers to Tavener's forbidding one.

"Though it would be more proper to have Lord Lynton present you," Mrs. Randall replied uncertainly, "I suppose Lord Tavener might do so. Might he not, Lady Maxwell?"

Thus appealed to, Mrs. Randall's friend turned to inspect the blond gentleman. "You're Wofford, Lady Martin's grandson, aren't you?" she asked.

"Indeed I am, ma'am," the blond man said with a bow. "You know my grandmother?"

"She was one of my bosom bows the year I made my come-out. Mrs. Randall, you may be quite easy about allowing Lord Tavener to present Wofford and his friend."

Tavener's expression did not lighten, suggesting he thought Lady Maxwell's quick acceptance of her friend's grandson rather precipitous. But with the three older ladies looking on expectantly, he briefly introduced Allegra to Lord Wofford and his companion, Sir Harry Miles.

Presentations performed, the older women resumed their conversation. "Miss Antinori, would you stroll with me to obtain a glass of wine before the next set?" Wofford asked.

"I'll keep you company and make sure Wofford minds his manners," Sir Harry said with a wolfish grin Allegra couldn't quite like.

Before she could decline, Tavener said, "You've been duly presented, gentlemen. Since the musicians will resume shortly, I suggest you go find another lady to entertain."

"Now, Tavener, that's hardly cordial!" Wofford protested. "You've monopolized Miss Antinori long enough. Why don't *you* go off and let us keep her company until the musicians begin."

Tavener balled one hand into a fist and casually rubbed the knuckles against his other palm. "'Tis never wise to outstay one's welcome, is it?" he asked in the same deceptively soft but menacing voice he'd used in the park.

Eyes going wide, the two men exchanged uneasy glances. Wofford cleared his throat. "When you put it like that, I suppose we'll just be on our way, eh, Sir Harry? Miss Antinori, a pleasure. Tavener."

Both men bowed and hastily walked away.

Watching these proceedings with a mingling of curiosity and indignation, Allegra murmured to Tavener, "Protecting me from more men I should not know?"

"I doubt Lady Maxwell knows what the grandson of her old friend has been doing since he grew up. Wofford's an infamous whoremon—womanizer, whereas Sir Harry, having depleted his late wife's dowry supporting a series of mistresses, is looking to marry into wealth again. They may be good ton, but they are not good men."

His obvious concern for her well-being stifled any further protest Allegra might have made about his high-handedness in dispatching the two men. "I suppose I must thank you for discouraging them, then." She gave him a tremulous smile. "You are as protective of me as Lynton."

He grinned. "My feelings for you are most unguardian-like, I assure you! But if scaring off the raff and scaff unworthy of your company earns me your gratitude, I am content…though I do wish Wofford had persisted. I've long wanted to plant my fist in the middle of that smug face."

Allegra was about to ask him why when suddenly Lynton appeared before her, wine in hand and a young gentleman in tow. Casting an aggravated glance at Mrs. Randall, he stopped short in front of Tavener.

"Lynton." Tavener bowed, an ironic gleam in his eyes.

"How fortunate you are just leaving," Rob replied, nodding a dismissal to Tavener as he handed Allegra a wineglass. "I have here a gentleman most desirous of making Miss Antinori's acquaintance."

"Since I am leaving, I suppose I should go," Tavener murmured. "Until later, Miss Antinori, Mrs. Randall."

Her cheeks warming with embarrassment and annoyance at Rob's rudeness, Allegra watched Tavener walk away. Suppressing with some difficulty the sharp rebuke she wanted to deliver to Rob, she willed a smile to her lips and turned to the gentleman Rob was pushing toward her.

As she curtseyed and murmured the usual polite responses to Sir Ralph Beckman's stammered greeting, her forced civility turned to compassion. Sir Ralph appeared younger than the youngest of the Marriage

Mart maidens on display here tonight and so embarrassed and inarticulate, she wondered that his mama let him out in polite company.

Blushing furiously, he opened and closed his mouth several times without producing more than a strangled bit of sound. Taking pity on him, Allegra initiated a one-sided conversation about the evening's entertainment and the other guests present to which the tongue-tied young man needed to contribute only an occasional nod.

Allegra had about run through her stock of conventional trivialities, but the young man, his cheeks still a furious red as he bobbed his head at her like a marionette on a string, showed no signs of leaving. Perhaps uttering goodbye was beyond him, she thought, suppressing a smile as, to her relief, she saw Lady Harrington proceeding to the center of the room.

"It appears the next set is beginning," Allegra said, inclining her head toward their hostess. "I must let you return to your seat. A pleasure to meet you, Sir Ralph."

While she curtseyed, Sir Ralph simply stood, his cheeks growing ruddier still. After clearing his throat, he seized her hand and kissed it before hurrying away.

"Really, Rob, you might have contributed something to the conversation," she murmured to her guardian as the young man scurried off. "Poor Sir Ralph! I don't think he liked me very much."

"Quite the contrary!" Rob replied. "He sought me out to tell me how much he admired you and begged me for an introduction. I will allow, not being much in the petticoat line, he...doesn't have much conversation. And though he appears rather young—"

"Young!" Allegra interrupted with a giggle. "He scarce looks old enough to be out of Eton."

"He comes from an ancient, well-respected family," Rob continued, frowning at her levity, "with an income of over twenty thousand pounds a year."

Allegra was about to reply that it was a shame his guineas couldn't talk, else he was going to have a hard time charming a wife, when their hostess clapped her hands.

"My lords and ladies, I regret to inform you that Alexandra Spolettini, our featured soprano this evening, has taken ill and will be unable to sing for us," Lady Harrington announced. "I was near despair at having to disappoint you when my dear friend Lady Lynton—" she nodded to Sapphira, who crossed the room to join her "—reminded me that we have among our guests someone almost as talented as La Spolettini. While the orchestra sets up in the gallery, would you not give us the pleasure of hearing you play, Miss Antinori?"

CHAPTER TEN

As ALLEGRA STOOD SPEECHLESS, Sapphira linked arms
with Lady Harrington. "Oh, pray do indulge us, Allegra,"
she said, a glittering, self-satisfied smile on her face.
Turning to the guests, she added, "With such a virtuoso
as her tutor, I'm sure Miss Antinori is a most accomplished performer."

"Shall we encourage her, my friends?" Lady Harrington asked. She nodded to Sapphira and the two
began to clap.

Immediately some of the other guests joined in.
From his position reclining against the wall, frankly in-
specting her, Lord Wofford called out, "Please, Miss
Antinori, *indulge* us."

"Hear, hear!" Sir Harry added.

So this was the reason Sapphira had been so anxious
for her to attend, Allegra thought, alarm and anger
flaring as she glanced over at her companions. Mrs.
Randall was looking distressed, Rob thunderous as he
cast a dagger glance at Sapphira, who ignored him and
continued to smile sweetly, apparently delighted to
have her relation show off her skill.

Allegra knew if Rob tried to refuse on her behalf, Sapphira would only remonstrate, stressing again her competence—and all but shouting a reminder of Allegra's lineage, which doubtless had been her goal from the start, whether Allegra ended up performing or not.

While the clapping quieted, Allegra placed a hand on Rob's arm. "It will cause less comment if I simply play and have done with it," she murmured.

He must have realized the truth of that, for despite looking as if he wished he might drag his stepmother from the room by her blonde locks, he gave a stiff nod. "Make it brief," he said tersely.

Her eyes on Sapphira's triumphant face, Allegra felt her anger intensify as she walked over. "I'm happy to oblige you, Aunt Sapphira. Being in deep mourning, I know you allow yourself few diversions." Relishing a few titters from the guests near enough to overhear her remark, Allegra proceeded to the pianoforte.

If Sapphira wished to brand her as a musician's daughter, Allegra thought mutinously as she seated herself, she would make her father proud.

Fingers hovering over the keyboard, she chose a challenging Bach concerto her father had made her practice over and over until his perfectionist's ear was satisfied.

Blazing fury drove her through the first few measures. But almost immediately, the beauty of the countermelodies intermingled with bittersweet memories of Papa standing beside the piano, tapping out the rhythm with his bow, transported her beyond the moment.

Sapphira's spitefulness faded away; the noise of the crowd dimmed. Caught up in the music that was almost a communion with the father she'd loved, Allegra played on, grief and joy and longing coursing from her heart through her fingers onto the keyboard that transformed her turbulent emotions into a glorious rhapsody of sound.

Hands stilled on the final chord, Allegra stared sightlessly over the instrument, scarcely hearing the enthusiastic applause of the crowd. Until a familiar voice, the tone honey-sweet, broke through her abstraction.

"Didn't I tell you she was accomplished?" Sapphira said. "Why, I'm sure she plays as well as any of the performers we've heard this evening."

Before Allegra could snap back a reply, Lord Tavener appeared beside the pianoforte. "Just couldn't bring yourself to play badly, could you?" he murmured in her ear.

Then he raised his voice to carry over the crowd as he addressed their hostess. "Lady Harringtton, I don't believe the orchestra is yet ready. Release Miss Antinori and I shall do my part to entertain. If you will permit?"

Lady Harringtton gave him a curious glance, but nodded. "If you wish to play as well, Lord Tavener, do proceed."

Allegra felt a zing of warmth as Tavener clasped her elbow, urged her up and gave her a little push toward Rob, who strode over to seize her arm and lead her away.

Mrs. Randall hurried over to meet them. "Should we leave at once?" she asked in an anxious whisper. "Lynton,

I'm so sorry! I never expected Allegra to be made a spectacle of like this."

"We'll leave as soon as practicable," Rob answered sotto voce. "I don't wish to attract notice by making too precipitous an exit." Turning to Allegra, he added with exasperation, "Couldn't you have chosen something simpler?"

Both hurt and angry that Rob dared reproach *her* when 'twas Sapphira who had set it all in motion, she flashed back, "I could never have embarrassed Papa by playing poorly."

He looked as if he meant to say more, but at that moment Lord Tavener began and the music drove all other thoughts from her head.

She listened, at first incredulous and then enthralled. If the concerto she'd played had been difficult, the piece Tavener selected was beyond the skill of all but a virtuoso. As well it might be, since it had been composed by one.

Grief and joy, gratitude and astonishment mingled in her breast as Tavener proceeded to give a masterful performance of the "Ode in B-flat minor," the pianoforte piece her father had written as a love song to her mother.

Tavener couldn't know that—could he? she wondered, pressing her lips together to keep back tears as the haunting melody wrapped around her. She could not wrest her gaze from Tavener, eyes closed in concentration as he bent over the keyboard, coaxing passion, tenderness and rapture from its keys.

For several moments after the last note faded, the guests sat in hushed silence. Then, amid a thunderous eruption of applause, Tavener stood and bowed.

Straightening, he held his hands in a palms-out request for silence. "Enough, my lords and ladies," he said when the din quieted. "We amateurs do but our poor best. Lady Harrington, if your guests would like to take some refreshment before the dancing begins, they should do so now. I believe the orchestra is almost ready."

An immediate hubbub filled the room as the guests rose from their seats, some milling about the ballroom while the orchestra in the gallery began tuning their instruments, some strolling toward the refreshment room. A small group tarried around Tavener at the pianoforte, shaking his hand or offering congratulations.

From over their heads, Tavener's gaze found Allegra's. A dazzling smile lit his face and he gave her a nod.

She nodded back, glad he required no more response of her. She wasn't sure she could have managed to coax a reply from her emotion-clogged throat.

"What a marvelous performance!" Mrs. Randall said.

"'Twas well-done of Tavener," Rob admitted. "Let us leave now, while attention is still focused on him."

Though she wished she might go express her thanks and gratitude immediately to the man whose brilliant performance had so neatly deflected the focus of the crowd, Allegra knew Rob was right. Regretfully responding to the pressure of his hand on her arm, she rose and was turning to follow him out of the room when several gentlemen blocked their path.

"Sir Thomas, Jessamyn, I didn't think to see you before we left," Rob said, his grim expression turning to a smile of surprise and pleasure as he greeted his friends.

"You mustn't leave yet! My compliments, Mrs. Randall," Colonel Jessamyn said before turning to Allegra. "Miss Antinori, you play like an angel!"

"Her skill is exceeded only by her beauty," Sir Thomas Reede said, bowing over her hand. "Lynton, would you allow me to escort your charming ward to the refreshment room?"

"Nay, mustn't let him monopolize the Diamond of the evening," Colonel Jessamyn objected. "Would have stopped by earlier, but Lady Lynton kept detaining us. Couldn't desert a poor grieving widow, you know. We'll both escort you, if you will permit us, Miss Antinori?"

Allegra glanced up at Rob, who shrugged and gave a nod of approval. Apparently they weren't leaving immediately after all. And though Allegra would have preferred to seek out Tavener, still surrounded by a group of well-wishers who included, she noted with an illogical flare of annoyance, a number of lovely ladies, she could not be rude to these gentlemen.

"A glass of wine would be most refreshing," she said.

"Capital," the colonel pronounced, taking her arm. "We shall bring her back safely in a moment."

"They will be clearing the floor of chairs so the dancing can begin, so Mrs. Randall and I might as well accompany you," Rob said. "That is, if you would like another glass of wine, ma'am?"

Mrs. Randall nodded her assent and took Rob's arm. Sparing one last wistful glance in Tavener's direction, Allegra let herself be led off with the group.

As they walked to the refreshment room, a number of the ladies and nearly all the gentlemen to whom she'd been introduced these last few weeks stopped her to offer compliments on her skill.

Allegra had to suppress a little smile. It appeared that Sapphira's scheme to discredit her had gone awry.

She hoped, after they finished their wine and the gentlemen went off, she might find a few minutes to speak with Rob alone and try to gauge how he felt about seeing her suddenly become the focus of admiring eyes. Would he be proud of her performance now? Despite his fine words about wanting her to meet a number of superior gentlemen, would he be as anxious to restrict the time she spent with the men of whom he approved as he was to bar her from seeing Tavener?

Soon after arriving in the refreshment room, they heard over the hubbub of voices the orchestra begin to play, signaling that the dancing had begun. A bubble of excitement rose in Allegra's belly. How she would love to twirl about the ballroom floor on Rob's arm! And if his friends should invite her to dance, she might discover if having another man so close to her moved him to jealousy.

To her consternation, though, Rob firmly declined

both men's suggestions that they return to the ballroom. Since Mrs. Randall was fatigued, he informed them, he meant to escort the ladies home as soon as they finished their wine. After exchanging goodbyes and promises to call, Rob's friends bowed and departed.

Hard put to maintain her cheerful expression, Allegra swallowed her disappointment along with the last of her wine before taking Rob's arm and allowing him to lead her out of the refreshment room.

During their transit down the stairs to claim their wraps, they were stopped by three more gentlemen proclaiming themselves eager to meet her. Allegra's mouth grew stiff from smiling, her neck sore from inclining her head—and her temper ruffled at the knowledge that the evening was being cut short before she'd had a chance to achieve one of her main purposes for coming here.

Rob's stated preference for meek, pretty-behaved maidens had already closed to her the avenue of flirtation. Lost now was the rare opportunity to savor the touch of his hand on hers when she danced with him. Where isolated from everyone by a canopy of sound, they might converse in relative privacy and she could attempt, without Mrs. Randall overhearing every word, to rekindle the admiration and camaraderie they'd shared in their youth.

A few moments later they reached the waiting carriage. "'Twas a close-run thing," Rob said as they settled themselves, "but I think the evening passed off well enough despite your performance, Allegra."

"Indeed, I believe her performance brought her the attention and admiration of more gentlemen than she would have had otherwise," Mrs. Randall observed.

So Rob still didn't admire her skill, Allegra thought regretfully. But another gentleman did and had shown his support by providing her the most timely of services. "You should thank Lord Tavener for playing immediately after—and far more brilliantly—than I did," Allegra reminded them.

"That was most chivalrous," Mrs. Randall said. "Perhaps it would have been safe for us to have remained for the dancing after all."

Rob shook his head. "'Tis best to beat a strategic retreat and leave your admirers wanting more."

"I'm sure you must be right," Mrs. Randall said. "Still, what a marvelous evening! That glorious music and all those charming gentlemen eager to meet you, Allegra."

"It was lovely," Allegra acknowledged. "I just wish," she added wistfully, looking up at Rob, "I'd been able to converse more with the charming gentleman who brought us."

Was there a hint of tenderness in the wide smile he gave her? "Nonsense!" he replied. "I can worship at your feet any day. I'm delighted you were able to meet so many excellent young men." His smile dimmed. "Men of better stamp than Tavener."

"That's hardly fair, Rob!" Allegra protested. "Not only did he shield me from scrutiny by his superior performance, while you were away procuring wine, he prevented Lord Wofford and Sir Harry Miles from lingering."

"Wofford and Miles—those two undesirables? Damn and blast!" he exclaimed. "They should never have had the effrontery to approach you—and I daresay they would not have, had Tavener's presence not encouraged them."

About to protest once again Rob's assessment of Tavener, Allegra was forestalled by Mrs. Randall, who cried, "Oh, Rob, are they not good ton? Lord Tavener did seem reluctant to present them to Allegra, but Lady Maxwell assured me that Wofford's being the grandson of one of her good friends made it all quite proper."

Rob hesitated—probably, Allegra speculated, trying to frame a reply that his gentle cousin would not take as a reproof. "I'm sure Lady Maxwell meant to be helpful," he said at last, "but in future, it's best to let me make such judgments. I am privy to information about society's gentlemen that a respectable lady wouldn't know. And yes, Allegra, I suppose Tavener did exercise good judgment by discouraging those two rogues. Though he probably just wanted free rein to flirt with you himself. You did well tonight, but you must still be very cautious to limit your contact with him."

Allegra's warm approval of Rob's gentle handling of his cousin cooled. Though she'd hoped he might be jealous of the dangerously attractive Tavener, she could not like his persistent refusal to acknowledge any good qualities in the baron. She opened her lips to disagree with him again, then shut them.

Thereafter, silence reigned in the vehicle, Mrs. Randall nodding off and Rob's eyes closing as well. Her mind and senses still aroused after the events of the evening, Allegra wasn't sleepy in the least.

If Rob chose to believe the worst of Tavener, she obviously wasn't going to dissuade him. Nor should she let his implacable disdain irritate her, since the lower Rob's opinion of her undesirable suitor, the more likely that alarm over Tavener's pursuit might propel Rob to a declaration.

Still, Rob was showing himself rather dictatorial and small-minded, his unfavorable opinion of Tavener so firmly fixed in his head that he refused to entertain any evidence to the contrary. By instinct and observation, Allegra knew Tavener to be a much finer man than Rob would allow.

Was she really sure she wanted to entice Rob into a proposal?

That errant thought shocked her so much that she gasped. Of course she still wanted to marry Rob! she assured herself, trying to calm her agitation. Granted, the golden hero of her childhood had obviously changed a bit, but hadn't she, as well? If he were now somewhat… firm in his views, 'twas understandable after all his years of commanding men in wartime. Besides, in her limited observation, most men believed they knew better than ladies what should be done in any situation—poor, misguided fools that they were.

Though Tavener might be a good man at heart, as well as a devastatingly attractive one, she mustn't lose sight of the fact that her future security and happiness were at stake here. Tavener may have beguiled her with his rogue's charm and innate kindness, but worldly wisdom said that sooner or later, he would focus his mesmerizing eyes, tender regard and devastating charm on some other susceptible female.

Once a rake, always a rake, a sorrowful Molly had told her. Rob seemed to share that opinion. Who was she to dispute their much greater knowledge of the world?

No, she would not let herself be distracted from her purpose by the allure of a rogue. Even a rogue who seemed to possess as many fine qualities as William Tavener.

CHAPTER ELEVEN

As HE HAD most of the evening when not by the lady's side, while Will nodded and smiled at his well-wishers, he watched Miss Antinori out of the corner of his eye. He'd hoped to speak with her again, but Lynton's friends—eminently respectable men both—were leading her away.

Perhaps later, he thought, not willing to leave the musicale while there was still the possibility of snagging her for a bit more of their delicious conversation. Since Lucilla had been obligated to attend another function tonight, he meant to take full advantage of this chance to focus upon Miss Antinori, free of his well-meaning cousin's urging that he seek out more "suitable" young ladies.

Now that Miss Antinori was out of black gloves, Will might even be able to claim her for a waltz.

Ah, that he might let his arm encircle her waist, clasp her hand while the movements of the dance brushed her body against him. Lust and longing blasted through him at the thought.

A simple conversation might be safer if he wished

to keep enough wits about him to charm her. He'd hardly exaggerated when he told her he had trouble thinking when she was near.

Trouble thinking of something appropriate, that is. The words that sprang to his lips weren't the politely superficial "I shall delight in calling upon you" she'd coached him to utter, but something simpler and more basic.

Like "Come with me." "Kiss me." "Stay with me." Just a glimpse of her from across the room was enough to set his body simmering. A mere touch of her hand whipped his smoldering desire back to full flame.

For a moment, he let himself imagine the splendor of satisfying the constant ache to possess her. The wonder of caressing the round of hip and provocative thrust of breasts beneath him, worshipping that velvet skin with his hands, his mouth, revealing to her the powerful release he knew awaited them both.

He couldn't remember ever craving a woman this badly, wanting to wind his arms and legs around her and bind her to him. To taste her, inhale her, absorb the essence of her into his skin, like a potent elixir that would cure the ills of isolation and loneliness that still plagued him deep within.

At the same time, he felt this powerful need to make her laugh, to shield her from unpleasantness and protect her from maggots like Wofford and Sir Harry.

Maybe from himself.

Hands shaking with the ferocity of the emotions she

roused in him, Will took a deep breath, realizing he hadn't heard a single word of the gushing compliments being paid him by the attractive young matron before him.

A matron who was well curved, full-bosomed and sending him every possible signal that she wished to discover if his reputation as an excellent lover was justified.

He vaguely remembered from their introduction earlier that she had an elderly husband secluded away at some country estate. Voluptuous, interested, available—she possessed all the attributes that normally would have prompted him to smile back at the invitation in her eyes.

It was not the vow he'd taken to remain celibate while looking about for a rich wife that prevented him from responding. With a jolt of panic, he realized Madame LushBosom, who was now leaning forward so he might have a better view of her assets, didn't tempt him in the least.

Curling his hands into fists, he made some excuse and walked away, leaving the woman gazing after him with a slightly piqued frown. Needing solitude in which to cool his overheated mind and body, Will escaped onto the balcony beyond the ballroom.

It appeared, he thought as he wrapped his fingers around the chill stone of the balustrade, that his first instinct had been correct. It would be safer for him to avoid Allegra Antinori.

But he knew in his next breath that he wouldn't. And

the wicked amusement he derived from aggravating Lynton by pursuing her no longer played any part in that decision.

Besides, Miss Antinori might have her heart set on winning Lynton's…but Will was certain Lynton had no such designs on his ward's. He'd watched them carefully tonight without ever seeing on that gentleman's face anything like the admiration and affection so nakedly visible on Miss Antinori's as she'd gazed at her guardian in the park. Perhaps Lynton was more circumspect in concealing his emotions than the passionate Miss Antinori, but Will didn't believe that was the reason for the man's lack of ardor.

Lynton's expression while Colonel Jessamyn conversed with his ward denoted approval and gratification—as if he were showing off a well-schooled colt. Where Will was inspired to almost snarling rage when Sir Thomas Reede bent over Miss Antinori's hand, his leering eyes trying to peer down her bodice with an insolence that made Will want to land him a facer, Lynton appeared not to have even noticed the baronet's effrontery.

Her guardian treated Allegra, Will concluded, like a valuable prize—but one he intended to award to some other fortunate contender.

Whereas if she were Will's to guide and protect, he could never persuade himself to give her up.

Will didn't know which of them was the bigger fool.

With his mind in turmoil, perhaps it would be best not to seek out Miss Antinori again tonight. Sighing with exasperation, Will wheeled around, stomped off the balcony and headed across the crowded ballroom floor.

Deciding to evade the pursuit of Madame Lush-Bosom—and put off to another evening the chore of trying to charm one of Lucilla's "suitable" maidens—he would visit the refreshment room for another free glass of his hostess's excellent wine before returning to his rooms.

He'd proceeded a few paces into the hallway when a touch to his shoulder made him stop.

"My, my," the amused voice said. "So absorbed in your reflections were you, my lord, I thought you had gone deaf. I nearly had to run to catch up with you."

Pouty pink lips curved in a smile, the low-cut bodice of her black silk gown drawing attention to the rapid rise and fall of her full breasts, Sapphira Lynton stepped around to face him. Slowly she slid her hand from his shoulder down his sleeve before tucking her hand under his.

"Shall we have a glass of wine? I wasn't able to penetrate the ranks of your admirers earlier to tell you how much I enjoyed your performance."

"Did you indeed?" he asked, resisting the urge to pull his hand away. Already disliking her for the way she treated Miss Antinori, he resented even more this obvious attempt to use her sensuality against him.

Though she'd flirted with him before—as she flirted with any man who came within her orbit—Lady Lynton had never before singled Will out. Wondering why she'd chosen to do so now, Will decided it would be wiser to swallow his distaste and play along. Perhaps he could find a way to scare her off persecuting Miss Antinori— or winkle out of her any other schemes she might be hatching to embarrass or discredit Lynton's ward.

"So ardent and unusual a piece," Lady Lynton was saying as she led him into the now nearly deserted refreshment room. "I've heard you write music. Was it your own composition?"

Will knew instinctively Miss Antinori wouldn't want him to share anything about her father with this woman. Especially not the work the maestro had composed for the courageous, beautiful lady who'd defied her family and deserted her world to marry him.

Did Miss Antinori know he'd played it just for her?

"Still abstracted, my lord?" Lady Lynton recalled him, the tiny frown on her forehead signifying she wasn't pleased at receiving less than his full attention.

Before he could dredge up some insincere apology, she continued, "'Tis no matter. Come, let us sit and chat." After the footman handed them each a wine-glass, she linked her arm in his and led him to a small sofa in the far corner of the room, strategically placed behind a pillar and hidden by a screen of plantings.

The furniture's location suggested it had been set there to encourage just such discreet encounters. Lady Lynton's familiarity with it indicated this might not be the first time she'd availed herself of the arrangement. Storing away that observation, Will waited for her to speak.

With an arch smile, she said, "After you've gone to

such lengths this evening to impress the lady, I imagine I can guess who occupies your thoughts. You must know I fully support your ambitions!"

"And which ambitions might those be?" he asked.

"Come now, you needn't be coy," she chided, tapping him with her fan. "I noticed your interest in Lynton's Tall Meg of a ward before tonight. I mean Allegra, of course."

So she thought he had played this evening simply to *impress* Allegra? He supposed that was part of it. Treading cautiously, he said, "And if I were attracted to the lady, what interest could that be of yours?"

She took a sip of her wine, then slowly licked an errant drop from the tip of her lip. Watching his reaction from under her lashes, she said, "I might be in a position to…further your aspirations. I could, for instance, arrange for you to visit the house while Allegra is home alone. A dark night, a candlelit bedchamber, no hovering chaperone…well, I imagine an attractive gentleman of your vast expertise would have little difficulty persuading her to give you what you desire."

The images she conjured up flooded over him. Allegra his, coming to him clad in nothing but a silk night rail, her lustrous dark hair unbound. Teasing and tempting her until passion glowed in her dark eyes as she came into his embrace. His fingers, clumsy with eagerness as they worked the ties of her garment…

It took several seconds for his indignant brain to wrench control back from his rampaging senses. In the aftermath of ardor, shock knifed through him. Had Lady Lynton truly meant what he thought she had?

Hardly able to credit such a thing, he said, "What exactly are you suggesting?"

She laughed softly. "Oh, I think you know exactly what I am suggesting. Do not fear. I would make sure you were not…interrupted, so there would be no unpleasant consequences afterward."

Though Allegra had told him Lady Lynton disliked her, Will could scarcely believe this woman graced with the beauty of an angel really wished him to commit so devilish a deed: to ravish a gently bred maiden under her roof.

"Why would you wish me to do this?"

She tossed her head. "A man of your breeding must have recognized at first glance, as I did, what she truly is. I've tried to encourage only the sort of men she deserves, like Wofford and Sir Harry, to seek her out. But—" she gave him a seductive smile "—clever girl that she is, she seems to prefer your company. If you were to keep her…occupied, I could relax my vigilance, knowing that she wouldn't be able to use those siren's looks to gull some respectable gentleman into offering for her."

"And why is that so important to you?"

"I should think that would be obvious," she replied impatiently. "An Italian menial's trollop daughter trying to jump above her station and marry into the ton—why, the very notion offends! Lynton would recognize her for what she is, too, if he weren't so blinded by a mawkish attachment dating back to his youth. Of course, my late husband encouraged him by tolerating the girl and her wretched family. Why, I cannot imagine."

"Perhaps because the late Lord Lynton was related to her mother?" Will suggested, struggling to keep his voice neutral as he suppressed the urge to tell this spoiled daughter of the ton that he did indeed recognize a trollop when he saw one—and it wasn't Miss Antinori.

Be cautious, he ordered himself, at least until you've discovered the whole of her scheme.

Mastering his contempt with an effort, he said, "As you pointed out, Lynton does have a fondness for the girl. What would happen if he discovered our…assignations? I have no desire to find myself on a grassy field some morning, sighting at him over the barrel of my pistol."

"I doubt it would come to that! Most likely if he did discover the liaison, he would finally have his eyes opened to the creature's true character. And if there should be…difficulties, you need only retire to the country for a time while the scandal blows over."

Will shook his head. "I've no desire to rusticate for years in rural obscurity, my lady."

She waved an impatient hand. "'Twould be no need for that. A fortnight's wonder it would be, if the on-dit lasted that long. Once the ton learned the particulars, they would think no more of it than if they discovered you'd taken some chit from the opera as your mistress. The *orchestra* is her proper milieu, after all," she said, her voice dripping scorn. "And of course, if you should need something to…sustain you during your short exile, I'm sure I could assist."

Her audacity and total lack of remorse almost choked him. Will had to swallow hard before he responded, "Pray remind me what I would derive from this scheme?"

"Beyond the immediate enjoyment, you mean?" When he said nothing, she slid closer to him. "If you require more…inducement, I understand you've turned your eye toward Dianthe Herndon. She's extremely fastidious about her lovers, but since she's a close friend of mine, I could whisper a word in her ear for you."

Trying to drive the scent of her perfume out of his nostrils, Will shook his head. "Kind of you, but I've no interest in the lady."

"Indeed?" Sapphira leaned toward him until her breasts brushed against his chest before looking up, her full lips almost touching his. "I might offer my own gratitude." She lowered her breathy tone to a whisper. "My very…personal…gratitude." She tilted her chin up and closed her eyes.

Though his body clamored for him to lean down the short distance that separated them and take the kiss she offered, he fought off the urge, reaching instead to intercept her hand before her groping fingers found his trouser flap.

The fact that she could use her sensuality to force a reaction from his body even though her proposition affronted him in every fiber of his being only increased his rage. Never in his life had he been so close to striking a woman. How he wished she were a man, not just so he would be immune to her sensual advances, but also so he might challenge her to meet him in the ring.

But, alas, Sapphira Lynton was a woman, beyond the ability of a gentleman not of her family to chastise. For a moment he marveled at the malice and self-centered arrogance that led her to believe she was justified in plotting to ruin a girl whose only crime was to be held in high regard by the family of whom she was a distant connection.

Perhaps, given her beauty and the hold she'd always maintained over society, it wasn't incredible that Sapphira rated her charms so high she expected the mere suggestion of being rewarded with her body would send him rushing off to do her bidding. It rankled, though, that she held so slight an opinion of his honor that she thought he could that easily be maneuvered into ruining an innocent.

After several moments, when he did not avail himself of her lips, she opened her eyes and looked at him, her expression puzzled.

That confusion turned to a surprise bordering shock when he thrust away the hand he'd seized and stood up.

"'Tis a very…interesting proposition, my lady. I shall ponder it with the gravity it merits."

Unable to tolerate the sight of her another moment, he bowed and strode away.

Breathing hard, his thoughts still scrambled by unwanted lust and searing rage, Will stalked down the stairs to claim his coat and escape the treacherous confines of the Harrington town house. Reaching the other side of the street, he waved away a linkboy's offer to find him a hackney and simply stood, exhaling in gusts that wreathed his head like smoke in the frigid night air.

Since he couldn't act upon his first impulse—to land a neat uppercut across Sapphira Lynton's devious lips—Will wasn't sure what he should do. His gaze went back to the town house, windows ablaze with light as glittering and artificial as the smiles of the ton members dancing within it, still trying to force out of his head the lingering images of Miss Antinori in her night rail.

No matter how much he hungered to make that dream a reality, there was no question of falling in with Lady Lynton's despicable plot. Miss Antinori's virtue should be her gift to her bridegroom on their wedding night. Playing the groom in *that* scenario was a role Will was finding increasingly attractive.

But in the meantime, what to do about Lady Lynton's proposal? Obviously accustomed to being granted her every wish, Sapphira Lynton was not a woman who would be easily discouraged. Once she realized Will did not intend to acquiesce to her bidding, would she recruit someone else?

Wofford's handsome, sensual countenance swam into his vision and Will felt sick in the pit of his stomach. Setting aside his chagrin at being considered a man of the same stamp, he realized both Wofford and his friend Sir

Harry would likely view Lady Lynton's proposal as a novel and delightful challenge. The prospect of sampling not just Miss Antinori's charms, but Lady Lynton's as well, would give additional piquancy to the task.

And if those two refused her, there were any number of other possibilities. Will's mind skittered back to the meeting in the park with Fitzhugh and Markham and the nausea in his gut intensified.

How could he protect Miss Antinori from Lady Lynton's schemes? He might try to warn Lynton. However, if confronted by her stepson, Sapphira Lynton would certainly deny Will's accusation. Given Lynton's dislike of Will, the man would be more likely to believe his stepmother's protestations of innocence than Will's slur against her character.

The only one who knew Sapphira Lynton—and Will—well enough to believe her capable of such outrage was Allegra Antinori herself. When he called on Miss Antinori tomorrow, he must find some opportunity to warn her that she now stood in more danger from her "aunt" than even she would have thought credible.

CHAPTER TWELVE

WILL'S HOPE before retiring that, in the prosaic light of morning, Lady Lynton's scheme would appear less threatening proved vain. After a fitful slumber, he rose early, his troubled mind continuing to recall yet more so-called "gentlemen" whom Sapphira Lynton would have no trouble enticing to carry out her plan.

Tempting as it was to pay a morning visit to Gentleman Jackson's, where he might distract himself by going a few rounds with whomever he could induce to spar with him, Will knew the only way to rid himself of the anxiety needling him would be to deliver his warning to Miss Antinori.

Since the Lynton drawing room today would likely be filled with admirers come to praise Miss Antinori's musical performance, Will also knew if he wished to find some way to obtain a few moments of private conversation with her, he would have to arrive in advance of usual calling hours. So as early as he thought he'd have some hope of being admitted, he set off for Upper Brook Street.

The startled footman who answered his knock dispelled one potential problem by confirming that Lady Lynton was certainly not receiving yet, as her ladyship never left her bedchamber until well past noon. Leaving him in an antechamber, the servant set off to discover if the other ladies of the house might be available.

A few minutes later, the man returned to usher him up to the drawing room. Will found Mrs. Randall seated at a small writing desk near the hearth while Miss Antinori occupied the sofa, a book in her hand.

After an exchange of greetings, Will took the chair Mrs. Randall indicated. As he seated himself, without conscious volition his gaze veered back, like a compass needle seeking north, to Miss Antinori.

How lovely she was in the morning light, the sheen of her deep green dress echoing the highlights in her glossy dark curls. Though he had to regret that, not being evening wear, her gown concealed the delectable expanse of neck, shoulder and bosom he'd so admired last night.

Suddenly realizing the ladies were gazing at him expectantly, Will pulled himself out of his abstraction. "Thank you both for receiving me so unfashionably early," he said. "But I didn't wish to miss this opportunity to tell you how much I enjoyed your company last night. Your performance, Miss Antinori, was marvelous."

"Not half as marvelous as yours, my lord," Allegra replied. "I can't thank you enough for…everything." The warmth of the smile she gave him sparked a rush of delight that momentarily overwhelmed Will's worry.

"'Twas a lovely evening, wasn't it?" Mrs. Randall said. "I thought you both played beautifully. But you speak of missed opportunities, Lord Tavener. Do you have business that will take you from town later?"

"Possibly," he evaded, dragging his mind back to the point of his visit. "Since the weather is so lovely this morning, before you are kept indoors by the others who will be coming to offer their compliments, might I invite you both to take a turn in the garden?"

If he could coax them outside, Will reasoned, he might be able to stroll Miss Antinori far enough ahead to be able to deliver his warning without Mrs. Randall overhearing.

"Is it not still rather chilly?" Mrs. Randall asked.

"Not excessively," Will replied.

"A walk sounds most refreshing," Allegra said. "Or—if you would rather not, Mrs. Randall, I'm sure Lizzie would accompany me. I know you have letters to finish and you probably will not have an opportunity to do so once other guests start arriving."

Bravo, Miss Antinori, Will thought, as cheered by her intervention as he was by the perception that she seemed as eager as he to engage in a more intimate chat.

Mrs. Randall's doubtful expression brightened. "Indeed, I would like to finish these. If Lizzie will walk with you, you may go."

"Excellent. Give me but a moment and I will gladly accompany you, Lord Tavener." Dipping Will a graceful curtsey, Miss Antinori walked from the room.

He was rewarded for his efforts in maintaining a flow of light conversation with her timid chaperone by her speedy return, the maid Lizzie following in her wake. Will's appreciation for the servant increased when, as soon as they reached the graveled paths of the small back garden, the girl fell discreetly behind, keeping them in sight as they strolled down the allées of neatly clipped boxwood but remaining a sufficient distance away that they would be able to converse in private.

With Miss Antinori beside him, all Will's senses heightened. The awareness that rioted through him the instant she placed her hand on his arm gradually calmed to a slow tingling that settled in his loins and radiated with the beat of his heart to every extremity. For a few moments, he simply reveled in her nearness before forcing his mind back to the matter that had compelled him to inveigle her away from Mrs. Randall.

Before he could order his thoughts, though, she said, "I must thank you again for so cleverly distracting the attention of the crowd last night. And your selection! 'Twas a sheer delight to have that particular work performed so beautifully."

"The maestro wrote it for your mother, did he not?"

Her eyes widened. "You knew?"

"I read the notes on the score. I hoped it would please you."

She took a deep breath, her eyes sheening as she looked up at him. "It did."

Before Will could pledge to play any piece she

wanted, whenever she wanted, if she would but gaze at him with the same tenderness now illumining her face, she tossed her head and laughed shakily.

"I must commend your behavior in the parlor just now," she said, her light tone breaking the mood. "Quite the admiring but proper suitor! Though your gaze never left me, your eyes remained fixed on my face, without straying…where they should not. Perhaps my tutoring is having some effect after all."

Accepting with a rueful smile the distance she'd put back between them, he tucked her hand more firmly under his arm. Would that he might beguile her again rather than deliver the warning he felt compelled to give her. "I regret to disabuse you of that optimistic assessment, but the fact that I was so proper should have warned you that I'd been distracted by some dire event."

Her expression immediately sobered. "Something is wrong, then? An illness or death in your family?"

He laughed shortly. "Nothing of that sort. Indeed, I hardly have any relations whose demise would cause me distress, save Lady Domcaster and her family, who were quite well as of yesterday. I'm worried about a danger to someone to whom I am not related. You."

Eyebrows lifting in surprise, she tilted her head up. "*Me,* in some danger? What danger?"

Briefly Will related what Sapphira had proposed. Rather than the tears or wails of alarm he'd braced himself for, Miss Antinori stopped short and stared at him, a righteous indignation filling her eyes.

"She actually enticed you to ruin me? Why, that despicable vixen! Little as I like her, I'm astonished she is willing to go that far."

But before he could reassure her he would do whatever was necessary to thwart Lady Lynton's plan, she shook her head and laughed. "Though that does sound exactly like the sort of tawdry scheme she'd concoct. Thank heavens she's never suspected my feelings for Rob. I shudder to think what she might have done to interfere."

"I beg you to focus on this current threat," Will replied, pushing out of mind the mention of her tendre for Lynton. "She wanted me, at the least, to…to dishonor you, at worst to have us discovered in flagrante delicto, after which I was to flee London and leave you to face humiliation and total ruin. As if I would stoop to such a thing! By heaven, if she were a man, I would have called her out for such an insult to my honor and yours."

Miss Antinori sighed. "I told you she hated me. But thank you for your kindness and courage in bringing me a warning. I'm chagrined that you were forced to concern yourself with so distasteful a matter."

They'd reached a bench at the end of the pathway next to the high wall that separated the garden from the street. Pulling Allegra aside, out of view of the dawdling maid, Will said urgently, "Lady Lynton's implacable animosity is what most worries me. Of course I wouldn't consider her despicable offer, but you are a very attractive lady. I'm afraid she may go on to involve men more unscrupulous than I—who would find her offer very tempting."

She angled a glance at him, a slight smile on her lips. "And you are…not tempted?"

"Not tempted!" he echoed, frustration and the ever-present scourge of desire sharpening his tone. "Of course I'm bloody well tempted! How could you doubt that?"

"Well, I know you tease and beguile and play the part of being enthralled by me. But those are just the tools of a rake's arsenal. I'm not sure I truly believe it."

Afterward he couldn't recall just what pushed him over the brink. Perhaps, aggravated by a deficiency of sleep and an excess of worry, his control slipped. Or maybe it was because she looked so delectable, her soft cheeks ruddy from the cold, her dark eyes sparkling a challenge. Or maybe he only followed the lead of the curving feather of her silly bonnet, which bobbed in the slight breeze to caress the cheek he yearned to touch. Whatever the spark that set him off, he found himself drawing her closer. "Believe it," he murmured.

Just a short, sweet sampling, he promised himself. With fingers that trembled as if he'd been waiting weeks, a lifetime, he tilted up her chin and gently brushed his lips over hers.

She tasted of tea and apricots, innocence and sensual power. The softness of her lips made his chest ache while her lavender scent encircled him, pulling him closer. When she didn't cry out or push him away, but instead uttered a little sigh that whispered from her lips to his, he lost completely the struggle to resist her.

Wrapping his arms around her, he pulled her hard against him, deepening the kiss, his eager tongue demanding, receiving entrance. The flame within him intensified as he plumbed the hot lush wetness of her mouth, then exploded into wildfire when her tongue, hesitant, tentative, sought out his.

'Twas impossible to know what idiocy he might have attempted had not the sharp crack of a whip, the shrill whinny of horses and the squeal of braking carriages on the other side of the garden wall not shocked him out of his sensual thrall. With shaking hands he pushed her back, then had to brace her upright when she swayed, seeming about to fall if he completely withdrew his support.

For a few moments, Will heard only the sound of their gasping breaths and the shouts of men trading insults in the street beyond before, in a jingle of harness and clop of hoofs, the vehicles drove off.

Miss Antinori's eyes were downcast and a rosy blush that owed nothing to the wind colored her cheeks. Clinging to his arm, she looked confused, aroused, adorable.

Allegra. The melody of her name singing in his head, he had to marshal every vestige of control to resist the overpowering compulsion to kiss her again.

Instead, he willed his heartbeat to slow, his voice to calm. And oh-so-regretfully released her the instant she tugged at his hand.

"Now," he said when he could speak again, "I shall

keep perfectly still so you may slap me." He turned his face to offer her better access.

She laughed unsteadily. "That wouldn't be very sporting, when I was almost as responsible for…what just occurred as you."

"If Lynton had been able to see us from the window, I should be awaiting much more than a slap."

She smiled. "As he left early this morning on a matter of business, you are safe."

"Safe." Will laughed wryly. "I think we've just established that with me, *you* are not safe at all. Which is despicable, when I came here today expressly to talk about safeguarding you."

Just then Will heard a loud cough. He looked over to find that the maid had nearly reached the bench where he stood with Allegra—in the wake of that kiss, he would never be able to think of her more formally again. In unspoken agreement, she gave him her arm and they set off again, turning the corner to start down the parallel allée.

"I'm very touched by your concern for my welfare," Allegra told him after they'd once again drawn ahead of her maid. "I just don't find the threat as credible as you do. Sapphira believes I'm such a lightskirt that I'll be helpless to resist the persuasion of the first handsome rogue who shows me any attention. I assure you—" she paused, her face coloring "—despite…what just occurred, neither my morals nor my intelligence are that deficient."

"I know they are not," Will reassured her. "Lady Lynton obviously assumes you possess no more character or honor than she does."

"Perhaps. But since we've both agreed that I will not be led astray, I'm in no danger. Once Sapphira discovers that I cannot be persuaded, she might try to entice some 'gentleman' to forcibly seduce me. But with Mrs. Randall or Lizzie or a servant always within calling distance whenever I stir from the house and a full staff nearby when I am within it, I cannot see how anyone could succeed in carrying me off. Sapphira may despise me enough to seek my ruin, but even I do not believe she would go so far as to hire some miscreant to attempt it."

"Probably not," Will allowed. "But a sufficiently motivated rogue might be able to overpower you before you could summon assistance."

"If in future I am prudent enough never to walk more than a few paces ahead of my maid, I should suffer no further…indignities," she said, softening the words by flashing him a swift, mischievous smile. "Besides, if it comes to that, I grew up around actresses. Though the world may doubt their honor, many are quite virtuous and have learned how to protect themselves, skills they passed on to me. I feel quite confident I could discourage any unwanted attentions."

"Even against a taller, more powerful man?"

"A taller, more powerful man would not expect me to know how to resist him," she pointed out. "Besides, since my friends among the staff here would not allow such a thing to happen under their very noses, nor have I any intention of driving with or strolling about with men I cannot trust, I doubt I shall have need of my skill. There, have I reassured you?"

"Somewhat. But do allow me to make you a list of men with whom you must never, ever ride or drive. I will not feel easy until I've done all I can to ensure your safety."

Her expression softened. "I truly am touched by your concern."

"You must know you are…special to me," Will replied, substituting that word at the last instant for the "precious" he'd been about to utter. "I only wish I could do more. I'd warn Lynton, but his dislike for me is so intense, I doubt he would believe me. And regrettably, I cannot…restrain Lady Lynton in the manner I should prefer."

Will didn't realize he'd instinctively tensed his hands into fists until Allegra began to gently straighten each clenched finger. Further conversation was impossible while he focused on the glorious sensation of her fingers stroking his.

He barely suppressed a sigh of disappointment when, her task concluded, she lowered her arm back to her side. "'Tis really best to do nothing," she advised.

When her words finally penetrated, Will shook his head in amazement. "How can you view her interference so calmly? I'd be ready to strangle her."

Allegra smiled ruefully. "What would you have me do? Rush into her chamber, burst into tears, beg her to treat me more charitably? I'd rather starve in the street."

"How about you rush into her chamber, drag her from bed by her hair and scratch her eyes out? Since, unlike we gentlemen, you cannot slap her face with your glove and demand that she name her seconds."

"How unfortunate that upon his return, Rob refused to continue the fencing lessons he'd begun with me years ago!" she said with a chuckle. "But little as I like it, Sapphira is Uncle Robert's widow and mistress of the house in which I dwell. I could hardly do anything significant enough to quell her without Rob finding out, and though she deserves no consideration, I'd rather not expose her machinations and create a dispute within the family."

"Perhaps I could entice her to a rendezvous on the pretext of discussing her scheme, then arrange to have us 'discovered,'" Will suggested.

Allegra shook her head. "That wouldn't wash. Sapphira would simply put it about that you lured her there on some pretext and being a grieving widow, she agreed, never imagining you would offer insult to a lady in her position. You might succeed in tarnishing her reputation, but 'tis more likely she would discredit you instead."

Will shrugged. "I expect I could bear the scandal."

"But you mustn't!" she replied, concern in her voice. "'Twould be most injurious to your hopes of wedding an heiress. Promise me you will do nothing of the sort."

Ah yes, those hopes—or rather, Lucilla's hopes. Will felt his chest tighten. Though he was becoming surer by the day that the only heiress he wished to wed was

Allegra, he knew instinctively that this was not the moment for such a declaration. Fumbling for something he could say, he finally replied, "If you insist, I will promise. By heaven, though, I wish something could be done. It grates exceedingly that Lady Lynton can contemplate perpetrating such an outrage with impunity."

"Perhaps I shall hit upon a suitable response," she said, a mischievous smile lighting her face.

"By all means do! The more nefarious the scheme, the more I should approve it."

Allegra chuckled. "For shame, my lord! A gentleman should not bloodthirstily envision a lady's discomfiture. But enough of Sapphira! Since we are speaking of nefarious schemes, what of your plans to take me driving? Perhaps, as you suggested last night, a public renewal of your pursuit would push Lynton into action."

Her sudden change of subject was like a slap, bringing Will back to the realization that, for Allegra, ensnaring Lynton was still the most important goal. An aching sadness pierced his heart, followed by a brief blaze of anger. What of the kiss they had shared a few minutes ago?

To be fair, he had surprised her with it. Since she'd avoided all but a brief mention of it since, clearly she didn't wish to even acknowledge her "unmaidenly" response. Thank heavens, then, that he hadn't blurted out his tangled feelings and embarrassed them both.

She had never strayed from the script they had written, so best he return to it as well. "I should be delighted to take you driving again. Let us go back in and I will propose an outing to Mrs. Randall at once."

No, he would not believe he saw disappointment in her eyes at his suggestion that they end their stroll. But having delivered his warning, 'twas no point lingering in the garden, where his restless body could remind him of the opportunities waiting round the turn of each allée when, for a few moments, they outdistanced the trailing maid. Especially when Allegra's mind was obviously fixed, not on the titillating prospect of feeling his lips on hers again, but on getting Lynton's ring on her finger.

Still, she should be safe now, so he should feel better. He did feel better. He just wished that the prospect of forwarding a scheme to get her into Lynton's arms didn't make that relief curdle in his gut.

MRS. RANDALL LOOKED UP as they reentered the parlor. "Ah, how fortuitous! I've just finished the last of my letters. Did you have a pleasant walk?"

"Very pleasant," Allegra replied.

"You didn't get too chilled?" her chaperone inquired.

To Will's gratification, a blush colored Allegra's cheeks. "No, the sun was quite warm."

Mrs. Randall frowned. "And I thought the sky had come over cloudy. Well, no matter. I do wish I might have joined you. Though London is full of amusements, I must admit that I miss the beauty and peace of the countryside."

A sudden, reckless idea formed in Will's head.

Allegra wanted to spend time in his company to provoke Lynton. Mrs. Randall pined for the country. And Will needed to do something quickly to squelch his growing compulsion to be near Allegra.

If the ladies agreed to it, this scheme was likely to inflame Lynton to the point of making some dramatic move to secure Allegra's affections—if he ever meant to. It might infuriate him enough that Will could maneuver him into a bout of fisticuffs, a prospect Will found vastly appealing. Bloodying her beloved's nose would probably give the bewitching Allegra a distaste for his company—if viewing his decrepit ruin of an estate didn't send her fleeing first. He would be left in peace to pursue one of Lucilla's approved heiresses.

He pushed aside the fact that pursuing other heiresses held no appeal at all.

"Miss Antinori and I have just been talking about taking a drive. But now that you mention a visit to the country, Mrs. Randall, what if we were all to ride out to Brookwillow? If we leave early enough, we can reach the estate by midday. The inn in the village has a tolerable lunch, and we could be back to London before nightfall."

Mrs. Randall sighed. "Oh, a day trip out of London does sound lovely! Where is your estate located?"

"In Hampshire, about five miles from Hemley."

"Hemley?" Mrs. Randall echoed. "Why, one of my dearest friends resides just south of the village!"

"Then we should certainly stop and call on her," Will replied. "Would you like to go, Miss Antinori?"

"I would indeed," she replied. "A day out of the smoke and crowds of London sounds delightful."

"If your estate is located near Amelia's home, 'tis rather ambitious to speak of driving there and back in a single day," Mrs. Randall said, frowning. "Oh, I've no doubt you do so often enough on horseback, but the journey by carriage would be slower."

Before Will could think of some other inducement, Mrs. Randall's brow smoothed. "But I'm sure Amelia would be happy to have Allegra and I stay the night with her. You could leave us at Pinetree Manor after we visit your estate and return the next day to escort us back to London, if that would be agreeable to you, Lord Tavener."

Two days out of London to walk with and talk with and tease Allegra Antinori. Even though his supposed goal was to put her at a distance, the prospect electrified Will. "That would doubtless make the excursion more comfortable," he replied. "Would you wish to undertake such a journey, Miss Antinori?" he asked, willing her to agree.

She opened her lips to answer and then hesitated, her eyes widening. Will knew the instant it occurred to her that spending two whole days, rather than just one, in his company would be even more of a goad to Lynton. Flashing him a look of understanding, she said, "If you are sure your friend would not find it an imposition— and Lord Tavener can be away from the city for another day, I should happily undertake the journey."

"Having an extra day at Brookwillow will allow me

to look into more estate business," he said. Or likely through it, he thought, envisioning the new holes that must have worked themselves into the roof by now.

"I'm sure Amelia would be happy to receive us," Mrs. Randall said. "I've already had two letters from her since arriving in London, chiding me for not yet paying her a visit. She suffers from a rheumatism that makes carriage travel quite painful, you see. I shall write her at once."

"I must send a note to my bailiff and can have my man deliver the letter to your friend," Will told her. Torn between the compulsion to push this matter to a conclusion and the wistful hope of retaining Allegra's favor, he felt compelled to add, "I must warn you, my estate is in rather poor condition. Still, its setting over-looking the river and the drive itself are both lovely."

"I would love to see your Brookwillow," Allegra said.

With those lustrous dark eyes gazing expectantly at him, for a moment Will wished despairingly that the estate to which he'd pledged to escort her was worthy of her obvious anticipation.

Idiot, he told himself, squelching the emotion. The whole purpose of his plan *was* to disappoint her, to make her withdraw from him at the same time they ma-neuvered Lynton closer into declaring for her. "I'll make the arrangements. Shall we say later this week?"

"I shall propose to Amelia that we set out in two days' time and let you know as soon as I have her reply, Lord Tavener," Mrs. Randall said.

"My man will come by to collect your letter this afternoon, ma'am," Will said.

A discreet knock at the door distracted them, followed by the entrance of the butler. "Colonel Jessamyn and Sir Thomas Reede to see you, Mrs. Randall, Miss Antinori."

Having accomplished what he'd come for, best that he take his leave—rather than remain to stoke his ire by watching Jessamyn and Sir Thomas pant over Allegra. Only the knowledge that she had no inclination toward either of them allowed him to calmly bow to Mrs. Randall before turning to take Miss Allegra's hand.

"Thank you for a most *warming* turn about the garden," he murmured, unable to leave without referring at least once to the unacknowledged passion between them. He brushed his lips over her gloved hand, savoring her lavender scent. "I await our outing with utmost anticipation."

A barely perceptible blush colored her cheeks and she raised her eyebrows in reproof. "As shall I, my lord."

Despite his ostensible purpose in conveying Allegra to Brookwillow, Will couldn't help the spring in his step as he descended the front steps of Lynton House and hailed a hackney. Two days in her company! 'Twas a boon he intended to relish…right up to the minute when her tour of Brookwillow ended her interest in him for good.

Arriving back at his modest rooms, he called for Barrows. "I've several letters to write and I'll need a runner to take them to Brookwillow. I'll be paying a brief visit later in the week."

"Very good, m'lord. Give me the letters when you've finished. In the meantime, I'll pack our bags."

"You won't need to accompany me. I'll be engaging a carriage and there won't be room."

About to exit, Barrows stopped short on the threshold. "Engaging a carriage? You do not intend to ride?"

"Mrs. Randall, Miss Antinori's chaperone, has a friend near Hemley whom she wishes to visit. Since I planned to go to Brookwillow anyway, I offered to escort the ladies."

Barrows stared at him for a long moment while Will felt his face heat. "You've been planning to visit Brookwillow? And I was unaware of that fact?"

Will took refuge in hauteur. "I don't tell you everything, Barrows."

"Apparently not. But you probably should. Shall I arrange for the carriage?"

"No, I'll take care of it. As for the packing, I'll only be gone for two days, so I won't need much."

"It would be better if I went along. The ladies will not be much impressed if you do not bring a valet."

"Not impressing them is the point," Will murmured. "In any event, it's already decided."

Barrows shook his head. "You're going to regret declining my assistance."

"Go!" Will said irritably, dismissing him. Sometimes he wondered which of them was master and which, employee. But given how uncomplainingly Barrows had shared his poverty and the very resourceful assistance he often provided, 'twas only natural he felt he ought to be part of whatever Will was planning.

Except that Will didn't think he could bear having even Barrows, who knew him perhaps better than anyone on earth, present to watch him tear his heart out while he drove Allegra away from him.

CHAPTER THIRTEEN

FROM THE MOMENT Hobbs escorted Lord Tavener out and Colonel Jessamyn and Sir Thomas in, Allegra was occupied by a steady stream of visitors. It seemed virtually everyone she knew in London had either attended the musicale or heard of it, and all were anxious to applaud her performance or inquire about the evening.

It wasn't until late afternoon that Allegra was able to get away to her own chamber to reflect upon Lord Tavener's warning. Though she'd known Uncle Robert's spiteful wife disliked her, she was genuinely surprised at the lengths to which Sapphira was apparently willing to go to discredit her.

It both angered and saddened her that Sapphira apparently felt compelled to use every means at her disposal to exclude from the society over which she reigned a person she judged unworthy of it. Thank heavens that, though a product of the same world, Uncle Robert had quite different standards!

He had continued to value her mother despite the choices she'd made and had always shown the greatest respect for Allegra's talented father. Once again, she was humbled that Uncle Robert believed her worthy of inclusion among the ton her mother had abandoned— despite the fact that it seemed increasingly likely that Allegra would never feel comfortable there. She was grateful, too, that if her dream of winning Rob's heart was not realized, she would have Uncle Robert's legacy to fall back on.

Should she eschew the polite world and settle on her country manor, she could think of few in society she would miss, save Rob—and Lord Tavener. She felt herself smile. Would he still deign to recognize a musician's daughter, even after he'd married an heiress?

Once she allowed herself to think of him, the indiscretion she'd fought all day to forget breached the barrier of will and came flooding back. Little shivers rippled across her skin as she remembered the feel of his lips on hers.

She'd never imagined such joy, such wonderment, such a powerful, compelling rush of sensation could result from the simple brush of a man's mouth over hers.

Not that she'd been able to limit herself to just that first gentle contact. No, having wondered so many times what it might feel like to kiss him, she'd been unable to resist the unexpectedly overwhelming response he evoked in her. No wonder Molly had been so captivated by her rogue!

She should have pushed him away after that first caress, but doing so became simply impossible once his tongue teased its way into her mouth, igniting a maelstrom of wicked, irresistible desires. Rather than step back, she'd wanted to press her body closer, deepen the kiss, nearly desperate to taste more of him, to urge his hands and mouth to continue their explorations.

No, it would not have been fair to slap him for his effrontery when all she'd wanted was still more of his delicious impropriety. Her face heated, her lips and nipples burned at the thought.

She put cool fingers to her flaming cheeks. It seemed she was even more susceptible to him than she'd thought.

And what if Rob *had* been home, had chanced to gaze out the library window and seen her, clinging to Lord Tavener like some Covent Garden strumpet?

The spiral of sensation in her gut abruptly stilled. At the least, Rob would have been disappointed; at worst, he might have felt she'd dishonored him and his household.

Proving Sapphira correct in her estimation of Allegra's character.

Well, such a thing must not happen again. She had a clearer knowledge now of the full extent of her weakness for Lord Tavener. She must not in future tease him into making advances she had just found, to her shame, that she was nearly incapable of resisting.

Did the necessity to be more circumspect mean she must give up his friendship, too? she wondered wistfully. It had been kind of him to worry about her so much he'd felt compelled to warn her against Sapphira. Not since Papa died had anyone been that protective of her welfare.

Though she had to laugh, recalling how, brow

creased and hands clenched into fists, he'd talked of wanting to deal with Lady Lynton himself. Uncle Robert's wife would probably faint dead away if she ever saw directed toward her the menacing look Allegra remembered upon Tavener's face when he'd scared off Lord Wofford last night. He truly was the most kind and chivalrous of gentlemen.

Resolving to figure out a way to remain his friend while resisting his appeal, Allegra forced her thoughts away from envisioning his all-too-compelling countenance and back to the problem of Sapphira.

What would be best to do about the woman? Reviewing Tavener's description of her tawdry scheme, Allegra felt her lip curl in contempt. Trust Sapphira to look for some dupe to maneuver into doing the disreputable work for her. Though as she'd told Tavener, Allegra was not particularly worried about the plan, if Sapphira did manage to recruit some unsavory gentleman to implement it, once he realized Allegra could not be easily seduced, he might become less genteel in his methods. Though she remained confident she would be able to escape such a man with her virtue intact, it was possible she might need help, and in coming to her aid, John Coachman or Hobbs or Lizzie might be injured. That, she couldn't allow.

Better, therefore, to make Sapphira see the wisdom of abandoning her scheme as soon as possible. Allegra set her lips in a firm line. She'd confront her this very day.

Allegra rang the bell and asked Lizzie to let her know

when Sapphira awakened from her afternoon nap. At that time, Lady Lynton usually lounged in her bed sipping chocolate and reading the society pages before summoning her maid to help her dress for the evening.

Alerted an hour later, Allegra walked down the hall, rapped twice and entered Lady Lynton's bedchamber.

Since she'd never before sought out her aunt, Allegra was not surprised to see that Sapphira looked startled before her eyes narrowed in annoyance.

"What do you think you're doing, invading my bedchamber?" Sapphira demanded.

"I should rather ask what you think you are doing," Allegra replied calmly. "But then, I already know. Lord Tavener told me what you proposed to him, madam. A dreadfully common scheme, don't you think, Aunt Sapphira?"

Sapphira's blue eyes opened wide. "Tavener told you…! Why, that…that brigand! I mean, how could you possibly believe anything said by a man of his stamp? If he speaks spitefully of me, 'tis only because I rebuffed his distasteful advances—"

"Oh, shut it," Allegra interrupted. "As I said nothing specific about what he'd alleged, your very denial convicts you, so spare me the protestations of innocence. You have done everything you could think of to ruin my presentation from the moment Rob informed you I was to have one. Thus far I have kept silent, but no longer. Your distasteful little game can be played by two, madam." Allegra fixed her unsmiling gaze on Sapphira and waited.

Lady Lynton lifted an imperious hand as if to dismiss her, then hesitated. Though Allegra doubted her glare was as forbidding as Tavener's, apparently it was well enough, for after a few moments of hard scrutiny, Sapphira broke the silence to ask, an edge of nervousness in her voice, "What do you mean to do?"

"If I learn you are hatching any more schemes to discredit me, I shall tell Rob what Lord Tavener told me."

Sapphira's eyes widened with dismay for an instant before she set her face in an expression of disdain that did not quite manage to mask her concern. "You wouldn't dare repeat such nonsense to Lynton. He'd dismiss it in a moment with the contempt it deserves."

"Would he? Recall that we grew up together, madam. If I were to appeal to him, which of us do you think he'd be more likely to believe?"

"You—lowborn daughter of a traveling musician!" Sapphira cried, rage distorting her lovely features. "Do you really dare threaten me?"

"Oh, I dare. Though even I am not quite so daring as you, my lady. Suppose I were to reveal to Rob what I know concerning events that transpired in this house before his father's death. Things I heard when I stepped out for air those evenings I kept vigil over Uncle Robert and you entertained the cicisbei come to console the distraught wife whose husband lay dying. The rustlings, the gasps, the little moans."

Though Allegra's words were a gamble based only on the little she'd overheard and her assessment of

Sapphira's character, she was close enough to the mark that a momentary flash of fear escaped Sapphira's pose of disinterest. "What you insinuate is preposterous!" she exclaimed. "Lynton would never believe you."

"Wouldn't he? You must know he doesn't like you. I fear you may have given him a disgust of you, trying out your wiles on him. With a bit more prodding he might decide it best for the family honor for you to leave London during your mourning period. I believe he mentioned Highbeck—'tis a fine manor near Ullswater in Cumbria, the Lynton ancestral home, though none of them have lived there in years. Such a lovely view of the fells! Rob always said he thought it a shame the place stood empty."

"C-Cumbria?" Sapphira repeated with horror.

"Or perhaps I need say nothing to Rob. Perhaps I shall only mention what I heard to Lizzie and let things take their course. 'Tis no controlling servants' gossip, you know—'twould be all over town in a trice."

Though Sapphira struggled to maintain her facade of unconcern, she began nervously twirling one golden curl around her finger. "No one listens to the chatter of underlings," she declared after a moment.

Allegra laughed. "No one but the entire ton! You should know better than most how much society delights in passing along deliciously scandalous news. Girls jealous of your beauty, maidens whose suitors you've lured away, men you've snubbed or slighted— do you truly think such as these would not rejoice to spread the word of your misdoings? Of course, you might be able to wait out the scandal and emerge with your prestige intact…but are you willing to gamble your place in society on that?"

All pretense of indifference gone now, Sapphira gave a little gasp of dismay. Allegra knew that for Sapphira, the possibility of no longer being one of the reigning Diamonds of the ton was far more frightening than the prospect of a chilly spring exile to Cumbria.

Taking advantage of Sapphira's momentary speechlessness, Allegra leaned toward her aunt, her face set in the most forbidding expression she could summon. "I have stood as much as I intend to stand, madam. Toy with me further and I promise, you will regret it."

After making Sapphira a deep curtsey, Allegra walked out. As the door closed, she caught one last glimpse of Lady Lynton, her lips half-open in a reply she had not been able to formulate, a troubled frown on her brow.

Allegra kept silent until she reached the sanctuary of her room where, the door firmly closed, she gave a whoop of glee. Whether or not Sapphira remained as cowed as she appeared at this moment, still it felt wonderful to stand nose to nose with the spoiled beauty and finally give her back for all the slights and abuses of the last six months.

If the cautionary effect of this little interchange abated, Allegra would just have to think of something else. But she felt sure she had just won herself some respite.

She recalled Tavener's comment and chuckled. Would he consider her stratagem sufficiently diabolical?

Laughing again, she clapped her hands together, the future suddenly seeming gloriously bright. She had Sapphira's malevolence stymied and the pleasing prospect of a long drive with Tavener during which she could relax and enjoy his company, Mrs. Randall's presence a guarantee she'd not succumb to temptation.

And taking a long *private* drive with the man Lynton most wanted her to avoid ought to propel Rob to action…if ever he meant to act, she thought, her euphoria dimming.

Impatiently she thrust away that dispiriting reflection. With the trip to Brookwillow imminent, she refused to let anything spoil her anticipation.

EARLY ON THE MORNING of the appointed day, Allegra, Mrs. Randall and Lord Tavener set off in a barouche for his country estate. Allegra figured he must have hired the carriage, which was well-appointed and far larger than a single gentleman would keep for his own use. He impressed her too by providing foot warmers, lap robes and mugs of spiced wine to ward off the morning chill as well as light refreshments to sustain them until they reached the inn where they would lunch before arriving at Brookwillow.

Once the vehicle emerged from the tangle of London streets and gained the countryside, Mrs. Randall sat up excitedly, her face pressed to the window glass. After an hour spent exclaiming over the beauty of budding trees, emerging bulbs and early wildflowers, she accepted a mug of wine from Lord Tavener. When she had finished that, the soporific effect of the rocking coach overcame her and she nodded off.

Allegra appreciated as much as her chaperone the unblemished beauty of the countryside passing beside them. With her lungs filled with the sweet scent of fresh country air, she too might have grown sleepy—but for the presence of Lord Tavener. Folding his tall frame onto a narrow carriage seat left his knees nearly touching hers, a fact that kept all her senses on edge.

Sternly forbidding herself to imagine sitting beside rather than opposite him, his arm, now draped casually along the back of the squabs, at her elbow to steady her against the bumps in the road, she once again gave thanks for the restraining presence of the dozing Mrs. Randall.

Smiling, Allegra looked from that lady's somnolent form to Lord Tavener—and caught him staring at her.

Her breasts tingled at the intensity of the gaze he had fixed on them. Her cheeks flushing as well, she said softly, "You are backsliding, sir."

His lazy gaze leapt to her face. "Backsliding?"

Allegra shook a finger at him. "You were staring at my…person again."

"How could you know? You've been gazing out the window."

"I just saw you," she pointed out.

He sighed and a little sparkle glittered in his eyes,

making him seem like a schoolboy caught out in some mischief. "Very well, but you must not be too severe with me. 'Tis your loveliness distracting me again, else I should have glanced away before you noticed. Besides, 'tis unreasonable to expect me to always resist the pleasure of looking at you. I'm but a man, after all."

"And therefore highly susceptible to temptation?"

He grinned. "Aren't we all, upon occasion?"

He must be referring to her response to him in the garden, she thought, her blush deepening. Restraining herself from remembering what his unwavering gaze teased her to recall, she wrapped her arms around her sensitized torso and said primly, "We must all resist temptation if we are to achieve our goals. If you wish to woo and win your heiress, you must learn more quickly. Since it appears such a daunting task, are you sure you want to attempt it?"

He shrugged. "I've no other recourse, if I am to salvage my estate."

"Is Brookwillow your family home?"

"I didn't grow up there, if that is what you mean. I was but a lad of five summers when my parents died, so spent most of my youth at school." The light in his eyes faded. "I've paid visits over the years, of course, but already by the time I left Oxford, the manor was too decrepit to inhabit. Nor does the land produce enough income to fund the necessary repairs."

His voice for once void of its usual teasing overtones, she caught an echo of despair in his reply. *He truly cares about Brookwillow,* she realized, a deep sympathy welling up within her. She wondered if Tavener realized how clearly his tone revealed the depth of his frustration at the deterioration of his estate.

"How is the manor situated?" she asked, aching for him and wanting to steer his mind to happier thoughts.

To her satisfaction, his expression brightened. "Brookwillow stands on a hill on the Hampshire downs," he replied, and from his faraway expression, she knew he must be picturing it in his mind. "A small river, hardly more than the brook for which it is named, runs at its feet and meanders through the surrounding farmland. The current building was erected on the ruins of a castle donjon, but it's Elizabethan, mostly."

"It sounds lovely."

He turned to her, the light in his eyes dimming again. "It used to be. I suppose it could be again, given an influx of enough cash and a knowledgeable manager."

"You know nothing of farming?"

His laughter had bitter overtones. "My guardian could not be bothered to teach me anything useful. But he paid my fees at Eton and Oxford, for which I must be grateful."

"In addition to music, Papa taught me Latin, mathematics and the classics. Mama drilled me in French, history and literature, so I'm more knowledgeable than most females, I suppose, but how I should have loved to go to Oxford! It seems so unfair that university learning is limited to gentlemen."

"'Tis much too dangerous for ladies to be educated," he responded. "You are already so much cleverer than men, you would soon take over the world." His eyes roamed her face to settle on her lips. "You've nearly conquered this bit of it already," he said softly.

Did he infer she'd conquered *him?* At the sudden heat in his powerful gaze, Allegra's lips burned and the breath caught in her throat.

"You will be…compassionate to the vanquished, I hope?" he whispered, leaning toward her.

She couldn't help it. Some irresistible impulse pulled her toward him, made her eyes flutter shut at the warmth of his breath on her cheeks. A sense of urgency churned in her belly as she anticipated his touch, his taste…

The carriage hit a rut that bounced them both into the air. He steadied her back to her seat as Mrs. Randall woke with a start.

"Dear me, I must have dozed off!" she exclaimed. "Are we near the inn yet?"

Though Allegra felt her cheeks flame hotter, Lord Tavener appeared perfectly composed. "We're almost there, ma'am," he said, smoothly picking up the conversation as if he hadn't just almost kissed her. "I trust you are rested and ready for luncheon. I promise the fare at The Brindled Mare will not disappoint you."

While he continued to talk to her chaperone with practiced ease, Allegra looked on, both frustrated and grateful at the fortuitous interruption of their little interlude. How could he look so cool and detached while, unsettled and still hungry for his touch, she burned?

Because, she answered herself acidly, despite the glimpse she'd had of the more complex man within, at heart he was still a rake. Only a man who, as he'd said, couldn't be blamed for taking advantage of the moment and a girl who was all too obviously susceptible to his charm.

Berating herself for allowing the fact of Mrs. Randall's presence to lull her into letting down her guard, Allegra vowed to conduct herself for the rest of this journey with the utmost propriety.

As if the rake's effect on her, she thought with more than a little disgruntlement, was as superficial and fleeting as hers seemed to be on him.

CHAPTER FOURTEEN

As THEY SAT AT A TABLE in the inn an hour later, Will's palms remained sweaty and his heart still thudded in his chest. He only hoped he'd forced down enough ham and ale to give credence to the claim he'd made to Mrs. Randall about the superiority of the Brindled Mare's luncheon.

What had he been thinking, to have subjected himself to the torture of riding for hours in a closed carriage with Allegra? He should have known that he'd not be able to content himself forever just with the pleasure of gazing at her, great as that pleasure was. Not when her lushly rounded body sat but a hand's reach away, her expressive dark eyes luring him closer as she captivated him with her smile, her lavender scent, her witty rejoinders.

It made his hands perspire anew to recall how close he'd come to wrapping her in his arms and kissing her until she begged for breath while her chaperone dozed not two feet away. Had he no control at all?

A review of how she'd looked in the carriage, the ebony curls peeking out beneath her bonnet, the satin skin of her countenance glowing from the crisp fresh air, those berry-red lips, was enough for his body to tighten again.

No, he possessed no control at all where Allegra was concerned.

Interestingly enough, it appeared she was also susceptible to him. Had that fortuitous bump in the road not prevented him from kissing her, he knew she would not have repulsed him, just as she had not slapped him in the garden at Lynton House.

He tried to damp down the thrill of purely masculine satisfaction at that realization and force himself instead to examine why, if the connection between them was so strong, she seemed so set on marrying Rob Lynton.

Of course, to ask that was to answer. For a lady of dubious connections who needed a secure position in the world, Lord Lynton had much more to offer than an impoverished baron with a crumbling estate. Allegra's senses might have other ideas, but her practical mind was set on what even he must admit was a more prudent and advantageous match.

Which probably explained why she'd grown so quiet since that almost-kiss in the carriage. Fortunately Mrs. Randall, full of excited chatter about her return to the country and the prospect of visiting her dear friend, hadn't seemed to notice the relative dearth of conversation produced by her two luncheon companions.

For another moment, Will let his gaze rest on Allegra's downturned face, the thick dark lashes painting two semicircles of shadow over her cheeks. A dull ache throbbed in his chest.

Assuming the man wasn't cloth-headed enough not to eventually recognize the treasure within his reach, would Lynton cherish that fiery passion just waiting to be awakened or Allegra's fiercely inquiring mind? Somehow, Will didn't think so—any more than he expected to thrill at possessing the well-dowered pinnacle of maidenly deportment Lucilla wanted him to wed.

Since the choice was out of his hands, he ought to concentrate on behaving as prudently as Miss Antinori. Mrs. Randall had finished her repast, her charge had pushed the food back and forth on her plate a sufficient number of times and heaven knows, he couldn't choke down another bite. Best to get them back on the road to his estate, the sooner to expose to his guests the full extent of his unsuitability, so that he might put an end to futile daydreams and painful imaginings.

And though the hiring of the carriage to bring them here today had severely diminished his reserve of coins, he vowed he would rent a horse to ride on the return journey even if it meant he must dine on whatever offerings were available at various gaming hells every night for a month.

WILL FOUND HIS NERVES winding tighter with every mile they drew closer to Brookwillow. On the other hand, each turn along the now-familiar road brought into view new vistas into woods he'd explored and

streams he'd fished on his infrequent but prized
holidays here, evoking a flow of fond memories. Odd,
to have so sharp a sense of belonging in a place in
which he'd spent comparatively little time. Perhaps it
was the warm welcome and straightforward acceptance
the Phillipses had always accorded him that made the
manor and its land so dear to him.

But drawing nearer also speeded him toward the
moment he'd have to gird himself for the dismayed
and perhaps disgusted reaction of the ladies, once they
viewed the true extent of Brookwillow's decrepitude.

The carriage turned off the main road and crossed a
narrow bridge over the lazy-flowing river. "The gatehouse is just ahead," he informed his companions, his
pulse quickening with anticipation and dread.

"Is this the brook for which the estate was named?"
Allegra asked. "'Tis lovely, and the woods also. Will we
be able to see the manor house from the drive?"

"Not until we are almost upon it. Though from the
manor one has a commanding view of the surrounding
countryside, from here the wood prevents one from
being able to see to the hilltop."

The carriage made a sharp turn to enter the drive.
Will sucked in a breath, fending off the tug of memory
and trying to see Brookwillow as his visitors must.

The tall brick wall that led away from the gatehouse
into the woods, lichen-coated and missing most of its
top course of bricks. The long-deserted gatehouse, its
windows empty of glass and part of its roof fallen in.

Only the drive, which received enough traffic to keep the grass beaten down, didn't look the picture of neglect.

They passed fields that had once, he vaguely remembered from childhood, been planted with gently waving rows of wheat, now grown up in weeds and bracken. As they climbed steadily upward, the tenant farms they skirted looked in better shape, with kitchen gardens neatly tended and new thatch on the roofs, the latter courtesy of a run of good luck he'd had at the tables in the early fall.

"The farms appear in good heart," Mrs. Randall said.

"I believe the land is quite fertile," he replied. "Not that I know much about agriculture."

Before she could answer him, the carriage crested the rise and suddenly, across an untidy meadow which had once been an expanse of parkland, he saw in the distance the stone and half-timbered manor house, the myriad panes of its mullioned windows winking in the sun as if waving a greeting. Despite the trial to come, a wave of affection swept through Will.

"How charming the house is!" Allegra exclaimed.

"You'll probably not find it so charming once you see how handily the rain penetrates the dining-room roof," he replied, the need to squelch his pleasure at her compliment making his tone sharper than he'd intended. "Though you mustn't fault the caretakers. Mr. and Mrs. Phillips have done all one could expect with what little funds were available to prevent the whole place from falling into ruin. They will have marshaled all their resources to provide as comfortable a reception for you as possible, so I beg you will not hold them responsible for Brookwillow's deficiencies."

Though Mrs. Randall looked a bit uneasy after that daunting speech, Allegra replied, "I am sure whatever they have arranged will be delightful."

Recalling the Adamesque elegance of Lynton House, Will wasn't so sure. The churning in his gut intensified and suddenly he regretted the crackbrained idea of inviting her here, exposing Brookwillow to her discerning eyes in all its shabbiness. He thought of the humble accommodations in the kitchen and the small parlor, the only rooms still in good enough repair to receive guests, the formal rooms beyond having been long since shut up, their hangings in tatters, their wall coverings spotted with damp. Anger and embarrassment flushing his face, he had the crazy desire to order the barouche to turn around immediately and head back to Hemley.

Taking a deep breath, he resisted the impulse. By now he ought to have squelched the pathetic desire to have her think well of him. The whole reason he'd brought her here was to let her see the worst, to give her such a distaste for him she'd have no desire even to remain his friend. And should Allegra be too loyal to cast him off, surely after viewing his crumbling estate, Mrs. Randall would be affronted enough at his audacity in calling himself a gentleman of property to deny him the house.

Which was just what he wanted, wasn't it?

Maybe not what he wanted, he conceded. But since

it was certainly what he needed, he silently vowed to master his cowardly reluctance and finish the business.

A few minutes later, the carriage passed the unused front entrance and pulled into the kitchen yard. A surge of gladness momentarily escaped his inner turmoil when, in a barking of dogs and banging of doors, Mr. and Mrs. Phillips emerged from the kitchen wing to greet them.

As soon as the carriage halted, Will leapt out. Wrinkled face wreathed in a smile, Phillips gave Will's hand a hearty shake while Mrs. Phillips captured him in a hug. "'Tis wondrous good to see you, Master Will!" she exclaimed. "Ye've been gone from home too long."

"'Tis good to be back," Will replied, surprised to realize he meant it, regardless of his reasons for returning. "Now, let me present my guests." He turned to assist the ladies from the barouche.

"I trust you can find a dry seat for the ladies and some meat and cheese to offer them," Will said to Mrs. Phillips after the brief introductions.

"Well, of course I can," she answered, giving him an indignant look before turning to his guests. "Ladies, you follow me out of this wind and we'll have you snug in the parlor in a trice! There's some good sharp cheese, meat pies and some of your favorite apple tarts, Master Will. By the looks of ye, you've need of some fattening. Just like when you was a lad. Gobbled up as many pies as I could make, he always did!"

Will followed them in, his expression grim. As she

gazed around the room, Mrs. Randall, widow and daughter of a gentleman, began to look properly appalled at realizing she was being received in what was clearly the servants' kitchen. Allegra merely looked thoughtful, but soon enough, Will thought, she too would progress from surprise to indignation. Feeling defensive in spite of himself, Will set his jaw.

Mrs. Randall rallied somewhat once Mrs. Phillips seated her on the divan in front of the cozy fire in the small adjoining parlor. Once the private domain of the butler and housekeeper, the Phillipses had converted the place into a sort of reception room for Will's use after it had become necessary to close up the rest of the house. Allegra's chaperone brightened further after Phillips entered bearing a tray loaded with cups, saucers, and covered dishes from which emanated the savory scent of warm meat pies and freshly baked apple tarts.

"You mean to stay a few days, Master Will?" Phillips asked. "The tenants was asking if ye'd be by to see 'em. 'Tis about time to start the spring planting."

"Yes, I'll be here a day or so while the ladies pay a visit in Hemley before I escort them back to London. Mrs. Randall, your friend is expecting you later this afternoon? Once you finish your tea, I can show you ladies about the house. A tour that, if we are prudent, I believe can be accomplished without either of you coming to harm on a rotting floorboard or a crumbled stair rail."

Mrs. Phillips gave him a distressed look. "'Tis not

much to see in there, Master Will. We closed it up tight like you ordered, moved the furniture out of the rooms where the roof leaks and put it under Holland covers, but there hasn't been nothing repaired since your last visit. The ladies be more comfortable staying here in the parlor. I can brew up another pot of tea and bring in some more apple tarts afore you drive back to Hemley."

Mrs. Randall, whose eyes had widened in alarm at Will's description of exploring the house, nodded vigorously. "If you don't mind, I should prefer to stay here and have another cup of tea, my lord."

"Having spent so much time cooped up in a carriage, I'm ready for a walk," Allegra said. "I would very much like to see the house and tour the grounds, too, if that wouldn't be too much of an imposition, Lord Tavener."

"The late Lady Tavener's flower beds aren't what they used to be, but the kitchen gardens be just as she planted them and the prospect from there is still fine," Mrs. Phillips interposed.

"Then if you are ready, my lord?" Allegra said, setting down her cup and reaching for her cloak.

Torn by a divisive mix of eagerness to be alone with her and humiliation at the prospect of displaying his disintegrating home, Will said, only a touch of irony in his voice, "'Twill be my pleasure."

It was a testament to how rattled Mrs. Randall had been by her unorthodox reception that she didn't think to ask for a maid to serve as Allegra's chaperone. That, or she figured the prospect of rotting floorboards and crumbling banisters would inhibit him from attempting to ravish her charge, Will thought acidly.

Silently he led Allegra from the warm parlor up a set of cold, narrow stairs to the first floor. "Behold the gate to my castle," he said, waving toward the entry.

She gave him a slight smile, her dark eyes doubtless taking in every detail of the dust-dulled marble floor, the wide oaken entry door and scarred wooden stairs draped with cobwebs that drifted down from the mullioned ceiling like ghostly scarves.

Best get this over with quickly, he told himself. Gritting his teeth, he seized her elbow and steered her to the doorway of the front parlor, its furniture muffled under heavy cotton covers, then to the mausoleum of a library with its linen-shrouded shelves, then back to the dining room and two reception rooms beyond it, all three barren of furniture, their faded wall hangings streaked with water marks and darkened by mold.

Glad now for Mrs. Randall's lapse in decorum, as he wasn't sure he could stand exposing himself any further, he said brusquely, "Since we have no chaperone, Miss Antinori, I won't suggest touring the rest of this floor or the bedchambers above—which for the most part are in the same condition as the rooms you've already seen." Amazing, he thought, how much of a curb humiliation was to the appetite, for he'd been able to link "Miss Antinori" and "bedchamber" within the same sentence without the least stirring of lust. "We can exit to the garden here."

Unable to bear looking at her face and seeing the distaste he knew must be reflected in her eyes, he took her arm again, escorting her outside and down the stairs from the back parlor toward the overgrown remains of his mother's flower garden. Allegra continued to walk silently beside him, doubtless too appalled by his ruin of a home to speak.

By now his chest hurt and he was breathing as hard as if he'd run a race. He'd never imagined it would be this painful to so baldly expose his poverty. He was surprised Allegra hadn't already drawn away from him in revulsion, begging to return to Mrs. Randall and the carriage that would transport her back to a household redolent of polished wood, shiny brass and pristine paint instead of mildew and rot.

Then she stopped, but instead of voicing a request to leave immediately, she ran her fingers through the silver-green needles of an overgrown rosemary bush in the garden bed beside them. "How clever the design is, alternating green, silver and blue-leaved plants," she observed. "The garden needs just a bit of care to set it to rights again."

"It was lovely indeed in my mother's day. Like everything else here, it's fallen into ruin from neglect and lack of funds," he replied, unable to keep the bitterness from his voice.

"But the garden, like the manor house, is basically well-designed and sound. Oh, 'tis true the roof needs work, but once that is repaired, one need only strip off the ruined wall coverings in the back rooms and apply new paper or paint. With some cleaning and polishing, that oak and marble entryway would be splendid! The wood carving of the ceiling is both unique and beautiful. No wonder you love Brookwillow so much, my lord."

Having braced himself to hear mockery in her voice, the sincerity of her tone surprised him so much he forgot his resolve not to look at her. Astoundingly, he found her expression to be as earnest as her voice.

"You find Brookwillow…beautiful?" he repeated incredulously.

"It certainly could be! If I were you, I should not be able to resist beginning its restoration immediately, even before I wed my heiress. There's plenty of timber in the woods and surely a carpenter from the village could be hired for a modest fee, or perhaps the tenants might help out for a reduction in their rents. And the view from here! I can't imagine how you ever make yourself go back to the fog and smoke of London."

"But the house is practically a ruin!"

Chuckling, she took his arm and tugged him into motion. "You should have seen some of the lodgings we rented when traveling with Papa! Mama always said one mustn't focus on how something appears at the moment, but rather imagine what it might become. And a restored Brookwillow could be magnificent."

He stared down at her face, glowing with genuine admiration. She wasn't just making polite conversation to salvage his pride. She really believed what she was saying.

His anger and humiliation faded away while something hard and cold deep within him melted in the warmth of her enthusiasm. He wanted to seize her in his arms and swing her around until she was dizzy.

Though he'd brought her here to reject him, now he wanted to hug her and never let go. It was all too easy to picture her here, her dark hair protected by a scarf, an apron over her gown, tackling every problem with her mother's cheerful and pragmatic efficiency.

With difficulty he reined in his wildly exuberant imagining. She might make a wonderful mistress for Brookwillow, but he mustn't forget that what *she* wanted was *Lynton,* not an invitation to help him restore his musty estate. Lest he lose sight of that fact, he'd better get her safely back to Mrs. Randall before he did something they would both regret.

To keep himself focused on that point, as he steered her out of the garden toward the kitchen, he said, "What did Lynton say about today's expedition?"

"Mrs. Randall only told him we were going to see her friend. He doesn't know yet that you escorted us."

"Ah, so the fireworks will happen later."

"I can't predict whether he will be furious—or indifferent," she said with a sigh. "Usually he seems to be more disapproving than jealous. But when I stay meekly at home, he doesn't intervene at all. I'm beginning to think he truly doesn't want me and never will."

Though he didn't really want to know, Will felt compelled to ask, "Do you love him?"

"I can scarcely remember a time when I didn't adore him or seek his approval. He's been my image of the *parfait, gentil* knight since I was a child. But except for keeping me from you, he seems more interested in foisting me on someone else than in claiming me himself."

Though that was precisely Will's impression, he couldn't bear the sadness that clouded her eyes as she confessed that conclusion. Even as he damned himself as an idiot for encouraging her hopes of wedding someone else—a hope he believed vain, to boot—he replied, "Most likely he's being noble, wanting to give you time to meet other gentlemen and make your own choice."

She rallied herself to smile. "I suppose when we get home and he learns you escorted us, we shall see."

"Even if Lynton doesn't offer for you," Will made himself point out, "I doubt you'll lack for admirers, despite Lady Lynton's efforts to discredit you."

She shrugged. "I've not met any other gentleman who so excited my admiration that I would willingly endure life in the ton to marry him. Indeed, every day I understand better why my mother chose to leave society and follow the man she loved. If…if Rob cannot return my affection, I think I shall quit London and use my inheritance to purchase a small country estate.

"Like Brookwillow," she continued, pirouetting as

she gestured toward the house, barns, fields and woods. "I'll plant a fine garden like this one. Raise chickens," she added with a smile, skirting a squawking cluster of hens that had escaped the poultry yard to approach them, perhaps hopeful they carried a handful of grain.

"A lady who'd rather raise chickens than spend a ton husband's blunt—amazing!" he said, admiration for her courage and independence resonating under the teasing tone. "I'm sure you'd make an excellent estate manager. Though I trust you'll purchase one in better repair."

She pressed his arm to halt him and turned her intent gaze up to his. "You mustn't despair! In the very timbre of your voice when you speak of it, one can hear how much you love Brookwillow. Somehow you will find the means to restore it."

She raised her hand and for a heart-stopping instant, Will thought she meant to stroke his face. Breath catching in his throat, he closed his eyes, every nerve alive with eagerness. Instead, he heard the small rustle of her gown as she let her hand fall back to her side.

He opened his eyes to see her curling her fingers into a fist—resisting the urge to touch him, perhaps?

"I think your lessons have progressed to the point where you may apply yourself more assiduously to finding that heiress," she said, avoiding his gaze. "We should start back to the village before the dusk is upon us. Thank you for bringing me. I understand better now why you decided to endure the shallowness of the ton in order to find the means to return Brookwillow to its former glory." Letting go his arm, she walked toward the kitchen entrance.

Allegra might want Lynton, but in this moment Will realized the only woman he wanted and would ever want, the lady who held his whole heart, was Allegra Antinori.

How could he settle for an infusion of money from an heiress for whom he felt only a tepid attachment? Without a loving, vibrant presence at its heart, even a restored Brookwillow would be more hollow facade than haven.

Wasn't there some way he could make Allegra his?

Excitement swelled Will's chest as the reckless, irresistible idea formed in his mind, perhaps propelled, as he would tell himself later, by the maddening frustration of sitting across from her all day long while being unable to touch or kiss her.

Without allowing himself time to think, he sped after her and seized her arm, forcing her to a halt. "Do you really wish to goad Lynton into deciding whether or not he wants you?"

Surprised, she looked up at him. "Goad him? What do you mean?"

In the dusty kitchen yard with the dogs milling about, Will dropped to one knee and took her hand. "Allegra Antinori, you've intrigued me since the moment I saw you. Though I've nothing but a ravaged estate to offer, would you do me the honor of marrying me?"

CHAPTER FIFTEEN

ALLEGRA STARED DOWN at him, shock on her face.
"Are you mad?"

Her fingers, which Will retained in a light grip,
trembled in his. Tightening his hold, he grinned at her.
"Probably. But you must admit, my offering for your
hand should propel Lynton into making a counteroffer,
if he ever intends to. Don't you agree?"

"Perhaps," she said after a moment. "And if he does
not?"

"You could always marry me. We deal well together,
don't we?" The very idea of claiming her for his own
made his body harden and sent the blood rushing
through his veins. "I think we've already had ample
proof of how much better we could deal with one
another…my sweet torment."

Her cheeks went rosy. "I know you find me…attrac-
tive, as you cannot help but know I find you, but I
hadn't any notion you were more than flirting. If you
have developed…deeper feelings, I certainly did not
mean to entice you to it."

It was the perfect opening to confess that he'd

needed no enticement, that he had begun falling top over tail in love with her since the first night they met. But as strongly as the emotions surged in his breast, the words to express them stuck in his throat.

Confessing he truly loved her would irretrievably alter the character of their relationship. If Lynton did surprise him and offer for her, she would at best feel uncomfortable about his declaration and at worst, might pity him. The notion made him writhe inside. Scarcely less revolting was the idea that, in the unlikely event Lynton blessed his suit, knowing his true sentiments might make her feel *obligated* to marry him.

Nor could he quite summon up the courage to plainly confess his emotions.

"Of course you didn't try to entice me," he answered finally. "In addition to finding you most attractive, I admire and respect you. And teasing aside, I have grown fond of you, a feeling that I flatter myself is mutual."

"It is," she acknowledged, pressing his hand. "After all, one does form a bond when one is able to reveal one's true self and work toward a common goal."

He had to steel himself not to flinch at that. "I know this is rather sudden. Why not pledge a temporary alliance? Keep the matter private between the two of us until after I call on Lynton and gauge his reaction. If he does not eject me from the house and come running to beg for your hand, we can consider then how to proceed. And if you decide you do not wish to continue the agreement, we'll cancel it with no one the wiser."

Her expression turned wistful. "You would do that for me?" Then she shook her head. "No, 'twould be an unthinkable imposition."

"No imposition," he argued. "Friends help friends. You would do all in your power to assist me, wouldn't you?"

Absently she nodded, then stared into the distance, her hand still clasped in his. Will resisted the urge to carry her hand to his lips.

"You truly wish to marry me?" she asked abruptly.

Once again, Will took refuge in a safe reply. "You're an heiress. I must wed one. Why not a lady whom I also happen to trust and esteem, one who shares my love for music—and tumbledown country houses?"

Chuckling, she nodded. "I did say we should be allies. And we do know where we stand with one another. Very well, Lord Tavener. I accept your 'temporary' offer."

Suddenly there didn't seem to be enough air to breathe. Scarcely believing he'd heard her aright, he struggled to draw in a lungful before saying, "Perhaps you'd better call me Will."

WHAT HAD SHE DONE? The thought consumed Allegra all during the carriage ride to the house of Mrs. Randall's friend, Lady Craig. Suddenly feeling shy around Lord Tavener—*Will*—she'd been relieved when he announced he would escort them there on horseback. Thankfully, since she was too rattled to make meaningful conversation, Mrs. Randall seemed content with the occasional murmurs of reply she managed to interject into that lady's monologue about dear Amelia and the times they'd shared at school and during their first Season.

Soon enough they arrived. Tavener declined Lady Craig's offer of refreshment, excusing himself with the need to return to his estate before darkness fell. Allegra felt both grateful and bereft at the idea of him leaving. After bidding everyone farewell, he clasped her hand once more before brushing a kiss over her knuckles.

Despite her gloves, she felt that touch all the way to her core, a fact which unraveled what little composure she'd managed to assemble during the drive. To her relief, Lady Craig did not detain them in the parlor, sending them instead up to their chambers to rest before dinner.

Once safe within the sanctuary of her room, Allegra was finally free to let her mind examine every detail of the walk in the garden that had culminated in that totally unexpected proposal. What should she make of it?

Seating herself before the chamber window, which offered a soothing prospect of the woods and hills beyond, she tried to take stock of her tangled emotions.

There'd been shock, certainly; dismay at having the casual equilibrium of their friendship upset—and a good deal of guilty delight at discovering that Lord Tavener truly did esteem her and had not just been toying with a maid who wasn't as discreet as she should be.

He'd referred to their mutual fondness, but the level of friendship demonstrated by his offer truly astounded her. He'd displayed his perceptive and caring character before, the night he'd played to distract the crowd, the day he'd come to warn her about Sapphira. But she was awed and humbled at realizing how far he was prepared to go to help her secure what she wanted.

When she considered the possible outcome of this ploy, her stomach plummeted and her knees turned to jelly.

Would Will's offer shake Rob from his seemingly impenetrable complacency? Shocked to discover she was sought by another, would he rush to declare his undying affection, confess he had loved her all these years, as she had loved him?

It had been a favorite illusion of her youth to imagine Rob riding in on a dashing steed and storming into Papa's presence to beg for her hand. That girlish dream had faded in recent years, not to be revived until her presentation catapulted the scenario out of fantasy into the realm of the possible.

A coil of fear wound in her stomach at the idea of forcing Rob's hand. What if he loved her, but was not ready yet to make a declaration? Would Will's pursuit cause him to back away?

But if he were not ready to claim her now, when would he be? Will was right; better to find out straightaway if in entertaining hopes of a proposal from her childhood hero, she'd merely been spinning castles in the air. She didn't really wish to wait any longer while she endured the small snubs, the whispering and the gossip of the ton—and the irritating necessity of appearing demure, modest and retiring. Nor did she relish remaining always on the alert lest Sapphira conceive some new plot to discredit her.

At that moment, a knock sounded, announcing the arrival of the maid Lady Craig had sent to help her dress for dinner and ending, for the moment, her ruminations. Though Allegra tried to keep the still-unresolved swirl of thoughts from her mind, as the evening progressed she blessed the fact that Mrs. Randall and Lady Craig were such good friends that they required only a modicum of dinner conversation from her. After that, she was able to take refuge at the pianoforte, playing through a repertoire of selections while they chatted.

Her fingers moving through the familiar pieces by rote, Allegra let herself contemplate again what she meant to do over the next several days. If Rob did beg for her hand, her future was settled. But…what if he did not?

Despite the fact that she was indeed fond of Will, should she really consider his offer? She was more than half convinced he'd tendered it only because, despite his assurances to the contrary, he didn't expect her to hold him to it. Even if he were seriously considering marrying her, she feared the modest sum Uncle Robert had bequeathed her wouldn't go very far in refurbishing his estate.

A true friend ought not to bind him to a promise that prevented him from making the much more advantageous match to which his birth and family connections entitled him.

Not until she returned to her bedchamber that night did she allow herself to contemplate the other implications of accepting his suit. Garbed in the thin silk of her night rail, she let herself imagine no longer having to fight her attraction to him, being free to let him kiss her whenever he wished, wherever he wished—being free to kiss him back. Envisioned letting his clever fingers and skilled lips roam from her mouth and shoulders down her torso, to stroke the breasts that now swelled and hardened at the thought of his touch. Visualized him loosening her stays, letting his fingers delve beneath the fabric of her chemise to stroke the naked flesh.

Her breath grew short, her skin sheened with moisture as she considered the feel of his hands as they slid down her naked hips and belly. Then thought of his fingers, his lips trailing lower still, where her flesh now throbbed with anticipation.

Ah, yes, she too understood how much better they might deal with one another.

But as much as the vision of surrendering to his sensual mastery thrilled her, as much as she genuinely liked him, enjoyed the way he engaged her mind and titillated her senses, she knew she needed more than the heady kisses and temporary loyalty of a rogue.

She needed, wanted, the kind of love and devotion Mama had felt for Papa and he for her. She refused to settle for less than an all-consuming passion of the sort that had led Mama to brave social disapproval and ostracization from her family in order to be with the man she adored. Though Lord Tavener had certainly inveigled his way into her affection and senses, Allegra didn't now feel that way about him. And if one did not love like that immediately, one never would—would one?

The possibility was even less likely on Will's part. Yes, he needed to marry an heiress; she "intrigued" him and certainly there was sensual fire between them. Nor did she doubt that he would always treat her with courtesy and kindness. But he'd made no promises beyond that.

A rogue who enjoyed pursuing women—who was enjoyed and pursued by them, as she'd witnessed with her own eyes—was hardly likely to give up that satisfying pastime simply because he'd taken to wife a lady he "admired and respected." Nor would anyone in the ton expect him to.

Slipping a ring on his finger would not be enough to persuade Will to change his ways. Only if he fell totally, hopelessly, irredeemably in love with someone did Allegra see any possibility that his commitment to his lady might be powerful enough to dissuade him from straying.

He'd vouchsafed no such emotion in asking for her hand.

She knew herself well enough to know that she would not be able to look the other way, as well-bred ton wives were supposed to do when their husbands dallied elsewhere. Nor could she bear to watch Will working his charm as he persuaded some other willing woman into his bed.

No, if Rob could not offer her the love she craved, better to live alone the rest of her life than accept Will's kind offer and subject herself to what she could already foresee would be the acutest of misery.

But even that rational conclusion did not succeed in banishing from her imagination the torrid visions she'd conjured of his hands and mouth on hers. For the rest of the night she tossed and turned, sleeping fitfully and unable to claim the peace of mind finalizing those decisions about her future should have afforded her.

The necessity of taking breakfast, nuncheon, dinner and tea with the ladies the next day did little to settle her. Restless, on edge and hard-put to respond with polite civility to the conversation of the gossiping friends, she was equally unable to engage herself in reading or needlework. Much of that interminable day she spent pacing the library or strolling the garden paths at a pace that left the maid Lady Craig had assigned to her breathless.

She arose the following morning both eager for and dreading the journey. To her annoyance, when Will arrived to escort them home, she felt her face flush and her pulse race as he walked into the room. The grin that broadened his face when, ever perceptive, he noticed her response made her want to both kiss him and slap him.

Their secret agreement heightening the connection between them, she was more conscious than ever of the burning imprint of his fingers as he helped her into the carriage. So 'twas probably for the best that he announced he intended to ride beside the carriage rather than sit within it. At the same time, she was most illogically disgruntled that he'd not chosen to remain near her, employing his teasing wit during the long journey to distract her from fretting over the events to come.

And it was downright silly, while she was on pins and needles with anticipation about eliciting an offer of marriage from another man, to miss his reassuring presence.

Fatigued after the constant chatting of her visit, Mrs. Randall dozed most of the way, leaving Allegra free to brood. Though for the most part, she spent that time playing over and over in her mind the possible scenarios once Rob learned of their trip and Will's offer, and she did make one other decision about the confrontation to come.

To preserve the secrecy of their bargain, but especially to prevent the possibility that Rob might deal insultingly with Will, she intended to speak with Lynton before Lord Tavener came to present his suit.

Upon their arrival at Upper Brook Street, Tavener declined Mrs. Randall's invitation to come in, saying he would call on them later. After standing by impatiently while that lady tendered him her effusive thanks and a polite farewell, Allegra contrived to detain him beside the carriage while Hobbs escorted Mrs. Randall in.

"Such a worried expression," he murmured, patting the hand she'd placed on his arm. "Courage, my sweet!

Lynton's unlikely to do anything more distressing than read you a severe scold once he discovers I escorted you."

"'Tis not that. We both know he dislikes you. After all you are doing for me, I should be very distressed if Lynton were to treat you…disrespectfully. Let me first inform him of your intentions. That alone may achieve the effect for which we hope. And if it does not—"

"No," Will interrupted, frowning. "I am quite capable of handling whatever Lynton might choose to say. The offer will carry more credence if I deliver it myself."

Aware she had mere seconds to conclude the matter, Allegra shook her head urgently. "I'm sorry, but I'm quite determined that unless you let me do this in my own way, I shall disavow our agreement this very moment."

Some strong emotion flitted across his face, so quickly she was unable to identify it. But she hadn't the time to figure it out; already Lizzie was at the entryway, about to descend and escort her in.

"Please, I cannot tarry any longer," she said. "Promise me you will not approach Lynton until after I've spoken with him. Promise!" she urged fiercely.

With Lizzie tripping down the steps, already smiling a greeting, he sighed. "Very well. I cannot like proceeding in so cowardly a manner, as if I were ashamed to approach him. But if you are adamant, I suppose there is nothing for me to do but acquiesce to your wishes."

Relieved, she squeezed his hand. "Thank you! I will send you word when…when I know how we should proceed."

As she turned away, he retained her. "Before you go, I want to hear you say my name."

She looked up into his face, the fierce blue gaze captivating her as always. "Thank you…Will," she murmured.

"Godspeed, Allegra." Smiling, he shook his head. "Even your name on my lips is music." With that, he tipped his hat and walked off to retrieve his horse.

While Lizzie swept her away, Allegra watched him go, excitement and nervousness already setting her stomach roiling and making her legs feel weak. A feeling that intensified when she looked up and realized Rob was watching them from the parlor window, his face grim.

A flutter in her stomach, Allegra mounted the stairs. She'd hoped to wait for just the right moment to approach Rob. Propitious or not, it looked as if that moment was going to be now.

CHAPTER SIXTEEN

HAVING ALREADY DETERMINED to get over heavy ground quickly, Allegra was relieved but not surprised when, a short time later, Rob summoned her to the library.

The curt tone of his voice when he bid her enter mirrored the aggrieved disapproval on his face as he motioned her to a chair. He looked, Allegra thought with a sinking heart, much more angry than jealous.

Omitting the courtesy of inquiring about her trip, he demanded, "Was that fellow's presence upon your return an indication that he accompanied you on your journey? If so, you can be sure that had my cousin informed me of that fact, I would never have allowed you to leave London!"

"If by 'that fellow,' you mean Lord Tavener, then yes, he did escort us. But if you feel compelled to scold someone, read your peal over me. I'm sure Mrs. Randall is not aware of the depth of your distaste for Lord Tavener."

"You certainly cannot claim that excuse. Good L— heavens, Allegra, what were you thinking? You cannot tell me you imagined I would favor such an expedition!"

Allowing her no time to reply, he stormed on, "How often must I warn that you cannot expect to attract the attention of worthy suitors if you allow that worthless fribble to hang about? I've had several eligible gentlemen inquire about you since the musicale last week, but no man of refinement will wish to pursue a closer association if your name is bandied about as Tavener's latest flirt!"

She'd hoped to inspire Rob's jealousy—not give him leave to abuse Will's character. Her temper flaring at his disparagement of a man who possessed qualities she'd come to appreciate and admire, Allegra said, "You wrong Lord Tavener by assuming he is merely flirting with me."

Stomach beginning to churn, she continued, "In fact, he intends to call on you to ask for my hand…in marriage," she added, just in case, in the intensity of his dislike, Rob should assume Tavener sought something else.

Eyes wide with a surprise that rendered him speechless, for a moment Rob merely stared at her. "He had the gall to think he might approach me about *marrying* you?" he said at last. "Why, the effrontery! As if I were sapskulled enough to throw my money away, putting it within the grasp of that doxy-chasing fortune hunter!"

Once again, Allegra had to rein in a heated reply. "Lord Tavener is a much finer gentleman than you give him credit for," she replied after a moment, striving to keep her voice even. "Besides, I believe 'tis *my* money that would be 'thrown away,' is it not?"

"'Tis *I* who decide how the funds of this estate should be managed," he flashed back, clearly as angry as she was. "I'll hear nothing more of Tavener, Allegra! I may have held the title only two months, but I know enough not to listen to a silly chit whose head has been turned by a skilled seducer. Much less to let her talk me into squandering the assets bequeathed me by furnishing a dowry for the benefit of a rogue who would abandon her as soon as he'd run through it!"

She'd opened her lips to utter a spirited rejoinder when suddenly the import of his words struck her. "I thought Uncle Robert had bequeathed those funds to *me,* to use as I see fit," she said slowly. "As a member of the family, someone he valued for having nursed him devotedly his last few months. Did he not do so?"

Rob opened his mouth, then closed it. "I'm sure he'd approve my arranging something," he began again, "though giving you money outright would hardly be appropriate."

Allegra felt suddenly chilled, then fever-hot. "He didn't leave me a bequest?" she asked again.

She must have looked as stricken as she felt, for Rob patted her hand. "I assure you, he truly appreciated—"

"Why did you let me believe he had done so?" she interrupted, pulling her hand back.

"What difference does it make? When we first discussed it and you assumed 'twas his idea, there seemed no reason to disabuse you of that notion."

"So sponsoring my Season," she said slowly, wanting to make sure she understood clearly this time, "offering me a dowry, that was all your idea?"

"A Season is necessary—"

"Why?" she interrupted again.

"I should think that would be obvious!" he retorted, running a distracted hand through his hair. "Surely you realized how desperate your situation was, your parents dying unexpectedly and leaving you with no near relations, no dowry, no recourse but to throw yourself upon Sapphira's uncertain mercy. You are blood kin, regardless of your mother's regrettable choice of husband. I thought the family owed you a chance to mingle with society and find a kind, forbearing gentleman perceptive enough to recognize you for the fine lady you've become in spite of your unfortunate connections. Of course, no gentleman could afford to do so unless you brought him at least a respectable dowry."

Her "unfortunate connections." So agonized was she by that punch to the gut that it took her a moment to realize the even more awful truth that must logically follow. For an instant she feared she might disgrace herself by becoming ill right there in the library.

Mastering the nausea with an effort, she forced herself to ask the question that would confirm the humiliating conclusion beyond any possibility of doubt. "So you never considered that you and I…" Unable to voice the rest, she let the sentence trail off.

"You and I?" he repeated, a perplexed look on his

face. The several seconds it took before he compre-
hended her meaning spoke volumes about just how un-
imaginable that eventuality seemed to him.

"Why, n-no!" he stammered, his face flushing. "I've
always seen you as my little cousin. It wouldn't have been
seemly for me to…to have that sort of interest in you."

His flush deepened, and Allegra realized wretchedly
that though she might have misjudged the depth of his
attachment to her, she had not been mistaken in thinking he found her attractive—on a base physical level.

So hearts really do break, she thought numbly. Or
was the shattered feeling within her caused by the razor-
edged shards of her splintering dream?

"In any event," he continued hurriedly, "last year I
received permission from the father of an exceptional
young lady that, should I return from the army intact,
I might begin to court. Indeed, had Evangeline's papa
not unfortunately passed away just a month ago, she
would have come to London for the Season and we
might even now be announcing our engagement—but
enough of that."

Her misery complete, all Allegra wished to do was
quit Rob's presence and seek the refuge of her chamber
where she might in solitude consider the implications
of what she'd just learned. Intending to flee before the
tears gathering at the corners of her eyes slid down her
cheeks to complete her humiliation, she rose unsteadily
from her chair.

Rob seized her hand, preventing her escape. "Just be-

cause my affections are already engaged does not mean
you should despair of finding a respectable husband! But
I simply will not countenance offers from out-and-out
rogues like Tavener. I always thought dear Mama displayed amazing tolerance, receiving Papa's beautiful
but feckless cousin whenever she chose to descend upon
the house. If, as I fondly hope, Evangeline and I marry,
I don't intend to force my wife to exercise similar re-
straint. I refuse to let you wed a ne'er-do-well who's
likely to leave you alone and penniless, as dependent
upon my charity as your mother was upon Papa's."

Allegra flinched at the words assaulting her ears. *It
was not like that with Mama!* she wanted to shriek back
at him. But 'twould serve no purpose; she doubted she
would have any more luck changing his view of her
mother than she'd had trying to sway his opinion of
Will's character.

The pretty phrases he'd fed her about having a
Season, everything she'd believed about herself, her
mother and the Lyntons, had been a lie. Rob saw her as
no more than a tedious obligation to be discharged so
he might get on with his life—and his marriage.

All she had ever wanted was his love and acceptance.
Instead, he offered her money to go away. Anger, pride
and the devastation of a bludgeoned heart warred with
humiliation as she struggled for words.

"If you wished to be rid of me," she said at last, "you
need only have said so. You didn't have to buy me a
husband." Yanking her hand free, she made for the door.

"Now, Allegra, don't go off in a pet!" Rob called from behind her. Not bothering to acknowledge him, she wrenched open the library door and fled to her room.

Writhing at Rob's axe blow to the heart, Allegra slammed shut and locked the door to her chamber, then fell upon her bed and let the storm of agony overwhelm her. Ignoring the occasional knock and later Lizzie's entreating voice begging entry, she wept until she was swollen-eyed and spent, then pulled herself up and stumbled to her desk.

Enough useless tears. She must examine all she had learned and decide dispassionately what to do next.

Humiliation swept through her again as she forced herself to acknowledge that Rob must never have had any inclination to wed her, that the partiality she'd tried to ascribe to him had been the product of her own hopeful imagination. Just as gut-wrenchingly painful— and more dire in its implications for her future—was the realization that Uncle Robert had not, out of love and appreciation for her presence, left her a bequest.

She possessed no assets at all. Certainly not the funds to purchase the small country estate she'd thought to acquire should she fail to win Rob's heart. There could be no home of her own, no safe place of refuge. She choked down another spasm of pain at relinquishing that dream.

The dowry she'd thought she owned actually belonged to Rob, a gift to be presented at his discretion should she marry a ton gentleman of whom he approved. A gift she would never earn, since from the beginning the only ton gentleman she'd wished to marry was Rob himself.

She'd not really expected a bequest from Uncle Robert. But Rob *was* wrong about her family, she thought fiercely, her anger reviving. She and Mama had never been "penniless" or "abandoned" by Papa; they had visited Uncle Robert between Papa's performances, when he was preoccupied composing a new work or rehearsing a new orchestra.

Far from "feckless," Mama was the most responsible and resourceful person Allegra had ever known. She had brought her daughter to visit her favorite cousin because she enjoyed his company—not to hang upon his charity.

And how dare Rob disparage her father! He, who had obtained his wealth by an accident of birth rather than by the exercise of his own talent and effort! She supposed being a competent army officer during a time of war meant he possessed abilities as well, but he had no right to look down upon a man as learned and accomplished as her father simply because he trod a different path in life. Whatever else she might be forced to admit, she would never concede that Mama's choice of Papa had been a mistake.

'Twas an error only by the standards of the ton—a society she disdained even more than Rob had her father. A society, she realized, she could not imagine joining.

She recalled Sapphira's beautiful, deceitful face, the fawning gallantry of the gentlemen who vied for Lady Lynton's favors. The condescending looks down long noses cast her way by overdressed, plume-headdressed matrons, the haughty glances of their richly gowned and bejeweled daughters. Anger flamed hotter, burning away some of her misery.

Only her delusions of a future with Rob had made tolerating that world possible. Though later, when it didn't hurt so much, she might give Rob credit for at least wanting to see her respectably settled, right now all she wanted was to escape both the ton and the Lyntons.

She was truly alone in the world now. But not entirely, she told herself, stemming the panicky feeling the thought engendered. Will would stand her friend.

That was it, she thought, a bubble of excitement rising. She could marry Will, have her country manor, help him rebuild Brookwillow and never visit London again.

But no, she couldn't. Will needed a bride with a dowry he could apply toward his estate's restoration. Rob had just confirmed beyond doubt that he would never give her funds to which Will might gain access. She must release Will from their agreement so he could pursue someone who really was an heiress.

Then what was she to do?

Another wave of anguish and fear threatened, but she pushed it back. "The fierceness of an Antinori," she reminded herself, imagining her father beside her, encouraging her with his pride and utter confidence in her ability to prevail.

Angrily she wiped away a tear. Time to muster up the "courage and intelligence" for which he'd praised her. She would simply do what she had planned, before Rob came home and dangled before her the illusion of a future that had proven no more real than a magician's trick.

Rob thought she was without talent or prospects, destined to become a permanent burden unless he contrived to marry her off to some gullible gentleman. She would show him she was not a helpless chattel, like a horse or a dog whose feed and maintenance he was obligated to provide.

She would show them all.

At her desk she pulled out pen, paper and ink.

She didn't wish to remain an hour longer than absolutely necessary under Rob's roof, nor could she bring herself to consider speaking with him again, lest she rant at him like the undisciplined child he sometimes accused her of being. She would leave him a note thanking him for his courtesy in trying to see her settled, but informing him she considered that he had fully discharged his responsibilities toward her. Nor did he need fear she would apply to him for assistance ever again.

However, she must gird herself to terminate her bargain with Will face-to-face. No matter how painful and humiliating it was going to be to reveal the truth to him.

After scribbling two other missives, she steeled

herself to pen Will a brief note asking that he meet her
in the park in an hour on a matter of utmost urgency,
though 'twas already almost dusk.

Fortunately, she need no longer concern herself
with society's rules about where she went and when.
Pleasant to discover one cheering thought in the midst
of this debacle.

Ringing for a footman, she unlocked her chamber
door to give him the folded notes with a coin and a
command that he deliver them without delay.

After his departure, she went to the wardrobe and
pulled her battered trunk from its depths. Swiftly she
packed the most simple and serviceable of her new gowns.

A nurse would have been paid a certain salary, she
reasoned, a welcome numbness overtaking her raw
emotions as she worked. She didn't think Uncle Robert
would begrudge her the gowns she was taking as recompense for her labors.

That task complete, she fished out the letter from Mr.
Waters at the employment agency, slipped through the
door and trod silently down the hall to the service stairs.

FROWNING, WILL READ through the note in his hand one
more time. Allegra urgently requested a brief meeting
with him in Hyde Park—he glanced at the mantel clock—
almost immediately. Setting down the card, he called for
Barrows to have his horse saddled and put on his coat.

Obviously Allegra—how he loved the sound of her
name, as lyrical and graceful as the lady herself—

must have had her meeting with Lynton. She'd wasted no time. He'd not even had the chance to call on her and try to talk her out of confronting her guardian before he did.

Had she requested this sudden, almost clandestine meeting so she might tell him Lynton had granted him permission to pay his addresses? Or would she announce that she'd received the offer for which she longed?

If she had, he must be happy for her. Even though his first and strongest impulse would be to beg her to cry off.

He didn't want to let her go to Lynton, even though he knew 'twas what she wanted. His mind still clung to the image of her at Brookwillow, praising the peeling marquetry work of the entry ceiling and the beautiful prospect from the flower garden. He wanted to take her there, to the place he most felt he belonged, and re-create from the ruins the house of loveliness and refinement she envisioned.

He wanted *her.*

Well, he wasn't going to get her. The woman he loved wanted something—and someone—else. Had his life not been full of such moments?

Enough whining. He would smile and wish her well and return to his rooms to polish off the brandy he would send Barrows to procure. Then once his head, if not his heart, stopped aching, he would present himself to Lucilla, ask her pardon for having abandoned her for two weeks and beg her to select a new lady for him to pursue.

It mattered little to him now which damsel she chose,

he thought as he turned his horse toward the park. In return for the funds to bring Brookwillow back to life, he would pledge to make some as yet unnamed heiress a kind and faithful husband, throw himself into the work at Brookwillow and try to forget he had ever hoped for more.

By the time he reached the appointed meeting place, he was frowning anew. What was Lynton thinking, allowing Allegra to set off through London in near-darkness? He was even more appalled when he spotted her descending from a hackney without even a maid to lend her countenance.

He loped toward her at a trot, anxious to reach her before some rascal lurking in the shrubbery noticed her unprotected state and tried to make off with her.

She hurried up to greet him. "Lord Tavener—Will! Thank you for meeting me on such short notice."

Bowing, he said, "I am yours to command. But, Allegra, what in heaven's name do you mean by taking a hackney at this time of day without even a maid to protect you? Lynton should be shot for treating your safety so lightly!"

He thought she flinched at the mention of her guardian's name, though it might have only been a trick of the fading light. But he was not imagining the trembling of her lips as she opened and closed them, nor her nervousness as she twisted her hands together.

Dread gathered in his gut as he grasped her hands, the fingers icy under his touch. "What's wrong, Allegra?"

She attempted a smile that didn't quite succeed. "As you may have guessed, I talked with Lynton. The results…weren't exactly what either of us had predicted."

"I can see he distressed you. What did he say?"

"You see, it seems there never was a legacy from the late Lord Lynton. Wishing to discharge what he perceived was his responsibility to me—despite my deplorable connections," she added, her voice bitter, "Rob took it upon himself to have me introduced and to provide me a dowry, as long as I married a man of whom he approved, who could be trusted to permanently relieve him of the burden of my care. I'll spare you the rest of his disparaging remarks, but he didn't consider you a credible candidate."

The enormity of it was too much to take in. "So—there is no dowry?" he repeated.

"Not if I choose to marry you. Of course, I release you from your pledge to do so. I wanted to tell you immediately, so you could redirect your efforts at once into charming a maiden who actually possesses a dowry."

Will shook his head, still trying to sort out all the implications. "Then Lynton did not ask—"

"No!" she cried out, wrenching her hands free and walking a few paces away. "That was all a s-silly illusion on m-my part. Lynton's affections are engaged elsewhere. In fact, he expects soon to be married."

Will could only imagine what a humiliating blow that must have been. "Allegra, I'm so sorry," he said softly.

"Oh, you needn't be!" she said brightly, looking back

at him. In the dim light he could see the glitter of tears on her lashes. "I know by now that I'm entirely unsuited for life in the ton, so 'tis for the best. Now I must go— but here, I nearly forgot the most important thing."

She rummaged in her reticule and drew out a folded sheet of paper. Holding it out, she said, "I've made you a list of those damsels whom I thought, from my limited time in London society, might be promising candidates for you to pursue. 'Twas the least I could do, after having you waste so much time in what turned out to be a fruitless effort."

She wrapped his fingers around the list. "Thank you for your friendship. 'Tis the only thing in the ton I shall regret leaving."

Then, before he had a hint of what she meant to do, she threw her arms around his neck and pulled him close. "Goodbye, Will," she whispered, and kissed him.

He might not yet have figured out what to do about the surprise she'd just sprung on him, but it took him no more than an instant to respond to the feel of her in his arms.

He bound her against him as if she belonged there, pressed to his side, her lips on his. Then gasped, nearly overwhelmed by a surge of desire as she shocked him by probing his lips with her tongue and delving within.

Lust and lack of air made him dizzy as, moaning deep in her throat, she kissed him with a desperate urgency he had no trouble reciprocating. Blood pounding through his veins, he devoured her lips with a greediness born of long denial. With her bonneted and buttoned up to the chin as she was, he invested into the only bit of her flesh he could touch all the passion and anguish of his love.

He could have kissed her forever while the stars glimmered toward full brilliance in the night sky, but all too soon, she pulled away.

Giving him a tremulous smile, she disengaged her arms from about his neck. "May you find a lady worthy of you, dear friend," she murmured, then turned and stepped away.

"Allegra, wait!" he cried as, off-balance and still dizzy, he managed to catch her shoulder. "You cannot go roaming about London in the dark. Let me escort you home."

Shaking her head, she detached his hand. "'Tis unnecessary. I paid the jarvey to wait. Will, I must go. I've a hundred things left to do and time is short."

Despite her obvious dismissal, he followed her back to where the carriage was indeed waiting. "What will you do?" he asked as he helped her into it.

"I'm not sure yet. I'll let you know when I decide."

In the soft glow of the carriage lamp, he saw both her cheeks and lashes were wet with tears. He wanted to seize her and pull her back into his arms, pledge to shelter and protect her, but before he could decide what to do, she shut the door and the jarvey whipped up his horses.

Will stood back as the carriage swept off into the deepening night. Not until he could no longer see its outline in the dark did he recall the note she'd pressed into his hand. With a violent oath, he balled up the paper and threw it to the ground.

CHAPTER SEVENTEEN

AN HOUR LATER, Will slumped at his desk back at his lodgings in Chelsea. After one look at his face, Barrows had set off for brandy, a bottle of which now sat at his elbow beside a half-full snifter. In front of him lay a blank piece of vellum, ready for him to compose the apology he owed Lucilla along with his promise to call on her.

He'd not yet written it because he hadn't been able to decide when he might pledge himself to call. Sighing, he gazed at the crumpled note Allegra had penned to him, which he'd smoothed out and propped against the back of his desk.

He smiled as he read down the list. He recognized the surnames, though he wasn't acquainted with the young ladies themselves. All came from wealthy families; all had been on the town for at least one Season and might therefore be expected to have grown less choosy about their suitors. To each name, Allegra had added a little note.

"Shy, but sweet-natured," read one. "Enamored of fashion, but modest and agreeable," read another. Each girl had been selected, she'd added in an addendum at the bottom of the page, because Allegra felt that the young lady possessed not only the necessary dowry, but also a kind disposition and cheerful spirit that should make her a comfortable wife—and lacked the vanity and self-importance that marred the character of so many ton Beauties.

Putting down his pen after once again not having written a syllable, Will took a sip of brandy and let the liquor's scorching heat slide down his throat. Though he knew he owed it to Brookwillow to marry an heiress like one on this list, his thoughts kept drifting back to Allegra.

He tried to imagine what it might feel like to learn that Brookwillow didn't belong to him after all, that owning it had merely been an illusion in which his guardian had allowed him to indulge, one that could be stripped from him if he did not meet the earl's expectations.

In which case, he would have lost it long since. The thought made him ill. Destitute though he was, he'd always known he owned *something* and might belong *somewhere*.

Allegra had literally been left with nothing.

Worse yet, she'd been beggared and repudiated by the very man she'd hoped would come to cherish her…who had struck the final blow by announcing his intention to marry someone else.

The more Will thought about it, the angrier he became. Bound by blood to the family, as devoted as a daughter to the late Lord Lynton, Allegra deserved better than this callous…betrayal. How could Lynton have so thoughtlessly wounded the girl whose care had been entrusted to him?

He could forgive Lynton wanting to see Allegra well settled. He could not forgive the man his indifference to her desires and his blind ignorance in failing to recognize the treasure right before his eyes.

For a few minutes, Will contemplated finding some pretext upon which to challenge Lynton to a bout at Gentleman Jackson's, where Will might repay in some small measure the pain Lynton had inflicted upon Allegra.

Then a much more intelligent idea occurred to him.

He could not help Allegra by marrying her. But perhaps, at the end of his fists if necessary, he might persuade Lynton to fulfill his duty to his kinswoman by giving her something that was truly her own.

A glance at the mantel clock informed him 'twas too late this evening to catch Lynton at home; Allegra's cousin, she had told him, always dined at his club.

After downing the last fiery sip, Will put the brandy away. He'd need a clear mind and a steady hand when, first thing in the morning, he called on Allegra's erstwhile guardian to see if he could persuade him into offering Allegra a fairer solution to her dilemma.

WILL'S KNOCK early the next morning was answered by Hobbs, who blinked in surprise at the visitor on his doorstep. "Lord Tavener!" he exclaimed. "I fear, my lord, that the ladies are still abed."

"I've not come to visit the ladies," Will said, walking

past Hobbs into the entry, "but to call on Lord Lynton. If *he* is still abed, I shall wait."

Hobbs bowed. "If you would step into the parlor, my lord, I'll inform the master of your arrival."

"Do that," Will replied. He'd chosen to come early so that the matter might be concluded, if possible, without the ladies learning anything about it. As he paced around the parlor to which Hobbs conducted him, tension and anticipation built within him, as they always did before a match.

He thought of Allegra in the dusky park, the tears on her lashes sparkling like the glimmer of the gathering stars, and his simmering anger intensified. Flexing his fists, he envisioned the satisfaction of planting them at the center of Lynton's smugly arrogant face.

Lynton must have been still abed as well, for 'twas nearly half an hour later when at last Will's quarry appeared on the threshold, his cravat, Will noted with amusement, looking as if it had been hastily tied. The expression on Lynton's face—a mixture of distaste and disdain, as if some disgusting rodent had invaded the pristine purity of his parlor—presented such a perfect invitation to fisticuffs that Will was hard-pressed not to slug him before even saying hello.

Regretfully choosing politeness, he bowed. "Lynton."

"Tavener," Allegra's guardian replied with an insultingly small inclination of his head. Without offering Will refreshment or a chair, he walked into the room.

"Please," he said, holding up a hand, "make me no speeches. Allegra has already informed me of your intentions. Rather than start a discussion which must be embarrassing for you and distasteful to us both, let me just state straightaway that under no circumstances would I give my permission for you to marry her. I am sorry you've roused yourself so early—or is it just that you've not yet been to bed?—upon what a man of any discernment would have known was a fool's errand. Good day, sir."

"You sanctimonious prig," Will said before Lynton could walk out. "Were you too stupid to recognize what that bequest meant to Allegra—or are you just too arrogant and selfish to care? Oh, yes," he continued, advancing on Lynton until they stood nose to nose, "I already know you refused to consider my suit."

Lynton stiffened in surprise, his sleepy eyes snapping open and his irritated expression turning to the alertness of an experienced commander sensing a battle to come. But although Will had all but raised his fists into a boxer's stance, he had to give Lynton credit, for the man neither flinched nor retreated an inch.

"If you mean to try to cajole me into reconsidering my decision, insulting me is hardly the way to go about it," Lynton said. "Unlike some men, I take my responsibility to my dependents quite seriously."

"Allegra is more than a 'dependent' and a 'responsibility,'" Will flashed back. "She is a person with a warm and caring heart who has lovingly devoted herself to this family. Have you the slightest idea how deeply you have wounded her?"

For the first time, Lynton looked uncomfortable. "You cannot take me to task for wounding sensibilities I gave her no encouragement to develop."

"Perhaps not. Emotions do not always need much 'encouragement.'" As he ought to know better than anyone. "This is more a matter of fairness, of discharging one's responsibilities *properly.* That is, if you flatter yourself by believing you *are* a responsible gentleman."

Lynton's face hardened. "What do you mean by that?"

"Allegra has never been your dependent. But she has unselfishly served your family, caring for your father before his death. You don't mean to deny that, I hope."

"I am well aware of the debt I owe her for her assistance to my father. 'Twas one of the reasons I sought to see her properly settled."

"How can you have known her all these years and still understand her so little? Being married off to a ton gentleman of your choosing might be proper recompense for most girls of gentle birth, but it's not right for Allegra. Surely you see she doesn't belong in the ton by either temperament or inclination. If you truly wish to discharge your obligation in a way that is suitable for her, give her outright the sum you meant to pledge as her dowry so she may purchase the rural manor she has always wanted."

"Give her money to buy property?" Lynton echoed. "Are you mad?"

"Has she never talked to you about this?" Will asked, incredulous. "Do you not even know that simple fact about the girl who is supposed to be your 'responsibility'? Ask her, then. And do the *right* thing by her."

"Ah, so that is your game," Lynton retorted. "You have the effrontery to come here and try to insinuate you know better than I how I should discharge my duty? You, a reprobate who spends his time carousing in gaming hells and seducing other men's wives? Well, your ploy will not work, Tavener. I won't fund your misspent life by giving Allegra funds or property you might later be able to wheedle her into turning over to you."

"You still don't understand, do you?" Will said with exasperation. "'Tis not my life I wish to secure, 'tis Allegra's. But perhaps there's another way to convince you." He assumed his stance and held up his fists.

After looking him up and down, Lynton sniffed. "Knowing you, I should have expected that if honeyed words failed, you'd try to start a common brawl."

"Knowing me and the reputation you witnessed me building at Eton, you should have expected me to defend what I believe is right. As I once defended your friend Warley, you may remember, when those bullies in First set upon him. You were not so quick to stand up for him, I recall. Or do you only fulfill your 'responsibilities' when 'tis easy and the cost is not too great?"

Anger flared in Lynton's eyes. "How dare you impugn my honor!"

"Oh, I dare impugn more than that. Are you too

dainty to lift your fists against me…or just too much of
a coward? As you were too cowardly to defend your
friend at Eton?"

Will had the satisfaction of seeing he'd finally penetrated Lynton's elephantine hide of superiority. Rage
flushing his face, Lynton spat out, "I, who faced the
charge of the Old Guard at Waterloo, afraid? Of the
likes of *you?* Never!"

"Prove it," Will said, and raised his fists again.

With a growl, Lynton swung at him. Dancing on his
toes, the blood singing in his veins at finally forcing the
fight he'd been thirsting for since Lynton's first con-
temptuous glance at him in Lady Ormsby's ballroom,
Will easily sidestepped the blow.

"If you mean to prove your mettle, we'd best shed
our jackets and secure the furniture. Unless you also
wish to fail in your 'responsibility' to protect the Lynton
estate's possessions."

In reply, Lynton tore off his coat and flung it on a
side chair, then dragged that chair to the edge of the
room. Grinning, Will stripped off his own coat and
pushed the sofa and several small tables out of the way.

With them both down to shirtsleeves and the center
of the room clear, Will raised his hands again. "So, you
will settle an inheritance upon Allegra?"

Stepping sideways, Lynton threw a left uppercut at
Will's jaw. "Never, you licentious wastrel!"

Will ducked out of reach and came back to land a
jab to Lynton's kidney. "Attach the stipulation that the

funds are meant to buy property. Name yourself as trustee to approve the purchase."

Grunting at the blow, Lynton gasped, "Impudent wretch! As if I need you…to instruct me…on managing my estate!"

"Thought you felt responsible for seeing her settled before you brought home your bride." Dancing past Lynton's next strike, Will said, "So purchase her some good fertile land. Something on which to plant a kitchen garden and a few crops. She'll manage it well."

"What good will her having a country property do you?" Lynton asked, then landed a punch to Will's side.

Moaning, Will ducked another blow, threw a hard left cross and missed. "I'd know she's provided for. With an income and independence no one can ever take from her."

"Supposing the idea did have merit," Lynton said. "I'd set it up such that you could never touch a penny." Following through Will's feint, he scored a solid hit to Will's jaw.

"Don't want your money," Will gasped, stars exploding behind his eyelids. "Just want her to be safe and happy."

"You really do care about her." A grudging respect dawned in Lynton's eyes before Will's left hook connected with his chin.

"Yes," Will replied, swinging back hard with his right and missing.

"Regrettable," Lynton said, staggering away before turning suddenly to slam Will with a blow to the torso.

Breath almost knocked from his body, Will rolled away. "Isn't it," he agreed when he could speak again, then closed to deliver his signature jab, uppercut and roundhouse blow to the side of Lynton's head that sent his opponent careening into the massed furniture.

There was the sharp snap of a table leg followed by the shattering sound of ripping inlay and smashing glass. Lynton landed in a sprawl on the floor atop the disintegrated side table while Will, holding his jaw, sank to his knees and rested his head against the couch.

From out in the hallway they heard Hobbs clear his throat. "Is something amiss, my lord?" he called.

Breathing heavily, Lynton raised his head and called back, "Nothing, Hobbs. We're having a…discussion." Looking over to Will, he said, "I cede your point."

Despite the pounding in his head, Will tried to focus on Lynton's face. "You'll make the arrangements?"

Lynton nodded. "I'll make the arrangements." Staggering upright, he came over and offered Will a hand.

Will struggled to his feet and shook it. "Good. But pray, lose no time in telling Allegra. She was distraught when she spoke to me last night. Proud and independent as she is, I dare not imagine what she might be planning."

"Hobbs," Lynton called. "Tell Miss Allegra I wish to see her here immediately." Turning to Will, he said, "You might as well remain while I inform her, since she has you to thank for the change in terms. Oh, and Hobbs," he called, raising his voice again, "send in James, please. There's been a slight accident."

WHILE THEY WAITED for Allegra to dress and come down, Lynton excused himself to repair his attire while Will did the best he could with his handkerchief and the cold water Hobbs provided. That task completed, Will accepted a glass of port and eased himself back on the sofa, rubbing his jaw where he knew a bruise was forming.

He'd have to avoid taking deep breaths for the next week, too, if past experience were any judge. Though the match had not lasted nearly as long as he would have liked, he had to admit that Lynton had acquitted himself well, once Will had finally goaded him into fighting. And at the end had finally, albeit grudgingly, accorded Will and his proposal the respect both deserved.

Will would have liked to have landed a few more of his blows—and to have absorbed two less—but he'd have gladly sustained a hundred more to have succeeded in convincing Lynton to provide for Allegra in a way that would leave her independent and happy.

Even though she would never be his.

Maybe he could visit her later, once he'd steeled himself to marry the heiress whose dowry would guarantee Brookwillow's restoration. They could take tea in her parlor, talk about corn planting and turnips.

Before he bid her a goodbye with a proper bow and returned to his wife.

For a moment he let himself remember the impassioned goodbye kiss she'd given him last night. Longing and a searing pain that had nothing to do with Lynton's skill at fisticuffs made him gasp.

Lynton reentered the parlor then, coat pristine and cravat expertly arranged, though he moved a bit stiffly and his cheek had already begun to swell. Before Will could compliment his adversary on his skill, the maid Will recognized as the girl who'd accompanied Allegra during their walk in the garden rushed into the room.

Hastily dipping a curtsey, she cried, "I'm sorry, my lord, but Miss Allegra won't be coming down!"

"Not coming?" Lynton frowned. "Why not? Is she ill?"

The girl twisted her hands in her apron. "I don't know, my lord. I couldn't find her! Her bed linens was pulled up, which weren't so unusual, for she don't like her chamber untidy and sometimes does that afore I can get to it, but I've looked everywhere in the house and she weren't anywhere. Then I found this on your desk in the library."

Advancing to Lynton, she handed him a folded note.

Dread keeping him silent, Will waited while Lynton read it. "It seems," he said, looking up from the missive, "that my cousin, after thanking me for my kind attentions in her regard, prefers to go her own way in the world."

"What does that mean?" Will burst out.

"I have no idea, except that she may have rushed off on some ill-judged start, just as she used to do when she was a girl. And you think I ought to give her the funds to live independently!" Lynton cast Will an exasperated glance. "What she needs is a sensible husband to curb her wild ways and teach her how to behave properly!"

Just then another servant rushed into the parlor, housekeeper's keys jangling at her waist. "Ah, Mrs. Bessborough," Lynton said, waving Allegra's note at the woman. "Perhaps you can shed some light on this mystery?"

Waving her hands in distress, the housekeeper said, "Miss Allegra's old bandbox is gone from the attic, along with a valise and a half-dozen gowns from her wardrobe. I do fear, my lord, that she has left us for good."

"Left?" Lynton repeated. "Are you sure, Bessie? She cannot have been so improper as to have departed alone, without even a maid to accompany her! How am I to find a respectable gentleman to take her off my hands when she comports herself like the veriest hoyden!"

"Why don't you worry about that after we find her," Will suggested through gritted teeth. Turning to the housekeeper, he said, "Mrs.—Bessborough, wasn't it? Have you any idea where Miss Antinori might have gone?"

"No! Oh, I do fear for her, my lord," the housekeeper wailed. "She's got no kin save the Lyntons and none of them high-and-mighty ton maidens was friendly enough for her to have gone to pay them a visit. Unless…"

"What?" Will demanded.

"Well, after the late Lord Lynton died, she did mention looking into a position as a governess. Now, if I can just recall the name of the agency…"

"I think I've heard enough," Lord Lynton interposed. "Damn the girl, running off in so hasty and intemperate a manner. And we were to dine with Lady Cowper tonight! How am I to explain her absence in a way that does not give the most grievous offence? I did my best by her, trying to gain her entrée back into the society her mother abandoned—at some risk to my own position, I might add. Funded it handsomely as well, and this is my thanks? Well, I wash my hands of her! I only hope Lady Cowper will not hold the insult against my dear Evangeline next Season."

"That certainly would be inconvenient," Will said.

"Indeed," Lynton replied, sublimely ignorant of the irony in Will's tone. "Good day, Tavener. Hobbs, if anything requires my attention, I shall be in the library."

"You don't intend to look for her?" Will asked.

About to leave the room, Lynton paused. "Allegra apparently left this house of her own free will. If she would rather ruin herself running off to become a governess than accept the arrangements I tried to make for her protection, there is nothing further to be done. I will not rush about the city like a looby, trying to discover her whereabouts so I may entreat her to return. She's made her choice and—" he waved the note at Will "—absolved me of all further responsibility. I shall take her at her word."

The housekeeper uttered a quickly stifled protest while the maid began to weep quietly. "Ass," Will muttered as Lynton exited, wishing they were still alone so he might leave the mark of his displeasure on that self-absorbed highbred brow. But now he had more pressing concerns.

"Think, Mrs. Bessborough," he urged, seizing the housekeeper's arm. "Try to remember the agency's name, so I may find Miss Antinori before anything happens to her."

"Oh, Mrs. B!" the maid interjected, raising her tear-stained face. "Might the name be Waters?"

"Waters, yes, that's it," the housekeeper cried. "Bless you, Lizzie! That would be Waters and Tremain in Lower Bond Street, my lord."

"Thank you both! I'll be off there directly. Pray that I may soon bring her safely home to you."

"Indeed I shall," Mrs. Bessborough said. "She's a good lass, no matter what some folk might say who should know better."

Striding into the hall, Will found Hobbs already on station. "Find her quickly, my lord," the butler urged in an undertone as he handed Will his hat and cane.

"I'll do my best," Will promised and hurried down the stairs to his waiting mount.

WILL HAD TO ASK directions twice before he found the offices of Waters and Tremain, "Furnishers of Genteel Employment for Ladies and Gentlemen." He entered a small anteroom to the jingle of a bell that roused a drowsy clerk at a desk opposite the entry.

"Lord Tavener to see Mr. Waters immediately on a matter of greatest urgency," he said, handing him his card.

"I'll see if he is available," the lad said and trotted off.

"He'd better be," Will muttered, in no frame of mind to be kept waiting.

Thankfully for Mr. Waters, since Will was prepared to storm into his office whether invited or not, the lad returned to usher Will into his employer's presence.

Will scarcely spared a glance for the spacious office to which the clerk escorted him, focusing instead on the thin man standing behind the desk. "I'm Tavener, sir, and I need your cooperation on a matter of utmost urgency."

"So my clerk said," Mr. Waters replied, bowing before he gestured Will to a chair. "With what can I assist you?"

"I have reason to believe a young lady has lately consulted you about employment. Due to a…misunderstanding with her family, she believed it necessary that she hire herself out as a governess. I wish to find her and bring her back home. The young lady's name is Allegra Antinori."

The man studied him. "I do not usually reveal the identities or the positions obtained by the individuals who use my service," he said.

Will took a menacing step closer. "Can I persuade you to make an exception to that policy?"

Not appearing alarmed in the slightest by Will's implicit threat, Mr. Waters said, a slight smile on his face, "Although I expect you could be very…persuasive, my lord, my recollection is that the young lady's

London relations are named 'Lynton,' not 'Tavener.' May I ask what your concern is in this matter?"

"I am a…close friend of the family and come on behalf of her guardian, who was…preoccupied with another matter."

"Of more pressing importance than recovering his ward?" Mr. Waters said.

"Nothing is more important to me," Will said flatly. "Please, tell me where she is."

For a long moment Mr. Waters studied him. Finally he said, "To prosper in my profession, one must make quick and accurate judgments about an individual's character. I believe you have a genuine concern for Miss Antinori."

"I wish her only the best," Will said.

The man nodded. "Then if what you conceive to be best for her is her return to Lynton House, I'm afraid I must disappoint you. 'Tis rather unusual to place an employee so quickly, but Miss Antinori had already been in contact with me concerning a position, and it so happened that a nearly ideal opening had just come up. Agreeing it would suit her talents and interests perfectly, last night she accepted a position as secretary to Sir Henry Malvern and governess to his daughter. Sir Henry wished to take his wife and child with him to see the lands he was unable, due to the unfortunate war just ended, to visit during his Grand Tour. They intended to leave this morning for Portsmouth, where he had booked passage to Italy."

"They left just this morning?" Will asked, focusing on the only part of the man's recitation that concerned him. "Then there may still be time to intercept her!"

Striding to the desk, he seized Mr. Waters's hand and gave it a brusque shake. "Thank you, sir."

"Good luck finding your lady, my lord," the man called behind him, for Will was already headed out the door.

Portsmouth, Will thought, his mind racing as he descended the stairs two at a time. Recovering his horse from the urchin he'd paid a penny to hold it, he leapt into the saddle. Though every impulse urged him to ride for Portsmouth at once, he knew he would have to delay long enough to make a few preparations.

Reaching Chelsea as swiftly as the crowded streets allowed, he sent Barrows out to pawn his ring and some of his mother's jewelry. He'd need cash to hire horses after his own was spent, for dinner and accommodations for Allegra at an inn before they started their journey back.

While he waited for Barrows, he packed a saddlebag of cheese, bread and ham, then headed into his chamber. He'd need to put together a razor and a change of clothing to make himself presentable when he escorted her home—before that starched-up prig Lynton reneged completely on the agreement Will had so recently coerced him into.

As he entered his chamber, Will saw, propped on his desk next to the crumpled list, a sealed note with his name in the same feminine hand. Pulse racing, he tore it open.

"Thank you again, dear Will, for your many kindnesses," he read. "You mustn't worry, for I have been fortunate enough to obtain a position which will exactly meet my needs. For some time, Sir Henry Malvern had been looking for a secretary fluent in Italian to accompany him and his family on a tour through Italy and the Levant. With his departure imminent, he had despaired of finding one. But after meeting him and his wife, I convinced them that I could handle the duties of secretary as well as assist his wife with their daughter Eliza, a charming little girl of four. We leave immediately for Rome.

"You may only imagine, after the—" there was a slight break where a word had been crossed out "—disappointments of London, how excited I am at the prospect of finally seeing my beloved father's homeland. The only thing I regret leaving in England, my dear Will, is our friendship. Thank you again, and adieu. Allegra."

He put the letter to his lips, where a faint trace of her lavender scent teased his nose. Then, carefully tucking it beside her list, he went to finish his packing.

He could understand her anticipation at visiting the land of her father. Hopefully, she would be even more enthusiastic about the prospect of purchasing the country manor about which she'd always dreamt.

Even if Will had to pummel Lynton again into honoring his commitment to provide her one.

CHAPTER EIGHTEEN

THE NEXT MORNING, Allegra sat at a table in the Malverns' private parlor at The Hoisted Anchor, gazing out at the ships in the harbor and enjoying the tangy scent of salt air through the open window while she waited for little Eliza to wake from her nap. After their arrival last night, the captain of the ship that was to take them to Italy informed Sir Henry that, if the weather continued fair, they would sail today on the afternoon tide.

Since the sun was shining brightly under a brisk blue sky, Allegra assumed they would indeed begin their journey today.

She leaned her face into the breeze, allowing herself to feel only anticipation. It was a relief beyond measure to have left London. To be leaving England.

She hoped her abrupt departure wouldn't come as a disappointment to Mrs. Randall. However, after witnessing that lady's delight at visiting Hemley, she trusted the joy of returning home to the country would offset any distress engendered by the premature ending of her London sojourn.

Allegra wished she might have been able to give her chaperone—and Bessie, Lizzie and Hobbs—a better goodbye than a note slipped under her chamber door, but time had been short. Nor did she think she would have been able to tolerate combating the objections they likely would have raised about her decision to abandon her Season.

As for Rob's reaction upon discovering her absence, the wound was still too deep and too raw for her to bear thinking about him at all.

She was glad she'd seen Will, though. Just remembering his vivid blue eyes and impudent smile lifted her spirits. She dipped her head to offer a fervent prayer that he might use her list to find a sunny-tempered lass with the intelligence to appreciate his clever wit, the wisdom to see beyond Brookwillow's current state of dilapidation and the industry to enjoy the challenge of helping him restore it.

Will would give his wife so much else to enjoy…. Allegra sighed, warmth rekindling within her as she remembered their kiss. He'd invested in it everything she'd sought and more, igniting the passion deep within her until the fury of it burned away, for those few moments at least, all the humiliation and heartache. She'd wanted it to go on forever, to give herself into his hands and let him teach her every delight possible between a skilled lover and an eager lass.

Thank heavens she'd chosen to kiss him in the park at dusk, where there'd been no possibility of abandoning herself completely to the agony searing her soul and the desire consuming her body. How difficult it had been to stop short of experiencing to the fullest the passion that she was giving up forever in choosing life as a governess. But she knew sometime later, when she could think more clearly, she'd be thankful she had not disgraced herself by tumbling him in a park corner like some Haymarket whore.

Though, in demanding his kiss, she'd still behaved like the veriest wanton. 'Twas a measure of the blessed numbness that still sustained her that she felt only a faint embarrassment at recalling it. If she wanted to keep her position, however, she would have to comport herself from now on with absolute propriety.

And she did wish to retain this position. Beyond the unparalleled opportunity to visit her father's country, she meant to enjoy every minute with Eliza. Teaching, tending and loving that delightful little girl was likely as close as she would ever come to having a child of her own.

She pushed aside that painful fact, along with a score of equally hurtful realizations she did not yet have the strength to contemplate. Raising her face once more, she willed the crisp breeze to blow through her mind as it was through her hair, carrying away distress, humiliation and regret, leaving only the determination to make the best of her situation, as Mama always had.

Perhaps in Italy, she might discover Papa's kin. Would they be as ashamed at finding they possessed a

half-English relation as her mother's aristocratic family
had always been of her Italian heritage?

All will be well in the end, Papa had promised. From
her reticule she took out her talisman, his last letter.
"'You have your mother's grace and the Antinori fierceness,'" she reminded herself, pressing the missive to her
lips. Closing her eyes, she tried to remember Papa as,
with vivid gestures and face alight, he'd described his
homeland to her.

She imagined herself already at the far side of the
Mediterranean, looking up from the ship's deck at an
endless spine of steep, sharp cliffs that towered over the
azure sea. Traveling inland to mountaintop cities with a
vista of gently rounded hills folding themselves into the
distance, their sides clothed in grapevines punctuated by
tall cypress trees, all of it shimmering in a clear, limpid
light unlike anything to be found in misty England.

She thought she could almost hear the lilting sound
of his native tongue, sweetly familiar to her ears. Until
with a start, she realized that she *was* hearing Italian,
words of inquiry and protest followed by loud, impatient
English replies, both emanating from the taproom below.

Curious, she quickly replaced the precious letter in
her reticule and went downstairs.

She met the innkeeper on the stairway, shaking his
head. "Pardon, sir," she hailed him, "but can I be of assistance? I couldn't help but overhear your discussion
and I speak Italian."

"That'd be a blessing, miss, for I couldn't make out

a thing that gent was asking. If foreigners want to traipse about the countryside, you'd think they'd trouble to learn the language first." Jerking his thumb toward the taproom, he said, "I left him in there."

Allegra continued into the public room where a dark-haired stranger sat at a table, what she recognized as a London guidebook in his hands. "Excuse me, sir," she began in her father's tongue. "I understand you are seeking information. May I be of some help?"

The man jerked his head up, a look of amazement and relief on his face. "Ah, signorina, at last a civilized person instead of these barbarous English! A thousand thanks for your assistance. From this book, I think I shall need to hire a carriage to get to London—and perhaps elsewhere in this benighted country, though I beseech the Holy Mother to let me find the gentleman I seek in that city! But excuse me, signorina," he said, jumping up to sweep her a bow. "Signore Luigi DiCastello, at your service."

Allegra returned him a curtsey. "You seek an Italian gentleman in London? Is he with the theater? Most of your countrymen here perform at the opera or upon the stage."

The visitor sniffed. "The man I seek is not a common performer, but a musician, a composer, a gentleman of genius! Might you know of this man? Let me show you his name, written by my master on letters addressed to him that I am entrusted to deliver."

Musician. Composer. Genius. Was it possible? But no, surely this man couldn't be seeking her father. The possibility was simply too far-fetched to belive. To her knowledge, there had been no letters from Italy in all the time she was growing up. Why might someone wish to contact him now?

Unless…this had something to do with the "great scheme" for their future to which Mama had alluded when she told Allegra Papa had refused her musician-suitor's request for her hand. "I should like to see the letters," Allegra replied.

Extracting a leather portfolio from his bag, Signore Di-Castello pulled out two sheaves of letters bound together with ribbon. "The man I seek," he said, holding them out to her, "is Signore Emilio Antinori. Here are the letters to him from my master. These others, written by Signore Emilio some years ago, were given to me so that I might verify his identity once I find him by matching his hand."

For a moment Allegra sat silent, astounded to discover her far-fetched speculation had turned out to be true. Following upon surprise came a surge of grief made more poignant by realizing that whatever Papa's grand project had been, now it would never reach fruition.

After taking a moment to compose herself, she said, "As impossibly coincidental as it seems, the gentleman you seek, Emilio Antinori, was my father. But I will not be able to conduct you to him. Sadly, I must tell you that he died of fever last fall in Bath."

The Italian stared at her. "You, the daughter of Signore Emilio? And he is dead? No," he exclaimed, dropping the letters back on the table, "this cannot be!"

He took an agitated pace away, then wheeled to face her. "It *must* not be! Shame on you, signorina," he declared, his voice rising as he shook his finger in her face, "to speak so beautifully my language and yet make sport of me, a poor foreigner!"

Before Allegra could try to calm him, Sir Henry strode in, frowning. "For heaven's sake, lower your voice, sir! You'll wake my daughter." Suddenly recognizing Allegra, he stopped short. "Miss Antinori, what is wrong? Is that gentleman accosting you?"

His finger still pointed at her accusingly, the man froze. "Miss Antinori?" he echoed. "It is truth, then? You *are* the daughter of Emilio Antinori?"

"I have that honor," Allegra replied in Italian. "Shall I show you a letter he wrote me?" Quickly she pulled it from her reticule. "You may see for yourself that it is in the same hand as the letters you carry."

While she held it out for the traveler's inspection, she said to Sir Henry, "It appears this gentleman has come to England seeking my father."

"*Cielo mio,* that *is* his hand!" DiCastello murmured. Then to her astonishment, the man fell on his knees at her feet, seized her hand and kissed it.

"Ah, yes, you do have the look of the Antinori about you!" he exclaimed. "I am honored, Duchessa! Now, you must promise to accompany me back to San Gregillio. Only the joyous news that he has so beautiful a granddaughter will assuage the grief of my master *il duce* when he learns his beloved son is dead."

"Your master—the duke?" Allegra repeated numbly.

"*Si,* Duchessa. Arturo Sergio Antinori, Duke of San Gregillio. And, it seems, your grandfather."

FOR THE NEXT HOUR, in the private parlor the Malverns kindly put at her disposal while they strolled with their daughter, Allegra sat at the table and listened to her grandfather's emissary. Still finding it difficult to believe what had unfolded this morning was real and not the most vivid of pleasant dreams, she struggled to comprehend all the implications of discovering her father's heritage.

Fortified by wine brought by Lady Malvern's maid, who at Signore DiCastello's insistence remained discreetly nearby to chaperone, the Italian related to her how her father came to be in England, estranged from his family.

Supremely gifted and interested only in his music, Emilio had not been content to be an amateur performer or a patron of the arts, as befitted one of his station. Determined to devote himself completely to music, he told his father he meant not only to perform with theater and opera orchestras, but to travel to England and study the works of the composers he most admired, Handel and Hayden.

When the duke adamantly refused to permit him to do either, declaring that an Antinori of San Gregillio must not perform on a public stage or chase after common musicians like a lackey, her father replied he would go with or without his parent's permission. The duke had cajoled, reprimanded and finally threatened to disown his son should he persist in carrying out his plans.

Her father left the following day. As proud and stubborn as his son, the duke did not try to stop him, nor did he attempt to even contact Emilio for the next several years. By the time increasing age along with the deaths of his wife and his other sons inspired the duke to relent, Napoleon's shadow had fallen over Italy. England's continental blockade and the necessity for the duke to scheme continually to keep his lands from being absorbed into the French-imposed Republic of Italy had forced the postponement of the duke's efforts to find his son.

Only now that Waterloo had determined the Emperor— and Italy's—fate had the Duke been able to send the emissary on his mission to seek reconciliation.

A reconciliation that was not to be. Allegra wondered if returning to seek the duke's forgiveness might have been the bold plan about which her mother had spoken, its implementation stymied by her parents' sudden, premature deaths. But now Signore DiCastello was saying that Allegra must make that journey to the family of her father, insisting she owed it to herself and the grandfather she had never met to become acquainted and to relate to the duke everything she could about the life of the son whose loss he would forever mourn.

As tempting as the invitation was, Allegra was trying

to explain to the Italian why she could not simply abandon the Malverns when Sir Henry, Lady Malvern and Eliza returned from their walk.

After an exchange of bows and curtseys, Lady Malvern said, "I understand you have received exciting news about your father's family, Miss Antinori."

Reaching over to take Eliza, who squealed with delight upon seeing her and thrust out her chubby arms, Allegra settled the child on her lap. "Yes, my lady. I've just discovered my grandfather is a...person of some importance. Signore DiCastello is pressing me to return with him to meet my grandfather and tell him about my father's years in England. I'm trying to make him understand that, regrettably, I cannot do so at this time, as I have pledged to assist you during your journey. 'Twould be impossible for you to secure a replacement for me now."

Lady Malvern exchanged a look with her husband. "We've just been discussing that, Miss Antinori," Sir Henry said. "Before your fortuitous appearance, I'd resigned myself to not having a secretary on the trip and Eliza won't truly need a governess for some time. We both feel it is important that you avail yourself of this opportunity to be escorted to your grandfather's home by a gentleman who knows both your family and the countryside. We shall travel to Rome together and insure you have a chaperone to accompany you for the rest of the journey, but we believe you should go to San Gregillio at once."

The wonder and excitement she'd been trying to suppress bubbled up. "You will release me from our agreement?" Allegra asked, not sure she dared believe it.

"You mustn't think we do not value your assistance," Lady Malvern assured her. "In the short time you've been with us, we've both been much impressed by your knowledge, intelligence and character."

"You've already won over Eliza—and she is an excellent judge," Sir Henry said, beckoning to his daughter.

"You are sure?" Allegra asked, setting the little girl down to run to her papa. "I must confess, I am anxious to meet my father's family and visit his childhood home."

"I should think so, when that 'childhood home' is a ducal court!" Lady Malvern said. "We are agreed, then?"

"If you are sure," Allegra replied. Though she didn't yet truly believe her abrupt change of fortune, just the thought of being welcomed as a cherished member of a family sent a thrill through her.

Perhaps she might finally have a place to belong.

"One other thing," Lady Malvern added. "Though I prefer the country, I have many friends who spend the Season in London, so I know something of your... situation. In view of that, I think it all the more important that you are reunited with your true family as quickly as possible."

Lady Malvern smiled impishly. "I can scarcely wait to write all my London friends that on my journey I was fortunate enough to make the acquaintance of Allegra Antinori, the Duchessa di San Gregillio!"

CHAPTER NINETEEN

LATE THAT AFTERNOON, mud-spattered and bone weary, Will finally trotted into Portsmouth on the last of the job horses he'd hired. Lack of sleep, hunger and the current nag's rough gait had left him with a pounding headache, which wasn't surprising, given everything that had gone wrong on the journey.

As desperately as he needed food, sleep and a bath, Will bypassed the numerous inns and continued on to the harbor. The bustle of sailors and the forest of masts of the ships anchored out revived his hope that Allegra might still be in the city. Perhaps within the very next hour he would find her and convince her to return to London with him. At the thought, his weary spirits revived.

After asking directions of a helpful stevedore, Will found the harbormaster's office, where he was fortunate enough to discover that official still at his post. Waiting in the anteroom, he recalled the frustrations of his journey.

Desperate to reach the port as speedily as possible, he'd intended to ride through the night, but once the sun went down he was beset by delays. The posting inn at his twilight stop had no horses available and he'd had to waste precious time visiting every establishment in town before finally finding a small inn able to provide him a mount.

He'd found the staff at the inn he reached after midnight all asleep, not surprising since the mail coach had long since passed through. Rousting out a groom to ready a horse and finding the proprietor to conclude the arrangements had devoured more precious minutes.

Then four miles out of town, the horse pulled up lame. After walking the beast to the nearest village, he'd once again banged on shuttered inn windows and bolted stable doors to rouse the owner who, irritated at having his sleep disturbed, had only with difficulty been persuaded to rent Will a horse.

As moonlit night gave way to dawn, he'd been able to change horses without further incident, but having lost so much time, Will had dared not stop for a meal. After disposing of the bread and cheese he'd brought with him, since early morning he'd existed on a few meat pies and several tankards of ale, as his growling stomach reminded him.

Just then the official walked out. "Sorry to keep you waiting, my lord. With what can I assist you?"

"Thank you for receiving me in all my dirt," Will replied, following him into his office. "I've just ridden in from London and urgently need some information. Could you tell me which ships in port are bound for Italy?"

"Certainly." The *Wentworth* and the *Westmoreland*

are bound for Genoa and Livorno, respectively, and the *Pride of Sussex* sailed this afternoon for Rome."

Will felt the pang of trepidation echo through his empty stomach. "Can you tell me if *Pride of Sussex* carried any passengers? I have vital news to convey to someone who arrived at Portsmouth yesterday and must discover whether or not they have already sailed."

The man nodded. "If you'll wait, I'll check my log."

Too agitated to sit despite his fatigue, Will paced the office while the harbormaster pulled a volume from the bookcase beside his desk and flipped through it. "According to my notes, that vessel carried a Sir Henry Malvern, his wife, Elizabeth, and daughter, Eliza, her nurse Harris, her governess Miss Antinori, the lady's maid Dorset, the gentleman's valet Stanley…"

The harbormaster continued to rattle off names, but Will stopped listening. Sagging back against the wall, he closed his eyes.

She was gone. From Portsmouth. From England. He would not be able to hurry her back to London and coerce Lynton, who'd already been positioning himself to disavow the bargain Will had forced, into honoring its terms.

"Are you all right, my lord?" The official's concerned voice penetrated his cloud of weary despair.

Will hauled himself upright. "Yes, yes, I'm fine." Fishing in his pocket, he pulled out a coin and pressed it into the harbormaster's hand. "Thank you for your trouble, sir."

"Happy to be of service, m'lord," the man said, pocketing the coin. "Hope you find that gent."

Slowly Will trudged out to retrieve his horse. Once the ton learned Allegra had left the Lynton family to take a post as a governess—news Sapphira would spread about gleefully—Lynton would contend 'twas next to impossible to reestablish her in society. Having thus recklessly cut herself off from the world he'd tried to help her enter, Lynton would doubtless feel justified in refusing to squander any more assets on someone who'd behaved in what he considered to be an overhasty, irrational manner.

Lynton wouldn't want Allegra back—but Will did. *He* could still go after her.

The idea fired through him, burning away his fatigue. He'd take the next ship for Rome and continue his search. Granted, he hadn't much to offer her at present, but surely getting a home of her own—albeit crumbling into ruin—and the title of Lady Tavener was preferable to spending the rest of her life as a low-paid, unappreciated servant.

She'd have a place to belong—and his undying love. Maybe, once she'd cleared Rob Lynton from her heart, he might have a chance of winning it.

Electrified by the image of placing his wedding ring on Allegra's finger and settling with her at Brookwillow for the rest of their days, he pulled up his horse. He'd go back to the harbormaster's office, ask him on which ship he'd need to book passage.

Even before he could turn his mount, the flame of excitement guttered. Baron Penniless of Rack-and-Ruin Manor hadn't the cash to book passage on a ship, much less to fund the rest of a potentially long and costly journey.

There could be no further pursuit. Allegra had chosen to go abroad as a governess and a governess she would remain. As he would remain alone, cut off from her by a sea of poverty and loneliness.

Through all the weary miles and hours, Will had spurred himself on by imagining Allegra claiming the brighter future he'd envisioned for her. As he let go of that dream, a weight of discouragement and fatigue heavier than a Corinthian's multi-caped greatcoat settled over him.

Instead of following the lady he loved, he'd look for an inn, use some of the modest reserve he'd hoarded to purchase Allegra's room and dinner to obtain those comforts for himself, then get some sleep before making his solitary way back to London.

Exhausted and heartsick, Will stopped at the first inn that looked respectable, engaged a chamber, wolfed down a bowl of the cook's hot stew and fell into bed.

SETTING OUT the next morning, Will spent the long hours in the saddle considering what he should do next.

First, finish his note to Lucilla—or better yet, deliver an apology in person. Perhaps he'd take along Allegra's list and solicit Lucilla's advice about it.

The mere thought inspired a wave of revulsion. Having so clearly envisioned Allegra as his wife, he couldn't imagine going through the travesty of paying court to another, nor did he feel capable of dredging up the charm necessary to captivate any of the ladies on that list.

Neither did the idea of resuming his previous life hold any appeal. He'd had enough of living from gaming win to gaming win, relieving the loneliness of his life by trysting with matrons eager to add his name to their list of conquests.

He craved rest and quiet and peace, a period of solitude in which to wean himself from the love he should somehow have prevented from developing in the first place.

He needed Brookwillow. Immersed in the soothing balm of its woods, river, and fields—fallow and growing up in weeds as they were—perhaps he could find himself and a new sense of purpose. He craved the company of honest folk like the Phillipses who valued him for who he was, not the arrogant Lyntons of the ton or the idle beauties who would seduce him to wound a former lover, to inspire jealousy in a potential one or simply to alleviate their boredom.

Perhaps he'd try taking Allegra's advice and see what he could do about restoring Brookwillow without the influx of funds from a rich wife's dowry. The Phillipses would assist him, he knew. Maybe there was a carpenter among the tenants who could work on the roof.

Will smiled. Maybe *he* could learn carpentry. Stonemasonry. Farm management. All useful skills that just might, over the course of years, allow him to gradually coax Brookwillow out of penury and ease it back along the road to becoming a productive estate.

A flicker of interest stirred in his despondent soul. He could observe the tenants' cottage gardens, visit the neighboring estates and talk to their managers. Read some books on agriculture; attend the Fall Meeting at Holkham…

If he spurned Lucilla's kindly-meant assistance, he'd never be a wealthy baron, Lord Tavener of Brookwillow, escorting his heiress wife to all the fashionable events of the London Season. But he also wouldn't have to spend a lifetime with a lady he couldn't love and didn't want.

A lady who wasn't Allegra.

As the miles passed by under the hoofs of one job horse after another, resolution became purpose and the sharp edge of his heartache eased. He would call on Lucilla, make arrangements to leave London, and be done with the ton, society and men like Lynton for good.

THE AFTERNOON AFTER his arrival back in London, Will set out to visit Lucilla. Replying this morning to the note he'd scrawled before falling into bed upon his return, she'd invited him to come by after the promenade hour in the park and remain for dinner.

He hoped she wouldn't be too upset when he turned down her offer after scarcely giving it a try, but the more he pondered returning permanently to Brookwillow, the more right and proper the decision seemed.

He also hoped Lucilla wouldn't question him too closely about why he suddenly had no interest in pursuing lovely women. The quiet agony smoldering in his soul at losing Allegra wasn't something he could bear to expose, not even to Barrows or his sympathetic cousin.

To his surprise, as he entered the parlor, Domcaster rose to greet him. "This is an unexpected pleasure," Will said, returning the earl's handshake. "I thought you'd returned to Waverley Hall for the rest of the spring."

"There's a matter before Parliament that needed my attention," his host said, waving him to a seat. "Besides which, you've turned out to be so indifferent an escort that Lucilla's threatening to cajole me into remaining for the rest of the Season. Instead of shaking your hand, I ought to box your ears."

Before Will could reply, his cousin entered in a rustle of skirts. "Will, dear, so nice of you to call—at last!" she exclaimed, offering him her cheek to kiss before joining her husband on the sofa. "What of our agreement? I excuse you for a few evenings when I was preoccupied elsewhere and you disappear!"

"You've every right to scold, and I do apologize. I didn't mean to be so neglectful. But…events transpired, and then I made that long-overdue trip to Brookwillow."

She narrowed her eyes at him. "In the company of a certain young lady, I understand."

"And her chaperone, who wished to visit a dear friend who lives in seclusion near Hemley. I thought it only courteous to offer my escort, since I was going in that direction anyway."

"Most gracious," Lucilla replied dryly, her tone telling Will she didn't believe his explanation for an instant. "Now that you have returned, let's move forward! We'll be dining en famille and can start planning at once."

"I'd be delighted to dine, but first I'd better warn you that, grateful as I am for your kindness in trying to make a respectable gentleman out of me, I…I must cry off our agreement. After attending a few ton gatherings, I've discovered, like Marcus, that I don't much enjoy them."

"Always said you were a man of sense, Will," Domcaster inserted with a grin.

While Lucilla shushed her husband, Will continued, "More to the point, after meeting several eligible ladies, I find it increasingly difficult to imagine myself cozening some poor innocent into marrying me so I can relieve her of her fortune and use it to restore my estate." He shook his head, a wry smile on his lips. "I can't do it, Lucilla."

For a long moment she studied him. Will hoped she could no longer read his thoughts as well as she'd been able when they were children.

"I see," she said at last. "What do you mean to do, then? Go back to gaming and forfeit any chance of finding a wife and having a family?" Putting a hand on her husband's arm, she added softly, "'Tis a blessing you cannot imagine, having never possessed one. Don't throw away the opportunity too hastily, Will."

"Oh, I'm not ruling it out altogether." 'Twas rather Allegra who had ruled it out for him, Will thought, wincing as pain slashed across his heart. "But as inured to poverty as I've become over the years, upon reflection I realized I don't want to bring a bride to the ruin Brookwillow has become and have her despise it upon sight. I'd rather try to bring it into some sort of order first."

He held up a hand before Lucilla could reply. "You're going to say I haven't enough capital to effect significant repairs, nor have I any knowledge of estate management, and you're correct. But I can learn. I want to learn. It will take years, I know, but I'm convinced that this is what I must do."

Looking at her frowning face, he sighed. "I am sorry, Lucilla. I don't expect you to understand why I'm turning down your offer—though Marcus might," he added, nodding to Domcaster. "I intend to leave for Brookwillow as soon as I settle my accounts in London. So if you wish to abuse me as an ungrateful wretch and throw me out before dinner, you've my leave to proceed."

Lucilla looked to her husband, as if asking whether she should argue further. After he gave her a minute, negative shake of the head, she turned back to Will.

"I am terribly disappointed. I had so been looking forward to watching you win the heart of some sweet-tempered maiden—and having her soften yours in return. I don't suppose this decision has anything to do with the interesting on-dit I heard this morning?"

"On-dit?" Will echoed in what he hoped was an innocent tone, though he suspected he knew what she'd learned.

"That Miss Antinori has abandoned her Season and left London. Now, some malicious tongues, encouraged by that viper Lady Lynton, no doubt, speculate that she became so…friendly with one or another of the rakehells pursuing her that she was obliged to leave—"

"The devil they are!" Will interrupted, fury suffusing him as he leapt to his feet, hands curled into fists. "Tell me who is spreading such scurrilous falsehoods! I promise you, when I am done with them they won't speak at all for a fortnight!"

Eyes going wide, Lucilla gasped at his vehemence while Domcaster put a restraining hand on his arm. "Sit down, Will," he said mildly. "As always with scurrilous rumors, 'tis best to do nothing. Those who were acquainted with the girl will know them to be ridiculous. Defending her would only prolong the talk."

Hard put to contain his anger, Will resumed his seat. "You are right, I suppose. Still…" Making his decision, he continued, "Probably many in the ton would consider what she really did as reprehensible as ruination by some scoundrel, but I would prefer you know the truth. Having decided that society was…not to her liking, she chose to take a position as governess with a family traveling to Italy. She wished to see her father's homeland."

"The ton probably would think succumbing to seduction less shocking than hiring herself out as a governess," Domcaster agreed. "I admire her independence, though."

"Do you know which family?" Lucilla asked.

"Sir Henry and Lady Malvern."

"I'm acquainted with Elizabeth," Lucilla said. "She has a darling little girl. Very well, when the subject arises, I shall inform everyone that Miss Antinori was invited to accompany the Malverns to the continent."

Smiling with real gratitude, Will said, "I would appreciate that."

"Putting that version of her story about may be easier than you imagine," Lucilla replied. "As I'm sure you will be pleased to know, Lady Lynton is soon to leave London. It seems Lynton departed the city right after Miss Antinori, telling Sapphira to vacate Lynton House as soon as possible since he meant to bring home a bride in the fall. I believe I heard something about Lady Lynton retiring to an estate in Cumbria…"

Leaning over to squeeze Will's hand, she added softy, "You mustn't despair, Will. Miss Antinori will return to England one day. Now, shall we dine?"

AFTER DINNER, Domcaster invited Will to share a brandy while his wife went up to freshen herself before the rout-party to which she was dragging her reluctant spouse.

"So you really intend to become a farmer?" Domcaster asked, handing him a snifter.

"Being one seems to agree with you."

Domcaster nodded. "I never had any interest in cutting a figure in society or in gaming and drinking away my nights. To me, nothing can equal the satisfaction of walking my fields in the morning mist. Watching seeds planted in spring sprout into tender shoots that turn to green waves of summer grain and then to the gold of harvest. Give me that, the laughter of my wife and children, and I ask no more of life."

It sounded good to Will as well—though he doubted he'd ever experience the bit about a wife and children's laughter. "I look forward to it."

"Whilst in town, I've consulted my man of business. I've been considering investing in additional acreage."

"Is there any suitable land adjacent to Waverley?"

"I've enough of my own to manage already. I was thinking not so much of purchasing more, but rather of acquiring an interest in other properties."

"With your expertise, I'm sure you'll soon discover something suitable."

"Especially if I'm assured of the honesty and good character of the estate manager. I'm thinking that for a property about the size of Brookwillow, ten thousand pounds should be sufficient to effect the most essential repairs and plant enough acreage to earn a profit."

Ten thousand pounds, the size of Allegra's supposed dowry—when she had one, Will thought, his attention so ensnared by bittersweet memory that at first he didn't fully comprehend what Domcaster had just said. Suddenly realizing it, he almost dropped his glass.

"Are you suggesting what I think you're suggesting?"

Domcaster smiled. "Why don't we say that before you leave London, I'll give you a draft on my bank for that amount? With interest at the going rate and flexible repayment terms, depending on the yields at harvest."

"But as yet I know nothing of managing a farm. Why would you take a chance investing in Brookwillow?"

"I've always liked you, you know. Even more so now that you're determined to eschew the easy path of wedding an heiress and work to restore the property yourself. Lucilla's always said that Brookwillow is a fine piece of land that only needs sufficient cash and attentive management to set it to rights. You provide the oversight and I'll supply the cash. You'll need a competent estate agent to advise you. I'll send over my manager's eldest son. He's a good lad and has been well-trained. I expect a handsome return on this investment, by the way."

Awed and humbled by Domcaster's generosity, Will said, "I hardly know what to reply."

Domcaster shrugged. "Needn't say anything. Family and all, you know. Just give me your hand on it and 'tis done. Then you can be off to Brookwillow to learn what your guardian should have made it his business to teach you years ago—how to profitably manage your birthright."

His mind still muddled with surprise, Will shook Domcaster's hand. From the turmoil of his thoughts, though, two sharply defined ideas emerged.

With such an influx of capital, he might accomplish at Brookwillow in a few years what would otherwise have required a decade. And once he'd made a good beginning, he would have the funds to pursue Allegra.

CHAPTER TWENTY

LAUGHTER AND THE MUSICAL babble of Italian conversation drifted on the night air from the ballroom into the garden where Allegra strolled with her cousin Alessandro, her duenna trailing a discreet distance behind. Breathing deeply of the blossom-scented air, she sighed. After three months in residence at her grandfather's estate crowning the summit of a Tuscan hill, the beauty of the palazzo and the gardens around it still enchanted her.

She would never forget her reception the balmy evening she arrived with Signore DiCastello and the Malverns' maid after their long dusty journey from Rome. Advised of her identity in a letter his servant had sent ahead by express messenger, her grandfather had been waiting on the terrace of the front entrance, just beyond where she now stood.

The duke himself had helped her from the carriage and stayed her at arm's length before she could curtsey, his eyes inspecting her face as avidly as she inspected his.

She saw in him the sharp aquiline outline of Papa's nose, the same dark, penetrating eyes gleaming with intelligence and fierce purpose, a high proud forehead now lined with age while his hair, wavy as Papa's, fell snowy white to his shoulders.

Though Allegra felt she favored her mother, there must have been sufficient echoes in her visage of her father, for the duke cried, "*Dio mio,* how I see Emilio in you!" Then he'd drawn her into his arms and wept.

"Wool-picking, Allegra?" Alessandro asked, recalling her to the present.

"Wool-gathering," she corrected, a tremor of laughter in her voice, "and yes, I'm afraid I was. Forgive me!" Alessandro, a serious young man who'd become even more intense, Allegra's Italian maid told her, after the death of his father made him heir to the Antinori title, liked to practice his English with her. In the new world Italy would build since ridding herself of the Napoleonic invaders, the next duke must prepare himself to deal with men of every country, he'd told her solemnly.

"'Tis well-known that a beautiful woman may be forgiven whatever she asks," he said, switching back to Italian as he smiled at her. "Did the press of visitors overwhelm you? I've noticed you often slip out to this garden after a day full of activities and callers."

"You've caught me out," she confessed. "With so discerning an eye, you shall make an excellent diplomat. And yes, I did feel the need for some quiet and solitude."

"Am I intruding? I can leave you to Signora Bertrude's company," he said, gesturing toward the duenna.

"No, please stay. Unlike so many…callers, you are

content to stroll in silence. And having your escort may discourage anyone else from joining me."

Alessandro laughed. "You cannot blame the young men of the district from clamoring to pay their respects to so lovely and charming a lady—especially when she is the long-lost granddaughter of the duke!"

"Which, I do not doubt, is why so many come clamoring," Allegra retorted. "Listening to so much talk sometimes makes my head hurt! And such a confusing mix of people, I'm still trying to sort them all out.

"Distant Antinori relations," she began, ticking them off on her fingers, "come to report on properties they manage for grandfather. Officials from the old French government who've stayed on and wish to ingratiate themselves with the aristocrats whose lands and titles they previously tried to confiscate. Poets and philosophers entreating grandfather to take up their causes. And now, the Austrians beginning their administration. I've tried asking grandfather to explain it all, but he merely says a lady needn't concern herself with political matters."

"'Tis true." Alessandro nodded. "Here, a maiden of good family occupies herself deciding which of her suitors might best please her as a husband, so she can persuade her guardian to accept his offer."

"I've no interest in marriage now," Allegra said, her exasperation increasing each time she had to repeat this apparently radical statement. "I am completely content to have found grandfather and my family again."

In the months since her fiasco in London, she'd achieved a certain measure of peace. Though she thought often and fondly of Will, even the idea of marriage was still too painful to contemplate.

"Perhaps, but as an Antinori, it will be your duty to marry well, just as it is mine," her cousin replied. "But then, you are half-English and must be allowed your sometimes odd ideas. Do English ladies interest themselves in politics rather than marriage?"

"Sometimes. Some become noted hostesses, inviting their husband's friends and allies to debate affairs of government as well as sponsoring poets and writers."

Alessandro frowned and shook his head. "I should not trust my wife among poets and writers. Inflammatory, unstable fellows. But one must tolerate them in the new Italy."

The sound of footsteps crunching on gravel behind them made them both turn. The duke was walking toward them, resplendent in black evening dress with a red sash about his waist, the jeweled crest of the Antinori family glittering on his lapel.

"Ah, here it is you are hiding," he said, coming over to take her arm. "Does the attention of these young pups fatigue you, dear one? If so, I shall send them home."

"I would not be so discourteous to your guests, *nonno*. Alessandro has been entertaining me quite well."

"Seeing you two in the distance, I could almost imagine it was your father Emilio strolling with your mother, Lady Grace, whom you so resemble."

The duke patted his pocket, where Allegra knew he kept the miniatures she'd given him of her parents, painted shortly after their marriage. "He was not much older than Alessandro when he left San Gregillio."

The duke sighed heavily. "Perhaps I erred, not letting him pursue his music here. I was also wrong not to trust him to remain faithful to his heritage, for he married your mother, a viscount's daughter. Though I am not wise in the ways of your country, I know she must have sacrificed much to wed one whom her society thought a mere musician. If only he had brought her back to San Gregillio, that they might have been accorded the place of honor they deserved!"

"I think they meant to do so, *nonno*," Allegra said, trying to ease the old man's distress. "Worldly esteem aside, Papa was very happy in their love and with his music. I am only sorry Mama was never able to meet you."

"I should resent her, for if my son had been unhappy, he might have returned sooner. But how can I be angry with the lady who made my Emilio content and gave me so lovely a *nipotina*, eh? Nor would my son have considered returning except in triumph.

"But enough of the sadness of the past. Will you let me return you to the ballroom where your admirers wait? I won't be here forever, and I wish for you to choose a fine young man to wed before I am gone."

It was a familiar theme. Much as she wanted to please this imperious old man whom she'd come to love, Allegra had to grit her teeth as the equally familiar ache passed through her. "Can I not remain here with you, *nonno?*"

"My darling *nipotina*, I love having you with me, but 'tis my duty to insure you a husband's protection, that you may never again have to hire yourself out as tutor to the children of others. No, I would surround myself with *your* children before I die. But I do not despair. It is only right that you are discriminating in your choice. Nor have you yet met all the eligible gentlemen in Tuscany. Surely one of them will catch your discerning fancy."

Repressing a sigh, Allegra refrained from arguing further. Perhaps eventually she might steel herself to marry. But not now. And if pressed too much upon that point, not sharing the duke's disdain at the notion of hiring herself out as a governess, she could always leave and make her own way in the world.

Retaining her independence and earning her own bread would be infinitely preferable to being bound for life to a man she knew little about and cared for even less.

Like the tall, elegantly dressed man making his way toward them, arrogant assurance in his walk. Both her grandfather and Alessandro stiffened at his approach, for this was a small family garden, not the formal one below the ballroom terrace that was illumined for the enjoyment of their guests. Allegra suspected her grandfather was not pleased that this guest dared trespass upon their privacy.

Count Hans von Strossen, the Austrian who'd recently been appointed governor of this portion of Italy, had quickly joined the court of her suitors and was fast taking persistence to the point of annoyance.

The air of ruthlessness about him made her almost as uncomfortable as the insolent way he inspected her when her grandfather wasn't watching, his eyes darkening with a lust he made no attempt to conceal. An unpleasant shiver passed over her skin at the thought of being near him on the darkened terrace, even with her grandfather and cousin beside her. Nor did she wish to do anything that might encourage in him the mistaken impression that she had the slightest desire for his company.

"Count von Strossen, you must have lost your way," Alessandro said pleasantly, though Allegra sensed her cousin had no more liking for the Austrian than she did. "This is but a small insignificant garden, unworthy of your notice. Let me lead you back to the south terrace. With the fountains at play, a stroll there is most refreshing."

"But the most delectable ornament in your garden is here. I should find a stroll with her much more…satisfying."

Even in the darkness, Allegra could see her cousin frown at the Austrian's provocative wording. With the fluid situation in Italy at this moment, the governments the French had imposed being dismantled and the local landowners dancing a delicate ballet with the Austrian powers who sought to replace the French, she knew her grandfather could not afford to antagonize the count.

Which doubtless accounted for the fact that the duke had not discouraged his frequent visits to the palazzo.

Before Alessandro could return a heated reply, she said quickly, "Overwhelmed as I am by your courtesy, Count, I fear I am fatigued. Grandfather and Duke Alessandro were just bidding me good-night before I retire."

As if he recognized and appreciated her sudden weariness for the tactic to avoid him it was, the count smiled. "Would that I might do my poor part to assist you, Duchessa," he murmured. "Another evening, perhaps. Another evening *soon.*"

Though she wasn't truly tired, Allegra had no more desire to return to the fawning attention and gallant compliments that awaited her in the ballroom than she did to suffer the count's lustful hand at her elbow. Leaning up to kiss her grandfather's cheek, she said, "Good night, *nonno,* Alessandro." According the count the smallest of nods, she turned away, her duenna hastening to follow.

From behind her came the count's soft laughter. "Ah, a disdainful woman," she heard him say to Alessandro as she hurried toward the entrance. "How much more satisfying to compel the surrender of such a one than to master any of those witless creatures so eager to please a man."

Closing the door upon his words, Allegra repressed another shiver. Sensitive situation or not, she vowed she'd risk creating a political incident before she'd allow the count to "compel" her "surrender."

Up in her room half an hour later, her formal dress discarded in favor of a silk night rail, Allegra leaned upon the stone balustrade of the balcony outside her chamber. She wasn't in the least sleepy, nor did she feel like perusing a book. The stars spangling the heavens and the faint sound of a plaintive melody emanating from the distant ballroom fueled a restless longing in her heart.

Wonderful as it had been to have spent the last three months in pampered luxury, she'd gradually come to think 'twas like living in a theater in which she was the principal player, surrounded by a cast of maids, dressers, friseurs and footmen who refused to let her do anything more useful than choose what new gown she would wear and which elegant hairstyle and bonnet would accompany it.

Though she felt guilty about the reaction after all the love and attention her grandfather had lavished upon her, she had come to feel more hemmed in than ever before in her life.

She'd thought the restrictions imposed upon her by the ton in London confining, but the limitations on a well-bred lady's behavior here were even greater. She soon discovered she was not permitted to walk a step outside the house without Signora Bertrude, a solemn older lady chosen by her grandfather specifically, Allegra surmised, judging by the duenna's sole topic of conversation, to school her in choosing a husband. Often when she walked in the gardens, the signora summoned a maid or a footman to join them as well.

With difficulty Allegra had persuaded her grandfather to allow her to ride about the grounds rather than be driven in a coach. But when she rode, she was preceded by an outrider and accompanied by at least two grooms.

When, feeling a compulsion to venture beyond the estate, she expressed a desire to visit the nearest town and inspect the shops, her duenna replied that the duchessa need only state what she required and the requisite tradesmen would be summoned to bring their wares to the palazzo for her consideration.

Though she supposed a gentleman had more freedom, Allegra was beginning to appreciate why her father had chosen to leave this house and pursue his music abroad.

She missed being able to ride and walk and shop without an entourage. And as much as Italy excited her admiration with its beauty and diversity, she was finding she missed the deep green hills and quiet dales of England.

Her grandfather's house was exquisite and the affection he'd shown her heartwarming, but the bitter truth was that she didn't feel she belonged here, either.

To her initial surprise but growing understanding, she'd also found that she did not miss Rob. Once the first wave of hurt and humiliation eased, she began to realize she had probably never felt more for him than the vestiges of youthful hero worship that, confused by grief and desperate for a home, she'd attempted, but never quite succeeded, to convince herself was love.

As had been brought so forcefully and painfully to her attention during her last interview with him, she hadn't really known the mature Rob at all, as he didn't know or appreciate her. Aside from a mutual grief over his father's death, they no longer had anything in common.

The new Lord Lynton had considered it inappropriate to ride with her or teach her fencing or billiards, as he'd done with careless grace when they were younger. Of course, she forced herself to recall, surprised to find the memory no longer stung so sharply, all along he'd been in love with another girl, one who, from what she'd gleaned, was as blond and proper and biddable as Allegra was not.

Despite their shared past, only in her wishful imagining had there ever been the possibility of a future with Rob. He'd seen her simply as a responsibility he needed to turn over to someone else so he might get on with his own life unencumbered.

Admitting that no longer hurt as it once had. In fact, she was beginning to develop a reluctant understanding of his position, though she still fiercely resented his characterization of her family.

She had to smile, recalling that the only man she'd had any interest in being turned over to was the one man in London Rob seemed most to dislike.

He was also the one person she'd missed most since leaving England. How many times had she met some unusual or interesting new personage, experienced a new sight or smell or taste, and wished Will were here to share it with her! How often she'd imagined his reaction to some new circumstance, wished she might have the benefit of his intelligent observations or smiled to think of the witty rejoinders he might have made.

She missed the friendship they'd developed, where she might express what she thought and felt without eliciting the alarmed or disapproving looks her comments sometimes evoked in her Italian family and servants.

Just as keenly, she missed the titillating warmth of being near Will, the velvet timbre of his voice that could send shivers of wicked delight across her skin, the look from those vivid blue eyes that made her lips and cheeks burn and her stomach churn with need.

She placed a hand over it now. If it had been Will instead of the count who wished to stroll in the dark garden with her, or tiptoe up to her chamber to help her into—or out of—her night rail, she would have had a very different response.

Where might he be now? she wondered. Waltzing across some ballroom with one of the ladies on her list? Or perhaps even engaged to be married?

If he wasn't yet, he soon would be. His love of Brookwillow was too strong for him to shrink from doing whatever he must to secure its restoration.

If she ever wished to contact him again, she should do so before he pledged his troth to another woman. Unlike Rob, who believed Will possessed no sense of honor, Allegra knew that once he exchanged his vows, though he might dally discreetly, he would never distress or embarrass his wife by openly corresponding with another woman.

Suddenly she felt the overwhelming need to share all that she'd experienced with Will before that event occurred. Besides, she'd promised to let him know how she was doing, hadn't she?

Fired by the greatest sense of enthusiasm and purpose she'd experienced since finding Papa's family, Allegra carried a brace of candles to her desk, took out a quill, ink and paper and began to write.

THREE WEEKS LATER, Will sat at his desk, reading through again the missive he'd received this morning from Allegra. His heart had leapt in his chest when Phillips had handed him the post and he'd seen the letter with his name upon it in her flowing hand. Wanting to savor it, he'd waited until after the day's work was completed to take it into the library where, glass of wine in hand, he meant to slowly devour every word.

Even after having read it through twice, though, the news she'd conveyed still astounded him. As the full import sank in, he threw back his head and laughed.

Allegra Antinori, scorned by the ton as the daughter of a lowly musician, was in truth the granddaughter of a duke. Indeed, a duchessa in her own right. The woman he'd once asked to marry him outranked him by several degrees!

The Malverns' travels must have taken them beyond the reach of the regular post, for surely they knew of this and if they'd conveyed the news to London, Lucilla would have heard it. He had no doubt that, knowing how isolated he was from ton gossip, she would have informed him at once.

As proud and fiercely grateful as he was to learn of her radical rise in station, the dismaying implications of her news soon sobered him.

'Twas unthinkable now to imagine going to Italy and begging Allegra to return with him as the wife of a lowly baron on an insignificant bit of English countryside. Not when her grandfather doubtless envisioned arranging a grand match for her with a gentleman of the highest rank.

For a moment, the pain that squeezed his chest robbed him of breath. As it eased, he picked up his wineglass with trembling hand and downed a large swallow. His hard work at Brookwillow, he thought sardonically, had done little to accomplish one purpose for which he'd originally thought to bury himself in the country. Allegra Antinori still had a stranglehold upon his heart.

Of course, he'd made no real attempt to free himself of his love for her. Instead, after leaving London he'd thrown himself into the work at Brookwillow, believing each step he took in its restoration brought him closer to the day when he might leave England to search for her.

With the aid of some tenants along with craftsmen hired from the city, the manor's whole roof and all the rotten wall beams had been replaced so that the structure was now secure against rain and wind. He'd sent the tenants back to their fields with the interior still incomplete, planning to reassemble the working party during the winter while the land lay fallow. Though much still needed to be done, he'd been able to have the furniture moved back into the rooms for which it had been designed and to open up the library for daily use.

The fields, too, had responded to the attention lavished on them. If the weather held fair and the summer rains were plentiful, Brookwillow should produce its first saleable crop since his father's death.

In fact, everything had been progressing toward realizing his dream for Brookwillow. Its fields would soon be waving with ripening wheat, its rooms repainted and repapered, its marble front hallway gleaming, the coffered ceilings restored to original splendor. He'd smiled as he went about his work, a glow of pride and anticipation warming him as he envisioned finding Allegra, rescuing her from a life of penury and bringing her home to be mistress of Brookwillow.

Except she no longer needed him to search for or rescue her. Brookwillow might be looking better than it had in years, but he could offer Allegra nothing to compare to the wealth, power or position she now enjoyed.

He swallowed hard, staring into his wineglass as he forced himself to face that bitter truth. He should reply to her letter, congratulate her on her good fortune, and finally begin the process he should have started months ago of trying to purge her from his mind and heart.

Except…except. Snatching up her letter, he reread the last part again. "My grandfather's estate at San Gregillio is so beautiful, Will," she wrote, "I would love you to see it. If you—and your new bride, for I know you must soon be married—should ever embark on a tour of the Continent, I do hope you'll stop and visit. I should be so delighted to meet you again and hear all the news of home…" After thanking him for his kindness, she had signed the letter, then added "Please do come if you can."

It seemed she was quite anxious for him to visit. Amid all the good news and the many and interesting experiences she recounted since leaving England, did he detect a note of homesickness? Might she be lonely, longing as desperately to see him as he was to see her?

Might he still have a chance to win her?

You, Will Tavener, are a hopeless dreamer, he told himself, throwing the letter down in disgust. *Reading between the lines of her note not what she's written but what you hope might be there.*

The paper drifted down to settle next to the list of eligible maidens she'd given him before her departure. He kept it propped on his desk in honor of the lady who'd inspired him to seize his life in his own hands and begin the restoration of Brookwillow.

With hard work—and Domcaster's funds—he'd accomplished more than he would have dreamed possible a year ago. Might he succeed too at the seemingly impossible task of winning her hand?

Was it even fair for him to attempt it, now that persuading her to come back to Brookwillow would mean so enormous a drop in status for her?

Unable to decide, he jumped up and paced the library, his thoughts zigzagging back and forth between the desire to seek her out and the resolution to refrain.

He was still pacing when Barrows entered to join him in a glass of brandy. Another benefit of living far from the censorious eyes of the ton, Will reflected, was being able to freely associate with this man who, like the Phillipses, had since boyhood been as much friend as servant.

Observing Will's activity and the expression on his face, Barrows raised his eyebrows as he walked over to pour himself a glass. "What catastrophe has befallen us now?" he asked. "Has Domcaster decided to call in his loan?"

"No disaster," Will replied. "At least, nothing of that sort."

"Then I must conclude this proclivity to frantic motion has something to do with the letter from Italy that arrived this morning. I hope the young lady hasn't fallen into difficulties."

Will laughed shortly. "Quite the opposite. It seems she rediscovered the family of her father—which just happens to possess a dukedom."

"How fortunate for the young lady," Barrows replied, studying Will's face. "You will offer her my congratulations when you send your own, I trust."

Will looked away. "I...I am considering delivering those congratulations in person. She's invited me to visit, you see," he said, striding over to his desk and holding up the letter. "To tour her grandfather's estate. With the work on the house on hold until winter and the crops already planted, I've half a mind to go. 'Twould be a marvelous opportunity to visit the Continent— and see how she is faring, of course."

Barrows uttered a long-suffering sigh. "I best begin packing our bags, then. No, not a word about leaving me to supervise the estate while you go loping off to Italy. You forced me to remain in London when you brought Miss Antinori to Brookwillow the first time, and see what a botch you made of that."

"It isn't as if I'll need your *expert* assistance to try to persuade her to come back with me," Will said irritably. "She's a bloody *duchessa* now, for heaven's sake. Besides, you've never before interfered in my affairs of the heart."

"I've never before had to serve you while you prowled around like a bear with a sore paw, snapping at everything. Oh, you've been better since we returned to Brookwillow, but if I were to let you go alone and you failed to win Miss Antinori this time, I daresay you'd be so intolerable upon your return to England that I might have to let the razor slip the first time I shaved you."

For a bleak moment, Will considered what his life would be, stripped of any hope of winning Allegra. "If I came back without her, I'd probably want you to."

Barrows tipped back the rest of the brandy. "Exactly," he said, setting down the glass. "So how soon do we leave?"

CHAPTER TWENTY-ONE

NEAR NOON TWO WEEKS LATER, Allegra strolled a graveled allée in the formal garden, relishing the shade provided by the sculpted yews and the wind-drifted moisture from the fountains. Already the afternoon promised to be scorching.

A reluctant Signora Bertrude sat on a nearby bench beside a wilted maid, both fanning themselves, having failed to persuade Allegra that 'twas already too hot to venture into the garden. But after being confined to the house all morning by visitors and feeling too restless to remain shuttered within until the evening cool made walking outside pleasant again, Allegra had insisted on coming now.

She was about to take pity on her attendants when a footman trotted up. "There's a gentleman come to see you, Duchessa," he said.

Allegra suppressed a groan. "Offer him refreshment, Federico, but tell him 'tis too sultry for me to receive any more visitors this morning. I shall see him tonight."

"So I already told him, Duchessa, but he was most insistent that I at least bring you his card." The footman held it out to her, shaking his head in disapproval. "A *foreign* gentleman, English, I think, who speaks our language not very well."

One special English gentleman came immediately to mind—but that was impossible. Still, a tremor of anticipation fluttered in her stomach as she seized the card—then uttered a cry of pure joy.

Will! Unbelievable as it seemed, it really was Will. Of course, she *had* invited him, so it wasn't totally beyond credibility that he'd come, but it had only been a few weeks since she'd written…

She took a deep breath and pulled her wits together. "Please escort him here immediately, Federico."

About to walk off, the footman stopped short. "Bring him here? Now? Are you sure, Duchessa?"

"Yes. At once."

Looking mystified, the footman bowed and went off.

Her heart commenced to pound and she could feel her cheeks flush. Suddenly nervous, Allegra smoothed her dress and patted her hair to make sure the chignon was still in place. If only this yellow morning gown wasn't already rumpled and she perspiring from the heat!

"You mean to receive the *foreigner* here?" Signora Bertrude walked to Allegra's side, disapproval on her face. "Please, Duchessa, not in the seclusion of the garden! Let us go into the house, where I may summon a footman—"

"Nonsense, signora," Allegra interrupted impatiently. "'Tis beautiful here and cool enough beside the fountains. Lord Tavener is not going to ravish me. Not on this hot a morning," she added, to the scandalized gasp of the duenna.

She could still scarcely believe Will was here. As she could scarcely prevent herself from running in to meet him, so eager was she to verify it really was him. Her nerves in knots, she made herself resume strolling.

What could have brought him here, almost as if the invitation in her letter had summoned him? Perhaps he was on his wedding trip…but no, he hadn't sent in his wife's card, which he surely would have done if he were married. He must have come alone.

And why now? When she'd last seen him, he'd been utterly determined, as well he should be, to do what he must to obtain the funds he needed for Brookwillow. Though she'd written in the wistful hope he might eventually visit, she'd never dreamed it would be this soon.

A sudden misgiving brought her pacing to a halt. Will depended on gaming for much of his income, she knew. Could he have suffered a run of losses so severe that he'd been forced to flee England to escape his creditors?

It seemed the only logical explanation for his sudden appearance. Otherwise he ought to still be occupied in charming his heiress, or if already wed, have returned with his bride to Brookwillow to begin the work of restoration.

Before she could puzzle it through, Will himself walked out onto the terrace, spotted her and smiled.

Her heart skipped a beat. It might be only the heat, to which she was not yet fully accustomed, but as he approached, the fiery blue of his gaze fixed upon her, Allegra felt hot, then cold, then dizzy. She reached out to steady herself on a bench, telling herself she absolutely would not swoon, like some silly heroine in a Minerva Press novel.

By the time he reached her side, every nerve was quivering. Somehow she managed to curtsey without falling over. "What a wonderful surprise, Will!" she said through the constriction in her throat. "But what brings you to San Gregillio?"

He took her hand and kissed it. For a moment Allegra feared she would faint after all.

"I seem to remember I received an invitation," he replied, amusement in his tone.

Her eyelashes drifted shut as she thrilled to the familiar sound of his voice. Which changed to a deeper, more intimate timbre as he continued, "Living at San Gregillio must agree with you, Allegra. You've never looked more beautiful. Ah, I can't tell you how wonderful it is to see you again!"

She looked back at him, knowing she must be grinning like a lunatic as she drank in every dearly remembered feature of his face—the waves of dark hair curling onto his forehead, the high cheekbones, patrician nose and purposeful chin, the sensuous, sculpted lips and mesmerizing eyes. Her gaze wandered downward over the powerful shoulders and muscled arms that could both threaten and protect, well displayed by his tight coat.

She couldn't seem to stop staring at him. Indeed, it was all she could do not to throw herself in his arms. How had she managed to exist so many months without him?

A loud "harrump" startled her into realizing that her duenna was standing beside them, a reproving frown on her face. "Um, Lord Tavener, may I present my chaperone, Signora Bertrude?"

"Un grande onore, Signora," Will said, bowing. "How gracious of you to receive me on such short notice, Duchessa. The garden is magnificent. Might you do me the honor of strolling with me?" He offered his arm.

Though Signora Bertrude would probably scold her for a week for not inviting him back into the coolness of the house—where a bevy of maids and footmen would watch their every move—Allegra couldn't make herself do it. Seizing this excuse to be with him, listen to his voice and feast her eyes upon his handsome face, she ignored the duenna's negative shake of the head.

"It shall have to be a brief walk," she said, "for 'tis almost one, when the afternoon rest begins." She placed her hand on his arm, reveling in the warmth and strength of it beneath her fingertips. "So, tell me all the London news!"

They set off at a leisurely pace, Allegra's disgruntled duenna reluctantly following. "I haven't much news, actually. I've…not been in London."

When he didn't add that he'd come from Brookwillow, a frisson of concern stirred within her. So he must be fleeing from gaming debts, then. Well, she'd insure that he found a safe haven here.

"I see," she said after a moment. "I hope you can make a lengthy visit. 'Tis expected here. One of grandfather's cousins arrived the same day I did and he is still with us. Oh, there's so much I want to show you!"

His smile turned tender. "Everything I want to see is before my eyes right now," he said softly.

Voice catching in her throat, Allegra felt heat suffuse her already flushed cheeks. Heavens, she felt as flustered as a schoolroom chit at her first ball.

"I see I shall have to continue my lessons on deportment, my lord, since you still manage so easily to put me to the blush. I must warn you, the rules are very strict here! You shall have to be on your best behavior."

"Lest your grandfather show me the door? Then I shall do my best to be perfectly conventional."

Allegra doubted he could manage that, but it was reassuring that he meant to try. "You must meet my cousin Alessandro, the duke's grandson and heir. He will be delighted to have a British guest, as he loves to practice his English. And Grandfather will be honored to host the gentleman who treated me with such kindness in London."

"I look forward to meeting them. Should I describe to the duke how impressed and honored I was to attend one of your father's concerts—or is his musical career not to be mentioned?"

"Grandfather will love hearing about it. He never

tires of asking me details about Papa's life in England. But…though of course I don't wish you to prevaricate, it might be best if you don't tell Grandfather about your losses. I shall avoid mentioning them to him as well."

"Losses?" Will repeated.

Allegra cast a quick glance at the duenna plodding behind them. She didn't think Signora understood much English, but 'twas better to be safe. Lowering her voice, she said softly, "Your gaming losses. 'Tis why you came to Italy now, isn't it, to avoid your creditors? It must have been most distressing to have to put off your plans for restoring Brookwillow."

Will opened his lips to reply, then closed them. Realizing she must have embarrassed him, Allegra went on quickly, "No matter. You must stay here until your fortunes are on the mend. The house is always full of guests, and many of the gentlemen play cards in the evenings, sometimes for quite high stakes. Once you've observed them and learned the rules, you could join their games and perhaps win enough to be able to return home. As long as he never suspects your financial straits, Grandfather will be happy to have a titled English gentleman staying with us. I'm sure you will charm him as you do everyone else."

By now they'd made a full circuit of the inner garden and were approaching the house. "We must go in now, Duchessa," Signora Bertrude said, giving Will a ferocious glance, as if daring him to contradict her. "'Tis late and you need your rest."

More likely, the signora needed hers. But much as Allegra would have preferred walking the garden the whole afternoon, keeping Will's company all to herself, she replied, "Very well, Signora. Escort me in, won't you, Lord Tavener? Gorgio, Grandfather's majordomo, will prepare a room and provide you a valet if you need one."

"Barrows accompanied me. By the way, he asked that I convey to you his congratulations."

Allegra felt a measure of relief. Things must not be quite so grim if Will had been able to bring his rascal of a servant with him. "Give him my thanks—but pray, don't let anyone see you hobnobbing with him. Such a thing is never done here! Now, I must go in."

Just then Signora bent down to remove a pebble from her shoe. Deciding on impulse to take advantage of the moment, Allegra went up on tiptoe and kissed Will's cheek.

"I'm so glad you're here," she said again. Then, re- luctantly releasing his arm, she entered the house and proceeded up to her room.

Giddy, Allegra danced around her chamber, her per- plexed maid following behind her, trying to remove her half-unfastened gown. It was as if her life had been suspended since she'd come to Italy, frozen into timeless immobility while she waited for something or someone to set it back in motion.

It seemed that something, that someone was Will. She couldn't wait to talk with him again, to walk with her hand on his arm, to share with him all her experiences.

Then she'd try to tactfully discover the true state of his affairs, so she might figure out how best to help him.

Guilty as it ought to make her feel, she rejoiced at the ill fortune that had forced him to leave England unwed and had brought him here. The sun had seemed brighter, the sky bluer, the birdsong more melodious because he'd walked beside her along the garden path.

The beauty of her grandfather's estate had soothed and delighted her since the moment she'd first seen it. But the prospect of sharing its wonders with Will multiplied that delight until her joy overflowed. Though it had brought her a deep satisfaction to discover she was not alone in the world after all, that she had a family, there had still been something missing.

Having Will here made her happiness complete.

By now her maid had finally succeeded in removing her gown and helping her into the light robe she wore over her chemise while she took her afternoon rest. After wishing her a good nap, the girl withdrew.

Hot as it was, Allegra wasn't drowsy. How could she sleep knowing Will was here in this very house? After months without him, it maddened her to know 'twas impossible to seek him out, that she must wait until evening to see him again, though he must even now be only a few rooms away.

Was he chatting with Barrows while the valet unpacked his belongings? Admiring the symmetry of the gardens outside his window? Or preparing, as she'd just done, to take an afternoon rest?

Ah, she thought with a wicked grin, that she might act his valet. She imagined removing his jacket, plucking open the buttons of his waistcoat, freeing his neck from the starched prison of his neckcloth…kissing the hollow of his naked throat, the pulse throbbing against her lips.

Like the throbbing that pulsed deep within her. Lips and breasts tingling, she remembered the kiss they'd shared in Hyde Park the night she'd said goodbye before leaving London. How she hungered to kiss him again under the stars—and this time, not have to stop.

Sighing with frustrated desire, she threw herself on the sofa and gazed out at the garden, shimmering with heat and shadow in the afternoon sun. How would she manage more than the quick peck on the cheek she'd just stolen, as encumbered as she was with duennas, maids and footmen? But manage it she would.

She intended to lick every droplet of pleasure she could savor from his visit. Indeed, if she could have her way, he would never leave again.

Suddenly the truth struck her with such blinding clarity, she sat bolt upright. How could she have been too dull-witted not to have realized it long ago?

It wasn't Rob she loved—and never had been. She was in love with Will. Once she admitted that, all the pieces of her emotional puzzle fell into perfect place.

That explained why his wit so amused her and his observations so intrigued her, why she wanted to share all her thoughts and experiences with him, why she felt so safe and at ease with him, why she preferred his company to anyone else's. 'Twas much more than the "friendship" she'd termed it that made her miss him so keenly, yearn for his company and ache for his touch.

How could she have thought she loved Lynton, when even as she contemplated marrying her cousin, her whole being had stirred at Will's presence and burned for his caress?

But how did Will feel about her? When he'd offered for her—it seemed a lifetime ago now—he'd assured her of his respect and affection. But did he love her? Was that why he'd come to Italy so quickly after receiving her invitation?

Allegra frowned, worrying her lip between her front teeth. If he loved her, she could imagine nothing more wonderful than spending the rest of her life with him. Except…though he'd not flirted with her comely young maid in the garden—who, she'd noticed, had watched Will with appreciative eyes—how could she determine if he'd given up his rogue's ways?

Knowing she loved him, she'd be even less able to endure infidelity than when he'd offered for her. Dare she risk marrying him?

But if he truly loved her…

If he truly loved her, if he burned for her as she did for him, if like her, he could imagine letting no one else share his bed and his life, it would be worth the risk. Especially if they spent their lives at Brookwillow, far from the blandishments of bored London matrons.

She knew he was as attracted to her as she was to

him. When they visited London, she'd just have to be so alluring and indefatigable that he was kept too busy—and satisfied—to have time or energy to respond to the lures cast his way by the aforementioned matrons.

Having gotten the idea of wedding Will into her head, she now seemed unable to pry it back out. She knew Grandfather would prefer her to marry an Italian. Though amenable to hosting her English gentleman, he would almost certainly forbid a marriage between them, especially if he learned of Will's financial difficulties.

But grateful as she was to her grandfather, this was her life and her happiness. Living in a pampered cocoon of wealth had been pleasant, but wealth alone, as she'd found these last three months, brought but a hollow satisfaction. Besides, she'd spent so little of her life in luxury that she'd not grown accustomed enough to miss it.

Not nearly as much as she would miss Will if she lost him again. More than she'd ever wanted anything, she realized with a wistful pang, she wanted to marry Will, return with him to Brookwillow and spend the rest of her life helping him restore it.

Which was probably the time it would require, since if Grandfather disapproved their match, he would not be disposed to settle any dowry on a granddaughter who, like his son, planned to abandon him and live in a foreign land.

She would regret disappointing him and would always be grateful for his loving welcome here. But she would not give up Will, no matter how much Grandfather objected.

But that was putting the cart in front of the horse. First, she needed to determine if Will returned her love.

Lounging back on the sofa, Allegra gazed out at the azure sky, pondering how best to proceed. Somehow she was going to have to figure out how a lady determined the depth of a gentleman's regard without asking him directly.

And no less than her entire future happiness depended upon succeeding.

CHAPTER TWENTY-TWO

IN THE ROOM to which the butler conducted him, Will stood before the glass, touching the cheek her lips had brushed. The skin seemed to burn against his fingers, as if still smoldering from her imprint.

At that proof of her gladness at seeing him again, he'd been tempted to wrap her in his arms and hug the breath from her, despite the presence of that disapproving dragon of a duenna.

How she'd dazzled him, walking in the blinding noon light in that pale yellow gown! So must the denizens of the ark of yore have felt when, after forty days of storm, they finally saw the sun crowning the heavens. His needy soul soaked up her radiance and thirsted for more.

Until he'd seen her today, he thought he'd been getting on with his life at Brookwillow. Now he realized he'd only been existing, marking time until he came again into the light of her presence.

Though the ducal palazzo of the Antinoris was even more opulent than he'd envisioned, making starker the contrast between what her family possessed and what he could offer her, seeing her again made his determination to win her all the stronger. And yet…

Sighing, he walked from the mirror to gaze out his window at the geometric precision of the formal flower gardens. The debate within him erupted again between whether to declare himself and ask for her hand, or simply drink in the pleasure of her company one last time before leaving her to a wealth and luxury far beyond what he could ever provide for her.

But he needn't make that decision now. He could take time to watch her, listen closely and determine if she seemed happy in her new life, or if beneath the pretty gowns and milling servants lay a reservoir of yearning.

For England…and for him?

At that moment, Barrows strolled in. "We've certainly landed in opulent surroundings this time, m'lord."

"Opulent indeed."

"I suppose you're already thinking it impossible to press your suit on so rich and privileged a lady."

Will sighed. "She would be coming down in the world."

"Depends on your outlook, my good sir. If I were of a philosophical turn of mind, I'd say that wealth alone is empty, that one's existence means nothing without love and purpose. Not, mind you, that I've ever possessed enough wealth to test the theory. I can affirm, however, that friendship ameliorates the despair of poverty and makes want bearable."

"She's hardly in want," Will observed.

Barrows shrugged. "Not by worldly standards, perhaps. But I recommend you watch and see."

"Thank you, Sir Philosopher. 'Tis what I'd just concluded. By the way," Will added with a chuckle, "she's taken it into her head that we're here because I lost what little fortune I possessed gaming and was forced to flee to the Continent. I suppose I ought to be insulted."

Barrows laughed. "You might, if the observation weren't so dangerously close to the mark! Knowing you'd pledged to marry and restore Brookwillow, 'tis not an unreasonable conclusion after our precipitous arrival."

"The misconception isn't that important. I can correct it whenever I wish."

"Indeed. First you must run the gauntlet of sufficiently impressing her grandfather and cousin so you may remain here long enough to discover if she loves you."

"I might succeed in getting invited to stay, but I'm not lovesick enough to imagine that, even apprised of my actual situation, the family that can provide so lavishly for her would ever countenance my suit."

"Don't bother about that yet. Keep your wits about you, observe keenly and await the right moment. I'll apply my perspicacity and acumen, too, of course."

Though Barrows had always shown himself to be innovative and resourceful, Will doubted his valet's skills extended to magically altering his circumstances enough to win the approval of Allegra's grandfather. But no sense giving up before he even began. "You do that."

THAT EVENING, to escape the press of guests and the stifling atmosphere of heat, smoke, candle wax and perfume, Will strolled out to the grand terrace. Watching the stars in the clear sky, he breathed deeply and flexed his shoulders, loosening the tension.

At dinner he'd finally met Allegra's grandfather, who had greeted him cordially and listened with what appeared to be genuine interest as Will described the concert by Emilio Antinori he'd once attended. After dinner, the duke had shown him a mark of favor by seeking him out when the gentlemen enjoyed their brandy and cigars, asking Will questions about his estate back in England.

From his conversation, the duke appeared to be a keen-witted, formidable man who earned Will's immediate respect. He liked Allegra's cousin, the young duke Alessandro, as well. Listening to the discussion among the guests this evening, he'd gleaned some insight into the tangled nature of local politics and sympathized with the difficulties that lay ahead for the young man, trying to preserve his heritage through what promised to be a turbulent future. Not envying him the task, Will offered the Almighty a silent thanks that Brookwillow was located in the relative peace and prosperity of England.

And as for Allegra—his heart expanded with love and longing just remembering her. She'd sat at the head of the table beside her grandfather, radiantly beautiful in an elaborate gown of pure white, the gracious hostess ever attentive to the duke's guests. She looked like an angel.

Would that she might be his!

So full of guests was the drawing room tonight, he'd not yet had a chance to speak with her. So when he spied her ahead of him on the terrace, trailed once again by her dour duenna, he went in pursuit.

"Good evening, Duchessa," he called to her. To his delight she turned and, recognizing him, stopped to wait for him. "'Tis a beautiful night, the stars gleaming like diamonds on velvet. May I walk with you?"

"I should be delighted, Lord Tavener," she replied.

She took his arm, capturing him in a haze of warmth and lavender scent. His body stirring, he nearly groaned at the pleasure of it. For several minutes they strolled in silence, wrapped in the magical mantle of night and starlight. Will could not help but remember the starry night she'd said goodbye to him…that unforgettable kiss that had shaken him to the core. Did she remember it, too?

He wanted nothing more than to kiss her again.

As if on cue, Barrows emerged from the shadows and approached the duenna, one hand grasping his other wrist as he held it up and out. From what he pantomimed to the duenna, he had cut himself and needed her assistance

Not easily distracted from her charge, the duenna seemed to be telling him where in the house to return for assistance, instructions Barrows apparently did not understand in the slightest. While he gestured to the agitated duenna, Will rounded the corner with Allegra.

For several precious seconds, they would be alone, hidden from view by the dark bulk of the sculpted yew.

As if by unspoken agreement, they both halted. Allegra looked up at him, a tremulous smile on her lips. Will took her chin in his hand and tipped it up so he could read her eyes. The yearning he saw there sent a thrill of anticipation and desire through him. Then she stepped closer and closed her eyes, apparently eager for the kiss he was more than ready to give her.

The first brush of his lips against hers was gentle, reverent. Then need and longing merged in an explosive imperative that compelled him to tighten his embrace while his lips on hers turned hard and urgent.

Instead of struggling or protesting, she leaned into him, a little moan escaping her lips.

Lost then, Will bound her to him, devouring her lips, invading her mouth, pursuing the tongue that fenced eagerly with his. There was a roaring in his ears and blood thundered through his veins in a fierce, primitive rhythm that said *mine, mine*.

She was his; she must be. One way or another, he was going to win her and bring her home.

Barrows's loud, theatrical cry of warning dragged him back to the present. Reluctantly, he broke the kiss.

Allegra stepped away from him as well, smoothing her gown before placing a trembling hand on his arm. Before he could decide whether or not to apologize, she nudged him into motion. "Your valet is a most valuable employee. I hope you pay him well."

"For allowing me moments like the one just past, I don't pay him nearly enough."

"Ah, for more such moments." Allegra sighed.

Hardly daring to hope, he said, "You would have more?"

"A lifetime," she murmured. "And you?"

"A lifetime is not long enough," he said with feeling.

Before Will could press her further, see if by her reply she meant what he hoped she did, footsteps approached from behind them. He turned to see Allegra's grandfather walking with a tall older man in evening dress, the jeweled medallion of some legion of merit hung on a ribbon about his neck.

"Ah, here you are, Allegra, Lord Tavener," the duke said. "Count von Strossen, allow me to present Lord Tavener, a friend of my granddaughter who is visiting us from England. Count von Strossen is the…local representative for the Austrian government, Lord Tavener."

It required only the moment it took Will to read the proprietary gaze the Austrian had fixed on Allegra for him to take a dislike to the man. Though the count gave Will a slight bow, his eyes remained on Allegra.

"My dear," her grandfather continued, "Alessandro needs your assistance in the ballroom."

"Then I shall go at once, *nonno*. Lord Tavener…" She pressed Will's hand before releasing it with obvious reluctance. "Thank you again for visiting, my lord. I hope to see much of you in the coming days."

"Let me walk you in," the count said.

"'Tis kind of you to offer, but I wouldn't dream of interrupting your conversation with Grandfather."

Will wondered if the coolness in her tone was as obvious to the Austrian as it was to him. Ebullient with relief, he relaxed. Covetous Von Strossen might be, but it was clear to Will that Allegra had no interest in him.

The count stood silently watching Allegra walk into the house before turning back to his host. "'Tis the loveliest bloom in your garden, my good sir. Enjoy it, for you shall not keep it long."

"Having just discovered so rare and lovely a blossom, I have no desire to lose it just yet," the duke replied.

"Ah, but a rose should be picked at its peak."

"'Tis well known that Antinori roses are always at their peak," the duke countered.

"You are correct, I am sure." The count gave the duke a thin smile. "However, its most ardent admirer is quite impatient to sample its fragrance."

"Patience and self-discipline will make the prize all the sweeter," the duke advised.

"But if the admirer becomes too impatient, he may feel compelled to pluck the rose whether the gardener is ready to relinquish it or not."

"Pluck the rose" indeed! Anger burned in Will as he listened, wishing he had the right to confront the count. But this was the duke's domain. He had no choice but to allow Allegra's grandfather to handle the man—with honeyed innuendo rather than the fists Will would have preferred.

"Such an admirer would do well not to provoke the wrath of the gardener, who guards his rose well," the duke was saying.

"A gardener who wished to prosper would be prudent not to foil the desires of one who has the power to strip from him both rose and garden," the count replied, his tone silky.

"A man who would yield his prize and his garden so meekly does not deserve either," the duke riposted.

"Indeed." The count's lips twitched as if he were suppressing a smile. "Let us hope this gardener has the wisdom to manage his garden prudently."

"Let us indeed," the duke agreed. He turned away from the count as a footman approached.

"Il Duce, some of the guests would like to pay their respects before returning home," the servant said.

The duke turned to Will and the count. "Excuse me, please, but I must go in. Do linger and enjoy the night air." With a bow to them both, the duke walked off.

Covertly Will inspected Von Strossen. He thought it unlikely that the count, who'd subjected Allegra to intense scrutiny, could have failed to notice that her treatment of Will was far warmer than the chilly indifference she offered him. So Will was not surprised when the count turned his penetrating gaze in Will's direction.

The man actually looked down his aquiline nose at Will, his expression haughtier and more disdainful than Lynton at his most imperious. Will curled his hands into fists, his fingers itching inside his gloves.

"Lord—Tavener, is it? You are English, no? I was at the Congress of Vienna and I do not recall hearing such a name. You must be a person of no great importance. Nonetheless, let me offer you a bit of friendly advice."

Will wished he might reply with the insult trembling on his tongue, but he didn't want to create an incident at the court of Allegra's grandfather. So instead he said, "And what would that be?"

"Do not turn your eyes to the Duchessa. She will be mine, and I do not suffer other men to approach her."

"How can you be so sure? She does not appear to hold you in much affection," Will pointed out.

The count shrugged. "Her opinion is of little importance. An alliance with the Antinoris would help solidify the position of my administration in this country, quiet some of the clamor of the lackwits who think Italy should be independent—as if this weak, puling mass of petty principalities could ever manage to shape itself into a nation! So for the advantage of us both, I have determined to take the Duchessa as my bride."

"Whether she wishes to be or not?"

"As I said," the count repeated a bit impatiently, "her wishes are of little importance. If her grandfather the duke knows what is good for him, he will see that she does her duty. And I must confess, a little resistance in a bride makes the game more satisfying. Ah, how I shall enjoy taming that one! She so whets my appetite with her constant temptation, I'm not sure how much longer I can wait to claim her. And so I warn you—set your eyes on another, or go back to your little island."

Ignoring with some difficulty the insults that speech had contained, Will said, "What if the lady has already made her choice—and acted upon it?"

Once more the count studied Will, as if he were an insect under glass. "Is this so, or do you say it to incite me? No matter. If she should come to me not entirely pure, that would be an…irritation. But it would not stay my purpose. Indeed, the prospect of punishing her for her indiscretion is quite…arousing. A punishment that would be severe enough to insure she does not stray again. There must be no question that the von Strossen sons she bears me are truly mine."

Just then, a man in a military uniform approached the count. Holding up a finger to halt the man, the Austrian bowed to Will. "A most illuminating conversation, Lord Tavener. I trust nothing more needs to be said."

"Of that you can be sure, Count von Strossen," Will replied, seething as he returned the count's bow.

Will had half a mind to follow the count into the ballroom and slap a glove in his arrogant face in front of all the assembled guests. But doing so would create the incident Will still wished to avoid.

But his threat—and his menace—were clear.

If the arrogant count ever got within a finger's reach of Allegra, it would be over Will's bloodless corpse.

Suddenly all the small details he'd overheard about

the current political situation in this region coalesced. Rather than protecting Allegra, her grandfather might be compelled to give her to this man if he wanted to preserve his birthright intact. Though looking well for his years, the duke was aging. The young grandson who would inherit the Antinori holdings would be no match for the count if, after the current duke's death, the ruthless von Strossen decided to strip the Antinoris of their lands.

Becoming the beloved wife of an obscure baron of a family of "no importance" would be far preferable to being forced to wed the repellant count.

If she were intent upon doing her duty to her new family, he might have to convince Allegra of that. He'd already hinted to her that he loved her and on the terrace tonight, she seemed to indicate she returned his affection.

There was but one certain way to insure she wed him and no one else. Allegra would never willingly give herself to another man once Will had made her his.

Desire long denied boiled up in him at the thought.

Nodding good-night to the guests he encountered, Will made his way to his room. He found Barrows on the balcony smoking a cheroot, gazing out at the night garden.

"Many thanks for your assistance," Will said.

Barrows bowed. "Thought a bit of obfuscation might do the trick. Devilish protective of their young maidens, these Italians."

"Indeed. Which is why I must once again call upon your expertise. I need to plan a seduction."

Tossing away the cheroot, Barrows grinned. "Pleased to be of service, my lord. When and where?"

CHAPTER TWENTY-THREE

MUCH LATER THAT NIGHT, Allegra returned to her chamber, the melody of the waltz she'd danced with Will still playing in her head. With his intelligent conversation and engaging wit, Will had impressed her grandfather and charmed the guests just as she'd expected he would. As she'd left to come upstairs, Alessandro had taken her aside to tell her he heartily approved of her cultured English lord.

And that kiss! 'Twas even more thrilling than the one in Hyde Park, for this time she was determined it should be but prelude and promise of the delights to come. She couldn't wait to kiss him again, to invite his caresses, to pledge her love before God and witnesses, so they might be bound together and never part again.

Her euphoria dimmed a little. Though Will seemed as avid for her company as she was for his, when she'd subtly pressed him, though he'd given her pretty words, he'd stopped short of a full declaration.

Might he be holding back because he now thought the disparity in their stations made a match between them impossible?

If so, then why had he told her "a lifetime would not be enough"? Too little time to love and protect her, she'd thought he meant. Could she be mistaken in thinking this? Did he want only a rogue's pleasure from her?

But when she thought of his kiss—tender, reverent and cherishing before passion ignited between them—she could not believe he'd simply been toying with her. With a certainty that went soul-deep, she knew he loved her.

So why hadn't he made a declaration? Might he have been about to speak when her grandfather and the count interrupted them on the terrace?

'Twas not the only time the count had interrupted her this evening, she recalled with a moue of distaste. He'd used his intimidating presence and slightly menacing gaze to chase every other eligible gentleman from her side—except, of course, for Will, who remained calmly impervious to both hints and threats.

Indeed, Allegra had the strong impression Will would welcome provoking the count into a round of fisticuffs so he might do some intimidating of his own. Of course, her grandfather would never tolerate such a quarrel among his guests, but how she would love to watch Will pummel some of the arrogance from the count's self-satisfied face!

Von Strossen was a troublesome presence she'd do well not to underestimate. Little as she liked him, he possessed the title, wealth and position to make him, in worldly terms, perhaps the most eligible of her suitors.

Suddenly she recalled Alessandro's comment that

she would be expected to marry well, just as he was, to advance the family's interests. An alliance with the new Austrian governor could be of great benefit to the Antinoris.

When the count made her an offer, which she was nearly certain he soon meant to do, would Grandfather expect her to accept it? *Require* her to accept it?

An unpleasant shiver rippled through her at the idea of being forced to marry the count. Allegra had come to love her grandfather and appreciated once again being part of a family, but she was not prepared to sacrifice herself to advance their political goals.

Grandfather had been wily enough to retain his title and keep his land while many aristocrats all over Italy had been stripped of both by the French and their local Jacobin allies. She had every confidence he would outwit the Austrian pretenders as well.

But she also sensed the count was not a man accustomed to being denied what he wanted. And he wanted her—whether or not she came willingly.

Was Will aware of the urgency of her situation?

If she wished to be sure of spending her life with the man she preferred, she couldn't wait until Will proceeded to a declaration at his own pace. She must discover without further delay whether he truly loved her and could be faithful to her.

And if he pledged that he did and he could… A thrill of excitement and desire shivered through her. There was only one sure way to bind herself to Will so inseparably that neither the count nor her grandfather would ever be able to part them. Despite the hovering presence of maids, footmen and duennas, she'd have to seduce him.

A little smile of anticipation playing about her lips, Allegra set her mind to figuring out how.

DETERMINED TO SECURE Allegra's safety before von Strossen could move against her, Will arose the next morning ready to put in motion the plan he'd formulated while lying sleepless through the night. Figuring it would be easier to spirit her away in daylight than after dark, when he risked alerting someone by stumbling around in unfamiliar surroundings, he decided to have her steal away this afternoon, while the heat drove everyone indoors.

He set Barrows to work investigating possible locations for the assignation, only to receive the inadvertent assistance of the duke himself. While the gentlemen partook of breakfast, the duke approached Will to thank him for his dinner conversation and invite him, as a fellow landholder, to tour his estate, that Will might compare the agricultural techniques employed at San Gregillio to those used in England.

And since his English guest seemed so appreciative of garden design, the duke added, Will mustn't miss viewing the garden house at the far end of the formal parterre. Within that small structure, a fountain surrounded by potted herbs and ferns refreshed air perfumed by the scent of jasmine, just now coming into full bloom.

Immediately after breakfast, Will sent Barrows to reconnoiter the spot. When his valet reported back that it seemed the perfect place for a secluded rendezvous, he told the man to make preparations and be ready to stand guard.

Next, Will penned Allegra a brief note begging her to meet him at three in the garden house. He sent Barrows to deliver it, trusting that the valet would be able to move about without suspicion in the afternoon while the guests were immured in their chambers. Whether Allegra would be able to steal away, he'd not discover until the rendezvous.

Confident she would come if she could, an hour after the guests retired, Will stealthily made his way to the garden house. He'd wait until dusk. If Allegra failed to arrive, he'd simply think of another plan for tomorrow.

Though the idea of finally being able to worship the body he'd yearned to caress for so long made him almost dizzy with need, Will also knew that making love to Allegra on the grounds of her grandfather's estate was dangerous. Should their tryst be discovered, they would be catapulted into a situation with immediate and unpredictable consequences.

Of one thing, however, he was sure. He must return to Brookwillow soon, and when he did, whatever he must do to accomplish it, Allegra was coming with him.

Hardly noting the charm of the little room or the enticing scent of jasmine, Will paced the travertine floor, anticipation, excitement and worry churning in his belly. He'd almost given up when a quick darting motion caught his eye—Allegra, moving along the screen of tall cypress trees that bordered both sides of the parterre.

As he waited for her to cross the last fifty yards, Will suddenly felt uncertain. Barrows, with his usual efficiency, had placed behind the garden bench several cushions and a thick, beautifully embroidered coverlet. The longer Will stared at them and the towels and water pitcher discreetly behind them, the more this looked like a crass, cold deflowering rather than a romantic rescue.

His attention distracted by that troubling image, Will jumped when a creak at the door announced Allegra's arrival. His heart lit with joy as she walked in.

"Thank you for coming," he said, taking her hand. "Did you have any difficulty—"

"No, everyone was sound asleep," she replied quickly. "Anyway, I should have done whatever it took to get here. Will, I've missed you so much! I thought I must go mad if I couldn't see you." With that, she came into his arms.

Grateful, greedy, he held her while she clung to him. She fit so perfectly there, he thought, listening to the thud of her heart beating against his. And suddenly, his doubts and worries vanished like spray from the fountains under the hot afternoon sun.

He didn't need to take her innocence by stealth, like a thief who filched what wasn't rightfully his. As if he were ashamed or afraid to confess his love to the world. No, he would announce his intentions boldly to her grandfather—and Count von Strossen.

If the Austrian tried to prevent Will from marrying Allegra, Will would be delighted to deal with him. As for her grandfather's objections, though Will would be sorry if he could not convince the duke to give them his blessing, the only consent he really needed was Allegra's.

He'd ask for her hand and if she accepted him, the pledging of her faith would be enough. He'd wait to enjoy her passion and innocence until their wedding night, when he would take her reverently, as a bridegroom should.

That resolution removing the weight that had burdened him, the loveliness of the garden house began to steal over his senses. Holding Allegra close, he let its magic wash over him: the dappled shadows cast by the trellises, the trickling play of the fountain, the heady scent of the delicate blooms peeping out from a swirl of glossy leaves.

Allegra pulled back within the circle of his arms. "It's lovely here, isn't it, Will? 'Tis one of my favorite places on the estate, especially with the jasmine in bloom. How I've longed to share it with you!"

"The loveliest thing on this estate is now in my arms," Will replied. Taking a deep breath, he went down on one knee before her. "Allegra, I've loved you since that first night at Lady Ormsby's rout. I loved you when I proposed the first time, though with you set on wedding Lynton, I dared not admit it. Let me joyfully affirm it now! Much as I love Brookwillow, I can offer you nothing to compare with what you have here, but if you marry me, you shall have my devotion in full measure. I shall work my whole life to make sure you never regret leaving this."

"Oh, Will," she whispered, her face luminescent. "I love you, too, so very much. There's nowhere I'd rather be than at your side. But…are you sure you could be faithful only to me? For I must warn you, I could not tolerate—"

"Idiot!" He chuckled as he stopped her lips with his finger. "How can you doubt that I want you and only you, for the rest of my life? But are *you* sure, my heart? Until recently, 'twas your cousin you'd always wanted."

"Please," she groaned, "don't remind me what a fool I was. But my blindness did serve some purpose. If I had realized sooner that I loved you instead of Rob, if I had accepted your first offer, we might have been wed and at Brookwillow when Signore DiCastello arrived in England. I might never have found Grandfather and Alessandro. Being away from you gave me time to purge my mind of my youthful delusions and learn who truly holds my heart. Indeed, should I meet Rob again, I could in all sincerity wish him happy with his chosen bride." She grinned. "With you beside me, I might even manage to be civil to Sapphira."

So thrilled was he by her affirmation that it took
him a moment to recall the one bit of London gossip
he knew she'd appreciate. Chuckling, he said, "You
shall not have to put civility to the test—yet. In anticipation of bringing home that bride, Lynton dispatched
his late father's widow to the family estate in Cumbria."

"Truly?" Allegra gasped. "Poor Sapphira! I can almost feel sorry for her. Well, I shall pray that her exile
leads her to revelations as wonderful as mine. Now, you
were about to ask me something?" she prompted.

"Indeed I was. Will you marry me, Allegra Antinori,
Duchessa di San Gregillio?"

"I will marry you gladly, Lord Tavener of Brookwillow. Now," she added, a naughty gleam in her eye,
"doesn't that call for a kiss?"

In no hurry, for she would be his now and they would
have all the time in the world—the rest of their lives—
he drew her chin down and touched her mouth with his.

More, more, his rampaging senses urged, but he tried
to ignore them. He could be patient. He could.

Well, perhaps a bit more, he conceded as Allegra's
tongue nudged his lips apart and slipped into his mouth.

Ah, he groaned at the pleasure of her tongue against
his. Soft, sibilant, stroking. The ravening beast of need
roared louder. Perspiration broke out on his brow, his
palms as he tried to resist it.

Knowing he could not stand much more temptation,
he drew back. But before he could imagine her intent,
Allegra started unknotting his cravat.

Uttering a strangled laugh, he caught her hands. "Allegra, what are you do—?"

She put her finger against his lips to still them. The knot disposed of, she began unwinding the neckcloth. He raised his hands again to stop her, then dropped them. The neckcloth was now ruined beyond repair anyway.

He took in a shuddering breath as, tossing the neck-cloth aside, she pulled open the top button of his shirt and placed her lips against the hollow of his throat.

"I've waited so long to do this," she murmured.

Heart hammering, his erection so hard its confinement within his breeches approached pain, he tried to protest. But his words died in a gasp as her tongue darted out to lick the moisture accumulating in the hollow of his throat.

He gasped again as, still kissing him, her busy fingers moved to unbutton his waistcoat. "'Tis too warm for this," she said.

Too warm indeed. He was afire with need, a controlled burning still, but all too close to exploding into raging conflagration.

Freeing him from his waistcoat, she started on the buttons of his shirt. Despite the fountain-moist air on his bare chest as she exposed more skin, the mere thought of her helping him disrobe nearly severed the few remaining fragments of his badly frayed control. This time, with trembling hands he made himself stop her.

"Don't, Allegra," he said urgently. "I've wanted you too badly for too long to resist much more. And I love you too dearly to take you for the first time here, on a garden-house floor. I want us to have a bed with fresh, flower-strewn sheets. I want to remove your wedding gown slowly, paying homage to each beautiful inch of you."

"I've wanted you just as long, Will," she countered. "And I don't want to wait. What could be lovelier than this place, spangled with sunlight and scented by jasmine? More important, I want to make sure that beginning today and forever after, I will belong to you and you alone."

"Because if I make you mine, you cannot be claimed by anyone else," he said, realizing then that she must be as aware of the danger posed by the count as he was. "So you *intended* me to…so that we—"

"Yes, and yes," she interrupted, smiling. "Love me now, Will. Please."

'Twas all he needed to evaporate his few remaining good intentions. Eagerly he raised his face to her kiss. Once again, he reveled in the dance of tongues, teasing, pursuing, evading, capturing. As he languidly explored her mouth, he began undoing the fastenings of her gown.

Fingers trembling, his breathing shallow, he freed her bodice as he tossed away his shirt. He made short work of her light stays, discarding them beside his shirt. And then drew back to admire the perfection of her full, plump breasts, clearly visible beneath the fine linen chemise.

Eyes glazed, her lips kiss-swollen, she gazed back at him. "Beautiful," he murmured and leaned forward to capture one dusky nipple.

She gasped as he used teeth and tongue, nibbling and suckling from areola to tip, dragging the wetted linen across her sensitized skin. She wrapped her fingers in his hair, holding his head to her breast.

She murmured in distress when he pulled away, then quieted as he spread the coverlet over the cool floor. The padded surface prepared, he guided her away from the bench and eased her down upon the soft embroidered cloth.

He paused long enough to reach toward the arbor and pluck one perfumed bloom. "The sweetness of the jasmine pales beside yours," he murmured, trailing the blossom across the rigid tips of her nipples before bending to follow with his lips the path of the flower. While he lavished his attention on her breast, he slid a hand under her skirts to caress her leg.

Suckling still, he stroked her thigh and hip, pushed the skirts up to expose the pale limbs beneath. Once again he drew the flower over her skin, from the round of her hip across the smooth inner thigh to nudge her legs apart.

He was trembling as much as she by the time he trailed the jasmine over her mound, down between her parted legs, over the fragrant moistness of her outer lips. Discarding the flower, with his fingers he cupped her, then rubbed gently as he moved his kiss back to her mouth.

He took her gasp on his tongue as he slowly parted the outer petals with his thumb and drew a finger over the rigid bud hidden within.

Ah yes, she was as passionate as he'd imagined, her breath turning to sobbing gasps as rhythmically he stroked within the tender folds. And while she hovered on the brink, he simply had to sample her, greedy to take the taste of her pleasure on his tongue and inhale her scent, more potent and heady than any flower.

She cried out when his mouth touched her. Fisting both hands in his hair, she began to undulate her hips rhythmically in time to his stroking tongue. Gauging his caresses to the rapidity of her movement and the raggedness of her breath, he kept her on the precipice, her cries of pleasure joyful in his ears before at last she crested, writhing with the intensity of climax.

Smiling, he kissed her eyelashes, her nose, her cheeks, then lay beside her and gathered her close, swallowing hard, his eyes wet with tears at the fierceness of the love swelling his chest.

For a few sweet minutes he watched her doze, so incredibly lovely with the dark moist tendrils curling upon her brow, her near-transparent chemise, damp from passion and his tender ministrations, molded around her ample breasts and luscious curves. He couldn't wait for her to awake so he might begin again.

As if upon the thought, her eyes fluttered open. Smiling, she touched his lips with her finger. "I love you, Will," she whispered. "Now let me love you." She reached for the straining buttons of his trouser flap.

Knowing his control would disintegrate the moment she touched him and wanting to make the wonder of this interlude last as long as possible, he seized her hand and kissed the fingers, then tucked it in his and bent to nibble her breasts. By the time he allowed her to free him from his breeches, he had once again used his lips and fingers on her breasts, her thighs, her slick inner passage to bring her a gasping, sobbing pleasure.

"Please, now, Will," she cried. "Make me yours."

Bracing himself with rigid arms, he positioned himself over her and slowly eased inside. Sweat popped out on his brow as he resisted the imperative to thrust hard and bury himself within her. "I...don't want...to hurt you," he gasped.

Apparently beyond speech, she shook her head and tilted her hips up to take him deeper. As gently as he could, he pressed down, until suddenly he passed the point of resistance and his cock descended in a slow satisfying slide to her very center.

She gasped, her nails biting into his back, then moved urgently beneath him. He moved with her, guiding her into the timeless rhythm of lovers' pleasure, gritting his teeth to stave off his own climax until he felt her cry out beneath him. And then gave himself up to the cataclysm.

Dizzy then, his heart hammering, he rolled over to his back, taking her with him to cradle against his chest. It seemed the most impossible of dreams come true that this beautiful, unabashedly passionate creature had pledged her heart and her future to him. Or that he would travel so far from Brookwillow to find the peace

ROGUE'S LADY

and joy of coming home to the place where he belonged, with her in his arms, pleasing her, delighting in her pleasure.

He must have dozed for a time as well, to awake weighted down by a sense of the most intense happiness. Then he realized Allegra, his beloved, soon to be his bride, lay against him, her head tucked on his shoulder.

"Incredible," he murmured, stroking the satin of her bare shoulder.

As she raised sleep-befuddled eyes to his, he whispered, "Time to wake, beloved. We must get you dressed as best we can and send you back before anyone misses you." After a lingering kiss that tempted him to begin all over again, he helped her to sit up.

"Not yet," she protested, tossing down the stays he handed her. "Oh, Will, you can't take me on the most exquisite, unbelievable journey I've ever experienced and expect me to simply go back to Signora Bertrude."

"But you must, my darling." Patiently he fitted the stays around her and fastened them.

"Well then, only if you promise to come to my room tonight," she said, reluctantly submitting to his ministrations.

"I cannot, my heart, and you mustn't tempt me," he said, slipping her bodice back up over her arms and haphazardly fastening the back. "When next we take that journey, I want you in my bed and I want you as my wife."

"That's all well and good, but when do you think you'll be able to afford for us to leave? We can't count on Grandfather's blessing and I fear Count von Strossen might interfere if we linger."

Will began to chuckle softly. "My impetuous darling, ready to run off in the face of your family's objections with a penniless rogue! At the risk of forfeiting your affection, I must confess that I didn't leave England under threat from the duns. Domcaster lent me the money to begin restoring Brookwillow. I had just completed the structural repair of the manor and put in my first crop when I received your letter. And then… well, even knowing how far above me you'd risen, having both the funds and your permission to visit, I couldn't resist trying to win you."

"So you didn't come here to escape your creditors?" Allegra asked.

"They are paid off to a man," he admitted. "Which only proves what little aptitude I have for becoming a fashionable member of the ton."

"So you came…only because you loved me?"

"Only because I couldn't face living without you."

At those tender words, Allegra balled one hand into a fist and slugged him in the side.

"What was that for?" he gasped.

"For not saying you loved me the instant you arrived!"

Rubbing his side, Will reached over to retrieve his shirt. "I intended to say nothing if you seemed happy here. Only when I felt you might return my love did I dare to declare myself. And speaking of declarations—" he paused to slip his shirt over his head "—I shall call upon your grandfather this very evening and ask for your hand."

He had just fastened the first button when a voice from the threshold roared, "A bit late for that!"

Allegra gasped and Will froze in horror as the garden-house door swung open and the duke strode in, his ferocious gaze moving from the rumpled coverlet upon which they sat to Will, his shirt mostly unbuttoned, cravat unraveled on the floor beside him, to Allegra, her bodice loose on her arms and her skirt bunched up above her ankles.

While Will hurriedly twitched her skirt back down and reached for his coat, Signora Bertrude rushed in behind the duke, to stop short as she spied them. Eyes widening, she emitted a piercing scream and fainted.

As if in the dreamy fog of a nightmare, Will saw behind the enraged duke a crowd of faces pressed to the garden-house windows, their expressions ranging from curiosity to shock to amusement.

And framed by the open doorway stood the furious figure of Count von Strossen.

CHAPTER TWENTY-FOUR

FOR ALLEGRA, what happened next transpired in a blur of shock and distress. Grandfather shooing away the gaping onlookers and bundling Allegra into his coat. Ordering a maid be sent to minister to the still-prostrate Signora. Barking at the count, who'd advanced on her, to take himself off with the others lest, as master of this estate, the duke have him thrown into irons. Finally, warning Allegra to keep silent and accompany him back to the house.

After commanding Will to remove himself at once, the duke refused to acknowledge him further. With equal stubbornness, though Will made no attempt to argue with her grandfather, he refused to leave her side.

After she'd shrugged on her grandfather's coat, Will defiantly seized her hand, placed it on his arm and informed her grandfather that unless they shot him first, *he* would escort his affianced bride back to the house.

For a terrified moment, Allegra feared the duke might take the little jeweled pistol he always carried and do just that. But then, with a curt nod, Grandfather indicated that they should follow him. In silence the three of them walked along the sunlit terrace back to the house, curious footmen and peeping maids scattering before the forbidding face of the duke.

Will walked her all the way to her bedchamber before relinquishing her hand. "Don't worry," he reassured her as he opened the door for her. "All will be well, I promise. I'll get word to you as soon as I can." Casting a challenging glance at the duke, he bent and kissed her cheek. "I'm sorry," he whispered.

"I'm not," she whispered back.

"I love you, my heart," she heard him say before the door closed behind her.

Though she wasn't happy that the most tender, thrilling afternoon of her life had ended in an ugly scene, she'd meant it when she assured Will she had no regrets. The hazy idea Molly's long-ago description had given her of lovemaking resembled the reality of her experience with Will only as a penny drawing by an itinerant artist compared to the finished oil of a master portraitist, the latter's breathtaking details and brilliant rendering making it almost impossible to believe both portrayed the same subject.

She would meet Will in the garden again in an instant if a hundred von Strossens glowered at her afterwards.

Knowing the glow of awe and pleasure wouldn't last forever, Allegra meant to enjoy it to the fullest. Humming to herself, she poured water into a basin and gently cleansed the sensitized flesh Will had worshipped with his hands and tongue, a tingle of arousal

stirring in her again at the memories. He'd demonstrated before on several occasions that he was thoughtful, kind, tender. But he'd proven that today on a
different, physical level beyond anything she had ever
experienced or imagined.

Will was a wonder. *Her* wonder. How proud she was
to love him, to have been claimed by him!

Grandfather would not see it that way, she knew. She
would regret leaving San Gregillio and the lavish, if
sometimes stifling, love of her family, but it seemed she
was truly her mother's daughter after all. Like Lady
Grace, she would abandon opulence and status without
a backward glance to follow the man she loved.

After finishing her ablutions, Allegra pulled her
battered trunk from the back of her wardrobe. She expected Grandfather would send her away before dawn
tomorrow, to spare the family the humiliation of having
their curious guests witness her banishment. While she
waited for Will to send her word, she folded and packed
the modest governess gowns she'd possessed when she
first arrived.

Will would be devising some plan for their return to
England. If her grandfather were angry enough to blacken
their name in the neighborhood, it might take him some
time to find a conveyance. But sooner or later, he would
bring her back to Brookwillow, the bride of his heart and
mistress of a country estate, just as she'd long hoped.

She placed a hand on her flat stomach and smiled.
Before their first child was born, she trusted.

A gust of wind rattled the shutters. She looked up to see that the sky had clouded over amid a distant rumble of thunder. A niggle of fear gathered in her stomach.

Things were done differently in Italy, she knew, recalling the elaborate entourage of duennas, maids, footmen and grooms that had shadowed her every step. What if, instead of simply sending her away, the duke prevented Will from accompanying her? What if, by law or tradition, Grandfather had the right to exact revenge upon the man who had disgraced his granddaughter? Might he even now be planning to harm Will?

The idea was so alarming, Allegra abandoned forthwith any notion of patiently waiting here until summoned. Dressing quickly in a simple gown, she left her room.

She thought first to seek out Will in his chamber—but she didn't know which room was his. The two servants she encountered quickly turned and walked in the opposite direction when they spied her, for which she couldn't blame them. 'Twas likely neither of them would have given her the information she sought anyway.

From halfway down the stairs she saw Barrows crossing the foyer. She beckoned urgently, then ran to meet him.

Looking haggard and shaken, the valet bowed low. "My most abject apologies, miss—that is, Duchessa. 'Tis my fault—all of it! I was to stand guard while you and the master…anyway, thinking the gardener might return, I watched the road to the barns. I never dreamed the duke would take it in his head to escort his guests to sniff his blasted night-scented jasmine! I can't beg pardon enough—"

"'Tis done now, so there's nothing to gain by repining," Allegra interrupted. "Where is your master?"

"The duke sent for him half an hour ago."

Fear, greater now that she'd had time to ponder the matter, caught in her throat. "Will he be h-harmed?"

Barrows shook his head miserably. "I don't know, Duchessa. I pray the duke merely gives him a thundering scold. If he should have him incarcerated or…disfigured—"

"Don't even think it." Allegra cut him off, shuddering. "I must do something!"

Picking up her skirts, she hurried down the hallway into the anteroom leading to the duke's office and library.

She stopped short on the threshold when she spotted Will staring out the window, his back to her.

"Will!" she cried, running over to him. "I've been so worried! I don't know the law here, but 'tis entirely possible Grandfather may be able to take some…unpleasant action against you. Don't see him! Let's leave together now, this very moment." She hugged him fiercely. "I cannot bear to be parted from you!"

"No, my darling," Will said, his smile tender as he detached her to kiss each hand, her forehead and then her lips. "We shall not run away like housebreakers who

have roused the dogs. I wronged your grandfather by
seducing you under his roof. It's only right that I stand
before him and accept the chastisement I've earned."

Even as he voiced it, Allegra had to acknowledge the
truth. "You are right," she said quietly. "But if you must
face him, then so must I. Indeed, mine is the greater
wrong, for I am blood kin."

As Will started to protest, Allegra put a finger over
his lips. "Do you mean to marry me, Will Tavener?"

"You know I do."

"If we are to be partners in life, then let us start
now—by going to see Grandfather together."

He studied her face for a moment. "Very well, my
love. We'll go in together."

Hand in hand, they approached the library door,
knocked once and entered.

The duke, who'd been studying some papers on his
desk, looked up. His expression of annoyance at being
interrupted fired to fury when he recognized them.

"How dare you barge in without my leave?" he
barked. "I summoned only the English devil, Allegra.
You, I shall deal with later."

"This 'English devil' will be my husband, *nonno*.
We came to beg your pardon and inform you we will
leave San Gregillio today. I'm sorry to disappoint you,
Grandfather. I know you are angry with us, and for
good cause, after we embarrassed you in front of your
guests. If I could do it over, I would choose for it not
to have happened like that—but if I could do it over,

I would always choose Will. I love him, *nonno*. And I will marry him."

"And you, Englishman?" the duke growled. "What have you to say?"

"That I, too, beg your pardon for having abused your hospitality. But I love Allegra and I mean to have her as my wife. We'd like to ask your blessing…though I know 'tis probably impossible, after everything that happened today."

The duke rose from his chair. "My *blessing!*" he thundered. "You have the audacity to ask for my blessing after your inexcusable, wanton, scandalous behavior?"

Gritting her teeth, Allegra squeezed Will's hand and braced herself for the tirade to come. Then, to her utter astonishment, the duke began to laugh.

Coming around from behind his desk, he swept Allegra into his embrace. "No, it is I who must beg pardon, my brave *nipotina!* I only hope *you* were not too embarrassed."

Setting her back on her feet, he continued, "Why do you think I urged your Englishman to visit the garden house? Do you suppose it was coincidence he found it unlocked this afternoon? Or that, in violation of custom, I roused my guests early from their slumbers to show them blossoms that will be just as fragrant later tonight?"

"You wanted us to…?" Allegra waved a hand, incredulous.

"And deliberately brought a crowd to discover us afterward?" Will asked, frowning.

Gesturing them to a sofa, the duke took a nearby armchair. "Did you think I did not know the danger that threatened you, my child? Did you imagine that after losing my son and finding you, I would let you go to that treacherous Austrian—that foul dog who dared to threaten he would seize my land if I should not yield you to him? Never!

"I knew he would force his will upon you and allow nothing to stand in his way. But he is also proud. Desire you as he does, he could not take to wife a woman at the center of so public a scandal, even though she be an Antinori. Now he must give up his designs on you."

Snuggling into the arm Will had wrapped around her, Allegra exclaimed, "Grandfather, you are a rascal!"

The duke shrugged modestly. "I did not survive the French nibbling at my estates and trying to devour my ancient title only to yield them to the Austrians. For over two hundred years, foreigners have dominated our land, but it will not always be so. I pray, in Alessandro's time if not in my own, our country will be united and free."

"I hope you are right, sir," Will said.

The duke nodded. "It will come to pass, but I shall not sacrifice you to that cause, Allegra. Once, when I was younger and not so wise, I stood between my son and what he loved—and lost him forever. I would not do so with his daughter. But for now, you must leave for England. Once von Strossen accepts that he

cannot force you to be his wife, he will see in your
disgrace other possibilities. I trust your Englishman
can deal with him, but 'twill be better if you were
both gone before he can marshal his resources here
against you."

The duke stood and held out his arms. Still marvel-
ing at her grandfather's wily, improbable scheme,
Allegra went into them willingly.

"If you send your man to the small shed behind the
stables," the duke told Will as he released Allegra, "he
will find a horse and carriage. Now, off with you both."

Crossing to his desk, the duke took a fat pouch jingling
with coins from a drawer and handed it to Will. "A small
gift for your wedding day. You should reach the village
on the road to Rome before nightfall. Stop at the Inn of
the Crossroads and tell Phillipo you are my guests."

"But what of my banishment?" Allegra asked. "Is
there not to be a public scene?"

The duke displayed what on a lesser man would
have been called a grin. "Indeed! When I summon you
to appear before me in the morning and you cannot be
found, there will be such a scene, no one at the palazzo
is likely ever to forget it. I shall roar and fume! Gnash
my teeth, curse your name and banish you forever. Ah,
such a performance it will be. I am quite looking forward to it. The Austrian will never be able to say we
Antinoris do not prize our honor, or that we stood in the
way of his desires. You will be safe, my child, and the
Antinori land as well."

Shaking her head, Allegra chuckled. "You truly are a rascal, Grandfather."

"No, 'tis you English who are knaves!" the duke said solemnly, pointing at Will. "Stealing my granddaughter *and* my carriage!"

"How can we thank you enough, sir?" Will asked.

"Make my *nipotina* happy. Go back to the green England for which she pines and build a life. Write to me, and when it's safe, when this Austrian has gone like the rest, come back and bring me your children to bless."

Taking Allegra's hand, he put it in Will's. "Go with him, my child. Both of you go with God."

She would marry Will—with her grandfather's blessing. Happiness swelled Allegra's heart so that, were it not for the sadness of leaving her grandfather, she felt she might float up to the clouds.

"It seems I'm the granddaughter of a rogue as well as a rogue's lady," she told Will after kissing the duke goodbye and asking him to convey her love to Alessandro. "Shall we find that carriage, my love?"

"I feel a wave of criminal impulses about to overcome me," Will said. Bowing to the duke, he led her away.

They slipped through the silent halls as daylight faded toward dusk. Will found Barrows and sent him ahead to load their luggage into the duke's carriage.

As the household began stirring, they tiptoed through the private garden beside the duke's wing that would lead them unobserved to the stables. From the window of his library, Allegra's grandfather waved goodbye.

Hand in hand, while the rays of the setting sun turned the fountain's spray to a sparkle of gold, Allegra and Will walked to the waiting carriage and into their future.

REQUEST YOUR FREE BOOKS!

2 FREE NOVELS
FROM THE ROMANCE/SUSPENSE
COLLECTION PLUS 2 FREE GIFTS!

YES! Please send me 2 FREE novels from the Romance/Suspense Collection and my 2 FREE gifts. After receiving them, if I don't wish to receive any more books, I can return the shipping statement marked "cancel." If I don't cancel, I will receive 4 brand-new novels every month and be billed just $5.49 per book in the U.S., or $5.99 per book in Canada, plus 25¢ shipping and handling per book plus applicable taxes, if any*. That's a savings of at least 20% off the cover price! I understand that accepting the 2 free books and gifts places me under no obligation to buy anything. I can always return a shipment and cancel at any time. Even if I never buy another book from the Reader Service, the two free books and gifts are mine to keep forever.

185 MDN EF5Y   385 MDN EF6C

Name _____ (PLEASE PRINT) _____

Address _____ Apt. # _____

City _____ State/Prov. _____ Zip/Postal Code _____

Signature (if under 18, a parent or guardian must sign)

Mail to **The Reader Service:**
IN U.S.A.: P.O. Box 1867, Buffalo, NY 14240-1867
IN CANADA: P.O. Box 609, Fort Erie, Ontario L2A 5X3

Not valid to current subscribers to the Romance Collection,
the Suspense Collection or the Romance/Suspense Collection.

Want to try two free books from another line?
Call 1-800-873-8635 or visit www.morefreebooks.com.

* Terms and prices subject to change without notice. NY residents add applicable sales tax. Canadian residents will be charged applicable provincial taxes and GST. This offer is limited to one order per household. All orders subject to approval. Credit or debit balances in a customer's account(s) may be offset by any other outstanding balance owed by or to the customer. Please allow 4 to 6 weeks for delivery.

Your Privacy: Harlequin is committed to protecting your privacy. Our Privacy Policy is available online at www.eHarlequin.com or upon request from the Reader Service. From time to time we make our lists of customers available to reputable firms who may have a product or service of interest to you. If you would prefer we not share your name and address, please check here. ☐

BOB07

JULIA JUSTISS

HQN™

We *are* romance™

www.HQNBooks.com

PHJJ1107BL